Rosamunde Pilcher was encouraged to write from an early age and had her first story published in *Woman and Home* at the age of eighteen. During the Second World War, she worked first in the Foreign Office, and then in the Women's Royal Naval Service, serving in Portsmouth and Trincomalee, Ceylon, with the East India Fleet. After the war she married and moved to Scotland. She and her husband today live near Dundee. They have four children and nine grandchildren. Throughout this time Rosamunde Pilcher has been writing continuously, for magazines as well as thirteen novels.

Her two bestselling novels, *The Shell Seekers* and *September*, captured the world's imagination and became the best-loved novels of the decade. Her short story collections, *The Blue Bedroom* and *Flowers in the Rain*, have also been wonderfully popular.

Praise for *September*.

'*September* has a classical sense of time and place. Elegantly unfolding, it's novel to wallow in like a finely scented bath'

Today

'An alluring sense of the Scottish Highlands is at the very core of this book . . . There is a comfortable pleasure to be had in following the interlocked lives of Violet Aird and her family and friends, with their numerous scandals and conflicts . . . Character is at the heart of a story, and this fine tale has plenty of that'

Belva Plain, *The New York Times Book Review*

'A wonderful, not-to-be-missed novel that is destined to provide many hours of pleasurable reading'

Woman and Home

'With the same effortless charm which made *The Shell Seekers* an international success, Rosamunde Pilcher draws enchanting cameos of family life in her new novel'

Annabel

'*September* has been awaited with baited breath. Could she carry on in the bestselling tradition with another remarkable novel or was it a one-off? The answer to this question must be "Yes, it is a big novel, and will delight her readers"'

Books

The Rosamunde Pilcher Collection

Featuring:
The Day of the Storm
Another View
Sleeping Tiger

CORONET BOOKS
Hodder & Stoughton

This collection copyright © 1991 by Rosamunde Pilcher
First published in Great Britain in 1991
By Coronet Paperbacks
A division of Hodder Headline

THE DAY OF THE STORM
Copyright © 1975 by Rosamunde Pilcher
First published in Great Britain in 1975 by William Collins Sons & Co Ltd

ANIOTHER VIEW
Copyright © 1968 by Rosamunde Pilcher
First published in Great Britain in 1990 by Coronet paperbacks

SLEEPING TIGER
Copyright © 1967 by Rosamunde Pilcher
First published in Great Britain in 1990 by Coronet paperbacks
A Coronet paperback original
New edition 2000

The right of Rosamunde Pilcher to be identified as the Author of
the Work has been asserted by her in accordance with the
Copyright, Designs and Patents Act 1988.

35 36 37 38 39 40

A CIP catalogue record for this book is available
from the British Library.

ISBN 0 340 55613 7

Printed and bound in Great Britain by
Mackays of Chatham plc, Chatham, Kent

Hodder and Stoughton
A division of Hodder Headline
338 Euston Road
London NW1 3BH

CONTENTS

ROSAMUNDE PILCHER

THE DAY OF THE STORM

1

It all started on a Monday at the end of January. A dull day at a dull time of the year. Christmas and the New Year were over and forgotten and yet the new season had not started to show its face. London was cold and raw, the shops filled with empty hope and clothes "for cruising". The trees in the park stood lacy and ·bare against low skies, the trodden grass beneath them dull and dead, so that it was impossible to believe that it could ever again be carpeted with drifts of purple and yellow crocus.

It was a day like any other day. The alarm woke me to darkness, but a darkness made paler by the wide expanse of the uncurtained windows, and through them I could see the top of the plane tree, illuminated by the orange glow of distant street lights.

My room was unfurnished, except for the sofa bed on which I lay, and a kitchen table which I was going to strip of paint when I had the time, and polish with a coat of beeswax. Even the floor was bare, boards stretching to the wainscoting. An orange box did duty as a bedside table, and a second one filled in for a chair.

I put out a hand and turned on the light and surveyed the desolate scene with the utmost satisfaction. It was mine. My first home. I had moved in only three weeks ago but it belonged entirely to me. With it, I could do as I pleased. Cover the white walls with posters or paint them orange. Sand the bare floor or stripe it in colour. Already I had started to acquire a proprietary interest in junk and antique shops, and could not pass one without scanning the window for some treasure that I might be able to afford. This was how the table had come into my possession, and

I already had my eye on an antique gilt mirror, but had not yet plucked up the courage to go into the shop and find out how much it was going to cost. Perhaps I would hang it in the centre of the chimney breast, or on the wall opposite the window, so that the reflections of the sky and the tree would be caught, like a picture, within its ornate frame.

These pleasant imaginings took some time. I looked again at the clock, saw that it was growing late, and climbed out of bed to pad, barefooted, across the floor and into the tiny kitchen, where I lit the gas and put the kettle on to boil. The day had begun.

The flat was in Fulham, the top floor of a small terrace house which belonged to Maggie and John Trent. I had met them only at Christmas, which I had spent with Stephen Forbes and his wife Mary and their large family of untidy children, in their large and untidy house in Putney. Stephen Forbes was my boss, the owner of the Walton Street bookshop where I had been working for the past year. He had always been enormously kind and helpful towards me and when he found out, from one of the other girls, that I would be on my own for Christmas, he and Mary had immediately issued a firm invitation – more an order, really – that I should spend the three days with them. There was plenty of space, he insisted vaguely, a room in the attic, a bed in Samantha's room, somewhere, but I wouldn't mind, would I? And I could always help Mary baste the turkey and pick all those torn bits of tissue paper off the floor.

Considering it from this angle, I finally accepted, and had a wonderful time. There's nothing like a family Christmas when there are children everywhere and noise and paper and presents, and a pine-smelling Christmas tree, glittering with baubles and crooked home-made decorations.

On Boxing Night, with the children safely in bed, the Forbeses threw a grown-up party, although we still seemed to continue playing childish games, and Maggie and John

Trent came to this. The Trents were young marrieds, she the daughter of an Oxford don, whom Stephen had known well in his undergraduate days. She was one of those laughing, cheerful, out-going people, and after she had arrived the party went with a swing. We were introduced but we didn't manage to talk until a game of charades, when we found ourselves side by side on a sofa, trying to guess, from the most incoherent gestures, that Mary was trying to act to us, in dumb show, the title of a film. "*Rose Marie!*" somebody yelled, for no apparent reason.

"*Clockwork Orange!*"

Maggie lit a cigarette and sank back on the sofa, defeated. "It's beyond me," she said. She turned her dark head to look at me. "You work in Stephen's shop, don't you?"

"Yes."

"I'll come in next week and spend all my Christmas book tokens. I've been given dozens."

"Lucky girl."

"We've just moved into our first house, so I want lots of coffee table stuff so that all our friends think I'm wildly intelligent . . ." Then somebody shouted, "Maggie, it's your turn," and she said "Cripes," and shot to her feet, and went stalking off to find out what she was going to have to act. I can't remember what it was, but watching her make a cheerful fool of herself, my heart warmed to her, and I hoped that I would see her again.

I did, of course. True to her word, she came into the shop a couple of days after the holiday wearing a sheepskin coat and a long purple skirt, and carrying a bulging handbag stuffed with book tokens. I wasn't serving anybody at that particular moment and I came out from behind a neat stack of shiny-jacketed novels and said, "Hello."

"Oh, good, there you are. I was hoping I'd find you. Can you help me?"

"Yes, of course."

Together, we chose a cookery book, a new autobiography which everybody was talking about, and a marvellously expensive volume of Impressionist paintings for the legendary coffee table. All this came to a little more than the book tokens did, so she groped around in that handbag and took out a cheque book in order to pay for the balance of the amount.

"John'll be furious," she told me happily, writing out the amount with a red felt pen. The cheque was yellow and the effect quite gay. "He says we're spending far too much money as it is. There." She turned it over to write her address. "Fourteen Bracken Road, SW6." She said it aloud in case I couldn't read her writing. "I haven't got used to writing it yet. We've only just moved in. Terribly exciting, we've bought it freehold, believe it or not. At least our parents chipped in with the deposit and John managed to con some building society or other into giving us a loan for the rest. But of course because of this, we've got to let the top floor to help pay the mortgage, but still, I suppose it'll all work out." She smiled. "You'll have to come and see it."

"I'd like to." I was wrapping her parcel, being meticulous about matching the paper and folding the corners.

She watched me. "You know, it's terribly rude, but I don't know your name. I know it's Rebecca, but Rebecca what?"

"Rebecca Bayliss."

"I suppose you don't know of a nice peaceful individual who wants an unfurnished flat?"

I looked at her. Our thoughts were so close I scarcely had to speak. I tied the knot on the parcel and snapped the string. I said, "How about me?"

"You? But are you looking for somewhere to live?"

"I wasn't until a moment ago. But I am now."

"It's only a room and a kitchen. And we have to share the bath."

"I don't mind if you don't. And if I can afford the rent. I don't know what you're asking."

4

Maggie told me. I swallowed and did a few mental calculations and said, "I could manage that."

"Have you got any furniture?"

"No. I've been living in a furnished flat with a couple of other girls. But I can get some."

"You sound as though you're desperate to get out."

"No, I'm not desperate, but I'd like to be on my own."

"Well, before you decide you'd better come and see it. Some evening, because John and I both work."

"*This* evening?" It was impossible to keep my impatience and excitement out of my voice and Maggie laughed.

"All right," she said. "This evening," and she picked up the beautifully wrapped parcel of books and prepared to depart.

I suddenly panicked. "I . . . I don't know the address . . ."

"Yes you do, silly, it's on the back of the cheque. Get a twenty-two bus. I'll expect you about seven."

"I'll be there," I promised.

Jolting slowly down the Kings Road in the bus I had to consciously damp down my enthusiasm. I was out to buy a pig in a poke. The flat might be totally impossible, too big, too small or inconvenient in some unimagined way. Anything was better than being disappointed. And indeed, from the outside, the little house was entirely unremarkable, one of a row of red brick villas, with fancy pointing around the doors and a depressing tendency towards stained glass. But inside Number 14 was bright with fresh paint and new carpets and Maggie herself in old jeans and a blue sweater.

"Sorry I look such a mess but I've got to do all the housework, so I usually change when I get back from the office. Come on, let's go up and see it . . . put your coat on the banisters, John's not home yet, but I told him you were coming and he thought it was a frightfully good idea . . ."

5

Talking all the time, she led the way upstairs and into the empty room which stood at the back of the house. She turned on the light. "It faces south, out over a little park. The people who had the house before us built an extension on underneath, so you've got a sort of balcony on its roof." She opened a glass door and we stepped together out into the cold dark night, and I smelt the leaf-smell of the park, and damp earth, and saw, ringed by lamplight from the streets all around, the stretch of empty darkness. A cold wind blew suddenly, gustily, and the black shape of the plane tree rustled and then the sound was lost in the jet roar of an aeroplane going overhead.

I said, "It's like being in the country."

"Well, next best thing perhaps." She shivered. "Let's go in before we freeze." We stepped back through the glass door, and Maggie showed me the tiny kitchen which had been fashioned out of a deep cupboard, and then, halfway down the stairs, the bathroom, which we would all share. Finally, we ended up downstairs again in Maggie's warm, untidy sitting-room, and she found a bottle of sherry and some potato crisps which she swore were stale, but tasted all right to me. "Do you still want to come?" she asked.

"More than ever."

"When do you want to move in?"

"As soon as possible. Next week if I could."

"What about the girls you're sharing with just now?"

"They'll find someone else. One of them has a sister who's coming to London. I expect she'll move into my room."

"And what about furniture?"

"Oh . . . I'll manage."

"I expect," said Maggie comfortably, "your parents will come up trumps, they usually do. When I first came to London, my mother produced the most wonderful treasures out of the attic and the linen cupboard and so . . ." Her voice died away. I watched her in rueful silence, and she finally laughed at herself. "There I go again, opening my mouth and putting my foot in

6

it. I'm sorry. I've obviously said something idiotically tactless."

"I haven't got a father, and my mother's abroad. She's living in Ibiza. That's really why I want somewhere of my own."

"I am sorry. I should have known, you spending Christmas with the Forbeses . . . I mean, I should have guessed."

"There's no reason why you should guess."

"Is your father dead?"

She was obviously curious, but in such an open and friendly way that all at once it seemed ridiculous to close up and shut up the way I usually did when people began asking me questions about my family.

"I don't think so," I said, trying to sound as though it didn't matter. "I think he lives in Los Angeles. He was an actor. My mother eloped with him when she was eighteen. But he soon got bored with domesticity, or perhaps he decided that his career was more important than raising a family. Anyway, the marriage lasted only a few months before he upped and left her, and then my mother had me."

"What a terrible thing to do."

"I suppose it was. I've never thought very much about it. My mother never talked about him. Not because she was particularly bitter or anything, just that when something was over and in the past, she usually forgot it. She's always been like that. She only looks forward, and always with the utmost optimism."

"But what happened after you were born? Did she go back to her parents?"

"No. Never."

"You mean, nobody sent a telegram saying 'Come back all is forgiven'?"

"I don't know. I honestly don't know."

"There must have been the most resounding row when your mother ran off, but even so . . ." Her voice trailed away. She was obviously unable to understand a situation

7

which I had accepted with equanimity all my life. ". . . what sort of people would do a thing like that to their daughter?"

"I don't know."

"You must be joking!"

"No. I honestly don't know."

"You mean you don't know your own grandparents?"

"I don't even know who they are. Or perhaps who they were. I don't even know if they're still alive."

"Don't you know anything? Didn't your mother ever say anything?"

"Oh, of course . . . little scraps of the past used to come into her conversation but none of it added up to anything. You know how mothers talk to their children, remembering things that happened and things they used to do when they were little."

"But – Bayliss." She frowned. "That's not a very usual name. And it rings a bell somehow but I can't think why. Haven't you got a single clue?"

I laughed at her intensity. "You talk as though I really wanted to know. But you see, I don't. If you've never known grandparents, then you don't miss them."

"But don't you wonder . . ." she groped for words ". . . where they *lived*?"

"I know where they lived. They lived in Cornwall. In a stone house with fields that sloped down to the sea. And my mother had a brother called Roger but he was killed during the war."

"But what did she do after you were born? I suppose she had to go out and get a job."

"No, she had a little money of her own. A legacy from some old aunt or other. Of course, we never had a car or anything, but we seemed to manage all right. She had a flat in Kensington, in the basement of a house that belonged to some friends. And we stayed there till I was about eight, and then I went to boarding school, and after that we sort of . . . moved around . . ."

"Boarding schools cost money . . ."

8

"It wasn't a very grand boarding school."

"Did your mother marry again?"

I looked at Maggie. Her expression was lively and avidly curious, but she was kind. I decided that, having gone so far, I may as well tell her the rest.

"She . . . wasn't exactly the marrying type . . . But she was always very, very attractive, and I don't remember a time when there wasn't some adoring male in attendance . . . And once I was away at school, I suppose there wasn't much reason to go on being circumspect. I never knew where I was going to spend the next set of holidays. Once it was in France, in Provence. Sometimes in this country. Another time it was Christmas in New York."

Maggie took this in, and made a face. "Not much fun for you."

"But educational." I had long ago learned to make a joke of it. "And just think of all the places I've seen, and all the extraordinary places I've lived in. The Ritz in Paris once, and another time a gruesomely cold house in Denbighshire. That was a poet who thought he'd try sheep farming. I've never been so glad in my life when that association came to an end."

"She must be very beautiful."

"No, but men think she is. And she's very gay and improvident and vague, and I suppose you'd say utterly amoral. Maddening. Everything is 'jokey'. It's her big word. Unpaid bills are 'jokey' and lost handbags and unanswered letters, they're all 'jokey'. She has no idea of money and no sense of obligation. An embarrassing sort of person to live with."

"What's she doing in Ibiza?"

"She's living with some Swedish man she met out there. She went out to stay with a couple she knew, and she met this guy and the next thing I knew I had a letter saying that she was going to move in with him. She said he was terribly Nordic and dour but he had a beautiful house."

"How long is it since you've seen her?"

"About two years. I eased out of her life when I was

seventeen. I did a secretarial course and took temporary jobs, and finally I ended up working for Stephen Forbes."

"Do you like it?"

"Yes. I do."

"How old are you?"

"Twenty-one."

Maggie smiled again, shaking her long hair in wonderment. "What a lot you've done," she said, and she did not sound in the least bit sorry for me but even slightly envious. "At twenty-one I was a blushing bride in a beastly busty white wedding dress and an old veil that smelt of mothballs. I'm not really a trad. person, but I've got a mother who is, and I'm very fond of her so I usually used to do what she wanted."

I could imagine Maggie's mother. I said, resorting to the comfort of clichés, because I couldn't think of anything else to say, "Oh, well, it takes all sorts," and at that moment we heard John's key in the lock and after that we did not bring up the subject of mothers and families again.

It was a day like any other day, but it had a bonus attached to it. Last Thursday I had worked late with Stephen, trying to complete the last of the January stocktaking, and in return he had given me this morning off so that I had until lunchtime to my own devices. I filled it in cleaning the flat (which took, at most, no more than half an hour), doing some shopping and taking a bundle of clothes to the launderette. By eleven thirty all this domesticity was completed so I put on my coat and set off, in a leisurely way, for work, intending to walk some of the way, and maybe stand myself an early lunch before getting to the shop.

It was one of those cold, dark, damp days when it never really gets light. I walked, through this gloom, up into the New Kings Road, and headed west. Here, every other shop seems to sell either antiques or second-hand beds

10

or picture frames, and I thought I knew them all, but all at once I found myself outside a shop which I had not noticed before. The outside was painted white, the windows framed in black, and there was a red and white awning pulled out as protection against the imminent drizzle.

I looked up to see what the shop was called and read the name TRISTRAM NOLAN picked out in neat black Roman capitals over the door. This door was flanked by windows filled with delectable odds and ends and I paused to inspect their contents, standing on the pavement bathed in brightness from the many lights which burned within. Most of the furniture was Victorian, re-upholstered and restored and polished. A buttoned sofa with a wide lap and curly legs, a sewing box, a small picture of lap dogs on a velvet cushion.

I looked beyond the windows and into the shop itself, and it was then that I saw the cherrywood chairs. They were a pair, balloon backed, with curved legs and seats embroidered with roses.

I craved them. Just like that. I could picture them in my flat, and I wanted them desperately. For a moment I hesitated. This was no junk shop and the price might well be more than I could afford. But after all, no harm could be done by asking. Before I could lose my nerve, I opened the door and went in.

The shop was empty, but the door opening and closing had rung a bell, and presently there was the sound of someone coming down the stairs, the woollen curtain that hung over the door at the back of the shop was drawn aside and a man came into view.

I suppose I had expected someone elderly and formally attired, in keeping with the ambience of the shop and its contents, but this man's appearance rocked all my vague, preconceived notions. For he was young, tall and long-legged, dressed in jeans – faded to a soft blue and clinging like a second skin – and a blue denim jacket, equally old and faded, with the sleeves turned back in a businesslike way to reveal the checked cuffs of the shirt he wore beneath it. A cotton handkerchief was knotted at his neck and on his feet he wore soft moccasins, much decorated and fringed.

That winter the most unlikely people were drifting around London dressed as cowboys, but somehow this one looked real, and his worn clothes appeared as genuine as he was. We stood and looked at each other, and then he smiled and for some reason this took me unawares. I don't like being taken unawares, and I said "Good morning" with a certain coolness.

He dropped the curtain behind him and came forward, soft footed. "Can I help you?"

He may have looked like a genuine, dyed-in-the-wool American, but the moment he opened his mouth it was clear that he was no such thing. For some reason this annoyed me. The life I had led with my mother had left me with a thick streak of cynicism about men in general, and phoneys in particular, and this young man, I decided then and there, was a phoney.

"I . . . I was going to ask about these little chairs. The balloon-back ones."

"Oh, yes." He came forward to lay his hand on the back of one. The hand was long and shapely, with spade-tipped fingers, the skin very brown. "There's just the pair of them."

I stared at the chairs, trying to ignore his presence.

"I wondered how much they were."

He squatted beside me to search for a price ticket and I saw his hair fell thick and straight to his collar, very dark and lustrous.

"You're in luck," he told me. "They're going very cheap because the leg of one has been broken and then not very professionally repaired." He straightened up suddenly, surprising me by his height. His eyes were slightly tip-tilted, and a very dark brown, with an expression in them that I found disconcerting. He made me uncomfortable and my antipathy for him began to turn to dislike. "Fifteen

12

pounds for the pair," he said. "But if you'd like to wait and pay a little more, I can get the leg reinforced, and perhaps a small veneer put over the joint. That would make it stronger and it would look better too."

"Isn't it all right now?"

"It would be all right for you," said the young man, ". . . but if you had a large fat man for dinner, he'd probably end up on his backside."

There was a pause while I regarded him – I hoped coldly. His eyes were brimming, with a malicious amusement which I had no intention of sharing. I did not appreciate the suggestion that the only men who would ever come and have dinner with me would necessarily be large and fat.

I said at last, "How much would it cost me to have the leg repaired?"

"Say five pounds. That means you get the chairs for a tenner each."

I worked this out, and decided that I could just afford them.

"I'll take them."

"Good," said the young man and put his fists on his hips and smiled amiably, as though this were the end of the transaction.

I decided he was utterly inefficient. "Do you want me to pay for them now, or to leave a deposit . . .?"

"No, that doesn't matter. You can pay for them when you collect them."

"Well, when will they be ready?"

"In about a week."

"Don't you want my name?"

"Not unless you want to give it to me."

"What happens if I never come back?"

"Then I expect they'll be sold to someone else."

"I don't want to lose them."

"You won't," said the young man.

I frowned, angry with him, but he only smiled and went to the door to open it for me. Cold air poured in, and outside the drizzle had started and the street looked dark as night.

He said, "Goodbye," and I managed a frosty smile of thanks and went past him, out into the gloom, and as I did so I heard the bell ring as he shut the door behind me.

The day was, all at once, unspeakable. My pleasure in buying the chairs had been wrecked by the irritation which the young man had generated. I did not usually take instant dislikes to people and I was annoyed not only with him, but with myself, for being so vulnerable. I was still brooding on this when I walked down Walton Street and let myself into Stephen Forbes's bookshop. Even the comfort of being indoors and the pleasant smell of new paper and printers' ink did nothing to dispel my wretched mood.

The shop was on three levels, with new books on the ground floor, second-hand books and old prints upstairs, and Stephen's office in the basement. I saw that Jennifer, the second girl, was busy with a customer, and the only other person visible was an old lady in a tweed cape engrossed in the Gardening section, so I headed for the little cloakroom, unbuttoning my coat as I went, but then I heard Stephen's heavy, unmistakable footsteps coming up from downstairs, and for some reason I stopped to wait for him. The next moment he appeared, tall, stooping and spectacled, with his usual expression of vague benevolence. He wore dark suits that always managed to appear as though in need of a good press, and already, at this early hour, the knot of his tie had begun to slip down, revealing the top button of his shirt.

"Rebecca," he said.

"Yes, I'm here . . ."

"I'm glad I've caught you." He came to my side speaking low-voiced, so as not to disturb the customers. "There's a letter for you downstairs; it's been forwarded on from your old flat. You'd better nip down and collect it."

I frowned. "A letter?"

"Yes. Airmail. Lots of foreign stamps. It has, for some reason, an air of urgency about it."

My irritation, along with all thoughts of new chairs, was lost in a sudden apprehension.

"Is it from my mother?"

"I don't know. Why don't you go and find out?"

So I went down the steep, uncarpeted stairs to the basement, lit, on this dark day, by long strip-lights let into the ceiling. The office was marvellously untidy – as usual – littered with letters and parcels and files, piles of old books, and cardboard boxes and ashtrays which nobody ever remembered to empty. But the letter was on the middle of Stephen's blotter and instantly visible.

I picked it up. An airmail envelope, Spanish stamps, an Ibizan postmark. But the writing was unfamiliar, pointed and spiky, as though a very fine pen had been used. It had been sent to the old flat, but this address had been crossed out and the address of the bookshop substituted in large, girlish, handwriting. I wondered how long the letter had lain on the table by the front door, before one of the girls realised that it was there and had taken the trouble to forward it on to me.

I sat down in Stephen's chair and slit the envelope. Inside, two pages of fine airmail paper, and the date at the head was the third of January. Very nearly a month ago. My mind sounded a note of alarm and, suddenly frightened, I began to read.

> Dear Rebecca,
>
> I hope you do not mind me calling you by your Christian name, but your mother has spoken to me of you a great deal. I am writing because your mother is very ill. She has been unwell for some time and I wished to write to you before but she would not let me.
>
> Now, however, I am taking matters into my own hands, and with the doctor's approval I am letting you know that I think you should come out to see her.
>
> If you can do this, perhaps you will cable me

the number of your aeroplane flight so that I can be at the airport to meet you.

I know that you are working and it may not be easy to make this trip, but I would advise you to waste no time. I am afraid that you will find your mother very changed, but her spirit is still high.

With good wishes.
Sincerely,
Otto Pedersen.

I sat in unbelief, and stared at the letter. The formal words told me nothing and everything. My mother was very ill, perhaps dying. A month ago I had been asked to waste no time but to go to her. Now it was a month later, and I had only just got the letter and perhaps she was already dead – and I had never gone. What would he think of me, this Otto Pedersen whom I had never seen, whose name, even, I had not known until this moment?

2

I read the letter again, and then again, the flimsy pages rustling in my hands. I was still there, sitting at his desk, when Stephen finally came downstairs to find me.

I turned to look up at him over my shoulder. He saw my face and said, "What is it?"

I tried to tell him, but could not. Instead I thrust the letter at him, and while he took it, and read it, I sat with my elbows on his desk, biting my thumbnails, bitter and angry, and fighting a terrible anxiety.

He was soon finished reading. He tossed the letter down on the desk between us, and said, "Did you know she was ill?"

I shook my head.

"When did you last hear from her?"

"Four, five months ago. She never wrote letters." I looked up at him and said, furiously, choked by the great lump in my throat, "That was nearly a *month* ago. That letter's been lying in the flat, and nobody bothered to send it to me. She may be dead by now and I never went, and she'll think I simply didn't care!"

"If she had died," said Stephen, "then we'd have surely heard. Now, don't cry, there isn't time for that. What we have to do is get you out to Ibiza with all convenient speed, and let . . ." he glanced down at the letter again ". . . Mr Pedersen know you're arriving. Nothing else matters."

I said, "I can't go," and my mouth began to grow square and my lower lip tremble as though I were a ten-year-old.

"Why can't you go?"

"Because I haven't got enough money for the fare."

"Oh, my dear child, let me worry about that . . ."

"But I can't let you . . ."

"Yes, you can, and if you get all stiff-necked about it then you can pay me back over the next five years and I'll charge you interest, if it'll make you feel happier, and now for God's sake don't let's mention it again . . ." He was already reaching for the directory, behaving in an altogether efficient and un-Stephen-like fashion. "Have you got a passport? And nobody's going to clamp down on you for smallpox injections or anything tiresome like that. Hello? British Airways? I want to make a reservation on the first plane to Ibiza." He smiled down at me, still fighting tears and temper, but already feeling a little better. There is nothing like having a large and kindly man to take over in times of emotional stress. He picked up a pencil and drew a sheet of paper towards him and began to make notes. "Yes. When? Fine. Can we have a reservation, please? Miss Rebecca Bayliss. And what time does it get to Ibiza? And the flight number? Thank you so much. Thank you. Yes, I'll get her to the airport myself."

He put down the receiver and surveyed, with some satisfaction, the illegible squiggles his pencil had made.

"That's it, then. You fly tomorrow morning, change planes at Palma, get to Ibiza about half past seven. I'll drive you to the airport. No, don't start arguing again, I wouldn't feel happy unless I saw you actually walk on to the aeroplane. And now we'll cable Mr Otto Pedersen . . ." he picked up the letter again ". . . at the Villa Margareta, Santa Catarina, and let him know that you're coming." He smiled down at me with such cheerful reassurance that I was suddenly filled with hope.

I said, "I can't ever thank you . . ."

"I don't ever want you to," said Stephen. "It's the least I can do."

I flew the next day, in a plane half-filled with hopeful winter holiday tourists. They even carried straw hats against

18

an improbably blazing sun, and their faces, as we stepped out into a steady drizzle at Palma, were disappointed but resolutely cheerful, as though, for certain, tomorrow would be better.

The rain never ceased, all the four hours I waited in the transit lounge, and the flight out of Palma was bumpy with thick, wet clouds. But as we rose above them and headed out across the sea, the weather brightened. The clouds thinned and broke, disclosing an evening sky of robin's egg blue, and far below the crumpled sea was streaked with the pink light of the setting sun.

It was dark when we landed. Dark and damp. Coming down the gangway beneath a sky full of bright southern stars, there was only the smell of petrol, but as I walked across the puddled tarmac towards the lights of the terminal building I felt the soft wind in my face. It was warm and smelt of pines, and was evocative of every summer holiday I had ever spent abroad.

At this quiet time of the year the plane had not been full. It did not take long to get through Customs and Immigration, and – my passport stamped – I picked up my suitcase and walked into the Arrivals Lounge.

There were the usual small groups of waiting people standing about or sitting hunched apathetically on the long plastic banquettes. I stopped and looked about me, waiting to be identified, but could see nobody who looked in the least like a Swedish writer come to meet me. And then a man turned from buying a newspaper at the bookstall. Across the room our eyes met, and he folded the newspaper and began to walk towards me, pushing his paper into his jacket pocket as though it were no longer of any use to him. He was tall and thin, with hair that was either blond or white – it was impossible to tell in the bright, impersonal electric light. Before he was halfway across the polished floor I smiled tentatively, and as he approached he said my name, "Rebecca?" with a question mark at the end of it, still not entirely certain that it was I.

"Yes."

"I'm Otto Pedersen." We shook hands and he gave a formal little bow as he did so. His hair, I saw then, was pale blond, turning grey, and his face was deeply tanned, thin and bony, the skin dry and finely wrinkled from long exposure to the sun. His eyes were very pale, and more grey than blue. He wore a black polo-necked sweater and a light oatmeal-coloured suit with pleated pockets, like a safari shirt, and a belt which hung loose, the buckle swinging. He smelt of aftershave and looked as clean as if he had been bleached.

Having found each other, it was suddenly difficult to find anything to say. All at once we were both overwhelmed by the circumstances of our meeting and I realised that he was as unsure of himself as I. But he was also urbane and polite, and dealt with this by taking my suitcase from me and asking if this was all my luggage.

"Yes, that's all."

"Then let us go to the car. If you like to wait at the door, I will fetch it and save you the walk . . ."

"I'll come with you."

"It's only across the road, in the car park."

So we went out together, into the darkness again. He led me to the half empty car park. Here, he stopped by a big black Mercedes, unlocked it, and tossed my case on to the back seat. Then he held the door open so that I could get in before coming around to the front of the car to settle himself beside me.

"I hope you had a good journey," he said, politely, as we left the terminal behind us and headed out into the road.

"It was a little bumpy in Palma. I had to wait four hours."

"Yes. There are no direct flights at this time of the year."

I swallowed. "I must explain about not answering your letter. I've moved flats, and I didn't get it till yesterday morning. It wasn't forwarded to me, you see. It was so

20

good of you to write, and you must have wondered why I never replied."

"I thought something like that must have happened."

His English was perfect, only the precise Swedish vowel sounds betraying his origins, and a certain formality in the manner in which he expressed himself.

"When I got your letter I was so frightened . . . that it would be too late."

"No," said Otto. "It is not too late."

Something in his voice made me look at him. His profile was knife sharp against the yellow glow of passing street lights, his expression unsmiling and grave.

I said, "Is she dying?"

"Yes," said Otto. "Yes, she is dying."

"What is wrong with her?"

"Cancer of the blood. You call it leukaemia."

"How long has she been ill?"

"About a year. But it was only just before Christmas time that she became so ill. The doctor thought that we should try blood transfusions, and I took her to the hospital for this. But it was no good, because as soon as I got her home again, she started this very bad nose bleed, and so the ambulance had to come and take her back to hospital again. She was there over Christmas and only then allowed home again. It was after that I wrote to you."

"I wish I'd got the letter in time. Does she know I'm coming?"

"No, I didn't tell her. You well know how she loves surprises, and equally how she hates to be disappointed. I thought there was a chance that something would go wrong and you wouldn't be on the plane." He smiled frostily, "But of course you were."

We stopped at a crossroads to wait for a country cart to pass in front of us, the feet of the mule making a pleasant sound on the dusty road, and a lantern swinging from the back of the cart. Otto took advantage of the pause to take a cheroot from the breast pocket of his jacket and light it from the lighter on the dashboard. The cart passed, we moved on.

"How long is it since you have seen your mother?"

"Two years."

"You must expect a great change. I am afraid you will be shocked, but you must try not to let her see. She is still very vain."

"You know her so well."

"But of course."

I longed to ask him if he loved her. The question was on the tip of my tongue, but I realised that at this stage of our acquaintance it would be nothing but impertinence to ask such an intimate and personal thing. Besides, what difference did it make? He had met her and wanted to be with her, had given her a home, and now, when she was so ill, was cherishing her in his own apparently unemotional manner. If that wasn't love, then what was?

After a little, we began to talk of other things. I asked him how long he had lived on the island, and he said five years. He had come first in a yacht and had liked the place so well that he had returned the next year to buy his house and settle here.

"You're a writer . . ."

"Yes, but I am also a Professor of History."

"Do you write books on history?"

"I have done so. At the moment I am working on a thesis concerned with the Moorish occupation of these islands and southern Spain."

I was impressed. As far as I could remember, none of my mother's previous lovers had been even remotely intellectual.

"How far away is your house?"

"About five miles now. The village of Santa Catarina was quite unspoiled when I first came here. Now, however, large hotel developments are planned and I fear it will become spoiled like the rest of the island. No, that is wrong. Like some parts of the island. It is still possible to be entirely remote if you know where to go and have a car or perhaps a motor boat."

It was warm in the car and I rolled down the window. The soft night air blew in on my face and I saw that we were in country now, passing through groves of olives, with every now and then the glimmering light of a farmhouse window shining beyond the bulbous, spiked shapes of prickly pear.

I said, "I'm glad she was here. I mean, if she has to be ill and die, I'm glad it's somewhere like this, in the south, with the sun warm and the smell of pines."

"Yes," said Otto. And then, precisely as ever, "I think that she has been very happy."

We drove on in silence, the road empty, telegraph poles rushing to meet the headlights of the car. I saw that now we were running parallel to the sea, which spread to an invisible, dark horizon and was dotted here and there with the lights of fishing boats. Presently there appeared ahead of us the neon-lighted shape of a village. We passed a sign reading SANTA CATARINA and then were driving down the main street; the air was filled with the smell of onions and oil and grilling meat. Flamenco music flung itself at us from open doorways, and dark faces, filled with absent curiosity, turned to watch us pass. In a moment we had left the village behind us, and had plunged forward into the darkness which lay beyond, only to slow down almost immediately to negotiate a steep corner which led up a narrow lane between orchards of almond trees. The headlights bored into the darkness, and ahead I saw the villa, white and square, pierced by small, secretive windows and with a lighted lantern swinging over the great, nailed front door.

Otto braked the car and switched off the engine. We got out, Otto taking my suitcase from the back seat and leading the way across the gravel. He opened the door and stood aside and I walked in ahead of him.

We were in a hallway, lit by a wrought-iron chandelier and furnished with a long couch covered in a bright blanket. A tall blue and white jar stood by the door containing a selection of ivory-handled walking sticks and sun umbrellas. As Otto closed the front door, another opened ahead of us and a small, dark-haired woman appeared, wearing a pink overall and flat, worn slippers.

"Señor."

"Maria."

She smiled, showing a number of gold teeth. He spoke to her in Spanish, asking a question to which she replied and then, turning, introduced me to her.

"This is Maria, who takes care of us. I have told her who you are . . ."

I held out my hand and Maria took it: we made friends by smiling and nodding. Then she turned back to Otto and spoke some more. Presently he handed her my suitcase, and she withdrew.

Otto said, "Your mother has been asleep but she is awake now. Let me take your coat."

I unbuttoned it, and he helped me off with it and laid it across the end of the couch. Then he went across the floor towards yet another door, motioning me to follow. I did, and was suddenly nervous, afraid of what I was going to find.

It was the salon of the house into which he led me. A long low-ceilinged room, whitewashed like the rest of the house, and furnished with a pleasing mixture of modern Scandinavian and antique Spanish. The tile floor was scattered with rugs, there were a great many books and pictures, and in the centre of the room a round table was laid out, seductively, with neatly ordered magazines and newspapers.

A wood fire burned in a great stone fireplace, and in front of this was a bed, with a low table alongside, holding a glass of water and a jug, a few pink geraniums in a mug, some books and a lighted lamp.

This lamp and the flicker of flames provided the only light in the room, but from the door I could see the narrow shape which humped the pink blankets and the attenuated

24

hand and arm which was extended as Otto came forward to stand on the hearth-rug.

"Darling," she said.

"Lisa." He took the hand and kissed it.

"You haven't been long after all."

"Maria says you have slept. Do you feel ready for a visitor?"

"A visitor?" Her voice was a thread. "Who?"

Otto glanced up at me, and I moved forward to stand beside him. I said, "It's me. Rebecca."

"Rebecca. Darling child. Oh, how blissfully jokey." She held out both arms to me, and I knelt down beside the bed to kiss her; her body gave me no resistance or support at all, so thin was she, and when I touched her cheek it felt papery beneath my lips. It was like kissing a leaf that has long since been wrenched by the wind from its parent tree.

"But what are you doing *here*?" She looked over my shoulder at Otto, and then back at me again. She put on the pretence of a frown. "You didn't *tell* her to come?"

"I thought you would like to see her," said Otto. "I thought it would cheer you up."

"But darling, why didn't you tell me?"

I smiled. "We wanted it to be a surprise."

"But I wish I'd known, then I could have looked forward to seeing you. That's what we always used to think, before Christmas. Half the fun was anticipation." She let me go and I sat back on my heels. "Are you going to stay?"

"For a day or so."

"Oh, how utterly perfect. We can have the most gorgeous gossips. Otto, does Maria know she's staying?"

"Of course."

"And what about dinner tonight?"

"It's all arranged . . . we'll have it together, in here, just the three of us."

"Well, let's have something now. A little drinkey. Is there any champagne?"

Otto smiled. "I think I can find a bottle. In fact, I

think I remembered to put one on ice for just such an occasion."

"Oh, you clever man."

"Shall I get it now?"

"Please, darling."

She slid her hand in mine and it was like holding chicken bones. "And we'll drink to being together."

He went away to fetch the champagne and we were alone. I found a little stool and pulled it up so that I could sit close to her. We looked at each other, and she could not stop smiling. The dazzling smile and the bright dark eyes were still the same, so was the dark hair that spread like a stain over the snowy pillowcase. Otherwise her appearance was horrifying. I had never known anyone could be so thin and still be alive. And to make it more unreal, she was not pale and colourless but quite brown, as though she still spent most of the day lying in the sun. But she was excited. It seemed she could not stop talking.

"So sweet of the darling man to know how much I would love to see you. The only thing is, I'm so boring just now, I don't feel like doing anything, he should have waited until I'm better and then we could have had some fun together, and gone swimming and out in the boat and had picnics and things."

I said, "I can come again."

"Yes, of course you can." She touched my face with her hand as though needing this contact to reassure her that I was really there. "You're looking gorgeous, do you know that? You've got your father's colouring, with those big grey eyes, and that corn-coloured hair. Is it corn, or is it gold? And I love the way you're doing it." Her hand travelled to the single plait which fell forward, like a rope over my right shoulder. "It makes you look like something out of a fairy story; you know, those old-fashioned books with the magical pictures. You're very pretty."

I shook my head. "No. I'm not."

"Well, you look it, and that's the next best thing. Darling, what are you doing with yourself? It's such ages

26

since I wrote or heard from you. Whose fault was that? Mine, I suppose, I'm hopeless at writing letters."

I told her about the bookshop and the new flat. She was amused by this. "What a funny person you are, building a little nest for yourself without anybody to share it with. Haven't you met anybody yet you want to marry?"

"No. Nor anyone who wants to marry me."

She looked malicious. "What about the man you work for?"

"He's married, he's got a charming wife and a brood of children."

She giggled. "That never bothered me. Oh, darling, what a dreadful mother I was to you, trailing you round in that reprehensible fashion. It's a wonder you haven't collected the most ghastly selection of neuroses or hang-ups or whatever they call them these days! But you don't look as though you have, so perhaps it was all right after all."

"Of course it was all right. I just grew up with my eyes open and that was no bad thing." I added, "I like Otto."

"Isn't he divine? So correct and punctilious and *northern*. And so blazingly intelligent . . . So lucky he doesn't want me to be intelligent too! He just likes having me make him laugh."

Somewhere, in the middle of the house, a clock struck seven, and as the last note chimed Otto came back into the room carrying a tray with the champagne bottle in a bucket of ice, and three wine glasses. We watched as he expertly loosened the cork and the golden foaming wine spilled into the three glasses, and we each took one and raised them, all of us smiling because it was suddenly a party. My mother said, "Here's to the three of us and happy times. Oh, so divinely jokey."

Later, I was shown to my bedroom, which was either simply luxurious or luxuriously simple, I couldn't decide which. A fitted bathroom led off it, so I showered, and changed into trousers and a silk shirt, and brushed my hair and replaited it, and returned to the salon. I found Otto and my mother waiting for me, Otto also changed for the evening, and Mother wearing a fresh bedjacket of powder blue with a silk shawl embroidered with pink roses flung across her knees, its long fringe brushing the floor. We had another drink and then Maria served dinner on a low table by the fire. My mother never stopped talking – it was all about the old days when I was growing up, and I kept thinking that Otto would be shocked, but he wasn't shocked at all, he was curious and much amused and kept asking questions and prompting my mother to tell us more.

". . . and that dreadful farm in Denbighshire . . . Rebecca, do you remember that terrible house? We nearly died of cold and the fire smoked whenever we lit it. That was Sebastian," she explained for Otto's benefit. "We all thought he was going to be a famous poet, but he wasn't any better at writing poetry than he was at sheep farming. In fact, if anything, worse. And I couldn't think how on earth I could leave him without hurting his feelings and then luckily Rebecca got bronchitis so I had the most perfect excuse."

"Not so lucky for Rebecca," suggested Otto.

"It certainly was. She hated it just as much as I did; anyway he had a horrible dog that was always threatening to bite her. Darling, is there any more champagne?"

She ate hardly anything, but sipped glass after glass of the icy wine while Otto and I worked our way steadily through Maria's delicious, four-course dinner. When it was finished, and the dishes cleared away, my mother asked for some music, and Otto put a Brahms concerto on the record-player, turned very low. Mother just went on talking, like a toy that has been overwound and will only stop whirring senselessly around the floor when it finally breaks.

Presently, saying that he had work to do, Otto excused himself and left us, first building up the fire with fresh logs and making sure that we had everything we needed.

"Does he work every evening?" I asked, when he had gone.

28

"Nearly always. And in the mornings. He's very punctilious. I think that's why we've got on so well because we're so different."

I said, "He adores you."

"Yes," said my mother, accepting this. "And the best bit is that he never tried to turn me into someone else; he just accepted me, with my wicked ways and my lurid past." She touched my plait again. "You're growing more like your father . . . I always thought you looked like me, but you don't, you look like him now. He was very handsome."

"You know, I don't even know what his name was."

"Sam Bellamy. But Bayliss is a much better name, don't you think? Besides, having you all on my own like that, I always felt you were my child and nobody else's."

"I wish you'd tell me about him. You never have."

"There's so little to tell. He was an actor, and too good-looking for words."

"But where did you meet him?"

"He came down to Cornwall with a Summer Stock company doing open-air Shakespeare. It was all terribly romantic, dark blue summer nights and the damp, dewy smell of the grass, and that divine Mendelssohn music and Sam being Oberon.

> Through the house give glimmering light
> By the dead and drowsy fire;
> Every elf and fairy sprite
> Hop as light as bird from brier.

It was magical. And falling in love with him was part of the magic."

"Was he in love with you?"

"We both thought he was."

"But you ran away with him, and married him . . ."

"Yes. But only because my parents left me with no alternative."

"I don't understand."

"They disliked him. They disapproved. They said I was

29

too young. My mother said why didn't I marry some nice young man who lived locally, why didn't I settle down and stop making an exhibition of myself? And if I married an actor, what would people say? I sometimes thought that was all she cared about, what people would say. As if it could possibly matter what anybody said."

It was, unbelievably, the first time I had ever heard her mention her mother. I said, cautiously prompting, "Didn't you like her?"

"Oh, darling, it's so long ago. It's so difficult to remember. But she stifled and repressed me. I sometimes felt she was trying to choke me with conventions. And Roger had been killed and I missed him so dreadfully. Everything would have been different if Roger had been there." She smiled. "He was so nice. Almost too nice. A real BV right from the very start."

"What's a BV?"

"Bitches' Victim. He always fell in love with the most impossible girls. And finally he married one. A little blonde doll, with dolly hair and dolly china blue eyes. My mother thought she was sweet. I couldn't stand her."

"What was she called?"

"Mollie." She made a face as though the very word tasted bad.

I laughed. "She can't have been as bad as all that."

"I thought she was. So maddeningly tidy. Always cleaning out her handbag or putting trees into her shoes, or sterilising the baby's toys."

"She had a baby then?"

"Yes, a little boy. Poor child, she insisted on calling him Eliot."

"I think that's a nice name."

"Oh, Rebecca, it's sickening." It was obvious that nothing Mollie had done could find favour in my mother's eyes. "I always felt sorry for the child, being saddled with such a dreadful name. And somehow he lived up to it, you know how people do, and after Roger was killed the poor scrap was worse than ever, always hanging round his mother's neck and having to have a light on in his room at night."

"I think you're being very unkind."

She laughed. "Yes, I know, and it wasn't his fault. He probably would have turned into quite a personable young man if his mother gave him half a chance."

"I wonder what happened to Mollie?"

"I don't know. I don't particularly care, either." My mother could always be cruelly off-hand. "It's like a dream. Like remembering dream people. Or perhaps . . ." her voice trailed away ". . . perhaps they were real and I was the dream."

I felt uncomfortable, because this was too near the truth that I was trying to keep at bay. I said quickly, "Are your parents still alive?"

"My mother died that Christmas we spent in New York. Do you remember that Christmas? The cold and the snow and all the shops full of the sound of 'Jingle Bells'? By the end of that Christmas I felt I never wanted to hear that damned tune again. My father wrote to me, but of course the letter didn't reach me until months later by which time it had followed me half round the world. And then it was really too late to write and say anything. Besides, I'm so useless about writing letters. He probably thought I simply didn't care."

"Didn't you ever write?"

"No."

"Didn't you like him either?" It seemed a sorry state of affairs.

"Oh, I adored him. He was wonderful. Terribly good-looking, attractive to women, frightfully fierce and frightening. He was a painter. Did I ever tell you that?"

A painter. I had imagined everything, but never a painter. "No, you never said."

"Well, if you'd had any sort of education at all you'd probably have guessed. Grenville Bayliss. Doesn't that mean anything to you at all?"

31

I shook my head sadly. It was terrible never to have heard of a famous grandfather.

"Well, why should it? I was never any good at trailing you round art galleries or museums. Come to think of it, I was never much good at anything. It's a wonder you've turned out so well on a solid diet of maternal neglect."

"What did he look like?"

"Who?"

"Your father."

"How do you imagine him?"

I considered the question and came up with Augustus John. "Bohemian, and bearded and rather leonine . . ."

"Wrong," said my mother. "He wasn't like that at all. He started off his life in the Navy, and the Navy left an indelible stamp on him. You see, he didn't decide to be a painter until he was nearly thirty, when he threw up a promising career and enrolled at the Slade. It nearly broke my mother's heart. And moving to Cornwall and setting up house at Porthkerris simply added insult to injury. I don't think she ever forgave him for being so selfish. She'd adored queening it in Malta, and probably fancied herself as wife to the Commander-in-Chief. I must say, he was tailor-made for the part, very blue-eyed and imposing and terrifying. He never lost what was known in those days as a quarter-deck manner."

"But you weren't terrified of him?"

"No. I loved him."

"Then why didn't you go home?"

Her face closed up. "I couldn't. I wouldn't. Terrible things had been said, by all of us. Old resentments and old truths had all come boiling up, and threats were made and ultimatums handed out. And the more they opposed me, the more determined I became, and the more impossible it was, when the time came, to admit that they'd been right, and I'd been wrong, and I'd made a hideous mistake. And if I had gone home, I would never have got away again. I knew that. And you wouldn't have belonged to me any more, you'd have belonged to your grandmother.

I couldn't have borne that. You were such a precious little thing." She smiled and added rather wistfully, "And we did have fun, didn't we?"

"Yes, of course we did."

"I would have liked to go back. Sometimes I very nearly did. It was such a lovely house. Boscarva it was called, and it was rather like this villa, standing square on a hill above the sea. When Otto first brought me here, it reminded me of Boscarva. But here it's warm and the winds are gentle; there, it was wild and stormy, and the garden was honeycombed with tall hedges to shelter the flower beds from the sea winds. I think the wind was the thing that my mother most hated. She used to seal all the windows and shut herself indoors, playing bridge with her friends or doing needlepoint."

"Didn't she ever do things with you?"

"Not really."

"But who looked after you?"

"Pettifer. And Mrs Pettifer."

"Who were they?"

"Pettifer had been in the Navy, too; he looked after my father and cleaned the silver and sometimes drove the car. And Mrs Pettifer did the cooking. I can't tell you how cosy they were. Sitting by the kitchen fire with them making toast and listening to the wind battering at the windows, knowing that it couldn't get in . . . it made you feel so safe. And we used to read fortunes from the teacups . . ." Her voice trailed off, memories uncertain now. And then, "No, that was Sophia."

"Who was Sophia?"

She did not reply. She was staring at the fire, her expression far away. Perhaps she had not heard me. She said at last, "After my mother died I should have gone back. It was naughty of me to stay away, but I was never over-endowed with what is known as moral fibre. But, you know, there are things at Boscarva that belong to me."

"What sort of things?"

"A desk, I remember. A little one, with drawers down

the side, and a lid that opened up. I think it's called a davenport. And some jade that my father brought home from China and a Venetian looking-glass. They were all mine. On the other hand, I moved around so much that they would just have been a nuisance." She looked at me, frowning a little. "But perhaps you don't think they are a nuisance. Have you got any furniture in this flat of yours?"

"No. Practically none."

"Then perhaps I'll see if I can get hold of them for you. They must still be at Boscarva, provided the house hasn't been sold or burned down or something. Would you like me to try and get hold of them?"

"More than anything. Not just because I need furniture, but because they belonged to you."

"Oh, darling, how sweet, too jokey the way you long for roots, and I could never bear to have any. I always felt they would just tie me down in one place."

"And I always feel that they would make me belong."

She said, "You belong to me."

We stayed talking until the early hours of the morning. About midnight, she asked me to refill her water-jug, and I found my way into the deserted kitchen and did this for her, and realised then that Otto, with gentle tact, had probably taken himself quietly off to bed, so that we could be together. And when at last her voice grew tired and her words began to trail off in a blur of exhaustion, I said that I was sleepy too, which I was, and I stood up, cramped from sitting, stretched, and put more logs on the fire. Then I took away her second pillow so that she lay, ready for sleep. The silken shawl had slipped to the floor, so I picked this up and folded it and laid it on a chair. It remained only to stoop and kiss her, turn off the lamp, and leave her there in the firelight. As I went through the door, she said, as she always used to say when I was a little girl, "Good night, my love. Goodbye until tomorrow."

The next morning I was awake early, aware of sunshine

streaming through the gaps in the shutters. I got up and went to open them, and saw the brilliant Mediterranean morning. I stepped out through the open windows on to the stone terrace which ran the length of the house and saw the hill sloping down to the sea, maybe a mile distant. The sand-coloured land was veiled in pink, the first tender blossoms of the almond trees. I went back into my room, dressed, and went out again – across the terrace, down a flight of steps, and through the ordered, formal garden. I vaulted a low stone wall, and walked on in the direction of the sea. Presently, I found myself in an orchard, surrounded by almond trees. I stopped and looked up at a froth of pink blossom and beyond it a pale and cloudless blue sky.

I knew that each flower would bear a precious fruit which, when the time came, would be frugally cropped, but even so I could not resist picking a single spray, and I was still carrying this when an hour or so later, having walked to the sea and back, I retraced my steps up the hill towards the villa.

It was steeper than I had realised. Pausing for breath, I looked up at the house, and saw Otto Pedersen standing on the terrace watching my progress. For an instant we both stood still; then he moved and started down the steps, and came down the garden to meet me.

I went on more slowly, still holding the spray of blossom. I knew then. I knew before he came close enough for me to see the expression on his face, but I went on, up through the orchard, and we met at last by the little dry-stone wall.

He said my name. That was all.

I said, "I know. You don't have to tell me."

"She died during the night. When Maria went in this morning to wake her . . . it was all over. It was so peaceful."

It occurred to me that we were not doing much to comfort each other. Or maybe there was no need. He put out a hand to help me over the wall, and kept my hand in his as we walked together up through the garden to the house.

She was buried, according to Spanish law, that very day, and in the little churchyard in the village. There was only the priest present, and Otto and Maria and myself. When it was all over, I put the spray of almond blossom on to her grave.

I flew back to London the next morning, and Otto drove me to the airport in his car. For most of the time we travelled in silence, but as we approached the terminal he suddenly said, "Rebecca, I don't know whether this has any significance, but I would have married Lisa. I would have married her, but I already have a wife in Sweden. We do not live together, and have not done so for a number of years, but she will not divorce me because her religion will not allow it."

"You didn't need to tell me, Otto."

"I wanted you to know."

"You made her so happy. You took such care of her."

"I am glad that you came. I am glad that you saw her."

"Yes." There was, all at once, a terrible lump in my throat, and my eyes filled and brimmed with painful tears. "Yes, I am glad too."

In the terminal, my ticket and my luggage checked, we stood and faced each other.

"Don't wait," I said. "Go now. I hate goodbyes."

"All right . . . but first . . ." He felt in his jacket pocket and took out three fine, worn silver bracelets. My mother had worn them always. She had been wearing them that last night. "You must have these." He took my hand and slipped them on to my wrist. "And this." Out of another pocket came a folded wad of British notes. He pressed it into my palm and closed my fingers over it. "They were in her handbag . . . so you must have them."

I knew they hadn't been in her handbag. She never had any money in her handbag except a few coppers for the next telephone call, and some dog-eared bills, long overdue. But there was something in Otto's face that I couldn't refuse, so I took the money and kissed him, and he turned on his heel, without a word.

I flew back to London in a state of miserable indecision. Emotionally I was empty, drained even of grief. Physically I found that I was exhausted but I could neither sleep nor face the meal that the stewardess offered me. She brought me tea and I tried to drink that, but it tasted bitter and I left it to grow cold.

It was as though a long-locked door had been opened, but only a crack, and it was up to me to open it wide, although what lay behind it was dark and fraught with uncertainty.

Perhaps I should go to Cornwall and seek out my mother's family, but the glimpses I had been given of the set-up at Porthkerris were not encouraging. My grandfather would be very old, lonely and probably bitter. I realised that I had made no arrangement with Otto Pedersen about letting him know that my mother was dead, and so there was the hideous possibility that if I went to see him, I should be the one who would have to break the news. As well, I blamed him a little for having let his daughter make such a mess of her life. I knew that she was impulsive and thoughtless, and stubborn too, but surely he could have been a little more positive in his dealings with her. He could have sought her out, offered to help, inspected me, his grandchild. But he had done none of these things, and surely this would always stand like a high wall between us.

And yet, I longed for roots. I did not necessarily want to live with them, but I wanted them to be there. There were things at Boscarva that had belonged to my mother, and so now belonged to me. She had wanted me to have them, had said as much, so perhaps I was under an obligation to go to Cornwall and claim them as my own, but to go only for this reason seemed both soulless and greedy.

I leaned back and dozed and heard again my mother's voice.

I was never frightened of him. I loved him. I should have gone back.

And she had said a name – Sophia – but I had never found out who Sophia was.

I slept at last and dreamed that I was there. But the house in my dream had no shape or form and the only real thing about it was the sound of the wind, battering its way inland, fresh and cold from the open sea.

I was in London by the early afternoon, but the dark day had lost its shape and meaning, and I could not think what I was meant to do with what remained of it. In the end I got a taxi and went to Walton Street to seek out Stephen Forbes.

I found him upstairs, going through a box of books out of an old house which had just been sold up. There was no one else with him, and as I appeared at the top of the stairs he stood up and came towards me, thinking that I was a potential customer. When he saw that I was not, his manner changed.

"Rebecca! You're back."

I stood there, with my hands in my coat pockets.

"Yes. I got in about two." He watched me, his face a question. I said, "My mother died, early yesterday morning. I was just in time. I had an evening with her, and we talked and talked."

"I see," said Stephen. "I'm glad you saw her." He cleared some books from the edge of a table, and leaned against it, folding his arms and eyeing me through his spectacles. He said, "What are you going to do now?"

"I don't know."

"You look exhausted. Why not take a few days off?"

I said again, "I don't know."

He frowned. "What don't you know?"

"I don't know what to do."

"What's the problem?"

"Stephen, have you ever heard of an artist called Grenville Bayliss?"

"Heavens, yes. Why?"

"He's my grandfather."

Stephen's face was a study. "Good Lord. When did you find that out?"

"My mother told me. I'd never heard of him," I had to admit.

"You should have."

"Is he well known?"

"He was, twenty years ago when I was a boy. There was a Grenville Bayliss over the dining-room fireplace in my father's old house in Oxford. Part of my growing up, one might say. A grey stormy sea and a fishing boat with a brown sail. Used to make me feel seasick to look at it. He specialised in seascapes."

"He was a sailor. I mean, he'd been in the Royal Navy."

"That follows."

I waited for him to go on, but he was silent. I said at last, "What am I to do, Stephen?"

"What do you want to do, Rebecca?"

"I never had a family."

"Is it so important?"

"Suddenly it is."

"Then go and see him. Is there any reason not to?"

"I'm frightened."

"Of what?"

"I don't know. Of being snubbed, I suppose. Or ignored."

"Were there dreadful family rows?"

"Yes. And cuttings-off. And never darken my door again. You know the sort of thing."

"Did your mother suggest that you went?"

"No. Not in so many words. But she said there were some things that belonged to her. She thought I should have them."

"What sort of things?"

I told him. "I know it's nothing very much. Perhaps not even worth making the journey for. But I'd like to have something that belonged to her. Besides . . ." I tried to turn it into a joke ". . . they might help to fill up some of the blank spaces in the new flat."

"I think collecting your possessions should be a secondary reason for going to Cornwall. Your first should be making friends with Grenville Bayliss."

"Supposing he doesn't want to make friends?"

"Then no harm has been done. Except possibly a little bruising to your pride, but that won't kill you."

"You're rail-roading me into this," I told him.

"If you didn't want my advice, then why did you come to see me?"

He had a point. "I don't know," I admitted.

He laughed. "You don't know much, do you?" and when at last I smiled back, he said, "Look. Today's Thursday. Go home and get some sleep. And if tomorrow's too soon, then go down to Cornwall at the weekend. Just go. See how the land lies, see how the old boy is. It may take a few days, but that doesn't matter. Don't come back to London until you've done all you can. And if you can get hold of your own bits and pieces, well and good, but remember that they're of secondary importance."

"Yes. I'll remember."

He stood up. "Then push off," he said. "I've got enough to do without wasting my time running a private Tell Auntie column on your account."

"Can I come back to work when all this is over?"

"You better had. I can't manage without you."

"Goodbye then," I said.

"Au revoir," said Stephen, and as if on an afterthought, leaned forward to give me a clumsy kiss.

"And Good Luck!"

I had already spent enough money on taxis, so, still carrying my case, I walked up to the bus stop and waited until one came, and lurched my way back to Fulham. Gazing, unseeing, out of the window at the grey, crowded streets, I tried to make some plans. I would go to Cornwall, as Stephen suggested, on Monday. At this time of year it shouldn't be difficult to get a seat on the train or find somewhere to stay when I finally got to Porthkerris. And Maggie would keep an eye on my flat.

Thinking of the flat made me remember the chairs I had bought before I had gone to Ibiza. That day seemed a lifetime ago. But if I did not claim them then they would be sold as the disagreeable young man had threatened. With this in mind, I got off the bus a few stops before my own so that I could call into the shop and pay for the chairs and thus be certain that they would be waiting for me when I returned.

I had steeled myself to do business once more with the young man in the blue denims, but as I let myself in and the bell rang with the opening and the closing of the door, I saw with some relief that it was not he who stood up from behind the desk at the back of the shop, but another man, older, with grey hair and a dark beard.

He came forward, taking off a pair of horn-rimmed spectacles, as I thankfully put down my suitcase.

"Good afternoon."

"Oh, good afternoon. I came about some chairs I bought last Monday. Cherrywood, balloon-back ones."

"Oh, yes, I know."

"One of them had to be repaired."

"It's been done. Do you want to take them with you?"

"No. I've got a suitcase. I can't carry them. And I'm going away for a few days. But I thought if I paid for them now, perhaps you'd keep them until I got back."

"Yes, of course." He had a charming, deep voice, and when he smiled his rather saturnine face lit up.

I began to open my bag. "Will it be all right if I write you a cheque? I've got a Banker's Card."

"That's all right . . . would you like to use my desk? And here's a pen."

I began to write. "Who shall I make it out to?"

"To me. Tristram Nolan."

I was gratified to know that it was he who owned this pleasant shop and not my mannerless, cowboy friend. I wrote the cheque and crossed it, and handed it to him. He stood, head down, reading it, and took so long that I thought I must have forgotten something.

"Have I put the date?"

"Yes, that's perfect." He looked up. "It's just your name. Bayliss. It's not very common."

"No. No it's not."

"Are you any relation to Grenville Bayliss?"

Having his name flung at me, just now, was extraordinary and yet not extraordinary at all, in the same way that a name, or a relevant item of news, will spring at you, unbidden, from a page of close print.

I said, "Yes, I am." And then because there was no reason why he shouldn't know, "He's my grandfather."

"Extraordinary," he said.

I was puzzled. "Why?"

"I'll show you." He laid my cheque down on his desk and went to pull out from behind a drop-leafed sofa table a large, sturdy oil painting in a gilt frame. He held it up, balancing one corner on his desk, and I saw that it was by my grandfather. His signature was in the corner, and the date below it, 1932.

"I've only just bought it. It needs cleaning, of course, but I think it's very charming."

I stepped closer to inspect it, and saw sand dunes in an evening light, and two young boys, naked, bent over a collection of shells. The work was perhaps old-fashioned, but the composition charming – the colouring delicate and yet somehow robust – as though the boys, vulnerable in their nakedness, were still tough, and creatures to be reckoned with.

"He was good, wasn't he?" I said, and could not hide the note of pride in my voice.

"Yes. A marvellous colourist." He put the picture back. "Do you know him well?"

"I don't know him at all. I've never met him."

42

He said nothing, simply stood, waiting for me to enlarge on this odd statement. To fill the silence I went on. "But I've decided that perhaps it's time I did. In fact, I'm going to Cornwall on Monday."

"But that's splendid. The roads will be empty at this time of the year, and it's a lovely drive."

"I'm going by train. I haven't got a car."

"It will still be a pleasant journey. I hope the sun shines for you."

"Thank you very much."

We moved back to the door. He opened it, I picked up my suitcase. "You'll look after my chairs for me?"

"Of course. Goodbye. And have a good time in Cornwall."

3

But the sun did not shine for me. Monday dawned grey and depressing as ever and my faint hopes that the weather would improve as the train rocketed westwards soon died, for the sky darkened with every mile and the wind got up and the day finally dissolved into pouring rain. There was nothing to be seen from the streaming windows; only the blurred shapes of hills and farmsteads, and every now and then the clustered roofs of a village flashed by, or we raced through the half-empty station of some small anonymous town.

By Plymouth, I comforted myself, it would be different. We would cross the Saltash Bridge and find ourselves in another country, another climate, where there would be pink-washed cottages and palm trees and thin winter sunshine. But of course all that happened was that the rain fell even more relentlessly; as I stared out at flooded fields and leafless wind-torn trees, my hopes finally died and I began to be discouraged.

It was nearly a quarter to five by the time we reached the junction which was the end of my journey, and the dark afternoon had sunk, already, into twilight. As the train slowed down alongside the platform, I saw an incongruous palm tree, silhouetted like a broken umbrella against the streaming sky, and the falling rain shimmered and danced in front of the lighted sign which said "St Abbotts, change for Porthkerris." The train finally stopped. I shouldered my rucksack and opened the heavy door which was instantly torn out of my grasp by the wind. The sudden impact of strong cold air, driven inland over the dark sea, made me gasp, and with some idea of making haste

I picked up my bag and jumped out on to the platform. I followed the general exodus of travellers up and over the wooden bridge to the station building on the far side. Most of the other passengers seemed to have friends to meet them, or else walked through the ticket office in a purposeful fashion, as though knowing that a car was waiting for them on the far side. Blindly, I followed them, feeling very new and strange but hoping that they would lead me to a taxi. But when I came out into the station yard, there were no taxis. I stood about, hopeful of being offered a lift, but too shy to ask for one, until the tail light of the last car, inevitably, disappeared up the hill in the direction of the main road and I was forced to return to the ticket office for help and advice.

I found a porter, stacking hen coops in a smelly parcels office.

"I'm sorry, but I have to get to Porthkerris. Would there be a taxi?"

He shook his head slowly, without hope, and then said, brightening slightly, "There's a bus. Runs every hour." He glanced up at the slow-ticking clock high on the wall. "But you've just missed one, so you'll 'ave to wait some time."

"Can't I ring up for a taxi?"

"Isn't much call for taxis at this time of the year."

I let my heavy rucksack slip to the floor and we gazed at each other, both defeated by the enormity of the problem. My wet feet were slowly congealing. As we stood there, there came, above the noise of the storm, the sound of a car, driven very fast down the hill from the road.

I said, raising my voice slightly in order to make my point, "I must get a taxi. Where could I telephone?"

"There's a box just out there . . ."

I turned to go in search of it, trailing my rucksack behind me, and as I did so I heard the car stop outside in the yard; a door slammed, footsteps ran, and the next moment a man appeared, banging the door open and shut against the icy wind. He shook himself like a dog before crossing the floor and disappearing through the open door of the Parcels Office.

I heard him say, "Hello, Ernie. I think there's a parcel here for me. From London."

"'Ullo, Mr Gardner. That's a dirty night."

"Filthy. The road's awash. That looks like it . . . that one over there. Yes, that's it. Want me to sign for it?"

"Oh, yes, you'll 'ave to sign. 'Ere we are . . ."

I imagined the slip of paper, smoothed on a table top, the stub of a pencil taken from behind Ernie's ear. And for the life of me I could not remember where I had heard that voice before, nor why I knew it so well.

"That's great. Thanks very much."

"You're welcome."

The telephone, the taxi, forgotten for the moment, I watched the door, waiting for him to reappear. When he did, carrying a large box stuck with red GLASS labels, I saw the long legs, the blue denims drenched in mud to the knee, and a black oilskin, beaded and running with rivulets of water. He was bare-headed, his black hair plastered to his skull, and he saw me for the first time and stopped dead, holding the parcel in front of him like an offering. In his dark eyes was first a flicker of puzzlement, and then recognition. He began to smile. He said, "Good God!"

It was the young man who had sold me the two little cherrywood chairs.

I stood open-mouthed, feeling obscurely that someone had played me a mean and unfair trick. If ever I was in need of a friend it was at this moment, and yet fate had chosen to send me possibly the last person on earth I ever wanted to see again. And that he should see me thus, drenched and desperate, was somehow the last straw.

His smile widened. "What a fantastic coincidence. What are you doing here?"

"I've just got off the train."

"Where are you going?"

I had to tell him. "To Porthkerris."

"Is someone coming for you?"

47

I very nearly lied and told him "yes." Anything to get rid of him. But I was always a useless fibber, and he would be bound to guess the truth. I said, "No," and then I went on, trying to sound competent, as though I could take good care of myself, "I'm just going to phone for a taxi."

"It'll take hours. I'm going to Porthkerris, I'll give you a ride."

"Oh, you don't need to bother . . ."

"No bother, I'm going anyway. Is that all your luggage?"

"Yes, but . . ."

"Come on then."

I still hesitated, but he seemed to consider the matter already settled, going over to the door to open it, and holding it open with his shoulder, waiting for me to follow. So eventually I did, edging past him, and out into the fury of the dark evening.

In the dim light I saw the Mini pick-up, parked, with the sidelights burning. Letting the door slam behind him, he crossed over to this, and gently loaded his parcel into the back, and then took my rucksack from me, and heaved this in too, covering the two bundles in a cursory fashion with an old piece of tarpaulin. I stood watching him, but he said, "Go on, get in, there's no point us both getting wet through," so I did as I was told, settling myself in the passenger seat with my bag jammed between my legs. Almost at once he had joined me, shutting his door with an almighty slam, and switching on the engine as though there were not a moment to be lost. We roared up the hill away from the station, and the next moment had turned on to the main road and were heading for Porthkerris.

He said, "Tell me more, now. I thought you lived in London."

"Yes, I do."

"Have you come down for a holiday?"

"Sort of."

"That sounds good and vague. Are you staying with friends?"

"Yes. No. I don't know."

"What does that mean?"

"Just that. It means I don't know." This sounded rude but it couldn't be helped. I felt as though I had no control over what I was saying.

"Well, you'd better make up your mind before you get to Porthkerris, otherwise you'll be spending the night on the beach."

"I . . . I'm going to stay in a hotel. Just for tonight."

"Well, that's great. Which one?"

I sent him an exasperated look and he said, reasonably enough, "Well, if I don't know which one, I can't take you there, can I?"

He seemed to have me cornered. I said, "I haven't booked in to any hotel. I mean, I thought I could do that when I arrived. There *are* hotels, aren't there?"

"Porthkerris is running with them. Every other house is a hotel. But at this time of the year most of them are closed."

"Do you know some that are open?"

"Yes. But it depends what you want to pay."

He glanced at me sideways, taking in my patched jeans, scuffed shoes, and an old fur-lined leather coat that I had worn for warmth and comfort. At the moment this garment looked and smelt like a wet dog.

"We go from one extreme to the other. The Castle, up on the hill, where you change for dinner, and dance the foxtrot to a three-piece orchestra, right down to Mrs Kernow who does Bed and Breakfast at Number Two, Fish Lane. Mrs Kernow I can recommend. She looked after me for three months or more before I got into my own place, and her prices are very reasonable."

I was diverted. "Your own place? You mean you live here?"

"I do now. Have done for the last six months."

"But . . . the shop in the New Kings Road . . . where I bought the chairs?"

"I was just helping out for a day or so."

We came to a crossroads, and, slowing down, he turned to look at me. "Have you got the chairs yet?"

"No. But I've paid for them. They'll still be there when I get back."

"Good," said the young man.

We drove for a little in silence. Through a village, and up over a wild bit of country high above the sea; then the road leaned down again, and there were trees on either side of us. Through these, through twisted trunks and branches tortured by the wind, there presently appeared, far below us, the twinkling lights of a little town.

"Is that Porthkerris?"

"It is. And in a moment you're going to have to tell me if it's to be The Castle or Fish Lane."

I swallowed. The Castle was out of the question, obviously, but if I went to Fish Lane I would necessarily place myself under an obligation to this managing person. I had not come to Porthkerris for any other reason than to see Grenville Bayliss, and I had an uncomfortable feeling that if I once got involved with this man he would stick like a burr.

I said, "No, not The Castle . . ." meaning to suggest some other, more modest establishment, but he cut me short.

"That's great," he said, with a grin. "Mrs Kernow of Fish Lane it is, and you won't regret it."

My first impression of Porthkerris, in the dark and the gusty rain, was confused to say the least of it. The town was, on this unsalubrious evening, nearly empty of people; the deserted streets gleamed wetly with reflected light, and the gutters ran with water.

At a great speed, we plunged down into a warren of baffling lanes and alleys, at one time emerging out on to the road which circled the harbour, only to turn back once more into the maze of cobbled roads and uneven, haphazard houses.

We turned at last into a narrow street of grey terrace houses, with front doors opening flush on to the pavement.

All was seemly and respectable. Lace curtains veiled windows, and there could be glimpsed statuettes of girls with dogs, or large green pots containing aspidistras.

The car slowed at last and stopped.

"We're here." He switched off the engine, and I could hear the wind and, above its whine, the nearby sound of the sea. Great breakers thundered up on to the sand, and there was the long hiss of the retreating waves.

He said, "You know, I don't know your name."

"It's Rebecca Bayliss. And I don't know yours."

"Joss Gardner . . . it's short for Jocelyn, not Joseph." With this useful bit of information he got out of the car and rang a bell in a door and, while waiting for an answer, went to retrieve my rucksack from underneath the tarpaulin. As he heaved it out, the door opened and he turned and was illuminated in a shaft of warm light which streamed from inside the house.

"Joss!"

"Hello, Mrs Kernow."

"What are you doing here?"

"I've brought you a visitor. I said you were the best hotel in Porthkerris."

"Oh, my soul, I don't belong to take visitors at this time of the year. But come along in now, out of the rain, what weather isn't it? Tom's down at the Coastguard lodge, been some sort of a warning up from the Trevose way, but I don't know, I haven't heard no rockets . . ."

Somehow we were all inside and the door shut and there was scarcely room for the three of us to stand in the narrow hall.

"Come along in by the fire . . . it's nice and warm, I'll get you a cup of tea if you like . . ." We followed her into a tiny, cluttered, cosy parlour. She knelt to poke the fire to

51

life and add more coal, and for the first time I was able to take a good look at her. I saw a small, bespectacled lady, quite elderly, wearing bedroom slippers and a pinafore over her good brown dress.

"We don't really want tea," he told her. "We just want to know if you can give Rebecca a bed – for a night or so."

She stood up from the fireplace. "Well, I don't know . . ." She looked at me doubtfully, and what with my appearance and the dog-smelling coat I didn't blame her for being doubtful.

I started to open my mouth, but Joss sailed in before I could say a word. "She's highly respectable and she won't run away with the spoons. I'll vouch for her."

"Well . . ." Mrs Kernow smiled. Her eyes were pretty, a very pale blue. "The room's empty, so she may as well have it. But I can't give her supper tonight, not expecting anybody, I haven't anything in the house but a couple of little pasties."

"That's all right," said Joss. "I'll feed her."

I started to protest, but once again I was overborne. "I'll leave her here to get settled in and unpacked, and then I'll be back about . . ." he glanced at his watch ". . . seven thirty, to pick her up. That all right?" he flung casually in my direction. "You're an angel, Mrs Kernow, and I love you like a mother." He put an arm around her and kissed her. She looked delighted; then he gave me a final, cheerful grin, said, "See you," and so departed. We heard his car roaring away down the street.

"He's a lovely boy," Mrs Kernow informed me. "I had him living here three months or more . . . now come along, pick up your little bag and I'll show you your room. 'Course it'll be cold, but I've got an electric fire you can have, and the water in the tank's nice and hot if you want a bath . . . I always say you feel so mucky coming off those dirty trains . . ."

The room was as tiny as all the other rooms in this little house, furnished with an enormous double bed which took

52

up nearly all the space. But it was clean and, presently, warm, and after Mrs Kernow had shown me where to find the bathroom she went back downstairs and left me to myself.

I went to kneel by the low window and draw back the curtains. The old frames had been jammed tight shut against the wind by rubber wedges, and the dark glass streamed with rain. There was nothing to be seen, but I stayed there anyway, wondering what I was doing in this little house, and trying to work out why Joss Gardner's sudden reappearance in my life had left me with this unexplained feeling of unease.

4

I needed defences. I needed to build up my confidence
and my self-esteem, disliking the role of rescued waif in
which I had suddenly found myself. A hot bath and a
change of clothes went a long way towards restoring my
composure. I did my hair, made up my eyes, splashed
on the last of a bottle of expensive scent and was halfway
towards being in charge again. I had already unpacked a
dress from the ubiquitous rucksack and hung it hopefully
to shed its wrinkles; now I put it on, a dark cotton with
long sleeves, and dark stockings, very fine, and shoes with
heels and old-fashioned buckles which I had found, long
back, on a stall in the Portobello Road . . . As I fastened
my pearl ear-rings I heard, over the rattle and bang of
the gusty wind, the sound of Joss Gardner's little van,
tyres drumming on the cobbles, coming up the street. It
screeched to a noisy halt outside the door, and the next
moment I heard his voice downstairs, calling first for Mrs
Kernow and then for me.

I continued, slowly, to screw the fastening of the last
ear-ring. I picked up my bag, and then my leather coat.
This I had draped near the electric fire in the hope that
it would dry off, but it hadn't. The heat had merely
emphasised the smell of a spaniel come in from a wet
walk, and it still weighed heavy as lead. Lugging it over
my arm, I went down the stairs.

"Hallo, there." Joss, in the hall, looked up at me. "Well,
what a transformation. Feel better now?"

"Yes."

"Give me your coat . . ."

He took it from me intending to help me on with it, and

instantly became a comic weightlifter, sagging at the knees with the sheer bulk of it.

"You can't wear this, it'll drive you into the ground. Anyway it's still wet."

"I haven't got another." Still toting the coat, he started to laugh. My self-esteem began to drain away and some of this must have showed on my face, because he suddenly stopped laughing and shouted for Mrs Kernow. When she appeared, with an expression both exasperated and loving on her face, he bundled my coat into her arms, told her to dry it for me, unbuttoned and removed his own black oilskin and laid it, with a certain grace, around my shoulders.

Beneath it he wore a soft grey sweater, a cotton scarf knotted at the neck. "Now," he said, "we are ready to go." He opened the door, on to a curtain of rain.

I protested, "But you'll get wet," but he only said "Scuttle" so I scuttled, and he scuttled too, and the next instant we were back in the van, scarcely wet at all, with the doors banged tight and shut against the storm, although small puddles of rain on my seat and at my feet gave rise to the suspicion that this staunch vehicle was no longer as watertight as it had once been. But he started the noisy engine and we were away, and with the volume of water both outside and inside the car it was a little like being taken for a fast ride in a leaky motor boat.

I said, "Where are we going?"

"The Anchor. It's just round the corner. Not very smart. Do you mind?"

"Why should I mind?"

"You might mind. You might have wanted to be taken to The Castle."

"You mean to foxtrot to a three-piece orchestra?"

He grinned. He said, "I can't foxtrot. Nobody ever learned me."

We flashed down Fish Lane, around a right-angled corner or two, beneath a stone archway and so out into a small square. One side of this was formed by the low, uneven shape of an old inn. Warm light shone from behind small windows spilled from a crooked doorway and the Inn sign over the door swung and creaked in the wind. There were four or five cars already parked outside, and Joss inserted the van neatly into a tidy space between two of them, turned off the engine, said, "One, two, three, run," and we both got out and sprinted the short distance between the car and the shelter of the porch.

There Joss shook himself slightly, brushed the rain from the soft surface of his sweater, took the oilskin off my shoulders and opened the door for me to go ahead of him.

It was warm inside, and low-ceilinged and smelt the way old pubs have always smelt. Of beer and pipe smoke and musty wood. There was a bar, with high stools, and tables around the edge of the room. Two old men were playing darts in a corner.

The barman looked up and said, "Hi, Joss." Joss put the oilskin up on a coat hook, and led me across the room to be introduced.

"Tommy, this is Rebecca. Rebecca, this is Tommy Williams. He's been here man and boy; anything you want to know about Porthkerris, or the people who live here, you come and ask Tommy."

We said, "How do you do." Tommy had grey hair and a lot of wrinkles. He looked as though he might be a fisherman in his spare time. We sat ourselves on two stools, and Joss ordered a Scotch and soda for me and a Scotch and water for himself, and while Tommy fixed these the two men began to talk, falling comfortably into conversation the way men in pubs always seem to.

"How are things going with you?" That was Tommy.

"Not too bad."

"When are you opening up?"

"Easter, maybe, with a bit of luck."

"Place finished is it?"

"More or less."

"Who's doing the carpentry?"

57

"Doing it myself."

"That'll save you something."

My attention wandered. I lit a cigarette and looked around me, liking what I saw. The two old men playing darts; a young couple, jeaned and long-haired, crouched over a table and a couple of pints of bitter, discussing, with avid and intense concentration – existentialism? Concrete painting? How they were going to pay the rent? Something. But it mattered, intensely, to both of them.

And then a party of four, older, expensively dressed, the men self-consciously casual, the women unwittingly formal. I guessed they were staying at The Castle, and out of boredom with the weather, perhaps, had come down the town for a spot of slumming. They seemed uncomfortable, as though they knew they looked out of place, and could scarcely wait to get back to the padded velvet comfort of the big hotel on the hill.

My eyes moved on around the room, and it was then that I caught sight of the dog. He was a beautiful dog, a great red setter, his coat handsome and shining, his tail a silken plume of copper fur against the grey flags of the floor. He sat very still, close to his master, and every now and then the tail would move slightly in a thump of approval, a private applause.

Intrigued, I inspected the man who appeared to own this enviable creature, and found him almost as interesting as the dog. Sitting, with an elbow on the table top, and his chin resting on his fist, he presented to me a clear and unblurred profile, almost as though he were posing for my inspection. His head was well shaped, and his hair had that thick silver-fox look of a person who has started to go grey early in life. The single eye which his profile allowed me was deep-set, and darkly shadowed, the nose was long and aquiline, the mouth pleasant, the chin strongly formed. And, from the length of his wrist, emerging from a checked shirt cuff and the sleeve of a grey tweed jacket, and the way he disposed of his legs beneath the little table, I guessed that he was tall, probably over six feet.

58

As I watched him, he laughed suddenly at something his companion had said. This drew my attention to the other man, and I felt a shock of surprise, because, for some reason, they did not match. Where the one was slender and elegant, the other was short, fat, red of face, and dressed in a tight-fitting navy blue blazer and a shirt collar that looked as though it were about to strangle him. It was not overly warm in the pub, but there was a shine of sweat on the ruddy brow, and I saw that the dark hair had been barbered with some ingenuity, so that a long oiled lock was combed up and over, concealing what would otherwise have been a totally bald head.

The man with the dog was not smoking, but the fat man suddenly crushed out his own cigarette in the brimming ash-tray on the table, as though emphasising some point that he was making, and almost instantly reached into his pocket for a silver case and another cigarette.

But the man with the dog had decided that it was time to go. He took his hand from his chin, pushed back his shirt cuff to consult his watch, and then finished his drink. The fat man, apparently anxious to comply with the other's arrangements, hastily lit the cigarette and then tossed back his whisky. They began to get up, pushing back their chairs with a hideous scraping sound. The dog stood up, his tail swooping in exultant circles.

Standing, one so short and fat and the other so tall and slim, the two men looked more ill-assorted than ever. The thin one reached for a raincoat which had been lying across the back of his chair and slung it over his shoulders like a cloak, and then turned towards us, heading for the door. For an instant I was disappointed, because full face, his finely drawn good looks did not live up to the promise of that intriguing profile. And then I forgot about being disappointed, because he suddenly saw Joss. And Joss, perhaps sensing his presence, stopped talking to Tommy Williams and turned to see who was standing behind him. For an instant they both looked disconcerted, and then the tall man smiled, and the smile etched lines down his thin brown cheeks and creased up his eyes, and it was impossible not to be warmed by such charm.

He said, "Joss. Long time no see." His voice was pleasant and friendly.

"Hi," said Joss, not getting off his stool.

"I thought you were in London."

"No. Back again."

The creaking swing of the door caught my attention. The other man, the fat man, had quietly left. I decided that he had an urgent appointment and thought no more about it.

"I'll tell the old boy I've seen you."

"Yes. Do that."

The deep-set eyes moved in my direction, and then away again. I waited to be introduced, but nothing happened. For some reason this lack of manners on Joss's part was like a slap in the face.

At last, "Well, see you around," said the tall man, and moved off.

"Sure," said Joss.

"Night, Tommy," he called to the barman as he pushed the door open and let the dog out ahead of him.

"Good night, Mr Bayliss," said the barman.

I felt my head jerk around as though someone had pulled a string. He had already disappeared, leaving the door swinging behind him. Without thinking, I slipped off the stool to go after him, but a hand caught my arm and restrained me, and I turned to find Joss holding me back. For a surprising second our eyes clashed, and then I shook myself free. Outside I heard a car start up. Now it was too late.

I said, "Who is he?"

"Eliot Bayliss."

Eliot. Roger's boy. Mollie's child. Grenville Bayliss's grandson. My cousin. My family.

"He's my cousin."

"I didn't know that."

"You know my name. Why didn't you tell him? Why did you stop me going after him?"

"You'll meet him soon enough. Tonight it's too late and too wet and too dark for family reunions."

"Grenville Bayliss is my grandfather, too."

"I thought there was probably some connection," said Joss coolly. "Have another drink."

By now I was really angry. "I don't want another drink."

"In that case, let's go and eat."

"I don't want to eat either."

I thought that I truly didn't want to. I didn't want to spend another moment with this boorish and overbearing young man. I watched him finish his drink and get down off his stool, and for an instant I thought that he was actually going to take me at my word; was going to drive me back to Fish Lane and there dump me, un-nourished. But, luckily, he did not call my bluff, simply paid for the drinks, and without a word led the way through a door at the far end of the bar, which gave on to a flight of stairs and a small restaurant. I followed him because there didn't seem to be anything else to do. Besides, I was hungry.

Most of the tables were already occupied, but a waitress saw Joss and recognised him and came over to say good evening, and led us to what was obviously the best table in the room, set in the narrow alcove of a jutting bay window. Beyond the window could be seen the shapes of rain-washed roofs, and beyond them again the liquid darkness of the harbour, a-shimmer with reflections from the street lamps on the quay and the riding lights of fishing boats.

We faced each other. I was still deeply angry and would not look at him. I sat, drawing patterns with my finger on the table mat, and listened to him ordering what I was to eat. Apparently I was not even to be allowed the right of making my own choice. I heard the waitress say, "For the young lady, too?" as though even she were surprised by his cursory behaviour, and Joss said, "Yes, for the young lady, too," and the waitress went off, and we were alone.

After a little I looked up. His dark gaze met mine, unblinking. The silence grew, and I had the ridiculous feeling that he was waiting for me to apologise to him.

I heard myself say, "If you won't let me talk to Eliot Bayliss, perhaps you'll talk about him."

"What do you want to know?"

"Is he married?" It was the first question that came into my head.

"No."

"He's attractive." Joss acknowledged this. "Does he live alone?"

"No, with his mother. They have a house up at High Cross, six miles or so from here, but about a year ago they moved into Boscarva, to be with the old·man."

"Is my grandfather ill?"

"You don't know very much about your family, do you?"

"No." I sounded defiant.

"About ten years ago Grenville Bayliss had a heart attack. That's when he stopped painting. But he always appears to have had the constitution of an ox, and he made a miraculous recovery. He didn't want to leave Boscarva, and he had this couple to take care of him . . ."

"The Pettifers?"

Joss frowned. "How do you know about the Pettifers?"

"My mother told me." I thought of the long-ago tea parties by the kitchen fire. "I never imagined they'd still be there."

"Mrs Pettifer died last year, so Pettifer and your grand-father were left on their own. Grenville Bayliss is eighty now, and Pettifer can't be far behind him. Mollie Bayliss wanted them to move up to High Cross and sell Boscarva, but the old man was adamant, so in the end she and Eliot moved in with him. Without noticeable enthusiasm, I may add." He leaned back in his chair, his long clever hands resting on the edge of the table. "Your mother . . . was she called Lisa?" I nodded.

"I knew Grenville had a daughter who'd had a daughter,

but the fact that you call yourself Bayliss threw me slightly."

"My father left my mother before I was born. She never used his name."

"Where's your mother now?"

"She died – just a few days ago. In Ibiza." I repeated, "Just a few days ago," because all at once it seemed like a lifetime.

"I'm sorry." I made some sort of vague gesture, because there weren't any words. "Does your grandfather know?"

"I don't know."

"Have you come to tell him?"

"I suppose I may have to." The idea of doing so was daunting.

"Does he know you're here? In Porthkerris?"

I shook my head. "He doesn't even know me. I mean we've never met. I've never been here before." I made the final admission. "I don't even know how to find his house."

"One way and another," said Joss, "you're going to give him something of a shock."

I felt anxious. "Is he very frail?"

"No, he's not frail. He's fantastically tough. But he's getting old."

"My mother said he was frightening. Is he still frightening?"

Joss made a gruesome face, doing nothing to comfort me. "Terrifying," he said.

The waitress brought our soup. It was oxtail, thick and brown and very hot. I was so hungry that I ate it right down to the bottom of the bowl without saying another word. As I finally laid down my spoon, I looked up and saw that Joss was laughing at me.

"For a girl who didn't want to eat, you haven't done so badly."

But this time I did not rise. I pushed the empty bowl away, and leaned my elbows on the table.

"How is it that you know so much about the Bayliss family?" I asked him.

63

Joss had not bolted his soup as I had. Now, he was taking his time, buttering a roll, being maddeningly slow.

"It's easy," he said. "I do a certain amount of work up at Boscarva."

"What sort of work?"

"Well, I restore antique furniture. And don't gape in that unattractive fashion, it does nothing for you."

"*Restore antique furniture?* You must be joking."

"I'm not. And Grenville Bayliss has a houseful of old and very valuable stuff. In his day he made a lot of money, and he invested most of it in antiques. Now, some of the things are in a shocking state of repair, not that they haven't been polished to within an inch of their lives, but then years ago he put in central heating and that wrecks old furniture. Drawers shrink and veneers curl and crack, and legs fall off chairs. Incidentally . . ." he added, diverted by the memory ". . . it was I who mended your cherrywood chair."

"But how long have you been doing this?"

"Let's see, I left school when I was seventeen, and I'm twenty-four now, so that makes it about seven years."

"But you had to *learn* . . ."

"Oh, sure. I did joinery and carpentry first, four years of it at a trade school in London, and then when I'd got that under my belt, I apprenticed myself for another couple of years to an old cabinet-maker down in Sussex. I lived with him and his wife, did all the dirty jobs in the workshop, learned everything I know."

I did a few sums. "That's only six years. You said seven."

He laughed. "I took a year off in the middle to travel. My parents said I was becoming parochial. My father has a cousin who runs a cattle ranch up in the Rockies, south-west Colorado. I worked as a ranch hand nine months or more." He frowned. "What are you grinning about?"

I told him. "That first time I saw you, in the shop . . . you looked like a ranch hand . . . you looked real. And somehow it annoyed me that you weren't."

He smiled. "And you know what you looked like?"

I cooled off. "No."

"The head girl of a nicely run orphanage. And that annoyed *me*."

A small clash of swords, and once more we were on opposite sides of the fence.

I eyed him with dislike as he cheerfully finished his soup; the waitress came to take away the empty plates, and to set down a carafe of red wine. I had not heard Joss ordering the wine, but now I watched him pour two full glasses and I saw the long spade-tipped fingers; I liked the idea of them working with wood and old and beautiful things, turning and measuring and oiling and coaxing into shape. I picked up the glass of wine and against the light it glowed red as a ruby. I said, "Is that all you're doing in Porthkerris? Restoring Grenville Bayliss's furniture?"

"Good God, no. I'm opening a shop. I managed to rent these premises down on the harbour six months or so ago. I've been here, off and on, ever since. Now, I'm trying to get it into some sort of order before Easter, or Whitsun, or whenever the summer business really starts."

"Is it an antique shop?"

"No, modern, furniture, glass, textiles. But antique restoring goes on in the background. I mean I have a workroom. I also have a small pad on the top floor which is where I now live, which is why you were able to take over my room at Mrs Kernow's. One day when you've decided that I'm trustworthy you can climb the rickety stairs and I'll show it to you."

I ignored this fresh little sally.

"If you work down here, what were you doing in that shop in London?"

"Tristram's? I told you, he's a friend; I drop in and see him whenever I'm up in town."

I frowned. There were so many coincidences. Our lives seemed to be tied up in them, like a parcel well-knotted with ends of string. I watched him finish his wine and once more was visited with the unease which I had known earlier in the evening. I knew I should ask him a thousand questions, but before I could think of one the waitress arrived at our table once more, bearing steaks and vegetables and fried potatoes and dishes of salad. I drank some wine and watched Joss, and when the waitress had gone I said, "What does Eliot Bayliss do?"

"Eliot? He runs a garage up at High Cross, specialises in highly-powered second-hand cars, Mercedes, Alfa Romeos. If you've got the right sort of cheque book he can supply you with practically anything."

"You don't like him, do you?"

"I never said I didn't like him."

"But you don't."

"Perhaps it would be nearer the mark to say he doesn't like me."

"Why?" He looked up, his eyes dancing with amusement. "I haven't any idea. Now why don't you eat up your steak before it gets cold."

He drove me home. It was still raining and I was, all at once, deathly tired. Outside Mrs Kernow's door Joss stopped the car, but left the engine running. I thanked him and said good night and began to open the door, but before I could do so he had reached across and stopped me. I turned to look at him.

He said, "Tomorrow. Are you going to Boscarva?"

"Yes."

"I'll take you."

"I can go alone."

"You don't know where the house is, and it's a long climb up the hill. I'll pick you up in the car. About eleven?"

Arguing with him was like arguing with a steamroller. And I was exhausted. I said, "All right."

He opened the door for me and pushed it open.

"Good night, Rebecca."

"Good night."

"I'll see you in the morning."

5

The wind did not drop during that night. But when I woke, the little window of my room at Mrs Kernow's gave me sight of a square of pale blue traversed by ballooning white clouds travelling at some speed. It was very cold, but bravely I got up and dressed and went downstairs in search of Mrs Kernow. I found her outside in the little yard at the back of the house, pegging out her washing on a line. At first, battling with flailing sheets and towels, she didn't see me, but when I appeared between a shirt and a modest lock-knit petticoat she gave a great start of surprise. Her own astonishment amused her, and she shook with shrill laughter, as though the two of us were a double act on the halls.

"You gave me some shock. I thought you were still asleep! Comfortable were you? That dratted wind's still around the place, but the rain's stopped, thank heaven. Want your breakfast do you?"

"A cup of tea, perhaps."

I helped her peg out the rest of the washing and then she picked up her empty basket and led the way back indoors. I sat at the kitchen table and she boiled a kettle and began to fry bacon.

"Have a good supper last night did you? Go to The Anchor? Tommy Williams keeps a good place there, always packed, winter and summer. I heard Joss bring you home. He's a lovely boy. I missed him when he moved out. Still, I go down sometimes to his new place, clean it up a bit for him, bring his washing home and do it here. Sad, a young man like that on his own. All wrong somehow, not having someone to take care of him."

"I should think Joss could take care of himself."

"It's not right a man doing woman's work." Mrs Kernow obviously did not believe in Women's Lib. "Besides, he's busy enough working for Mr Bayliss."

"Do you know Mr Bayliss?"

"Everyone knows he. Lived here nearly fifty years now. One of the old ones, he is. And some lovely painter he was before he took ill. Used to have an exhibition every year, and all sorts used to come down from London, famous people, everybody. 'Course, lately we don't see so much of him. He can't walk up and down the hill like he used to, and it's a bit of a business Pettifer getting that great car down these narrow lanes. Besides, in the summer, you can't move for traffic and visitors. The place is teeming with them. Sometimes you'd think half the population of the country is jammed into this little town."

She flipped the bacon on to a warm plate and set it in front of me. "There now, eat that up before it gets cold."

I said, "Mrs Kernow, Mr Bayliss is my grandfather."

She stared at me, frowning. "Your grandfather?" Then, "Whose child are you?"

"Lisa's."

"Lisa's child." She reached for a chair and slowly sat down upon it. I saw that I had shocked her. "Does Joss know?"

It seemed irrelevant. "Yes, I told him last night."

"She was a lovely little girl." She stared into my face. "I can see her in you . . . except that she was so dark and you're fair. We missed her when she went, and never came back. Where is she now?"

I told her. When I had finished she said, "And Mr Bayliss doesn't know you're here?"

"No."

"You must go now. Right away. Oh, I wish I could be there to see the old man's face. He worshipped your mother . . ."

A tear gleamed. Quickly, before we were both awash with sentiment, I said, "I don't know how to get there."

68

Trying to tell me, she confused the two of us so much that finally she found an old envelope and the stub of a pencil and drew a rough map. Watching her I remembered Joss's promise to come at eleven o'clock and take me to Boscarva in his ramshackle van, but suddenly it seemed a much better idea to go at once, on my own. Besides, last night I had been altogether too meek and compliant. It would do Joss's boundless ego no harm to arrive here and find me already gone. The thought of this happening cheered me considerably and I went upstairs to fetch my coat.

Outside I was instantly buffeted by the wind which tunnelled down the narrow street like the draught in a chimney. It was a cold wind, smelling of the sea, but when the sun burst out from behind the racing clouds the brightness was dazzling, full of glare, and overhead gulls screamed and floated, their wings white sails against the blue of the sky.

I walked and soon I was climbing. Up narrow, cobbled streets, between haphazard lines of houses. Up flights of steps, and leaning alleys. The higher I went the stronger became the wind. As I climbed the town dropped below me, and the ocean revealed itself, dark blue, streaked with jade and purple and flecked with white horses. It spread to the horizon where the sky took over, and below me the town and the harbour shrank to toy-size, to insignificance.

I stood looking at it, catching my breath, and all at once a funny thing happened. For this new place was not new to me at all, but totally familiar. I felt at home, as though I had returned to somewhere I had known all my life. And though I had scarcely thought of my mother since making the decision to come to Porthkerris, she was suddenly beside me, climbing the steep streets, long-legged, breathless, and warm with exertion as I was.

I was comforted by this sense of *déjà-vu*. It made me feel less lonely and much more brave. I went on and was glad I had not waited for Joss. His presence was disturbing, but I could not for the life of me decide why.

He had, after all, been quite open with me, answering questions, giving perfectly believable reasons for his every action.

It was obvious that there was no love lost between himself and Eliot Bayliss, but I could easily understand this. The two young men would have nothing in common. Eliot, albeit unwillingly, was living at Boscarva. He was a Bayliss and the house was, for the time being, his home. On the other hand Joss's occupation in the house would give him the freedom to come and go in his own time. Be found, unexpectedly, at odd hours of the day, perhaps when his presence was neither convenient nor welcome. I imagined him on easy terms with everybody, sometimes getting in the way, and worst of all, blithely unaware of the trouble he was causing. A man like Eliot would resent this and Joss, in return, would react to his resentment.

Busy with these thoughts and the exertion of climbing, I did not observe my surroundings, but now the road levelled off beneath my feet, and I stopped to look around and take my bearings. I was on top of the hill, that was for sure. Behind and below me lay the town; ahead stretched the rugged coastline, curving away into the distance. It bordered a green country, patchworked with small farms and miniature fields, traversed by deep valleys, thick with hawthorn and stunted elm, where narrow streams channelled their way down to the sea.

I looked about me. This too was country. Or a year ago it had been. But since then a farm, perhaps, had been bought out, the bulldozers brought in, old hedges demolished, the rich earth torn up and flattened, and a new housing estate was in the process of being erected. All was raw, stark and hideous. Cement mixers churned, a lorry ground through a sea of mud, there were piles of brick and concrete, and in front of it all, like a proud banner, a hoarding which announced the man responsible for this carnage.

ERNEST PADLOW
DESIRABLE DETACHED HOUSES
FOR SALE
Apply Sea Lane, Porthkerris
Telephone Porthkerris 873

The houses were certainly detached, but only just. Scarcely three feet lay between them, and one window stared straight into another.

My heart mourned for the lost fields and the lost opportunities. As I stood there, mentally redesigning the entire project, a car came up the hill behind me, and drew to a halt in front of the hoarding. It was an old Jaguar, navy blue, and the man who stepped out of it, shutting the door behind him with a resounding thump, wore a workman's donkey jacket and carried a clip board and a lot of papers which fluttered in the wind. He turned and saw me, hesitated for only a second and then walked towards me, trying to flatten his hair down over his bald head.

"Morning." His smile was familiar as though we were old friends.

"Good morning."

I had seen him before. Last night. At The Anchor. Talking to Eliot Bayliss.

He glanced up at the hoarding.

"Thinking of buying a house for yourself?"

"No."

"You should. Get a good view up here."

I frowned. "I don't want a house."

"Be a good investment."

"Are you the foreman?"

"No." He glanced, with some pride, up at the hoarding which reared above us. "I'm Ernest Padlow."

"I see."

"Lovely site this . . ." He looked around at the devastation with some satisfaction. "Lot of people after this site, but the old girl who owned the land was a widow, and I managed to charm her into letting me have it."

71

I was surprised. As he spoke he reached for and lit himself a cigarette; he did not offer me one, his fingers were stained with nicotine and he seemed to me the most uncharming man I had ever met.

He turned his attention back to me. "Haven't seen you around, have I?"

"No."

"Visiting?"

"Yes, perhaps."

"It's better out of season. Not so crowded."

I said, "I'm looking for Boscarva."

Caught unawares, the bonhomie slid from his manner. His eyes were sharp as pebbles in his florid face. "Boscarva? You mean old Bayliss's place?"

"Yes."

His expression became wily. "Looking for Eliot?"

"No."

He waited for me to enlarge on this. When I didn't he tried to make a joke of it. "Well, I always say, least said, soonest mended. You want Boscarva, you go down that little lane. About half a mile. You'll see the house down towards the sea. It's got a slate roof, a big garden round it. You can't miss it."

"Thank you." I smiled politely. "Goodbye."

I turned and began to walk, feeling his eyes on my back. Then he spoke once more and I turned back. He was smiling, all friends again.

"You want a house, make up your mind quickly. They're selling like hot cakes."

"Yes, I'm sure. But I don't want one. Thank you."

The lane led downhill towards the great blue bowl of the sea, and now I was truly in the country, in a farmland of fields grazed by sweet-faced Guernseys. Wild violets and primroses grew in the grassy hedges, and the sun came out and turned the rich grass to emerald. Presently, I came around a corner and saw the white gates, set between low dry-stone walls; a driveway curved down, out of sight, and there were high hedges of

72

escallonia and elm trees, tortured to unnatural shapes by the relentless winds.

I could not see the house. I stood at the open gates and looked down the drive, my courage seeping away like bathwater after the plug has been pulled out. I could not think what I was meant to do, nor what I was going to say once I had done it.

My mind was, unexpectedly and mercifully, made up for me. Down by the house, out of sight, I heard a car start up and come at some speed up the drive towards me. As it approached, a low-slung open sports car of some age and style, I stood aside to let it flash past between the gate posts and up the hill in the direction from which I had come, but still there was time to see the driver and the great red setter sitting up on the back seat, with the deliriously joyful expression of any dog being taken for a ride in an open car.

I thought that I had not been noticed but I was wrong. A moment later the car stopped with a screech of brakes and a shower of small stones flung from the back wheels. Then it went into reverse, and returned, with scarcely less speed back to the spot where I stood. It stopped, the engine was killed, and Eliot Bayliss, leaning an arm on the driving wheel, surveyed me across the empty passenger seat. He was bare-headed and wore a sheepskin car coat, and his expression was one of amusement, perhaps intrigue.

"Hello," he said.

"Good morning." I felt a fool, bundled in my old coat, with the wind blowing stray strands of hair over my face. I tried to push them away.

"You look lost."

"No. I'm not."

He continued to regard me, frowning slightly. "I saw you last night, didn't I? At The Anchor? With Joss."

"Yes."

"Are you looking for Joss? As far as I know he's not arrived yet. That is, if he's decided to come today."

"No. I mean I'm not looking for him."

73

"Then who – " asked Eliot Bayliss gently, "are you looking for?"

"I . . . I wanted to see old Mr Bayliss."

"It's a little early for that. He doesn't usually appear till mid-day."

"Oh." I had not thought of this. Some of my disappointment must have shown in my face, for he went on, in the same gentle and friendly voice, "Perhaps I could help. I'm Eliot Bayliss."

"I know. I mean . . . Joss told me last night."

A small frown appeared between his eyebrows. He was obviously and naturally puzzled by my relationship with Joss.

"Why did you want to see my grandfather?" And when I did not reply, he suddenly leaned across to open the door of the car and said, with cool authority, "Get in."

I got in, closing the door behind me. I could feel his eyes on me, the shapeless coat, the patched jeans. The dog leaned forward to nuzzle my ear; his nose was cold and I reached over my shoulder to stroke the long, silky ear.

I said, "What's he called?"

"Rufus. Rufus the Red. But that doesn't answer my question, does it?"

I was saved by another interruption. Another car. But this time it was the Post Office van, rattling scarlet and cheerful, down the lane towards us. It stopped, and the postman rolled down the window to say to Eliot, good naturedly, "How can I get down the drive and deliver the letters if you park your car in the gateway?"

"Sorry," said Eliot, unperturbed, and he got out from behind the driving wheel and went to take a handful of mail and a newspaper from the postman. "I'll take it – it'll save you the trip."

"Lovely," said the postman. "Be nice if everyone did my job for me," and with a grin and a wave he went on his way, presumably to some outlying farmstead.

Eliot got back into the car.

"Well," he said, smiling at me. "What am I going to do with you?"

But I scarcely heard him. The pile of mail lay loosely in his lap, and on the top was an airmail envelope, postmarked Ibiza, and addressed to Mr Grenville Bayliss. The spiky handwriting was unmistakable.

A car is a good place for confidences. There is no telephone and you can't be unexpectedly interrupted. I said, "That letter. The one on the top. It's from a man called Otto Pedersen. He lives in Ibiza."

Eliot, frowning, took up the envelope. He turned it over and read Otto's name on the back. He looked at me. "How did you know?"

"I know his writing. I know him. He's writing to . . . to your grandfather to tell him that Lisa is dead. She died about a week ago. She was living with Otto in Ibiza."

"Lisa. You mean Lisa Bayliss?"

"Yes. Roger's sister. Your aunt. My mother."

"You're Lisa's child?"

"Yes." I turned to look directly at him. "I'm your cousin. Grenville Bayliss is my grandfather, too."

His eyes were a strange colour, greyish-green, like pebbles washed by some fast-moving stream. They showed neither shock nor pleasure, simply regarded me levelly without expression. He said at last, "Well I'll be damned."

It was hardly what I expected. We sat in silence because I could think of nothing to say, and then, as though coming to a sudden decision, he tossed the pile of mail into my lap, started the car up once more, and swung the wheel around so that once more we were facing the drive.

"What are you doing?" I asked.

"What do you think? Taking you home of course."

Home. Boscarva. We came around the curve of the drive and it was there, waiting for me. Not small, but not large either. Grey stone, smothered in creeper, grey slate roof, a semicircular stone porch with the door open to the sunshine, and inside a glimpse of red tiles, a clutter of

75

flowerpots, the pinks and scarlets of geranium and fuchsia. A curtain fluttered at an open upstairs window and smoke plumed from a chimney. As we got out of the car the sun came out from behind a cloud and, caught in the spread arms of the house, sheltered from the north wind, it was suddenly very warm.

"Come along," said Eliot and led the way, the dog at his heels. We went through the porch and into a dark, panelled hallway illuminated by the big window on the turn of the stairs. I had imagined Boscarva as being a house of the past, sad and nostalgic, filled with the chill of old memories. But it wasn't like that at all. It was vital, humming with a sense of activity. There were papers lying on the table, a pair of gardening gloves, a dog's lead. From beyond a doorway came the kitchen sounds of voices and the clatter of crockery. From upstairs a vacuum-cleaner hummed. And there was a smell compounded of scrubbed stone and old polished floors, and years of woodfires.

Eliot stood at the foot of the staircase and called, "Mamma." But when there was no answer, only the continued hum of the vacuum-cleaner, he said, "You'd better come this way." We went down the hall and through a door which led into a long, low drawing-room, palely panelled and sensuous with the brightness and scent of spring flowers. At one end, in a fireplace of carved pine and Dutch tiles, a newly lit fire flickered cheerfully, and three tall windows, curtained in faded yellow silk, faced out over a flagged terrace, and beyond the balustrade of this I could see the blue line of the sea.

I stood in the middle of this charming room as Eliot Bayliss closed the door and said, "Well, you're here. Why don't you take your coat off?"

I did so. It was very warm. I laid it over a chair where it looked like some great, dead creature.

He said, "When did you get here?"

"Last night. I caught the train from London."

"You live in London?"

"Yes."

"And you've never been here before?"

"No. I didn't know about Boscarva. I didn't know about Grenville Bayliss being my grandfather. My mother never told me till the night before she died."

"How does Joss come into it?"

"I . . ." It was too complicated to explain. "I'd met him in London. He happened to be at the junction when my train got in. It was a coincidence."

"Where are you staying?"

"With Mrs Kernow in Fish Lane."

"Grenville's an old man. He's ill. You know that, don't you?"

"Yes."

"I think . . . this letter from Otto Pedersen . . . we'd better be careful. Perhaps my mother would be the best person . . ."

"Yes, of course."

"It was lucky you saw the letter."

"Yes. I thought he would probably write. But I was afraid that I would have to break the news to you all."

"And now it's been done for you." He smiled, and all at once he looked much younger . . . belying those strange-coloured eyes and the thick silver-fox hair. "Why don't you wait here and I'll go and find my mother and try to put her in the picture. Would you like a cup of coffee or something?"

"Only if it's not a nuisance."

"No nuisance. I'll tell Pettifer." He opened the door behind him. "Make yourself at home."

The door closed softly, and he was gone. Pettifer. *Pettifer had been in the Navy too, he looked after my father and sometimes drove the car and Mrs Pettifer did the cooking.* So my mother had told me. And Joss had told me that Mrs Pettifer had died. But in the old days she had taken Lisa and her brother into the kitchen and made hot buttered toast. She had drawn the curtains against the dark and the rain, and made the children feel safe and loved.

Alone, I inspected the room where I had been left to

wait. I saw a glass-doored cabinet filled with Oriental treasures, including some small pieces of jade, and wondered if these were the ones that my mother had mentioned to me. I glanced around, thinking that perhaps I might find the Venetian mirror and the davenport desk as well, but then my attention was caught by the picture over the mantelpiece, and I went to look at it, all else forgotten.

It was a portrait of a girl, dressed in the fashion of the early 1930s, slender, flat-chested, her white dress hanging straight to her hips, her dark, bobbed hair revealing with enchanting innocence the long, slender neck. She sat, in the picture, on a tall stool, holding a single long-stemmed rose, but you could not see her face, for she was looking away from the artist, out of some unseen window, into the sunshine. The effect was all pink and gold, with sunlight filtering through the thin stuff of her white dress. It was enchanting.

Behind me the door opened suddenly and I turned, startled, as an old man came into the room, stately, bald-headed, a little stooped, perhaps; treading cautiously. He wore rimless spectacles and a striped shirt with an old-fashioned hard collar, and over it all a blue and white butcher's apron.

"Are you the young lady wanting a cup of coffee?" He had a deep, lugubrious voice, and this, with his sombre appearance, made me think of a reliable undertaker.

"Yes, if it's not too much trouble."

"Milk and sugar?"

"No sugar. Just a little milk. I was looking at the portrait."

"Yes. It's very pleasing. It's called 'Lady Holding a Rose'."

"You can't see her face."

"No."

"Did my . . . Did Mr Bayliss paint it?"

"Oh yes. That was hung in the Academy, could have been sold a hundred times over, but the Commander would never part with it." As he said this, he carefully took off his spectacles, and was now staring at me intently. His old eyes were pale. He said, "For a moment, when you spoke, you reminded me of someone else. But you're young and she'd be middle-aged by now. And her hair was dark as a blackbird. That's what Mrs Pettifer used to say. Dark as a blackbird's wing."

I said, "Eliot didn't tell you?"

"What didn't Mr Eliot tell me?"

"You're talking about Lisa, aren't you? I'm Rebecca. I'm her daughter."

"Well." Fumbling a little he put his spectacles back on again. A faint gleam of pleasure showed on his gloomy features. "I was right then. I'm not often wrong about things like that." And he came forward, holding out a horny hand. "It's a real pleasure to meet you . . . A pleasure that I never thought I should have. I thought you'd never come. Is your mother with you?"

I wished that Eliot had made it a little easier for me.

"My mother's dead. She died last week. In Ibiza. That's why I'm here."

"She died." His eyes clouded. "I'm sorry. I'm really sorry. She should have come back. She should have come home. We all wanted to see her again." He took out a copious handkerchief and blew his nose. "And who . . ." he asked ". . . is going to tell the Commander?"

"I think . . . Eliot's gone to fetch his mother. You see, there's a letter for my grandfather in the post, it came this morning. It's from Ibiza, from the man who was . . . taking care of my mother. But if you think that wouldn't be a very good idea . . ."

"What I think won't make no difference," said Pettifer. "And whoever tells the Commander, it's not going to lessen his sorrow. But I'll tell you one thing. You being here will help a lot."

"Thank you."

He blew his nose again and put away his handkerchief.

"Mr Eliot and his mother . . . well, this isn't their home. But it was either the old Commander and me moving up to High Cross or them coming here. And they wouldn't be here if the doctor hadn't insisted. I told them we could manage all right, the Commander and me. We've been together all these years . . . but there, we're neither of us as young as we used to be, and the Commander, he had this heart attack . . ."

"Yes, I know . . ."

"And after Mrs Pettifer passed on, there wasn't anyone to do the cooking. Mind, I can cook all right, but it takes me a good part of my time taking care of the Commander, and I wouldn't want to see him going about the place looking shabby."

"No, of course not . . ."

I was interrupted by the slam of a door.

A hearty male voice called, "Pettifer!" and Pettifer said, "Excuse me a moment, Miss," and went out to investigate, leaving the door open behind him.

"Pettifer!"

I heard Pettifer say, with what sounded like the greatest satisfaction, "Hello, Joss."

"Is she there?"

"Who, here?"

"Rebecca."

"Yes, she's right here, in the sitting-room . . . I was just going to get her a cup of coffee."

"Make it two would you, there's a good chap. And black and strong for me."

His footsteps came down the hall, and the next moment he was there, framed in the doorway, long-legged, black-haired, and it was obvious – angry.

"What the hell do you think you're doing?" he demanded.

I could feel my hackles rising, like a suspicious dog. Home, Eliot had said. This was Boscarva, my home, and whether I was here or not was nothing to do with Joss.

"I don't know what you're talking about."

"I went to pick you up and Mrs Kernow told me you'd already left."

"So?"

80

"I told you to wait for me."

"I decided not to wait."

He was silent, fuming, but finally appeared to accept this inescapable fact.

"Does anyone know you've arrived?"

"I met Eliot at the gate. He brought me here."

"Where's he gone?"

"To find his mother."

"Have you seen anyone else? Have you seen Grenville?"

"No."

"Has anyone told Grenville about your mother?"

"A letter came by this morning's post, from Otto Pedersen. But I don't think he's seen it yet."

"Pettifer must take it to him. Pettifer must be there when he reads it."

"Pettifer didn't seem to think that."

"I think it," said Joss.

His apparently outrageous interference left me without words, but as we stood glaring at each other across the pretty patterned carpet and a great bowl of scented narcissus, there came the sound of voices and footsteps down the uncarpeted staircase and along the hall towards us.

I heard a woman's voice say, "In the sitting-room, Eliot?"

Joss muttered something that sounded unprintable, and marched over to the fireplace where he stood with his back to me, staring down into the flames. The next instant, Mollie appeared in the doorway, hesitated for a moment and then came towards me, hands outstretched.

"Rebecca." (So it was to be a warm welcome.) Eliot, following behind her, closed the door. Joss did not even turn round.

I worked it out that by now Mollie must be over fifty, but this was hard to believe. She was plump and pretty, her fading blonde hair charmingly coiffed, her eyes blue, her skin fresh and lightly scattered with freckles which helped to create this astonishing illusion of youth. She wore a blue skirt and cardigan and a creamy silk blouse; her legs were slim and shapely and her hands beautifully manicured, decorated with pale pink fingernails, and many rings and fine gold bracelets. Scented, immaculately preserved, she made me think of a charming little tabby cat, curled precisely in the centre of her own satin cushion.

I said, "I'm afraid this is something of a shock."

"No, not a shock, but a surprise. And your mother . . . I'm so dreadfully sorry. Eliot's told me about the letter . . ."

At this Joss swung around from the fireplace.

"Where is the letter?"

Mollie turned her gaze upon him, and it was impossible to guess whether this was the first time she had realised he was there, or whether she had seen him and simply decided to ignore him.

"Joss. I didn't think you were coming this morning."

"Yes. I just got here."

"You know Rebecca, I believe."

"Yes, we've met." He hesitated, seeming to be making an effort to pull himself together. Then he smiled, ruefully, turned to lean his broad shoulders against the mantelpiece and apologised. "I'm sorry. And I know it's none of my business, but that letter that came this morning . . . where is it?"

"In my pocket," said Eliot, speaking for the first time. "Why?"

"It's just that I think Pettifer should be the one to break the news to the old man. I think Pettifer is the only person to do it."

This was greeted by silence. Then Mollie let go of my hands and turned to her son.

"He's right," she said. "Grenville's closest to Pettifer."

"That's all right by me," said Eliot but his eyes, on Joss, were cold with antagonism. I did not blame him. I felt the same way myself – I was on Eliot's side.

Joss said again, "I'm sorry."

Mollie was polite. "Not at all. It's very thoughtful of you to be so concerned."

"None of my business, really," said Joss. Eliot and his mother waited with pointed patience. At last he took the hint, heaved his shoulders away from the mantelpiece, and said, "Well, if you'll excuse me, I'll go and get on with some work."

"Will you be here for lunch?"

"No, I can only stay a couple of hours. I'll have to get back to the shop. I'll pick up a sandwich at the pub." He smiled benignly at us all, not a trace of his former temper showing. "Thanks all the same."

And so he left us, modest, apologetic, apparently cut down to size. Once more the young workman, an employee, with a job to do.

6

Mollie said, "You must forgive him. He's not always the most tactful of men."

Eliot laughed shortly. "That's the understatement of the year."

She turned to me, explaining, "He's restoring some of the furniture for us. It's old and it had got into bad repair. He's a marvellous craftsman, but we never know when he's going to arrive or when he's going to go!"

"One day," said her son, "I shall lose my temper with him and punch his nose into the back of his neck." He smiled at me charmingly, his eyes crinkling, belying the ferocity of his words. "And I'm going to have to go too. I was late as it was, now I'm bloody late. Rebecca, will you excuse me?"

"Of course. I'm sorry, I'm afraid it was my fault. And thank you for being so kind . . ."

"I'm glad I stopped. I must have known how important it was. I'll see you . . ."

"Yes, of course you will," said Mollie quickly. "She can't go away now that she's found us."

"Well I'll leave the two of you to fix everything up . . ." He made for the door, but his mother interrupted gently.

"Eliot." He turned. "The letter."

"Oh yes, of course." He took it from his pocket, the fateful letter, a little crumpled now, and handed it to Mollie. "Don't let Pettifer make too big a meal of it. He's a sentimental old chap."

"I won't."

He smiled again, saying goodbye to both of us. "See you at dinner."

85

And he was gone, whistling up his dog as he went down the hall. We heard the front door open and shut, his car start up. Mollie turned to me.

"Now," she said, "come and sit by the fire and tell me all about it."

I did so, as I had already told Joss and Mrs Kernow, only this time I found myself stumbling a little when I got to the bit about Otto and Lisa living together, as though I were ashamed of it, which was a thing which I had never been. As I talked and Mollie listened, I tried to work this out, and to understand why my mother had disliked her so much. Perhaps it was simply a natural antipathy. It was obvious that they would never have had anything in common. And my mother had never had much tolerance for women who bored her. Men, now, were different. Men were always amusing. But women had to be very special for my mother to be able to tolerate their company. No, it could not all have been Mollie's fault. Sitting across the fireside from her, I resolved that I would be friends with her, and perhaps compensate, in a small way, for the short shrift she had received from Lisa.

"And how long are you going to be able to stay in Porthkerris? Your job . . . do you have to get back?"

"No. I seem to have been given a sort of indefinite leave."

"You'll stay here, with us?"

"Well, I've got this room with Mrs Kernow."

"Yes, but you'd be much better here. There's not a lot of space, that's the only thing; you'll have to sleep up in the attic, but it's a dear little room if you don't mind the sloping ceilings and you manage not to bump your head. You see, Eliot and I seem to have filled up the guest rooms, and as well I've got my niece staying for a few days. Perhaps you'll make friends with her. It'll be nice for her to have someone young about the place."

I wondered where the niece was. "How old is she?"

"Only seventeen. It's a difficult age, and I think that her mother felt it would be a good thing if she was out of

86

London for a little. They live there, you see, and of course she has so many friends, and there is so much going on . . ." She was obviously finding it difficult to find the right words ". . . Anyway, Andrea's down here for a week or two to have a little change, but I'm afraid she's rather bored."

I imagined myself at seventeen, in the unseen Andrea's shoes, staying in this warm and charming house, cared for by Mollie and Pettifer, with the sea and the cliffs on my doorstep, the countryside inviting long walks, and all the secret crooked streets of Porthkerris waiting to be explored. To me it would have been heaven, and impossible to be bored. I wondered if I would have very much in common with Mollie's niece.

"Of course," she went on, "as you've probably gathered, Eliot and I are only here because Mrs Pettifer died and really the two old men couldn't manage on their own. We've got Mrs Thomas, she comes in each morning to help do the housework, but I do all the cooking, and keep the place as bright and pretty as I can."

"The flowers are so lovely."

"I can't bear a house without flowers."

"What about your own house?"

"My dear, it's empty. I shall have to take you up to High Cross one day to show it to you. I bought a pair of old cottages just after the war and converted them. Even though I shouldn't say so, it is very charming. And, of course, it's so handy for Eliot's garage; as it is, living here, he seems to be perpetually on the road."

"Yes, I suppose so."

I could hear footsteps coming down the hall again; in a moment the door opened, and Pettifer edged around it, cautiously, carrying a tray laden with all the accoutrements of mid-morning coffee, including a large silver pot with steam drifting from its spout.

"Oh, Pettifer, thank you . . ."

He came forward, stooped with the weight of the tray, and Mollie got up to fetch a stool and place it swiftly beneath the tray so that the old man could put it down before it tilted so sharply that everything on it went hurtling to the floor.

"That's splendid, Pettifer."

"One of the cups was for Joss."

"He's upstairs working. He must have forgotten about the coffee. Never mind, I'll drink it for him. And, Pettifer . . ." He straightened, slowly, as though all his old joints were aching. Mollie took the letter from Ibiza off the mantelpiece where she had placed it for safety. "We thought, all of us, that perhaps it would be the best if you told the Commander about his daughter and then gave him this letter. It would be best, we thought, coming from you. Would you mind?"

Pettifer took the thin blue envelope.

"No, Madam. I'll do it. I'm just on my way up now to get the Commander up and dressed."

"It would be a kindness, Pettifer."

"That's all right, Madam."

"And tell him that Rebecca is here. And that she's staying. We'll have to make up the bed in the attic but I think she'll be quite comfortable."

Again a gleam came into Pettifer's face. I wondered if he ever really smiled, or whether his face had dropped permanently into those lugubrious lines and a cheerful expression had become physically impossible.

"I'm glad you're staying," he said "The Commander will like that."

When he'd gone, I said, "You'll have a lot to do. Shouldn't I go, and get out from under your feet?"

"You'll have to collect your things from Mrs Kernow anyway. I wonder how we could manage that? Pettifer could take you, but now he'll be occupied with Grenville and I must speak to Mrs Thomas about your room and then start thinking about lunch. Now what are we going to do?" I could not imagine. I was certainly not going to be able to carry all my belongings up the hill from the town. But luckily Mollie answered her own question. "I know. Joss. He can take you and bring you back up the hill in his van."

"But isn't Joss working?"

"Oh, for once we'll interrupt him. It's not often he's asked to put himself out – I'm sure he won't mind. Come along, we'll go and find him."

I had thought that she would take me to some forgotten outhouse or shed where we would find Joss, surrounded by wood shavings and the smell of hot glue, but to my surprise, she led me upstairs, and I forgot about Joss, because these were my first impressions of Boscarva, where my mother had been brought up, and I didn't want to miss a thing. The stairs were uncarpeted, the walls half panelled and then darkly papered above and hung with heavy oil paintings. All was at variance with the pretty, feminine sitting-room which we had left downstairs. On the first-floor landing passages led to left and right, there was a tallboy of polished walnut, and bookcases heavy with books, and then we went on again, up the stairs. Here was red drugget, white paint, again the passages led away to either side, and Mollie took the right-hand one. At the end of this passage was an open door, and from behind it the sound of voices, a man's and a girl's.

She seemed to hesitate and then her footsteps quickened, determined. Her back view became, all at once, formidable. With me following she went down the passage and through the door, and we were in an attic which had been converted, by means of a skylight, to a studio, or perhaps a billiard room, for against one wall was a massive, leather-seated sofa with oaken arms and legs. Now, however, this cold and airy room was being used as a workshop, with Joss in the middle of it, surrounded by chairs, broken picture frames, a table with a crooked leg, some scraps of leather, tools and nails, and a gimcrack gas ring on which reposed an unsavoury-looking glue pot. Wrapped in a worn blue apron, he was carefully fitting beautiful scarlet hide over the seat of one of the chairs, and as he did this, was being entertained by a young and female companion, who turned, disinterested, to see who had come into the room, and was so breaking up this cosy *tête-à-tête*.

Mollie said, "Andrea!" And then, less sharply, "Andrea, I didn't realise you were up."

"Oh, I've been up for hours."

"Did you have any breakfast?"

"I didn't want any."

"Andrea, this is Rebecca. Rebecca Bayliss."

"Oh, yes," she turned her eyes on to me. "Joss has been telling me all about you."

I said, "How do you do." She was very young and very thin, with long seaweedy hair that hung on either side of her face, which was pretty, except for her eyes which were pale and slightly protuberant, and not improved by a great deal of clumsy mascara. She wore, inevitably, jeans, and a cotton tee-shirt which did not look entirely clean and which revealed, with no shadow of a doubt, the fact that she wore nothing beneath it. On her feet were sandals which looked like surgical boots that had been striped in green and purple. There was a leather bootlace around her neck upon which hung a heavy silver cross of vaguely Celtic design. Andrea, I thought. So bored with Boscarva. And it made me uncomfortable to think that she and Joss had been discussing me. I wondered what he had said.

Now, she did not move, but stayed where she was, legs straddled, leaning against a heavy old mahogany table.

"Hi," she said.

"Rebecca's going to stay here," Mollie told them. Joss looked up, his mouth full of tacks, his eyes bright with interest, a lock of black hair falling over his forehead.

"Where's she going to sleep?" asked Andrea. "I thought we were a full house."

"In the bedroom along the passage," her aunt told her crisply. "Joss, would you do a favour for me?" He spat the tacks neatly into his palm and stood up, pushing his hair back with his wrist. "Would you take her, now, down to Mrs Kernow, and tell Mrs Kernow that she's coming here, and then help her with her suitcases and bring her back up to Boscarva again? Would that be very inconvenient?"

"Not at all," said Joss, but Andrea's face assumed an expression of bored resignation.

"It's a nuisance, I know, when you're busy, but it would be such a help . . ."

"It's no trouble." He laid down his little hammer and began to untie the knot of his apron. He gazed at me. "I'm getting quite used to carting Rebecca about."

And Andrea gave a snort, whether of disgust or impatience it was impossible to tell, sprang to her feet and marched out of the room, leaving the impression that we had been lucky to escape without a monumentally slammed door.

And so I was back where I started, with Joss, crammed into the ramshackle little van. We drove in silence away from Boscarva, through Mr Padlow's building estate, and on to the slope of the hill that led down to the town.

It was Joss who broke the silence.

"So, it all worked out."

"Yes."

"How do you like your family?"

"I haven't met them all yet. I haven't met Grenville."

He said, "You'll like him," but the way he said it, he made it sound, "You'll like *him*."

"I like them all."

"That's good."

I looked at him. He wore his blue denim jacket, a navy polo-necked sweater. His profile was impassive. I felt it would be easy to be maddened by him.

"Tell me about Andrea," I said.

"What do you want to know about Andrea?"

"I don't know. I just want you to tell me."

"She's seventeen, and she thinks she's in love with some guy she met at Art School, and her parents don't approve so she's been rusticated with Auntie Mollie. And she's bored stiff."

"She seems to have taken you into her confidence."

"There's no one else to talk to."

"Why doesn't she go back to London?"

"Because she's only seventeen. She hasn't got the money. And I think she hasn't quite got the courage to stand up to her parents."

"What does she do with herself all day?"

"I don't know. I'm not there all day. She doesn't seem to get up until lunch-time, and then she sits around watching television. Boscarva's a house of old people. You can't blame her for being bored."

I said, without thinking, "Only the boring are bored." This had once been drummed into me by a wise and well-meaning headmistress.

"That," said Joss, "sounds uncomfortably sanctimonious."

"I didn't mean it to."

He smiled. "Were you never bored?"

"Nobody who lived with my mother was ever bored."

He sang, "You may have been a headache, but you never were a bore."

"Exactly."

"She sounds great. Exactly my sort of female."

"That's what most men thought about her."

When we got to Fish Lane Mrs Kernow was out, but Joss seemed to have a key. We let ourselves in and I went upstairs to pack my rucksack while Joss wrote Mrs Kernow a note to explain the new arrangements.

"How about paying her?" I asked as I came downstairs, bumping the rucksack behind me.

"I'll fix that when I next see her. I've told her so in the note."

"But I can pay for myself."

"Of course you can, but let me do it for you." He took my rucksack and went to open the door, and there did not seem to be opportunity for further argument.

Once more my belongings were heaved into the back of the little truck, once more we headed for Boscarva, only this time Joss took me round by the harbour road.

"I want to show you my shop . . . I mean, I just want to show you where it is. Then if you want to get hold of me for any reason, you'll know where to find me."

"Why should I want to get hold of you?"

"I don't know. You might need wise counselling; or money; or just a good laugh. There it is, you can't miss it."

It was a tall narrow house, boxed in between two short fat houses. Three storeys high with a window on each floor, and the ground floor still in a state of reconstruction, with new wood unpainted and great circles of whitewash splashed over the plate glass of the shop window.

As we flashed past it, tyres rattling on the cobbles, I said, "That's a good position, you'll get all the visitors coming in to spend their money."

"That's what I hope."

"When can I see it?"

"Come next week. We'll be more or less straight then."

"All right. Next week."

"It's a date," said Joss, and turned the corner by the church. He put the little truck into second gear and we roared up the hill with a noise like a badly tuned motor bicycle.

Back at Boscarva, it was Pettifer who, hearing our arrival, emerged from the front door as Joss lifted my rucksack from the back of the truck.

"Joss, the Commander's downstairs and in his study. He said to bring Rebecca in to see him just as soon as you arrived."

Joss looked at him. "How is he?"

Pettifer ducked his head. "Not too bad."

"Was he very upset?"

"He's all right . . . now you leave that rucksack, and I'll carry it upstairs."

"You'll do no such thing," said Joss, and for once I was glad that he was being his usual bossy self. "I'll take it up. Where's she sleeping?"

"In the attic . . . the other end from the billiard room, but the Commander did say, right away."

"I know," Joss grinned, "and naval time is five minutes beforehand. But there's still time to take the girl up to her room, so stop fussing, there's a good man."

Leaving Pettifer still mildly protesting, I followed him up the two flights of stairs that I had already climbed this morning. The sound of the vacuum had stopped, but there was the smell of roasting lamb. I realised then that I was very hungry and my mouth watered. Joss's long legs sped ahead of me, and by the time I reached the slope-ceilinged bedroom which was to be mine, he had set down the rucksack and gone to fling wide the dormer window, so that I was met by a blast of cold, salty air.

"Come and look at the view."

I went to stand beside him. I saw the sea, the cliffs, the gold of bracken and the first yellow candles of gorse. And below was the Boscarva garden which, because of the stone balustrade of the terrace, I had not been able to see from the drawing-room window. It had been built in a series of terraces, dropping down the slope of the hill, and at the bottom, tucked into a corner of the garden wall, was a stone cottage with a slate roof. No, not a cottage, perhaps a stable, with a commodious loft above it.

I said, "What's that building?"

"That's the studio," Joss told me. "That's where your grandfather used to paint."

"It doesn't look like a studio."

"From the other side it does. The entire north wall is made of glass. He designed it himself, had it built by a local stonemason."

"It looks shut up."

"It is. Locked and shuttered. It hasn't been opened since he had his heart attack and stopped painting."

I shivered suddenly.

"Cold?" asked Joss.

"I don't know." I moved away from the window, undoing my coat, dropping it over the end of the bed.

The room was white, the carpet dark red. There was a built-in wardrobe, shelves full of books, a washbasin. I went over to wash my hands, turning the soap beneath the warm water. Over the basin was a mirror which gave me back a reflection both dishevelled and anxious. I realised then how nervous I was of meeting Grenville for the first time, and how important it was that he should get a good impression of me.

I dried my hands, went to unbuckle my rucksack, and found a brush and comb. "Was he a good painter, Joss? Do you think he was a good artist?"

"Yes. The old school, of course, but magnificent. And a marvellous colourist."

I pulled the rubber band from the end of my plait, shook the coils free, and went back to the mirror to start brushing. Over my reflected shoulder I could see Joss watching me. He did not speak while I brushed and combed and finally re-plaited my hair. As I fastened the ends, he said, "It's a wonderful colour. Like corn."

I laid down the brush and comb. "Joss, we mustn't keep him waiting."

"Do you want me to come with you?"

"Please."

I realised then that this was the first time I had ever had to ask him to help me.

I followed him downstairs, down the hall and past the sitting-room, to a door which stood at the end of the passage. Joss opened it and put his head around.

He said, "Good morning."

"Who's that? Joss? Come along in . . ." The voice was higher pitched than I had imagined, more like the voice of a much younger man.

"I've brought someone to see you . . ."

He opened the door wide, and put his arms behind me to propel me gently forward into the room. It was a small room, with french windows leading out on to a paved terrace and a secret garden, warm with trapped

sunshine, and enclosed by dense hedges and escallonia.

I saw the fire flickering in the grate; the panelled walls
covered either with pictures or books; the model, on the
mantelpiece, of an old-fashioned naval cruiser. There were
photographs in silver frames, a table littered with papers
and magazines, and a blue and white Chinese bowl filled
with daffodils.

As I entered, he was already heaving himself – with the
aid of a stick – out of a red leather armchair, which stood
half turned towards the warmth of the fire. I was amazed
that Joss did nothing to help him, and I began to say, "Oh,
please don't bother . . .." but by then he was on his feet
and erect, and a pair of blue eyes surveyed me calmly from
beneath jutting brows and bristling white eyebrows.

I realised then that I had steeled myself to finding him
pathetic in some way, old, infirm, perhaps a little shaky.
But Grenville Bayliss, at eighty, was formidable. Very tall,
very upright, starched and barbered, smelling faintly of
Bay Rum, he was a credit to his servant Pettifer. He wore a
dark blue blazer, of naval cut, neatly creased grey flannels,
and velvet slippers with his initials embroidered in gold. He
was also very tanned, his bald head brown as a chestnut
beneath the thinning strands of white hair, and I imagined
him spending much time in that little sunny secret garden,
reading his morning paper, enjoying a pipe, watching the
gulls and the white clouds scudding across the sky.

We looked at each other. I wished that he would say
something but he simply looked. I hoped that he liked
what he saw, and was glad I had taken the time to brush
my hair. And then he said, "I've never been in this situation
before. I'm not quite sure how we're meant to greet each
other."

I said, "I could give you a kiss."

"Why don't you do that?"

So I did, stepping forward and raising my face, and he
stooped slightly and my lips touched the smooth clean skin
of his cheek.

"Now," he said, "why don't we sit down? Joss, come and sit down."

But Joss excused himself, said that if he didn't start work soon then he would have done nothing all day. But he stayed long enough to help the old man back into his chair, and pour us both a glass of sherry from the decanter on the side table, and then he said, "I'll leave you. You'll have a lot to talk about," and with a cheerful wave of his hand, slipped away. The door closed quietly behind him.

Grenville said, "I believe you know him quite well."

I pulled up a stool so that I could sit and face him. "Not really. But he's been very kind, and . . ." I tried to think of the right word. "Convenient. I mean, he always seems to be there when people need him."

"And never when they don't?" I was not sure if I could entirely agree with this. "He's a clever boy, too. Doing up all my furniture."

"Yes I know."

"Good craftsman. Lovely hands." He laid down his sherry glass, and once more I was subjected to that piercing blue stare. "Your mother died."

"Yes."

"Had a letter from this Pedersen fellow. He said it was leukaemia."

"Yes."

"Did you meet him?"

I told him about going to Ibiza and the night I had spent with Otto and my mother.

"He was a decent chap, then? Good to her?"

"Yes. He was immensely kind. And he adored her."

"Glad she ended up with somebody decent. Most of the chaps she picked on were just a lot of bounders."

I smiled at the old-fashioned word. I thought of the sheep-farmer, and the American in his Brooks Brothers shirts, and wondered how they would have liked being called bounders. They probably wouldn't even have known what it meant.

I said, "I think she sometimes got a little carried away."

97

A gleam of humour showed in his eyes. "You seem to have adopted a fairly worldly attitude?"

"Yes. I did. Long ago."

"She was a maddening woman. But she'd been the most enchanting little girl it was possible to imagine. I painted her often. I've still got one or two canvases of Lisa as a child. I'll have to get Pettifer to look them out, show them to you. And then she grew up and everything changed. Roger, my son, was killed in the war, and Lisa was always at loggerheads with her mother, rushing off in her little car, never coming home at night. Finally she fell in love with this actor fellow, and that was it."

"She really *was* in love with him."

"In love." He sounded disgusted. "That's an overrated expression. There's a lot more to life than just being in love."

"Yes, but you have to find that out for yourself."

He looked amused. "Have you found it out?"

"No."

"How old are you?"

"Twenty-one."

"You're mature for twenty-one. And I like your hair. You don't look like Lisa. You don't look like your father either. You look like yourself." He reached for his sherry glass, raised it carefully to his mouth, took a sip, and then replaced the glass on the table by his chair. In such cautious actions did he betray his age and his infirmity.

He said, "She should have come back to Boscarva. At any time we would have welcomed her. Come to that, why didn't *you* come?"

"I didn't know about Boscarva. I didn't know about you until the night before she died."

"It was as though she'd put the past out of her life. And when her mother died and I wrote to tell her, she never even replied."

"We were in New York that Christmas. She didn't get your letter till months later. And then it seemed too late to write. And she was so bad at writing letters."

"You're standing up for her. You don't resent the fact that she kept you from this place? You could have been brought up here. This could have been your home."

"She was my mother. That was the important thing."

"You seem to be arguing with me. Nobody argues with me nowadays. Not even Pettifer. It gets very dull."

Once more I was fixed with that blue stare. "Have you met Pettifer? He and I were in the Navy together about a century ago. And Mollie and Eliot? Have you met them?"

"Yes."

"They shouldn't be living here at all, of course, but the doctor insisted. Doesn't make that much difference to me, but it's hard luck on poor Pettifer. And Mollie's got a niece here as well, dreadful child with sagging breasts. Have you seen her?"

I managed not to giggle. "Yes, for a moment."

"A moment would be too long. And Boscarva. What do you think of Boscarva?"

"I love it. What I've seen of it, I love."

"The town's creeping out over the hill. There was a farm at the top, belonged to an old lady called Mrs Gregory. But this builder fellow talked her into selling up to him and now they've bulldozed the fields flat as a pancake and they're putting up houses nineteen to the dozen."

"I know. I saw them."

"Well, they can't come any further, because the farm at the back of this place and the fields on either side of the lane belong to me. Bought them when I bought Boscarva, back in 1922. Wouldn't like to tell you how little it cost me. But a bit of land around you gives you a feeling of security. Remember that."

"I will."

He frowned. "What's your name again? I've forgotten it already."

"Rebecca."

"Rebecca. And what are you going to call me?"

"I don't know. What do you want me to call you?"

"Eliot calls me Grenville. You call me Grenville too. It sounds more friendly."

"All right."

We drank our sherry, smiling, content with each other. Then, from the back of the house, came the sound of a gong being struck. Grenville put down his glass and got painfully to his feet, and I went to open the door for him. Together, we went down the passage towards the dining-room and family lunch.

7

Exhaustion hit me at the end of that long, eventful day, and unfortunately in the middle of dinner. Luncheon had been a sustaining, homely meal, eaten at a round table set in the bay window of the big dining-room. This had been laid with a simple checked cloth, and everyday china and glass, but dinner was a different affair altogether.

The long, polished table in the middle of the room was set for the five of us, with fine linen mats, and old silver and glass sparkling in the candlelight.

Everybody, it seemed, was expected to change in honour of this apparently nightly ritual. Mollie came downstairs in a brocade housecoat the colour of sapphires, which emphasised the brightness of her eyes. Grenville wore a faded velvet dinner jacket and Eliot a pale flannel suit in which he looked as elegant as a greyhound. Even Andrea, probably under much protest, had put on a different pair of trousers and a blouse of broderie anglaise which looked as though it could have done with a press, or a wash, or maybe both. Her lank hair was tied back with a scrap of velvet ribbon, the expression on her face continued to be one of resentful boredom.

Not in the habit of attending formal dinner parties, I had nevertheless packed a garment which would obviously have to appear every evening as long I stayed in this house, for I had no other. It was a caftan of soft brown jersey wool, with silver embroidery at the neck and the wrists of the flowing sleeves. With it, I wore my silver bracelets and a pair of hoop earrings which my mother had given me for my twenty-first birthday. Their weight, on this occasion, gave me odd comfort and confidence, two things which I badly needed.

I did not want to have dinner with my newly acquired family. I did not want to have to make conversation, to listen, to be intelligent and charming. I wanted to go to bed and be brought something undemanding, like Bovril or a boiled egg. I wanted to be alone.

But there was soup and duckling, and red wine, dispensed by Eliot. The duckling was rich and the room very warm. As the meal slowly progressed I felt more and more strange, disembodied, light-headed. I tried to concentrate on the flames of the candles in front of me, but as I stared at them they separated and repeated themselves, and the voices around me became blurred and unintelligible, like the hum of conversation heard from a distant room. Instinctively, I pushed my plate away from me, knocked over the wineglass, and watched, in hopeless horror, as the red wine spread amongst the shattered splinters of glass.

In a way the accident was a blessing, for they all stopped talking and looked at me. I must have gone quite pale, for Eliot was on his feet in an instant and at my side . . .

"Are you all right?"

I said, "No, I don't think I am. I'm sorry . . ."

"Oh, my dear." Mollie flung aside her napkin and pushed back her chair. From across the table Andrea eyed me with chill interest.

"The glass . . . I'm so sorry . . ."

From the head of the table Grenville spoke. "It doesn't matter about the glass. Leave the glass. The girl's exhausted. Mollie, take her up and put her to bed."

I tried to protest, but not very hard. Eliot drew back my chair and helped me to my feet, his hands firm beneath my elbows. Mollie had gone to open the door, and cooler air moved in from the hall – already I felt better, as though, perhaps, after all, I was not going to faint.

As I passed Grenville, I said, "I'm sorry," for the third time. "Forgive me. Good night." I bent and kissed him, and left them all. Mollie closed the door behind us and came upstairs with me. She helped me undress and get into bed, and I was asleep before she had even turned off the light.

I slept for fourteen hours, waking at ten o'clock. I had not slept so late for years, and beyond my window the sky was blue and the cold bright northern light reflected from the sloping white-painted walls of my room. I got up, pulled on a dressing-gown and went and had a bath. Dressed, I felt wonderful, apart from the sinking sensation of shame at my behaviour the night before. I hoped they had not all thought that I was drunk.

Downstairs, I finally ran Mollie to earth in a little pantry, arranging a great mass of purple and pink polyanthus in a flowered bowl.

"How did you sleep?" she asked at once.

"Like the dead. I'm sorry about last night . . ."

"My dear, you were tired out. I'm sorry I didn't realise before. You'll want some breakfast."

"Just coffee."

She took me into the kitchen and heated coffee while I made some toast. "Where is everybody?" I asked.

"Eliot's at the garage, of course, and Pettifer's taken the car to Fourbourne to do some shopping for Grenville."

"What can I do? There must be something I can do to help."

"Well . . ." she debated. I looked at her. This morning she wore a cashmere sweater the colour of caramel and a slender tweed skirt. Immaculately made up, with every strand of hair in place, she seemed almost inhumanly neat. "You could go and fetch the fish for me in Porthkerris. The fishmonger rang up to say he'd got some halibut and I thought we'd have it for dinner. I could lend you my little car. Do you drive?"

"Yes, but couldn't I walk down? I like walking and it's such a lovely morning."

"Of course, if you want to. You could take the short cut over the fields and along the cliff. I know . . ." she appeared to be suddenly struck by inspiration ". . . take Andrea with you, and then she can show you the way, and show you where the fish shop is. Besides, she never takes any exercise if she can possibly help it and a walk would do her good." She made Andrea sound like a lazy dog. I did not particularly relish the idea of Andrea's company for the entire morning but I was sympathetic to Mollie, being encumbered by this unengaging girl, so I said that I would do as she suggested, and when I had finished my breakfast went in search of Andrea whom Mollie had last seen out on the terrace.

I found her bundled in a rug, lying on a long cane chair in a patch of sunshine, and peevishly regarding the view, like a seasick passenger on a liner.

"Will you walk down to Porthkerris with me?" I asked her.

She fixed me with her protuberant stare. "Why?"

"Because Mollie's asked me to go and pick up some fish and I don't know where the shop is. Besides, it's a lovely morning, and she thought we might go down to the cliffs."

She considered my suggestion, said, "All right," uncoiled herself from the rug and stood up. She wore the same dirty jeans as yesterday and a vast black and white sweater which reached below her narrow hips. We went back to the kitchen to fetch a basket and then set out, by way of the terrace and the sloping garden, down in the direction of the sea.

At the bottom of the garden, stone steps led up and over the wall, and Andrea went ahead of me, but paused because I wanted to inspect the studio from this new angle. It was, as Joss had said, locked and shuttered, and somehow desolate, and the great window on the north wall had been closed off by tightly-drawn curtains so that not a chink presented itself to any inquisitive passer-by.

Andrea stood on the top of the wall, her gaze following mine.

"He never paints now," she told me.

"I know."

"I can't think why. There's nothing wrong with him."
She jumped, hair flying, down off the wall, and totally
disappeared. I took a last look at the studio and then
followed her and we took a trodden path that led down
through small, irregular fields, and came out at last,
through the hazard of some waist-high gorse bushes, to
a stile, and so on to the cliff path.

This was obviously a favourite walk with visitors to
Porthkerris, for there were seats set in sheltered view
points, and litter bins for rubbish, and notices warning
people not to go too near the edge of the cliff which was
likely to collapse.

Andrea instantly went to the very edge and peered over.
Gulls wheeled and screamed all around her, the wind tore
at her hair and the baggy sweater, and from far below came
the distant thunder of surf on rocks. She flung her arms
wide and teetered slightly as though about to fall over
the edge, but when she saw that I didn't care whether she
committed suicide or not, she returned to the path, and in
single file we walked on, Andrea in front.

The cliff curved and the town came into view in front of
us, the low grey houses nestled around the sweep of the
bay and climbing the steep hill to the moor behind. We
went through a gate, and were now on to a proper road,
and so able to walk side by side.

Andrea became conversational.

"Your mother's just died, hasn't she?"

"Yes."

"Aunt Mollie was telling me about her. She said she was
a tart."

Painfully, I remained serene. It would have been instant
victory for Andrea if I had been anything else.

"She didn't really know her. They hadn't seen each other
for years."

"Was she a tart?"

"No."

"Aunt Mollie said she lived with men."

I realised then that Andrea was not merely trying to needle me, she was genuinely curious, and there was envy there as well.

I said, "She was very gay and very loving and very beautiful."

She accepted this. "Where do you live?"

"In London. I've got a little flat."

"Do you live alone, or with somebody?"

"No, I live alone."

"Do you go to parties and things?"

"Yes, if someone asks me and I want to go."

"Do you work? Do you have a job?"

"Yes. In a bookshop."

"God, how grim."

"I like it."

"Where did you meet Joss?"

Now, I thought, we're getting down to business, but her face was empty of expression.

"I met him in London . . . he mended a chair for me."

"Do you like him?"

"I don't know him well enough to dislike him."

"Eliot hates him. So does Aunt Mollie."

"Why?"

"Because they don't like having him around the place all the time. And they treat him as though he should call them Sir and Madam, and of course he doesn't. And he talks to Grenville and makes him laugh. I've heard them talking."

I imagined her creeping up to closed doors, listening at keyholes.

"That's nice, if he makes the old man laugh."

"He and Eliot had a terrible row once. It was about some car that Eliot had sold to a friend of Joss's and Joss said it wasn't roadworthy and Eliot called him an insolent, interfering bastard."

"Did you listen in to that one as well?"

"I couldn't help hearing. I was in the loo and the window was open and they were out on the gravel by the front door."

"How long have you been staying at Boscarva?" I asked, curious to know how long it had taken her to dig all these skeletons out of the family cupboards.

"Two weeks. It seems like six months."

"I should have thought you'd have loved coming down."

"For heaven's sake, I'm not a child. What am I meant to do with myself. Go bucket and spading on the beach?"

"What do you do in London?"

She kicked a pebble, viciously, hating Cornwall. "I was at an art school, but my parents *didn't approve* . . ." she put on a mealy voice ". . . of my friends. So they took me away and sent me here."

"But you can't stay here for ever. What are you going to do when you go back?"

"That's up to them, isn't it?"

I felt a twinge of pity for her parents, even parents who had somehow raised such an obnoxious child.

"I mean, isn't there anything you *want* to do?"

"Yes, just get away, be on my own, do my own thing. Danus, this fabulous chap I went around with, he had a friend who was running a pottery on the Isle of Skye, and he wanted me to go and help . . . It sounded super, you know, living in a sort of commune, and right away from everybody . . . but my grotty mother shoved her great oar in and spoiled it all."

"Where's Danus now?"

"Oh, he went to Skye."

"Has he written to tell you about it?"

She tossed her head, fiddled with her hair, would not meet my eye. "Yes, actually, long letters. Reams of them. He still wants me to go there, and I'm going to, just as soon as I'm eighteen and they can't stop me any more."

"Why don't you just go back to art school first, and get some sort of a qualification . . . that'd give you time . . ."

She turned on me. "You know something? You talk like all the rest of them. How old are you anyway? You sound like someone with one foot in the grave."

"It's crazy to wreck your life before it's even started."

"It's my life. Not yours."

"No, it's not my life."

Having thus stupendously quarrelled, we continued our walk into the town in silence, and when Andrea did speak again, it was to say, "That's the fish shop," and wave a hand in its direction.

"Thank you." I went in to collect the halibut but she stayed, pointedly, outside on the cobbled pavement. When I emerged again, she had gone, only to appear the next moment from a paper-shop next door, where she had been buying a lurid magazine called *True Sex*.

"Shall we go back now?" I asked her. "Or do you want to do more shopping?"

"I can't shop, I haven't any money. Only a few pence."

I was suddenly, irrationally, sorry for her. "I'll stand you a cup of coffee if you'd like one."

She looked at me with sudden delight and I thought she was going to gleefully accept my modest offer, but instead she said, "Let's go and see Joss."

I was taken unawares. "Why do you want to go and see Joss?"

"I just do. I often go and see him when I come down to the town. He's always pleased to see me. He made me promise always to go and see him if I'm down here."

"How do you know he'll be there?"

"Well, he's not at Boscarva today, so he must be at the shop. Have you been there? It's super, he's got a sort of pad on the top floor, just like something out of a magazine, with a bed that's a sort of sofa and masses of cushions and things, and a log fire. And at night . . ." her voice became dreamy ". . . it's all closed-in and secret, and there's nothing but firelight."

I tried not to gape. "You mean . . . you and Joss . . ."

She shrugged, tossing her hair. "Once or twice, but nobody knows. I don't know why I told you. You won't tell the others, will you?"

"But don't they . . . doesn't Mollie . . . ask questions?"

108

"Oh, I tell her I'm going to the cinema. She doesn't seem to mind me going to the cinema. Come on, let's go and see Joss . . ."

But after this revelation, nothing would have induced me to go near Joss's shop. I said, "Joss will be working, he won't want to be interrupted. And anyway there isn't time. And I don't want to go."

"You said there was time for coffee, why isn't there time for Joss?"

"Andrea, I told you, I don't want to go."

She began to smile. "I thought you liked Joss."

"That's not the point. He doesn't want us under his feet every time he turns round."

"Do you mean me?"

"I mean *us*." I was beginning to be desperate.

"He always wants to see me. I know he does."

"Yes, I'm sure," I said gently. "But let's go back to Boscarva."

I reminded myself that from the very start I had not liked Joss. Despite his concern and apparent friendliness he had always left me with that strange sensation of disquiet, as though someone were creeping up behind my back. Yesterday I had begun to forget this initial antipathy, even to like him, but after Andrea's confidences it was not hard to whip back to life my first distrust of the man. He was too good-looking, too charming. Andrea could be a liar, but she was no fool; she had pigeon-holed the rest of the family with disconcerting accuracy, and even if there was only a grain of truth in what she said about Joss, I wanted to have no part of it.

If I had known him and liked him better, I would have taken him aside and taxed him with what she had said. As it was, he held no importance for me. Besides, I had other things to think about.

Grenville did not come down for lunch that day.

"He's tired," Mollie told us. "He's having a day in bed.

Perhaps he'll join us for dinner. Pettifer's going to take him up a tray."

So the three of us ate lunch together. Mollie had changed into a neat woollen dress and a double string of pearls. She was going, she said, to play bridge with friends in Fourbourne. She hoped that I would be able to occupy myself.

I said that of course I would be perfectly all right. Across the table, we smiled at each other and I wondered if she had really told Andrea that my mother was a tart, or if this was simply Andrea's interpretation of some vague euphemistic explanation that Mollie had given her. I hoped it was the latter, but still I wished that Mollie had not found it necessary to discuss Lisa with Andrea. She was dead now, but once she had been funny and enchanting and full of laughter. Why couldn't she be remembered that way?

As we sat around the table, the day outside changed its face. A wind got up from the west, and with great speed a bank of grey cloud sped over the blue sky, obliterating the sunshine, and presently it started to rain. It was in this rain that Mollie set off for her bridge party, driving her little car, and saying that she would be home about six. Andrea, perhaps exhausted by her morning's exercise, but more likely bored to death with my company, disappeared up to her bedroom with her new magazine. Alone, I stood at the foot of the stairs, wondering how to amuse myself. The silence of the gloomy afternoon was broken only by the ticking of the grandfather clock and small, occupied sounds which came from the direction of the kitchens, and which, investigated, proved to be Pettifer, seated at a wooden table in his pantry and cleaning silver.

He looked up as I put my head around the door.

"Hello. I didn't hear you."

"How's my grandfather?"

"Oh, he's all right. Just a bit weary after all the excitement of yesterday. We thought it would be better if he had a day with his toes up. Has Mrs Roger gone?"

"Yes." I pulled up a chair and sat opposite him.

110

"Thought I heard the car."

"Do you want me to help you?"

"That'd be very kind . . . those spoons there need a good rub up with the shammy. Don't know how they get so marked and stained. But, there, I do know. It's this damp sea air. One thing silver really hates it's damp sea air." I began to rub at the thin worn bowl of the spoon. Pettifer looked at me over the top of his glasses. "Funny to have you sitting there after all these years. Your mother used to spend half her life in the kitchen . . . When Roger went off to boarding school there wasn't anyone else for her to talk to. So she used to come and spend her time with Mrs Pettifer and me. Taught her to make fairy cakes, Mrs Pettifer did, and how to play two-handed whist. We had great times. And on a day like this, she used to make toast at the old range . . . mind, that's gone now, we've got a new one and good thing too . . . but that old range was cosy, with the fire burning behind the bars, and all the brass knobs polished up lovely."

"How long have you been at Boscarva, Pettifer?"

"Ever since the Commander bought it, back in 1922. That was the year he left the Navy, decided to be a painter. Old Mrs Bayliss didn't like that. For three months or more she wouldn't even talk to him."

"Why did she mind so much?"

"She'd been with the Navy all her life. Her father was the Captain of the *Imperious* when the Commander was First Lieutenant. That was how they met. They were married in Malta. A lovely wedding with an arch of swords and all. Being with the Navy meant a lot to Mrs Bayliss. When the Commander said he was going to leave they parted brass rags good and proper, but she couldn't make him change his mind. So we left Malta, for good and all, and the Commander found this house, and then we all moved down here."

"And you've been here ever since?"

"More or less. The Commander enrolled at the Slade, and that meant working in London, so he had this little *pied-à-terre*, just off St James's it was, and when he went up to London I went too, to keep an eye on him, and Mrs Pettifer stayed here with Mrs Bayliss and Roger. Your mother wasn't born then."

"But, when he'd finished at the Slade . . .?"

"Well, then he came back for good. And built the studio. That was when he was painting at his best. Lovely stuff he did then, great seascapes, so cold and bright you could smell the wind, feel the salt on your lips."

"Are there many of his pictures in this house?"

"No, not many. There's the fishing boat over the dining-room fireplace, and one or two little black and white drawings along the upstairs passage. He's got three or four in his study, and then there's a couple in the room where Mrs Roger sleeps."

"And the one in the drawing-room . . ."

"Oh, yes, that one of course. 'Lady Holding a Rose.'"

"Who was she?"

He did not reply; was, perhaps, preoccupied with his silver, rubbing away at a fork as though determined to flatten the pattern.

"Who was she? The girl in the picture?"

"Oh," said Pettifer. "That was Sophia."

Sophia. Ever since my mother had fleetingly mentioned her I had wanted to know about Sophia and now here was Pettifer bringing up her name as though it were the most natural thing in the world.

"She was a girl who used to model for the Commander. I think she first worked for him in London when he was a student, and then she used to come down here sometimes during the summer months, take lodgings in Porthkerris and work for any artist who was ready and able to pay her."

"Was she very beautiful?"

"Not my idea of a beauty. But lively, and what a talker! She was Irish, she'd come from County Cork."

"What did my grandmother think of Sophia?"

112

"Their paths never crossed, any more than your grand-mother would have had social dealings with the butcher or the girl who did her hair."

"So Sophia never came to Boscarva?"

"Oh, yes, she used to come and go. She'd be down at the studio with the Commander, and then he'd get tired, or lose his patience with her, and call it a day, and she'd come up the garden and through the back door calling out, 'Any chance of a cup of tea?' and because it was Sophia, Mrs Pettifer always had the kettle on."

"She used to tell fortunes from teacups."

"Who told you that?"

"My mother."

"That's right, she did. And wonderful things she told us were going to happen to us all. 'Course, they didn't, but it was fun listening to her, just the same. She and your mother were great friends. Sophia used to take her down to the beach and Mrs Pettifer would pack a picnic. And if it was stormy weather they'd go for long walks up on the moor."

"But what was my grandmother doing all this time?"

"Oh, playing bridge or mah-jong most afternoons. She had a very select circle of friends. She was a nice enough lady, but not really interested in children. Perhaps if she'd been more interested in Lisa when she was a child, they'd have had more in common when Lisa grew up, and maybe your mother wouldn't have run off like that, breaking all our hearts."

"What happened to Sophia?"

"Oh, she went back to London, she got married and she had a baby, I think. Then, in 1942, she was killed in the Blitz. The baby was down in the country and her husband was overseas, but Sophia stayed in London because she was working in a hospital there. We didn't hear about it for a long time, till long after it happened. Mrs Pettifer and I felt as though a light had gone out of our lives."

"And my grandfather?"

"He was sorry, of course. But he hadn't seen her

113

for years. She was just a girl who'd once worked for him."

"Are there any more pictures of her?"

"There's pictures of Sophia in provincial art galleries up and down the country. There's one in the gallery in Porthkerris if you want to go and look at that. And there's a couple upstairs in Mrs Roger's bedroom."

"Could we go and look at them now?" I sounded eager and Pettifer looked surprised, as though I were suggesting something faintly indecent. "I mean Mrs Bayliss wouldn't mind, would she?"

"Oh, she wouldn't mind. I don't see why not . . . come on."

He got laboriously to his feet, and I followed him upstairs and along the first-floor passage to the bedroom over the drawing-room, which was large and furnished in a very feminine fashion with old-fashioned Victorian furniture and a faded pink and cream carpet. Mollie had left it painfully neat. The two little oil paintings hung side by side between the windows, one of a chestnut tree with a girl lying in its shade, the other of the same girl hanging out a line of washing on a breezy day. They were scarcely more than sketches, and I was disappointed.

"I still don't know what Sophia looks like."

Pettifer was about to reply when, from the depths of the house, came the ringing of a bell. He cocked his head, like a dog listening. "That's the Commander, he's heard us talking through the wall. Excuse me a moment."

I followed him out of Mollie's room and closed the door behind me. He went on down the passage a little way and opened a door, and I heard Grenville's voice.

"What are you two muttering about in there?"

"I was just showing Rebecca the two pictures in Mrs Roger's room . . ."

"Is Rebecca there? Tell her to come in . . ."

I went in, past Pettifer. Grenville was not in bed, but sitting in a deep armchair with his feet propped up on a stool. He was dressed, but there was a rug over his

114

knees and the room was cheered by the flicker of a fire. Everything was very neat and ship-shape and smelt of the Bay Rum he put on his hair.

I said, "I thought you were in bed."

"Pettifer got me up after lunch. I get bored stiff lying in bed all day. What have you been talking about?"

"Pettifer was showing me some of your pictures."

"I expect you think they're very old-fashioned. They're going back to realism now, you know, these young artists. I knew it would come. You'll have to have one of my pictures. There are racks of them in the studio that have never been sorted out. I closed the place up ten years ago, and I haven't been there since. Pettifer, where's the key?"

"Put safely away, sir."

"You'll have to get the key off Pettifer, go down and nose around, see if there's anything you'd like. Got anywhere to hang it?"

"I've got a flat in London. It needs a picture."

"I thought of something else sitting here. That jade in the cabinet downstairs. I brought it back from China years ago, gave it to Lisa. Now, it belongs to you. And a mirror that her grandmother left her – where's that, Pettifer?"

"That's in the morning-room, sir."

"Well, we'll have to get it down, give it a clean. You'd like that, wouldn't you?"

"Yes, I would." I felt greatly relieved. I had been wondering how to bring up the subject of my mother's possessions, and now, without any prompting, Grenville had done it for me. I hesitated and then, striking while the iron was hot, mentioned the third thing. ". . . and there was a davenport desk."

"Hm?" He fixed me with his ferocious stare. "How do you know?"

"My mother told me about the jade and the mirror, and she said there was a davenport desk." He continued to glare at me. I wished all at once that I had said nothing.

115

"I mean, it doesn't matter, it's just that if nobody did want it . . . if it wasn't being used . . ."

"Pettifer, do you remember that desk?"

"Yes, I do, sir, now you come to mention it. It was up in the other attic bedroom, but I can't remember having seen it lately."

"Well, look for it some time, there's a good fellow. And put another bit of wood on the fire . . ." Pettifer did so. Grenville, watching him, said suddenly, "Where is everybody? The house is quiet. Only the sound of the rain."

"Mrs Roger's out to a bridge party. I think Miss Andrea's in her room . . ."

"How about a cup of tea?" Grenville cocked an eye at me. "You'd like a cup of tea, wouldn't you? We haven't had the chance of getting to know each other. Either you're keeling over in the middle of dinner, or I'm too old and infirm to get out of bed. We make a fine pair, don't we?"

"I'd like to have tea with you."

"Pettifer will bring up a tray."

"No," I said. "I will. Pettifer's legs have been up and down these stairs all day. Let's give him a rest."

Grenville looked amused. "All right. You bring it up, and let's have a good big plateful of hot buttered toast."

I was to wish, many times over, that I had never brought up the subject of the davenport desk. Because it could not be found. While Grenville and I ate our tea, Pettifer began to look for it. By the time he came to take the tray away, he had combed the house from top to bottom, and the desk was nowhere.

Grenville scarcely believed him. "You've just missed it. Your eyes are getting as old as mine."

"I could scarcely miss seeing a desk." Pettifer sounded aggrieved.

"Perhaps," I said, trying to be helpful, "it was sent away to be mended or something . . ." They both looked at me as though I were a fool, and I hastily shut up.

"Would it be in the studio?" Pettifer ventured.

"What would I do with a desk in the studio? I painted there, I didn't write letters. Didn't want a desk cluttering the place up . . ." Grenville was getting quite agitated. I stood up, "Oh, it'll turn up," I said in my best, soothing voice, and picked up the tea-tray to carry it downstairs. In the kitchen I was joined by Pettifer, upset by what had happened.

"It's not good for the Commander to get worked up about anything . . . and he's going to go after this like a terrier after a rat. I can tell."

"It's all my fault. I don't know why I ever mentioned it."

"But I remember it. I just can't remember having seen it lately." I began to wash the cups and saucers and Pettifer picked up a tea towel in order to dry them. "And there's another thing. There was a Chippendale chair that used to go with it . . . mind, they didn't match, but the chair always sat in front of that desk. It had a tapestry seat, rather worn, birds and flowers and things. Well, that's gone, too . . . but I'm not going to tell the Commander that and neither are you."

I promised that I wouldn't. "Anyway," I said, "it doesn't matter to me one way or the other."

"No, but it matters to the Commander. Artistic he may have been, but he had a memory like an elephant and that's one thing he hasn't lost." He added gloomily, "I sometimes wish he had."

That evening when I went downstairs, changed once more into the brown and silver caftan, I found Eliot in the drawing-room, alone except for that inevitable companion, his dog. Eliot sat by the fire with a drink and the evening paper, and Rufus was stretched, like some glorious fur, on the hearth-rug. They looked companionable, caught in the light of the lamp, but my appearance disturbed the peaceful scene, and Eliot stood up, dropping the paper behind him on the seat of the chair.

"Rebecca. How are you?"

"I'm all right."

"I was afraid last night that you were going to be ill."

"No. I was just tired. I slept till ten o'clock."

"My mother told me. Would you like a drink?"

I said that I would and he poured me some sherry and I went to crouch by the fire and fondle the dog's silky ears.

As Eliot brought me my drink I asked, "Does he go everywhere with you?"

"Yes, everywhere. To the garage, to the office, out to lunch, into the pubs, anywhere I happen to be going. He's a very well-known dog in this part of the world."

I sat on the hearth-rug, and Eliot subsided once more into his chair and picked up his drink. He said, "Tomorrow I have to go over to Falmouth, see a man about a car. I wondered if you'd like to come with me, see a bit of the country. Does that appeal to you?"

I was surprised by my own pleasure at this invitation. "I'd love it."

"It won't be very exciting. But perhaps you can amuse yourself for an hour or two while I'm doing business, and then we'll stop at a little pub I know on the way home. They serve delicious sea food. Do you like oysters?"

"Yes."

"Good. So do I. And then we'll come home by High Cross, and you can see where we normally live, my mother and I."

"Your mother told me about it. It sounds charming."

"Better than this mausoleum . . ."

"Oh, Eliot, it's not a mausoleum . . ."

"I was never much of a one for Victorian relics . . ."

Before I could protest further, we were joined by Grenville. At least, we heard him coming, step by step downstairs; heard him talking to Pettifer, the high-pitched voice and the low growl; heard them coming down the hall, the tap of Grenville's stick on the polished wood.

Eliot made a small face at me and went to open the door, and Grenville moved in, like the prow of some great, indestructible ship . . .

"That's all right, Pettifer, I can manage now." I had got up from the hearth-rug, wanting to help push forward the chair which he had used the night before, but this seemed to madden him. He was obviously not in a good mood.

"For God's sake, girl, stop fussing around. Do you think I want to sit *in* the fire, I'll burn to death sitting there . . ."

I edged the chair back to its original position and finally Grenville reached it and sank into it.

"How about a drink?" Eliot asked him.

"I'll have a whisky . . ."

Eliot looked surprised ". . . Whisky?"

"Yes, a whisky. I know what that fool of a doctor said but tonight I'm having a whisky."

Eliot said nothing, just nodded his head in patient acquiescence and went to pour the drink. As he did so Grenville leaned round the edge of the chair and said, "Eliot, have you seen that davenport desk around the place?" and my heart sank into my shoes.

"Oh, Grenville, don't start that again . . ."

"What do you mean, start that again? We've got to find the damned thing. I told Pettifer just now, got to go on looking till we've found it."

Eliot came back with the glass of whisky. He drew up a table and set the glass within Grenville's reach.

"What davenport desk?" he asked patiently.

"Little davenport desk, used to be in one of the bedrooms. Belonged to Lisa and now it belongs to Rebecca. She wants it. She's got a flat in London, wants to put it there. And Pettifer can't find it, says he's been through the house with a toothcomb, can't find it. You haven't seen it, have you?"

"I've never set eyes on it. I don't even know what a davenport desk is."

"It's a little desk. Got drawers down the side. Bit of tooled leather on the top. They're rare now, I believe. Worth a lot of money."

"Pettifer's probably put it somewhere and forgotten."

"Pettifer doesn't forget things."

"Well, perhaps Mrs Pettifer did something with it and forgot to tell him."

119

"I've already *said*; he doesn't forget things."

We were joined at this moment by Mollie, who appeared, smiling determinedly, as though she had heard the angry voice raised beyond the closed door, and was about to spread oil on troubled waters.

"Hello, everybody, I'm afraid I'm a little late. I had to go and do some very exciting things to that delicious piece of halibut Rebecca bought for me this morning. Eliot, dear . . ." she kissed him, apparently seeing him for the first time that evening. "And Grenville . . ." she stooped to kiss him too ". . . you're looking more rested." Then, before he could contradict her, she smiled across the top of his head at me. "Did you have a good afternoon?"

"Yes, thank you. How was the bridge?"

"Not too bad. I won twenty pence. Eliot darling, I'd love a drink. Andrea's just coming. She won't be a moment . . ." But she finally ran out of defensive small talk, and Grenville instantly opened fire. "We've lost something," he told her.

"What have you lost? Your cuff-links again?"

"We have lost a davenport desk."

It was becoming ludicrous.

"You've *lost* a davenport desk?"

For her benefit, Grenville went through the whole rigmarole. On being told that it was I who had precipitated this crisis, Mollie looked at me with some reproach, as though she thought this a poor way to return her hospitality and kindness. I was inclined to agree with her.

"But it must be somewhere." She took her glass from Eliot, drew up a stool and sat, all ready to work the whole thing out. "It must have been put somewhere for safety."

"Pettifer has looked for it."

"Perhaps he hasn't seen it. I'm sure he should get his glasses changed. Perhaps it's been put somewhere and he's forgotten."

Grenville thumped the arm of his chair with a balled fist. "Pettifer does not forget things."

120

"In fact . . ." said Eliot coolly ". . . he forgets things all the time."

Grenville glared at him. "And what does that mean?"

"Nothing personal. Just that he's getting older."

"I suppose you're blaming Pettifer . . ."

"I'm not blaming anybody . . ."

"You just said he's too old to know what he's doing. If he's too old what the hell do you think I am?"

"I never said that . . ."

"You blamed *him* . . ."

Eliot lost his patience. "If I was going to blame anybody," he said, raising his voice almost to the pitch of Grenville's, "I'd ask a few questions of your Joss Gardner." There was a pause after he'd come out with this. And then, in a more controlled, reasonable voice, he went on. "All right, so nobody wants to accuse another man of stealing. But Joss is in and out of this house all the time, in and out of all the rooms. He knows what's in this place better than anybody. And he's an expert, he knows what it's worth."

"But why should Joss take a desk?" asked Mollie.

"A valuable desk. Don't forget that. It's rare and it's valuable, Grenville just said so. Perhaps he needed the money. To look at him he could do with a bit of extra cash. And he's an expert. He's up and down to London all the time. He'd know where to sell it."

He stopped, abruptly, as though realising that already he had said too much. He finished his whisky, and went, without speaking, to pour himself a second glass.

The silence became uncomfortable. To break it, Mollie said, briefly, "I don't think that Joss . . ."

"Just a lot of poppycock," Grenville interrupted her savagely.

Eliot set down the whisky bottle with a thump.

"How do you know? How do you know anything about Joss Gardner? He turns up, like a hippy, out of nowhere, says he's going to open a shop, and the next thing you've opened up the house to him and given him the job of patching up all the furniture. What do you know about Joss? What do any of us know about him?"

"I know that I can trust him. I was trained to judge a man's character . . ."

"You could be wrong . . ."

Grenville raised his voice and rode over Eliot's, ". . . and it would be no bad thing if you were to take a few lessons in choosing your companions."

Eliot's eyes narrowed. "What does that mean?"

"It means that if you want to be made a fool of, try doing business with that little shyster Ernest Padlow."

If I could have escaped at that moment, I would. But I was caught, jammed into the corner behind Grenville's chair.

"What do you know about Ernest Padlow?"

"I know you've been seen around with him . . . drinking in bars . . ."

Eliot shot a glance at me, and then said, under his breath, "That bastard Joss Gardner."

"It wasn't Joss who told me, it was Hargreaves, at the bank. He came up for a glass of sherry the other day. And Mrs Thomas came in to do my fire this morning, she'd seen you with Padlow, up at that gimcrack nightmare he calls a housing estate."

"Back-stairs gossip."

"You hear the truth from truthful people. It doesn't matter in which direction they live. And if you think I'm selling up my land to that jumped-up little beachsweeper, you're wrong . . ."

"It won't always be your land."

"And if you're so sure it will be yours, all I can say is, don't count your chickens before they're hatched. Because you, dear boy, are not my only grandchild."

And at this dramatic moment, like a nicely stage-managed play, the door opened and Andrea appeared to tell us that Pettifer had told her to tell us that dinner was ready.

8

It was hard to sleep that night. I tossed and turned, fetched a glass of water, paced the floor, looked out of the window, climbed back into bed and tried once more to compose myself, but always, when I closed my eyes, the evening came back to me like a film played over and over, voices drummed in my ears, and would not be stilled.

All right, so nobody wants to accuse another man of stealing. What do any of us know about Joss?

If you want to be made a fool of, try doing business with that little shyster Ernest Padlow. And if you think I'm selling my land to that jumped-up little beachsweeper, you're wrong . . .

It won't always be your land . . .

. . . you, dear boy, are not my only grandchild.

Dinner had been a gruesome meal. Eliot and Grenville had scarcely spoken a word from beginning to end. Mollie, to make up for their silence, had kept up a patter of meaningless conversation to which I had tried to respond. And Andrea had watched us all, a gleam of triumph in her round, seeking eyes, while Pettifer trod heavily to and fro, removing dishes, handing round a lemon soufflé rich with whipped cream, which nobody seemed to want.

When at last it was over, they had all dispersed: Grenville to his bedroom, Andrea to the morning-room from whence we presently heard the blare of the television set. Eliot, with no explanations, put on a coat, whistled up his dog and banged out of the front door. I guessed he had gone to get drunk and didn't entirely blame him. Mollie and I ended up in the drawing-room, one on either side of the fire. She had some tapestry and seemed quite prepared to sit and sew in silence, but this would have been unbearable. I said, plunging straight in with the apology which I felt I owed her, "I am sorry about this evening. I wish I'd never mentioned that desk."

She did not look at me. "Oh, it can't be helped."

"It was just that my mother had mentioned it to me, and when Grenville spoke about the jade and the mirror, well, it never occurred to me that I'd start such a storm in a teacup."

"Grenville's a strange old man. He's always been stubborn about people, he'll never see that there can be two sides to every situation."

"You mean about Joss . . ."

"I don't know why he's so taken with Joss. It's frightening. It's as though Joss were able to exert some hold over him. Eliot and I never wanted him in and out of the house this way. If Grenville's furniture needed to be repaired, surely he could have come and fetched it in his van and taken it down to his workshop, like any other tradesman would do. We tried to talk Grenville out of it, but he was adamant, and, after all, this is his house. It isn't ours."

"But it will be Eliot's one day."

She sent me a cold look.

"After this evening, one wonders."

"Oh, Mollie, I don't want Boscarva, Grenville would never leave a place like this to me. He just said that to win a point; perhaps it was the first thing that came into his head. He didn't mean it."

"He hurt Eliot."

"Eliot will understand. You have to make allowances for old people."

"I'm tired of making allowances for Grenville," said Mollie, viciously snapping at a strand of wool with her silver scissors. "My life has been disrupted by Grenville. He and Pettifer could have come and lived at High Cross; that's what we wanted. The house is smaller and more convenient and it would have been better for everybody. And Boscarva should have been made over to Eliot years

124

ago. As it is, death duties are going to be exorbitant. Eliot is never going to be able to afford to keep it going. The whole situation is *so* unrealistic."

"I suppose it's hard to be realistic when you're eighty and you've lived in a place most of your life."

She ignored this. "And all that land, and the farm. Eliot is simply trying to make the best of it all, but Grenville won't see that. He's never shown any interest, never encouraged Eliot in any way. Even the garage at High Cross, Eliot got that going entirely on his own. At the beginning, he asked his grandfather to help, but Grenville said he wasn't going to have anything to do with second-hand cars, and there was a row, and finally Eliot borrowed the money from someone else, and he's never asked his grandfather for a shilling since that day. You'd think he'd deserve some credit for that."

She was pale with anger on Eliot's account – a little tigress, I thought, fighting for her cub, and I remembered my mother's low opinion of the way in which she had possessed and molly-coddled the young Eliot. Perhaps neither of them had ever grown out of the habit.

To change the subject I told her about Eliot's invitation for the next day. "He said he'd take me into High Cross on the way home."

But Mollie was only momentarily diverted. "You must go in and see the house, Eliot's got the key. I go up most weeks to make sure everything's all right, but really I get so depressed having to leave my darling little house and come back to this gloomy place . . ." and then she laughed at herself wryly. "It's getting me down, isn't it? I must try to pull myself together. But really I'll be glad when it's all over."

When it's all over. That meant when Grenville finally died. I didn't want to think about him dying any more than I wanted to think about Joss coupled with the unsavoury Andrea; any more than I wanted to think about Joss helping himself to a davenport desk and a Chippendale chair, heaving them into the back of his little truck, and selling them to the first dealer who made him a good offer.

What do you know about Joss? What do any of us know about him?

For my part I wished I knew nothing. I turned in bed, thumped at the pillows, and waited, without much hope, for sleep.

It rained in the night, but the next morning it was still and clear, the sky a pale, washed blue, everything wet and shining, translucent in the cool spring light. I leaned out of the window and smelt the dampness, mossy and sweet. The sea was flat and blue as a sheet of silk, gulls drifted lazily over the rim of the cliff, a boat moved out from the harbour, heading for distant fishing-grounds, and so still was the air that I could hear the distant chug of its engine.

My spirits rose. Yesterday was over, today would be better. I was glad to be getting out of the house, away from Mollie's reproach and Andrea's unsettling presence. I bathed and dressed and went downstairs and found Eliot in the dining-room, eating bacon and eggs, and looking – I was thankful to see – cheerful.

He looked up from the morning paper. "I wondered," he said, "if I was going to have to come and wake you up. I thought perhaps you'd forgotten."

"No, I didn't forget."

"We're the first down. With any luck we'll be out of the house before anyone else appears." He grinned, ruefully, like a repentant boy. "The last thing I want on a beautiful morning like this is recriminations."

"It was all my fault, mentioning that stupid desk. I said I was sorry last night to your mother."

"It'll all blow over," said Eliot. "These little differences of opinion always do." I poured myself a cup of coffee. "I'm just sorry that you were involved."

We left straight after breakfast, and there was a marvellous feeling of relief to be in his car, with Rufus perched on the back seat, and to be escaping. The car roared up the hill away from Boscarva; the wet road was blue with reflected sky, and the air smelt of primroses. As we climbed up and over the moor, the view spread and dipped before us – there were hills topped by ancient cairns and standing stones, and tiny forgotten villages, tucked into the folds of unexpected valleys where little rivers ran, and ancient clumps of oak and elm stood clustered by narrow, hump-backed bridges.

But I knew that we could not enjoy our day together, that we could not be entirely at ease, until I had made my peace with him.

I said, "I know that it'll blow over, and that perhaps it *wasn't* important, but we have to talk about last night."

He smiled at me, glancing sideways. "What do we have to say?"

"Just that, what Grenville said about having another grandchild. He didn't mean it. I know he didn't mean it."

"No, perhaps he didn't. Perhaps he was just trying to set us against each other, like a pair of dogs."

"He'd never leave me Boscarva. Never in a thousand years. He doesn't even know me, I've only just come into his life."

"Rebecca, don't give it another thought. I'm not going to."

"And, after all, if it is going to be yours one day, I don't see why you shouldn't start thinking about what you're going to do with it."

"You mean Ernest Padlow? What a lot of gossips those old people are, carrying tales and making mischief. If it isn't the bank manager it's Mrs Thomas, and if it isn't Mrs Thomas it's Pettifer."

I made myself sound casual. "Would you sell the land?"

"If I did I could probably afford to live at Boscarva. It's time I set up on my own."

"But . . ." I chose my words tactfully ". . . but wouldn't it be rather . . . spoiled . . . I mean, living there with rows of Mr Padlow's little houses all round you?"

127

Eliot laughed. "You've got entirely the wrong end of the stick. This wouldn't be a building estate like the one at the top of the hill. This would be high-class stuff, two-acre lots, very high specifications as to the style and the price of the houses built on them. No cutting down of trees, no despoiling of the amenities. They'd be expensive houses for expensive people, and there wouldn't be a lot of them. How does that sound to you?"

"Have you told Grenville this?"

"He won't let me. He won't listen. He's not interested and that's it."

"But surely if you explained . . ."

"I've been trying to explain things to him all my life and I've never got anywhere. And now, is there anything else you want to discuss?"

I considered. I certainly didn't want to discuss Joss. I said, "No."

"In that case shall we forget about last night and enjoy ourselves?"

It seemed a good idea. We smiled at each other. "All right," I said at last. We crossed a bridge and came to a steep hill, and Eliot changed down, expertly, with the old-fashioned gear stick. The car purred up the savage slope, its long, elegant bonnet seeming to point straight to the sky.

We got to Falmouth about ten o'clock. While Eliot attended to his business I was turned loose to explore the little town. Facing south, sheltered from the north wind, with gardens already filled with camellias and scented daphne bushes, it made me think of some Mediterranean port, and this illusion was strengthened by the blue of the sea on that first warm spring day, and the tall masts of the yachts which lay at anchor in the basin.

I felt, for some reason, impelled to shop. I bought freesias for Mollie, tightly in bud with their stalks wrapped in damp moss so that they would not wither before I got home, a box of cigars for Grenville, a bottle of fruity sherry for Pettifer, a record for Andrea. The sleeve portrayed a

128

transvestite group with sequined eyelids. It seemed to me to be right up her street. And for Eliot . . . I had noticed that his watch strap was wearing thin. I found a narrow strap in dark crocodile, very expensive, exactly right for Eliot. Then I bought a tube of toothpaste for myself, because I needed one. And for Joss , . .? Nothing for Joss.

Eliot picked me up, as we had arranged, in the lounge of the big hotel in the middle of town. We drove very fast out of the town and through Truro, and down into the little maze of lanes and wooded creeks that lay beyond until we came to a village called St Endon, where there were white cottages, palm trees and gardens full of flowers. The road wound down towards the creek, and at the very bottom was a little pub, right on the water's edge, with the high tide lapping at the wall below the terrace. Kittiwakes perched along the top of it, their eyes bright and friendly, unlike the greedy, wild gulls of Boscarva.

We sat out in the sunshine, drinking sherry, and I gave Eliot his present, then and there; he seemed inordinately delighted, ripping off the old watch strap right away and fitting on the new, shining leather one, adjusting the little clips with the blade of his penknife.

"What made you think of giving me that?"

"I noticed your old one was worn. I thought perhaps that you might lose your watch."

He leaned back in his chair, watching me across the table. It was so warm that I had pulled off my sweater and rolled up the sleeves of my cotton shirt. He said, "Did you buy presents for everybody?"

I was embarrassed. "Yes."

"I thought you had a lot of parcels. Do you always buy presents for people?"

"It's nice to have people to buy presents for."

"Isn't there anyone in London?"

"Not really."

"No one special?"

"There's never been anyone special."

"I can't believe it."

"It's true." I could not think why I was confiding in him this way. Perhaps it had something to do with the warmth of the day, surprising me by its beneficence, lowering all my guards. Perhaps it was the sherry. Perhaps it was simply the intimacy of two people who had weathered such a storm as the row that had taken place last night. Whatever the reason, it was easy that day to talk to Eliot.

"Why is that?" he asked.

"I don't know. It may have something to do with the way I was brought up . . . my mother lived with one man after another, so I lived with them too. And there's nothing like living at close quarters with people to destroy that marvellous illusion of romance."

We laughed. "That could be a good thing," said Eliot. "But it could be a bad thing, too. You mustn't close up altogether. Otherwise nobody's ever going to get near you."

"I'm all right."

"Are you going back to London?"

"Yes."

"Soon?"

"Probably."

"Why not stay for a bit?"

"I don't want to wear out my welcome."

"You won't do that. And I've hardly spoken to you. Anyway, how can you go back to London and leave all this behind you . . .?" His gesture included the sky, the sun, the quiet, the lap of water, the promise of the coming spring.

"I can, because I have to. I've a job to get back to and a flat that needs painting, and a life to pick up and start all over again."

"Can't that wait?"

"Not indefinitely."

"There's no reason to go." I did not reply. "Unless," he went on, "you were put off by what happened last night." I smiled and shook my head, because we had promised not to mention that again. He leaned on the table, his chin on his fist. "If you really wanted a job you could get one here. If you wanted a flat of your own you could rent that too."

"Why should I stay?" But I was flattered at being so persuaded.

"Because it would be good for Grenville, and for Mollie, and for me. Because I think we all want you to stay. Particularly me."

"Oh, Eliot . . ."

"It's true. There's something very serene about you. Did you know that? I noticed it that first evening I saw you before I even knew who you were. And I like the shape of your nose, and the sound of your laugh, and the way you can look marvellously ragamuffin one minute, in jeans and with your hair coming all unravelled, and then, the next minute, like a princess in a fairy story, with your plait over your shoulder and that stately gown you wear in the evenings. I feel as though I'm finding out new things about you every day. And this is why I don't want you to go. Not just yet."

I found that I could think of no rejoinder to this long speech. I was touched by it, and embarrassed too. But still, it was gratifying to be liked and admired, and even more gratifying to be told so.

Across the table, he began to laugh at me. "Your face is a picture. You don't know where to look and you're blushing. Come along, finish your drink and we'll go and eat oysters. I promise I'll not pay you any more compliments!"

We lingered over lunch in the small, low-ceilinged dining-room, eating at a table which wobbled so much on the uneven floor that Eliot was forced to prop up one of the legs with a scrap of folded paper. We ate oysters and steak and a fresh green salad and drank our way through a bottle of wine. We took our coffee back into the sunshine, and sat on the edge of the terrace wall, watching two boys, sunburned and barelegged, rig up a dinghy and take her sailing out on to the blue waters of the creek. We saw the striped sail fill with some mysterious, unfelt breeze, as the

131

dinghy heeled and went away from us, around the tip of a wooded promontory. And Eliot said that if I stayed in Cornwall, he would borrow a boat and teach me to sail; we would go mackerel fishing from Porthkerris – in the summer he would show me all the tiny coves and secret places which the tourists never found.

At last it was time to go, and the afternoon wound itself in like a long, shining ribbon. I was sleepy and replete when he drove me slowly back to High Cross, taking the long road that led through forgotten villages and the heart of the country.

When we got to High Cross, I realised that it stood at the very summit of the peninsula, so that the village had two aspects, one north to the Atlantic, the other south to the Channel; it was like being on an island, swept with clean winds and ringed by the sea. Eliot's garage stood in the middle of the village street, a little back from the road, with a cobbled forecourt set about with tubs of flowers, and inside the glass-fronted showroom stood the gleaming, racy cars. Everything was very new and expensive-looking and immaculately kept. I wondered, as we crossed the forecourt towards the showrooms, how much Eliot had had to sink into such a venture, and why he had decided that it was a viable proposition to open such a specialised garage in this out-of-the-way spot.

He pulled one of the sliding glass doors aside and I went in, my feet making no sound on the highly polished rubber floors.

"Why did you decide to start your garage here, Eliot? Wouldn't it have been better in Fourbourne or Falmouth or Penzance?"

"Psychological selling, my dear. Get a good name for yourself and people will come from the ends of the earth to buy what you've got to sell." And he added with disarming candour, "Besides, I already owned the land, or at least my mother did, which was an excellent incentive to build the garage here."

"Are all these cars for sale?"

132

"Yes. As you can see we concentrate on continental and sports cars. We had a Ferrari in last week, but that was sold a couple of days ago. It had been crashed, but I've got this young mechanic working for me, and by the time he'd finished with it it was as good as new . . ."

I laid my hand on the gleaming yellow bonnet. "What's this?"

"A Lancia Zagato. And this is an Alfa Romeo Spyder, only two years old. Beautiful car."

"And a Jensen Interceptor . . ." That was one that I recognised.

"Come and see the workshop." I followed him through another sliding door at the back of the showroom and decided that this was more like my idea of a garage. Here was the usual clutter of dismantled engines, oil cans, long flexes trailing from the ceiling, naked bulbs, tool benches, old tyres and trolleys.

In the middle of all this a figure was stooped over the stripped-down engine of a skeletal car. He wore a welding mask which made him appear monstrous, and worked with the roaring blue flame of a welding gun. The noise of the gun was overlaid by non-stop blaring music from a surprisingly small transistor radio perched on a beam above him.

Whether or not he saw us coming was anybody's guess, but it was only when Eliot switched off the radio that he shut off his gun and straightened up, pushing the welding mask up and back off his face. I saw a thin, dark young man, oil-stained and in need of a shave, his hair long, his eyes sharp and bright.

"Hello, Morris," said Eliot.

"Hello."

"This is Rebecca Bayliss, she's staying at Boscarva."

Reaching for a cigarette, Morris looked my way and gave me a nod. I said, "Hello," just to be friendly, but got no more response. He lit his cigarette, then slipped the fancy lighter back into the pocket of his oily overalls.

133

"Thought you'd be coming in this morning," he told Eliot.

"I told you I was going over to Falmouth."

"Any luck?"

"A 1933 Bentley."

"What sort of condition?"

"Looked OK. A bit of rust."

"Get the old paint spray out. There was a chap in the other day, wanting one of them."

"I know, that's why I bought it. Thought we'd take the transporter over, tomorrow or the next day, pick her up."

They fell silent. Morris went to his transistor and turned it on again, if anything louder than before. I looked down at the confusion of engineering on which he had been working and finally asked Eliot what sort of a car it had originally been.

"A 1971 Jaguar XJ6 4.2 litre, if you really want to know. And it will be again when Morris has finished with it. This is another that was in a crash."

Morris came back to stand between us.

"What exactly are you doing to it?" I asked him.

"Straightening out the chassis, fixing the wheel alignment."

"What about the brake shoes?" said Eliot.

"It could have done with new brake shoes, but I fixed the old ones to cover us for the guarantee . . . and Mr Kemback rang up from Birmingham . . ."

They began to talk shop. I drifted away, deafened by the sound of rock, went back through the showroom and out into the forecourt where Rufus waited, with dignity and patience, behind the driving wheel of Eliot's car. Together we sat there until we were rejoined by Eliot. "Sorry about that, Rebecca; I wanted to check on another job. Morris is a good mechanic, but he gets shirty if he's expected to answer the telephone as well."

"Who's Mr Kemback? Another customer?"

"No, not exactly. He was down here last summer on

134

holiday. He runs a motel, a garage, just off the M6. He's got quite a selection of old cars. Wants to start a museum, you know, a sort of sideline to the bacon-and-egg trade. He seems to want me to run it for him."

"You mean go and live in Birmingham?"

"Doesn't sound very tempting, does it? Anyway, that's it. Let's go and look at my mother's house."

We walked there, just a little way down the street, then up a short lane and through a double white gate, and the path sloped up to a long, low white house, which had been converted from two ancient thick-walled stone cottages. Eliot took a key out of his pocket and opened the door and inside it was cold, but not musty or damp. It was furnished like an expensive London flat, with pale, thick, fitted carpets and pale walls and sofas upholstered in mushroom-coloured brocade. There were a great many mirrors and little crystal bag chandeliers hanging from the low-beamed ceilings.

It was all charming, and just what I had imagined, and somehow wrong. A kitchen like an advertisement, a dining-room furnished with gleaming mahogany, upstairs there were four bedrooms and three bathrooms, a sewing-room and a linen cupboard of mammoth proportions, richly smelling of soap.

At the back of the house was a little patio, and then a long garden sloped up to a distant hedge. I looked at the patio and could see Mollie out there, entertaining her friends, with cane furniture set out on the flagstones, and martinis to drink, served from an expensive glass trolley.

I said, "It's a perfect house," and meant it. But I did not love it as I loved Boscarva. Perhaps because it was too perfect.

We stood in the elegant out-of-place drawing-room and eyed each other. Our day together seemed to have come to an end. Perhaps Eliot felt this too and wanted to postpone it, for he said, "I could put on a kettle and make you a cup of tea, only I know that there's no milk in the fridge."

"I think we should go home." I was surprised by an

enormous yawn, and Eliot laughed at me. He took my shoulders between his hands. "You're sleepy."

"Too much fresh air," I answered. "Too much wine."

I tipped my head back to look up into his face, and we were very close. I could feel his fingers tighten over my shoulders. He wasn't laughing any more, but his deep-set eyes held an expression as gentle as anything I had ever seen.

I said, "It's been a wonderful day . . ." but that was as far as I got, because he kissed me then, and for some time I was not able to say anything at all. When at last he drew away I was so shaken that all I could do was lean limply against him, wanting to cry, feeling a fool, knowing that the situation was fast slipping out of my control. My cheek was against his coat, and his arms around me held me so close that I could feel, like the throb of a drum, the solid beating of his heart.

Over the top of my head, I heard him say, "You mustn't go back to London. You mustn't ever go away again."

9

The shopping which I had done in Falmouth proved to be an unexpected blessing. I must have been inspired, for, without thinking, I provided exactly the small talking point we all needed to smooth over the embarrassment of the previous uncomfortable evening. Mollie was charmed with her freesias; she couldn't grow them at Boscarva, she explained, the winds were too cold, the garden too exposed. She paid me the compliment of arranging them with more artistry than one would have thought possible, and finally giving them the place of honour in the middle of the mantelpiece in the drawing-room. They filled the room with their rich romantic scent, and the cream and the violet and the deep pink drew one's eye, quite naturally, up to the portrait of Sophia. The flowers seemed to complement the glowing skin tones and the fragile shimmer of the white dress.

"Beautiful," said Mollie, standing back, but I could not be sure whether she was referring to the flowers or the portrait. "It was sweet of you to bring them. And did Eliot take you to see my house? So now you can understand how I feel about having to live in this great place." She regarded me thoughtfully, her eyes narrowed. "You know, I believe the day has done you good. I could even imagine you've caught the sun. You've got quite a good colour. The air must agree with you."

Pettifer accepted his sherry with dignity, but I could tell that he was pleased. And Grenville was wickedly delighted with his cigars, for the doctor had warned him against smoking and Pettifer had hidden his usual supply. I understood that he was parsimonious about doling them

137

out. Grenville took and lit one instantly, puffing away with immense satisfaction and leaning back in his big chair like a man without a care in the world. Even with Andrea I had for once done the right thing. "*The Creepers!* How did you know they're my favourite group? Oh, I wish there was a record-player here, but there isn't and I left mine in London. Gosh, aren't they fabulous, groovy . . .?" And then she came down to earth again, searching for the price tag. "That must have cost you something."

It was as though, with peace offerings, we had all formed an unspoken pact. Last night was never discussed. There was no mention of the davenport desk, of Ernest Padlow, of the possible sale of Boscarva Farm. There was no mention of Joss. After dinner Eliot set up a table, and Mollie got out the rosewood box containing the mah-jong set, and we played until bed-time, Andrea sitting with Mollie in order to learn the rules.

I caught myself thinking that, if a stranger were to come, unexpectedly, upon us, how he would be charmed by the picture we made, caught, like flies in amber, in the pool of light from the standard lamp, absorbed by our timeless occupation. The distinguished painter, mellow in the twilight of his years, surrounded by his family; the pretty daughter-in-law and the handsome grandson – and even Andrea, for once alert and interested, absorbed by the intricacies of the game.

I had played as a child with my mother, sometimes making up a foursome with two of her friends, and found myself comforted by the remembered touch of the ivory and bamboo tiles, by their beauty, and the satisfying sound they made, like sea pebbles disturbed by the tide, as we stirred them around in the middle of the table.

At the start of each round we built the four walls, two tiles high, and closed them together into a tight square, "to keep the evil spirits out," we were told by Grenville, who had learned to play as a young sub-lieutenant in Hong Kong and knew all the traditional superstitions of the ancient game. I thought how easy it would be, how safe, if ghosts and doubts and skeletons-in-the-cupboard could be thus shut out and kept at bay.

The travel brochures and holiday posters of Porthkerris inevitably portrayed a place where the sea and the sky were always a bright and unsullied blue, the houses white with sunshine, the odd palm tree in the foreground lending that suggestion of Mediterranean glamour. The imagination was led, naturally, to visions of fresh lobster, eaten out of doors; artists with beards and paint-stained smocks; and weather-beaten fishermen, picturesque as pirates, sitting on bollards, smoking their pipes and discussing last week's catch.

But Porthkerris, in February, in a north-east gale, had no shred of connection with this nebulous paradise.

The sea, the sky, the very town were grey, the maze of baffling, narrow streets subjected to onslaughts of bitter wind. The tide was high; the waves broke against the sea-wall and splashed across the road, misting the windows of the houses opposite with salt, and filling the gutters with yellow foam, like dirty soapsuds.

It was as though the place were under some sort of a siege. Shoppers were wrapped, buttoned, scarved in every sort of protective clothing, their faces half hidden by hoods or deep coat collars, their bodies bundled into ambiguity, so that men and women all looked alike, gumbooted and shapeless.

The sky was the colour of the wind, the air filled with flying flotsam, old leaves, twigs, scraps of paper, even tiles torn from roofs. In the shops, people forgot what they had come to buy, the talk was all of the weather, the wind, the damage the storm was going to do.

I had come, once more, to shop for Mollie, fighting my way down the hill in borrowed raincoat and rubber boots, because I felt safer on my feet than I would have driving Mollie's insubstantial car. Now that I was more familiar with the town I no longer needed Andrea to show me the way . . . anyway Andrea was still in bed when I left

Boscarva, and for once I did not blame her. The day was not inviting and it was hard to believe that only yesterday I had been sitting out, in my shirtsleeves, basking in a sun as warm as May.

The last of the shopping completed, I emerged from the baker's as the clock in the tower of the Norman church struck eleven. Normally, under such conditions, I would have headed straight back up the hill to Boscarva, but I had other plans. With my head down, the heavy basket over one arm, I made for the harbour.

The Art Gallery, I knew, was housed in an old Baptist Chapel, somewhere in the maze of streets which lay to the north of the town. I had thought that I would simply go and look for it, but as I braved the harbour road, battling with alternate assaults of wind and spray, I saw the old fisherman's lodge which had been converted to a Tourist Information Bureau and decided that I would save myself both time and effort if I made a few enquiries.

Inside, I found an unenthusiastic girl huddled over a paraffin stove; booted and shivering, she looked like the sole survivor of some Arctic expedition. When I appeared she did not move from her chair but said, "Yes?" and stared at me through a pair of unbecoming spectacles.

I tried to feel sorry for her. "I'm looking for the Art Gallery."

"Which one did you want?"

"I didn't know there was more than one."

Behind me the door opened and shut and we were joined by a third person. The girl looked over my shoulder and a faint interest gleamed behind her pebble glasses.

"There's the Town Gallery and the New Painters," she said, much more lively.

"I don't know which I want."

"Perhaps," said a voice behind me, "I can help."

I swung around and Joss stood there, in rubber boots and a streaming black oilskin, a fisherman's cap jammed down on to his head. His face was wet with rain, his hands jammed into the deep pockets of the coat, his dark eyes glinting with amusement. One half of me could see exactly why the sluggish girl behind the counter had suddenly come to life. The other half was maddened by his extraordinary ability to turn up just when I was least expecting him.

I remembered Andrea. I remembered the desk and the chair. I said, coolly, "Hello, Joss."

"I saw you come in. What are you wanting to do?"

The girl chipped in. "She wants the Art Gallery."

Joss waited for me to enlarge on this and, thus cornered, I did so.

"I thought perhaps there might be some pictures of Grenville's there . . ."

"You're quite right, there are three. I'll take you . . ."

"I don't need to be taken, I just want to be told how to get there."

"I'd like to take you . . . here . . ." he removed my heavy basket from my arm, smiled at the girl and went to open the door. A howl of wind and a blast of spume-laden air poured in from the outside and a pile of leaflets flew and scattered from the counter all over the floor. Before we could do any more damage, I hurried out, and the door swung shut behind us. As though it were the most natural thing in the world, Joss took my arm and we made our way down the middle of the cobbled road, Joss carrying on a cheerful conversation despite the fact that the wind tore the words from his mouth, and that, even with his arm in mine, it was taking all my efforts to progress at all.

"What on earth brings you down to the town on a day like this?"

"You're carrying it. Mollie's shopping."

"Couldn't you have brought the car?"

"I thought I might get blown off the road."

"I love it," he told me. "I love a day like this." He looked as though he loved it too, wind-whipped and wet and bursting with vitality. "Did you have a good day yesterday?"

"What do you know about yesterday?"

"I was up at Boscarva and Andrea told me you'd gone

141

to Falmouth with Eliot. Don't imagine you can keep any secrets in this place. If Andrea hadn't told me, Pettifer would, or Mrs Thomas, or Mrs Kernow, or Miss Bright-Eyes in the Information Bureau. It's part of the fun of living in Porthkerris, everybody knows exactly what everybody else is up to."

"I'm beginning to realise that."

We turned away from the harbour and began to climb a steep cobbled hill. Houses closed in on either side of us, a cat flashed across the street and disappeared through a crack in a window. A woman in a pot-hat and a blue apron was scrubbing her steps. She looked up and saw us, and said, "'Ullo my lover," to Joss; her fingers were like a bunch of pink sausages, made so by the hot water and the cold wind.

At the end of the street, we found ourselves in a little square which I had not seen before. One side of this was taken up by a large barn-like structure, with arched windows set high along the wall. By the door was a sign, PORTHKERRIS ART GALLERY, and Joss let go of my arm, pushed open the door with his shoulder and stood aside to let me go ahead of him. Inside it was bitterly cold, draughty, totally empty. The white walls were hung with paintings, of all sorts and shapes and sizes, and two great abstract sculptures were marooned in the middle of the floor, like rocks exposed by an ebb tide. There was a table by the door, with neat stacks of catalogues and folders and copies of the *Studio*, but despite this window-dressing the gallery stayed thick with the atmosphere of joyless bygone Sundays.

"Now," Joss put down my basket and took off his cap, shaking it free of rain as a dog shakes its coat, "what do you want to see?"

"I want to see Sophia."

He glanced at me sharply with a sudden turn of his head, but in the same instant smiled and put his hat on his head again, pulling the peak down over his eyes, like a guardsman.

"Who told you about Sophia?"

I smiled sweetly. "Perhaps it was Mrs Thomas. Perhaps it was Mrs Kernow. Perhaps it was Miss Bright-Eyes in the Information Bureau."

"Insolence will get you nowhere."

"There *is* a portrait of Sophia here. Pettifer told me."

"Yes. It's over this way."

I followed him down the length of the floor, our rubber-booted footsteps sounding loud in the emptiness.

"There," he said. I stopped beside him and looked up, and she was there, sitting in a beam of lamplight with some sewing in her hands.

I stared at it for a long time and finally let out a long sigh of disappointment. Joss looked down at me from under the ridiculous peak of his cap.

"What's that sigh for?"

"You still can't see her face. I still don't know what she looks like. Why didn't he ever paint her face?"

"He did. Often."

"Well, I still haven't seen it. It's always the back of her head or her hands or else she's so small a part of the picture she doesn't have a face at all, just a blob."

"Does it matter what she looked like?"

"No, it doesn't matter. It's just that I want to know."

"How did you know about Sophia in the first place?"

"My mother told me about her. And then Pettifer, and the picture of her – the one at Boscarva in the drawing-room – is so charming and feminine, one feels she must have been beautiful. But Pettifer says that she wasn't beautiful at all. Just very charming and attractive." We looked again at the picture. I saw the hands, and the shine of lamplight on her dark hair. "Pettifer says that art galleries up and down the country have portraits of Sophia hanging on their walls. I shall just have to go on from Manchester to Birmingham, to Nottingham, to Glasgow, until I find one that isn't of the back of her head."

"What will you do then?"

"Nothing. Just know what she looks like."

I turned from my disappointment and began to walk back to the door where my laden basket waited for me, but Joss was there first, stooping to swing it up and out of my reach.

I said, "I must go back."

"It's only . . ." he consulted his watch ". . . half past eleven. And you've never seen my shop. Come back with me and let me show it off, and I'll make you a cup of coffee and drive you home. You can't possibly walk up the hill with this great weight on your arm."

"Of course I can."

"I won't let you." He opened the door. "Come along."

I couldn't go without the basket and he obviously wasn't going to give it up, so, resigned and reluctant, I went with him, pushing my hands into my pockets so that he could not take my arm. He seemed in no way put out by my ungraciousness, which in itself was disconcerting, but when we got back to the harbour and were once more in the teeth of the wind, I nearly lost my balance with the unexpectedness of it, and he laughed and pulled my hand out of my pocket, taking it in his own. It was hard not to be disarmed by this protective and forgiving gesture.

As soon as the shop came in view, the tall narrow house shouldering up between the two short fat ones, I saw that indeed changes had taken place. The window frames were now painted, the plate glass had been cleared, and a sign put up over the door. JOSS GARDNER.

"How does that look?" He was full of pride.

"Impressive," I had to admit.

He took a key out of his pocket and unlocked the door and we went into the shop. Packing cases stood about on the flagged floor, and around the walls, shelving was being erected in varying widths, up to the ceiling. In the centre of the room was another structure, rather like a child's climbing frame, and this had already been set out with modern Danish glass and china, cooking pots in bright colours, and brightly striped Indian rugs. The walls were

144

white, the woodwork had been left in its natural state, and this and the grey floor provided a simple and effective background to the bright wares which he had to sell. At the back of the shop an open staircase rose to the upper floors, and beneath this was another door, ajar, leading down into what appeared to be a dark cellar. "Come upstairs . . ." He led the way.

I followed him. "What's that door there?"

"That's my workshop. It's in a dreadful mess, I'll show you that another time. Now this . . ." we emerged on to the first floor, and could scarcely move for baskets and wickerwork ". . . I haven't exactly got this straight but, as you can see, this is where you buy baskets for logs, clothes pegs, shopping, babies, laundry, anything you care to put in them."

None of it was very spacious. The narrow house was just a glorified staircase with a landing on each floor.

"Up again. How are your legs? Now we come to the *pièce de résistance*, the owner's palatial living quarters." I passed a tiny bathroom squeezed into the turn of the stairs. And lagging behind Joss's long legs found myself remembering Andrea's yearning descriptions of his flat, and hoping it would not be the way she had described it to me, but entirely different, so that I would know that her imagination had taken control, and that she had made the whole thing up. *Just like something out of a magazine. With a bed that's a sort of sofa and masses of cushions and things and a log fire.*

But it was just the way she had said. As I came up the last stairs, my fleeting hope swiftly died. And there *was* something closed-in and secret about it, with the ceiling sloping down to the floor and a dormer window set into the gable with a seat below it. I saw the little galley, enclosed behind a counter, like a bar, and the old Turkish carpet on the floor, and the divan, red-blanketed, pushed against the wall. As she had said, it was scattered with cushions.

Joss had put down my basket and was already divesting

himself of his wet clothes and hanging them on an old-fashioned cane hat-stand.

"Take your things off before you die of cold," he told me. "I'll light a fire . . ."

"I can't stay, Joss . . ."

"No reason not to light the fire. And please, take off that coat."

I did, unbuttoning it with frozen fingers, pulling off my damp woollen hat and shaking my plait down over my shoulder. While I hung these up beside Joss's things, he was busy at the fireplace, snapping twigs, balling paper, scraping together the ashes from some previous fire, lighting it all with a long taper. When it was crackling he took some pieces of driftwood, tar-soaked, from a basket by the fireplace, and stacked them round the flames. They spat, and spluttered, and swiftly caught. And the room, by firelight, sprang to life. He stood up and turned to face me.

"Now, what do you want? Coffee? Tea? Chocolate? Brandy and soda?"

"Coffee?"

"Two coffees coming up." He retired behind his counter, filled a kettle and lit the gas. As he collected a tray and cups, I went over to the window, knelt on the seat and looked down through the fury of the storm to the street below, washed by spray as the waves broke over the sea wall. The boats in the harbour bobbed about like demented corks, and huge herring gulls floated over their swinging mastheads, screaming at the wind. Absorbed in the task of making our coffee, Joss moved with economy from one side of the galley to the other, neat-fingered and self-sufficient as a single-minded yachtsman. So occupied, he appeared harmless enough, but the disconcerting point about Andrea's revelations was that they all seemed to contain an element of truth.

I had known Joss for only a few days, but already I had seen him in every sort of mood. I knew he could be charming, stubborn, angry, and downright rude. It was not difficult to imagine him as a ruthless and passionate lover, but it was distasteful to imagine him with Andrea.

He looked up suddenly and caught my eye. I was embarrassed, caught with my thoughts. I said, quickly, to divert us both, "In good weather you must have a lovely view."

"Clear out to the lighthouse."

"In the summer it must be like being abroad."

"In the summer it's like Piccadilly Underground at rush hour. But that only lasts for two months." He came out from behind his counter, carrying a tray with the steaming cups, the sugar bowl and the milk jug. The coffee smelt delicious. He pulled forward a long stool with his foot, set the tray at one end of it and himself at the other. Thus, we faced each other.

"I want to hear more about yesterday," said Joss. "Where did you go besides Falmouth?"

I told him about St Endon and the little pub by the water's edge.

"Yes, I've heard about it, but I've never been there. Did you get a good lunch?"

"Yes. And it was so warm that we sat out in the sunshine."

"That's the south coast for you. And what happened then?"

"Nothing happened then. We came home."

He handed me my cup and saucer. "Did Eliot take you to High Cross?"

"Yes."

"Did you see the garage?"

"Yes. And Mollie's house."

"What did you think of all those elegant, sexy cars?"

"I thought just that. That they were elegant and sexy."

"Did you meet any of the guys who work for him?"

His voice was so casual that I became wary.

"Who, for instance?"

"Morris Tatcombe?"

"Joss, you didn't ask me here for coffee at all, did you? You're pumping me."

147

"I'm not. I promise I'm not. It's just that I wondered if Morris was working for Eliot."

"What do you know about Morris?"

"Just that he's rotten."

"He's a good mechanic."

"Yes, he is. Everybody knows that, and it's the only good thing about him. But he's also totally dishonest and vicious to boot."

"If he's totally dishonest, why isn't he in jail?"

"He's already been. He's just come out."

This took the wind out of my sails, but I soldiered bravely on, sounding more sure of myself than I felt.

"And how do you know he's vicious . . .?"

"Because he picked a quarrel with me one night in a pub. We went outside and I punched him in the nose, and it was lucky for me I hit him first, because he was carrying a knife."

"Why are you telling me this?"

"Because you asked. If you don't want to be told things, you shouldn't ask questions."

"And what am I meant to do about it?"

"Nothing. Absolutely nothing. I'm sorry I brought it up. It was just that I'd heard Eliot had given him a job and I hoped it wasn't true."

"You don't like Eliot, do you?"

"I don't like him, I don't dislike him. He's nothing to do with me. But I'll tell you something. He picks bad friends."

"You mean Ernest Padlow?"

Joss sent me a glance that was full of reluctant admiration.

"You don't waste much time, I'll say that for you. You seem to know it all."

"I know about Ernest Padlow because I saw him with Eliot that first night when you gave me dinner at The Anchor."

"So you did. That's another rotten egg. If Ernest had his way the whole of Porthkerris would be bulldozed into

148

car parks. There wouldn't be a house left standing. And we would all have to go up the hill and live in his fancy little semis which in ten years' time will be leaking, leaning, cracking up and generally bagging at the knees."

I did not reply to this outburst. I drank my coffee and thought how pleasant it would be to have a conversation without being instantly drawn into longstanding vendettas which had nothing to do with me. I was tired of listening to everybody I wanted to like running down the reputations of everybody else.

I finished my coffee, set down the cup and said, "I must get back."

Joss, with an obvious effort, apologised. "I'm sorry."

"Why?"

"For losing my temper."

"Eliot's my cousin, Joss."

"I know." He looked down, turning his cup in his hands. "But, without meaning to, I've become involved with Boscarva, too."

"Just don't take your prejudices out on me."

His eyes met mine. "I wasn't angry with you."

"I know." I stood up. "I must go," I said again.

"I'll drive you back."

"You don't have to . . ." But he paid no attention to my protest, just took my coat from its hook and helped me on with it. I pulled the wet woollen hat over my ears and picked up the heavy basket.

The telephone rang.

Joss, in his oilskin, went to answer it, and I started downstairs. I heard him call, just before he took the receiver off the hook, "Rebecca, wait for me. I won't be a moment . . ." and then, into the telephone, "Yes? Yes, Joss Gardner here . . ."

I went down to the ground floor and the shop. It was still raining. Upstairs I could hear Joss deep in conversation.

Bored with waiting for him, perhaps a little curious, I pushed open the door of the workshop, turned on the light, and went down four stone steps. There was the usual confusion, benches, woodshavings, scraps, tools, vices; over all hung the smell of glue, of new wood, of polish. There was also a clutter of old furniture, so dusty and ramshackle it was impossible to tell whether it was of any value or not. A chest of drawers missing all its handles, a bedside cupboard without a leg.

And then, at the very back of the room, in the shadows, I saw them. A davenport desk, in apparently perfect repair, and alongside it a chair in the Chinese Chippendale style, with a tapestry seat, embroidered in flowers.

I felt sick, as though I had been kicked in the stomach. I turned and went up the steps, turning off the light and closing the door, going through the shop and out into the bitter windblast of that wicked February day.

My workshop's in a dreadful mess, I'll show you that another time.

I walked and then found that I was running up towards the church, into a warren of little lanes where he would never find me. I was running, always uphill, encumbered by the shopping basket, heavy as lead, and my heart pounded in my chest and there was the taste of blood in my mouth.

Eliot had been right. It was too easy for Joss and he had simply taken his chance. It was my desk; it was *my* desk that he had taken, but he had taken it from Grenville's house, flinging the old man's trust and kindness back in his face.

I could imagine killing Joss, and it was easy. I told myself that I could never speak to him, could never bear to be near him again. I had never been so angry in my life. With him; but worse with myself, for having been taken in by his empty charm, for having been proved so totally wrong. I had never been so angry.

I stumbled on up the hill.

But if I was so angry, then why was I crying?

150

10

It was a long and exhausting climb back to Boscarva, and I have never found it possible to sustain extreme emotion for more than ten minutes. Gradually, fighting my way up the hill against the weather, I calmed down, wiped my tears away with my gloved hand, pulled myself together. In an apparently intolerable situation, there is nearly always something one can do, and long before I reached Boscarva I had decided what it was. I would go back to London.

I left the shopping basket on the kitchen table and went upstairs to my room, took off all my drenched clothes, changed my shoes, washed my hands, carefully re-plaited my hair; thus calmed I went in search of Grenville and found him in his study, sitting by the fire and reading the morning paper.

He lowered this and looked over the top of it as I came in.

"Rebecca."

"Hello. How are you this wild morning?" I sounded determinedly cheerful, like a maddening nurse.

"Full of aches and pains. The wind's a killer even if you never go out in it. Where've you been?"

"Down in Porthkerris. I had to do some shopping for Mollie."

"What time is it?"

"Half past twelve."

"Then let's have a glass of sherry."

"Is that allowed?"

"I don't give a damn if it's allowed or not. You know where the decanter is."

I poured two glasses, carried his over and set it carefully

151

down on the table by his chair. I pulled up a stool and sat facing him. I said, "Grenville, I have to go back to London."

"What?"

"I have to go back to London." The blue eyes narrowed, the great jaw thrust out; I hastily made Stephen Forbes my scapegoat. "I can't stay away for ever. I've already been away from work nearly two weeks, and Stephen Forbes, the man I work for, he's been so good about it, I can't just go on taking advantage of his kindness and generosity. I've just realised that it's Friday already. I must go back to London this weekend. I must be back at work on Monday morning."

"But you've only just come." He was obviously thoroughly disgusted with me.

"I've been here three days. After three days fish and guests stink."

"You're not a guest. You're Lisa's child."

"But I still have commitments. And I like my job and I don't want to stop working." I smiled, trying to divert him. "And now I've found the way to Boscarva, perhaps I can come again, when I've got more time to spare, to spend with you."

He did not reply but sat, looking old and grumpy, staring into the fire.

He said dismally, "I may not be here then."

"Oh, of course you will be."

He sighed, took a slow, shaky mouthful of sherry, set down his glass, and turned to me, apparently resigned.

"When do you want to go?"

I was surprised, but relieved, that he had given in so easily.

"Perhaps tomorrow night. I'll get a sleeper. And then I can have Sunday to get myself settled into my flat."

"You shouldn't be living in a flat in London on your own. You weren't made for living alone. You were made for a man, and a home, and children. If I were twenty years younger and could still paint, that's how I'd show you to

152

the world, in a field or a garden, knee-deep in buttercups and children."

"Perhaps it'll happen one day. And then I shall send for you."

His face was suddenly full of pain. He turned away from me and said, "I wish you'd stay."

I longed to say that I would, but there were a thousand reasons why I couldn't. "I'll come back," I promised.

He made a great and touching effort to pull himself together, clearing his throat, re-settling himself in his chair. "That jade of yours. We'll have to get Pettifer to pack it in a box, then you can take it with you. And the mirror . . . could you manage that on the train, or is it too big? You ought to have a car, then there would be no problems. Have you got a car?"

"No, but it doesn't matter . . ."

"And I suppose that desk hasn't . . ."

"It doesn't matter about the desk!" I interrupted, so loudly and so suddenly that Grenville looked at me in some surprise, as though he had not expected such bad manners.

"I'm sorry," I said quickly. "It's just that it really doesn't matter. I couldn't bear everybody to start quarrelling about it again. Please, for my sake, don't talk about it, don't think about it any more."

He regarded me thoughtfully, a long unblinking stare that made me drop my eyes.

He said, "You think I'm unfair to Eliot?"

"I just think that perhaps you never talk to each other, you never tell each other anything."

"He'd have been different if Roger hadn't been killed. He was a boy who needed a father."

"Couldn't you have done as a father?"

"Could never get near him for Mollie. He was never made to stick to anything. Always chopping and changing jobs and then he started that garage up three years ago."

"That seems to be a success."

153

"Second-hand cars!" His voice was full of unjustified contempt. "He should have gone into the Navy."

"Suppose he didn't want to go into the Navy?"

"He might have, if his mother hadn't talked him out of it. She wanted to keep him at home, tied to her apron strings."

"Oh, Grenville, I think you're being thoroughly old-fashioned and very unfair."

"Did I ask you for your opinion?" But already he was cheering up. A good argument was, to Grenville, like a shot in the arm.

"I don't care whether you asked for it or not, you've got it."

He laughed then, and reached forward to gently pinch my cheek. He said, "How I wish I could still paint. Do you still want one of my pictures to take back to London with you?"

I was afraid that he had forgotten. "More than anything."

"You can get the key of the studio from Pettifer. Tell him I said you could have it. Go and nose around, see what you can find."

"You won't come with me?"

Again the pain came into his face. "No," he said gruffly, and turned away to take up his sherry. He sat, looking down at the amber wine, turning the glass in his hand. "No, I won't come with you."

At lunch he broke the news to the others. Andrea, livid that I was going back to London while she had to stay in horrible, boring Cornwall, went into a sullen sulk. But the others were gratifyingly dismayed.

"But do you have to go?" That was Mollie.

"Yes, I really must. I've got a job to do and I can't stay away for ever."

"We really love having you here." She could be charming when she wasn't aggressive and possessive about Eliot, resentful of Grenville and Boscarva. I saw her again as a pretty little cat, but now I was aware of long claws hidden in the soft velvet paws, and I knew that she had no compunction about using them.

"I've loved it too . . ."

Pettifer was more outspoken. After lunch I went out to the kitchen to help him with the dishes, and he minced no words.

"What you want to go away for now, just when you're settling down and the Commander's getting to know you – well, it's beyond me. I didn't think you were that sort of a person . . ."

"I'll come back. I've said I'll come back."

"He's eighty now. He's not going to last for ever. How are you going to feel, coming back and him not here, but six feet under the ground and pushing up the daisies?"

"Oh, Pettifer, *don't*."

"It's all very well saying 'Oh, Pettifer, *don't*.' There's nothing I can do about it."

"I've got a job. I must go back."

"Sounds like selfishness to me."

"That's not fair."

"All these years he's not seen his daughter, and then you turn up and stay three days. What sort of a grandchild are you?"

I didn't reply because there was nothing to say. And I hated feeling guilty and being put in the wrong. We finished the dishes in silence, but when they were done and he was wiping down the draining board with a damp cloth, I tried to make my peace with him.

"I'm sorry. I really am. It's bad enough having to go without you making me feel a brute. And I will come back. I've said I will. Perhaps in the summer . . . he'll still be here in the summer, and the weather will be warm and we can do things together. Perhaps you could take us out in the car . . ."

My voice trailed away. Pettifer hung his cloth neatly over the edge of the sink. He said, gruffly, "The Commander said you were to have the key of the studio. Don't know

155

what you'll find down there. A lot of dust and spiders, I should think."

"He said I could have a picture. He said I could go and choose one."

He slowly dried his worn, gnarled hands. "I'll have to find the key. It's put away for safe keeping. Didn't want it lying around where anyone could get their hands on it. There's a lot of good stuff down in the studio."

"Any time will do." I could not bear his disapproval. "Oh, Pettifer, don't be angry with me."

He melted then. "Oh, I'm not angry. Perhaps it's me who's being selfish. Perhaps it's me who doesn't want you to go."

I saw him suddenly, not as the ubiquitous Pettifer around whom this household revolved, but as an old man, nearly as old as my grandfather and probably as lonely. A stupid lump came into my throat and for a terrible moment I thought I was going to burst into tears, which would have made it the second time that day, but then Pettifer said, "And don't go choosing one of them nudes, they wouldn't be suitable," and the dangerous moment was behind me and we were smiling, friends again.

That afternoon Mollie lent me her car, and I drove the five miles to the railway junction and there bought myself a ticket back to London and reserved a sleeper for the night train on Saturday. The violence of the wind had dropped a little, but it was still wild and stormy, with trees down and devastation everywhere, smashed greenhouses, broken branches, and fields of early spring bulbs flattened by the gales.

I got home to find Mollie in the garden at Boscarva, bundled up against the weather (even Mollie could not look elegant on such a day) and trying to tie up and rescue some of the more fragile shrubs that grew around the house. When she saw the car, she decided to call it a day, for as I put it away and walked back towards the house I met her coming towards me, stripping off her gloves and tucking a strand of hair into her head-scarf.

"I can't bear it a moment longer," she told me. "I hate wind, it exhausts me. But that darling little daphne was being snapped to ribbons. and all the camellias have been burnt by this wind. It turns them quite brown. Let's go in and have a cup of tea."

While she changed I put the kettle on, and set out cups on a tray. "Where is everybody?" I asked her when she reappeared, miraculously neat once more, down to her pearls and her matching ear-rings.

"Grenville's having a nap and Andrea's up in her room . . ." she sighed. ". . . I must say, she really isn't the easiest of girls. If only she'd do something to amuse herself instead of skulking around in this tiresome manner. I'm afraid it's not doing her any good being down here, I didn't think it would, to be quite honest, but my poor sister was quite desperate." She looked around the comfortable kitchen. "This is cosy. Let's have our tea in here. The drawing-room's so draughty when the wind's from the sea, and we can scarcely draw the curtains at half past four in the afternoon . . ."

She was right, it was cosy in the kitchen. She found a cloth and laid the tea, setting out cakes and biscuits, sugar bowl and silver milk jug. Even for kitchen tea, it appeared, her standards were meticulous. She pulled up two wheel-back chairs, and was in the act of reaching for the teapot when the door opened and Andrea appeared.

"Oh, Andrea, dear, just in time. We're having kitchen tea today. Do you want a cup?"

"I'm sorry, I haven't got time."

This unexpectedly mannerly reply made Mollie look up sharply. "Are you going out?"

"Yes," said Andrea, "I'm going to the cinema."

We both stared at her like fools. For the impossible had happened – Andrea had suddenly decided to take much trouble with her appearance. She had washed her hair and tied it back off her face, found a clean polo-necked tee-shirt, and even, I was delighted to see, a bra to wear beneath it. Her Celtic cross hung around her neck on its thread of leather, her black jeans were neatly pressed, her clumpy shoes polished. Over her arm was a raincoat and a fringed leather handbag. I had never seen her look so presentable. And, best of all, the expression on her face was neither sulky nor malevolent, but . . . demure? Could one possibly describe Andrea as looking demure?

"I mean," she went on, "if that's all right by you, Auntie Mollie."

"Well, of course. What are you going to see?"

"*Mary of Scotland*. It's on at the Plaza."

"Are you going by yourself?"

"No, I'm going with Joss. He rang me while you were out gardening. He's going to give me supper afterwards."

"Oh," said Mollie, faintly. And then, feeling that further comment was expected of her, ". . . how are you going to get down there?"

"I'll walk down, and I expect Joss will drive me home . . ."

"Have you got some money?"

"I've got 50p. I'll be all right."

"Well . . ." But Mollie was defeated. "Have a good time."

"I will," she flashed us both a smile. "Goodbye."

The door swung to behind her.

"Goodbye," said Mollie. She looked at me. "Extraordinary," she said.

I was concentrating on my cup of tea. "Why so extraordinary?" I said casually.

"Andrea and . . . Joss. I mean he's always been quite polite to her, but . . . to ask her out . . .?"

"You shouldn't sound so surprised. She's attractive when she cleans herself up and bothers to smile. Probably she smiles at Joss all the time."

"You think it's all right, letting her go? I mean I do have responsibilities . . .?"

"Honestly, I don't see how you could have stopped her going. Anyway she's seventeen, she's not a child. She can surely look after herself by now . . ."

"That's just the trouble," said Mollie ". . . That's always been the trouble with Andrea."

"She'll be all right."

She would not be all right, and I knew this, but I could not disillusion Mollie. Besides, what did it matter? It was no business of mine if Joss chose to spend his evenings making firelit love to an adolescent nymphomaniac. They were two of a kind. They deserved each other. They were welcome to each other.

When we had finished tea, Mollie tied a neat apron around her waist and started preparing dinner. I cleared away the cups and saucers and washed them up. As I was drying the last plate, and putting it away, Pettifer appeared, bearing in his hand a large key which looked as though it might unlock a dungeon.

"I knew I'd put it somewhere safely, found it in the back of a drawer in the Commander's bureau . . ."

"What's that, Pettifer?" Mollie asked.

"The key to the studio, Madam . . ."

"Heavens, who wants that?"

"I do," I said. "Grenville said I could go down and choose a picture to take back to London."

"My dear child, what a task you'll have. The place must be in the most terrible mess, it hasn't seen the light of day for ten years."

"I don't mind." I took the key which weighed heavy as lead in my hand.

"Are you going now? It's getting dark."

"Aren't there any lights?"

"Oh, yes, of course, but it's very cheerless. Wait till tomorrow morning."

But I wanted to go now. "I'll be all right. I'll put on a coat."

"There's a torch on the hall table, you'd better take that as well, the path down the garden is quite steep and slippery."

And so, buttoned into my leather coat, and armed with the torch and the key, I set off, letting myself out of the

159

house by the garden door. The wind from the sea was still violent, carrying with it squalls of thin, cold rain, and I had to struggle to get the door closed behind me. The dismal afternoon was turning early to darkness, but still there was enough light to pick my way cautiously down the sloping garden, and I did not turn on the torch until I reached the studio when I needed its beam to find the keyhole.

I fitted the key and it turned reluctantly, needing oil; the door swung inwards, creakingly. There was a damp and musty smell, a suggestion of cobwebs and mould, and I quickly put my hand inside and felt for the light switch. At once a single naked bulb, high in the roof, sprang to a chill and insubstantial life, and I was surrounded by leaping shadows, for the draught caused the long flex to swing to and fro like the pendulum of a clock.

I went in and shut the door behind me and the shadows, slowly, were stilled. Around me, dust-covered shapes loomed in the half-light, but across the room was a standard lamp, with a crooked, broken shade. I picked my way over to this, found the switch and turned that on, and at once everything looked a little less forlorn.

I saw that the studio had been designed on two levels with a sleeping gallery at the south end, reached by a stair like a ship's ladder.

I went halfway up the ladder and saw the divan and the striped blanket. Over the bed was a window tightly shuttered, and a pillow had shed feathers, perhaps the work of some marauding mouse. The remains of a small dead bird lay, twig-like and dehydrated, in the corner of the floor. I shuddered slightly at the desolation, and descended again to the studio.

The wind banged and rattled at the huge north window. A complicated contraption of strings and pulleys worked the long curtains, and I struggled with these for a moment, but was finally defeated by their mechanics and left the curtains closed.

In the middle of the floor was a model's throne, with a sheeted shape in the middle which proved to be an ornate gilt chair. The mice had been at the seat of this, too – scraps of red velvet and horsehair were scattered about, along with mouse-droppings and a great deal of dust.

Under another sheet I found Grenville's workbench; his brushes, his trays of paint-tubes, palettes, knives, bottles of linseed oil, piles of unused canvases, grimy with age. There was also a little collection of *objets trouvés*, small things which, perhaps, had taken his fancy. A sea-polished stone, half a dozen shells, a bunch of gulls' feathers, probably collected for the practical purpose of cleaning his pipe. There were curling, faded snapshots, of nobody I recognised, a blue and white Chinese ginger jar filled with pencils, some bottles of fossilised Indian ink, a scrap of sealing wax.

It was like prying, as though I were reading another person's diary. I put back the sheet and went on to the true purpose of my visit, which was the stack of unframed canvases standing around the wall, each with its face turned inwards. These had been dust-covered too, but the sheets had slipped, draping themselves about the floor, and as I dislodged the first pile my fingers touched cobwebs, and a huge, disgusting spider went scuttling across the floor and lost itself in the shadows.

It was a slow business. Five or six at a time, I lifted out the pictures, dusted them off, leaned them in rows against the model's throne, shifting the rickety standard lamp so that the light should shine on them. Some were dated, but they were stacked away in no sort of chronological order, and for the most part I could tell neither when nor where they had been painted. I only knew that they encompassed the whole of Grenville's professional life and all his interests.

There were landscapes, seascapes – the ocean in all its moods, charming interiors, some sketches of Paris, some that looked like Italy. There were boats and fishermen, street scenes of Porthkerris, a number of rough charcoal sketches of two children, whom I knew were Roger and Lisa. There were no portraits.

I began to make my selection, setting aside the pictures

which I found particularly engaging. By the time I had reached the final pile, there were half a dozen of them propped against the seat of a sagging couch, and I was dirty and cold, with grimy hands and cobwebs clinging to my clothes. With the good feeling of a task nearly completed I went to sort out the last pile of canvases. There were three pen and ink drawings, and a view of a harbour with yachts at anchor. And then . . .

It was the last canvas and the biggest of all. It needed two hands and all my efforts to lift it out of its dark corner and turn it around to face the light. I held it upright with one hand and stood back, and the face of the girl leapt out to meet me, the dark, tip-tilted eyes smiling with a vitality undimmed by the dust of the years that passed. I saw the dark hair and the bumpy cheek-bones and the sensuous mouth, not smiling, but seeming to tremble on the brink of laughter. And she wore the same fragile white dress, the dress that she had worn for the portrait that hung over the fireplace in the drawing-room at Boscarva.

Sophia.

Ever since my mother had mentioned her name I had been fascinated by her. The frustrations of never knowing what she looked like had only increased my obsession. But now that I had found her and we were face to face at last, I felt like Pandora. I had opened the box and the secrets were out, and there was no way in the world of packing them back and locking the lid once more.

I knew that face. I had talked to it, argued with it; seen it scowl and smile; seen the dark eyes narrowed in anger and glint with amusement.

It was Joss Gardner.

11

All at once I was bitterly cold. It was dark now and the
studio was icy, but as well I could feel the blood drain
from my face like water out of a basin; I could hear
the laboured thumping of my own heart, and I started,
violently, to shiver. My first instinct was to put the portrait
back where I had found it, pile some other canvases on top
of it and hide it, like a criminal trying to conceal a body, or
something worse.

But in the end I reached for a chair and arranged it
carefully, so that it supported Sophia's portrait like an
easel, and then I backed away on shaking legs and carefully
lowered myself on to the sagging seat of the aged sofa.

Sophia and Joss.

Sophia the enchanting, and the baffling Joss, who I had
finally learned was not to be trusted.

*She went to London, she got married, she had a baby, I
think*, Pettifer had told me. Then in 1942 she was killed in
the Blitz.

But he had not mentioned Joss. And yet Joss and Sophia
were so obviously, inextricably linked.

And I thought of my desk, my mother's desk that she
meant me to have, hidden away at the back of Joss's
workshop.

And I heard Mollie's voice. *I don't know why Grenville's
so taken with Joss. It's frightening. It's as though Joss were
able to exert some hold over him.*

Sophia and Joss.

It was dark now. I had no watch and I had lost all track of
time. The wind drowned all other sound, so that I did not

hear Eliot coming down the garden from the house, picking his way through the darkness because I had taken the torch. I did not hear anything until the door burst open, as though on a gust of wind, causing the light to start up its demented swinging, and frightening me nearly out of my wits. The next instant Rufus bounded in and flung himself up on the sofa beside me, and I realised that I had company.

My cousin Eliot stood in the open doorway framed in darkness. He wore a suede jacket and a pale blue polo-necked sweater and he had slung a raincoat around his shoulders like a cloak. The cruel light drained all the colour from his thin face, and turned his deep-set eyes into two black holes.

"My mother told me you were down here. I came to . . ."

He stopped, and I knew that he had seen the portrait. I couldn't move, I was too petrified with cold, and anyway, now it was too late to do anything about it.

He came into the studio and closed the door. The leaping shadows, once more, were slowly stilled.

We neither of us said anything. I held Rufus's head, instinctively seeking comfort in his soft, warm fur, and watched while Eliot shrugged off his raincoat, dropped it across a chair, and came slowly to sit beside me. His eyes never left the portrait.

At last he spoke. "Good God," he said.

I said nothing.

"Where did you find that?"

"In a corner . . ." My voice came out as a croak. I cleared my throat and tried again. "In a corner, behind a lot of other canvases."

"It's Sophia."

"Yes."

"It's Joss Gardner."

There was no denying it. "Yes."

"Sophia's grandson, do you suppose?"

"Yes. I think he must be."

"Well, I'll be damned." He leaned back, and crossed his

long, elegant legs, suddenly relaxed, like a knowledgeable art critic at a private view.

His obvious satisfaction puzzled me, and I did not want him to think that I shared it.

I said, "I wasn't looking for it. I've been wanting to know what Sophia looked like, but I had no idea there was a portrait of her down here. I just came to look for a picture because Grenville said I could have one to take back to London."

"I know. My mother told me."

"Eliot, we mustn't say anything."

He ignored this. "You know, there was always something funny about Joss, something unexplained. The way he turned up in Porthkerris, out of the blue. And the way Grenville knew that he was there; the way he gave him a job, and the run of Boscarva. I never trusted Joss farther than I could see him. And the desk disappearing – the desk that should have come to you. It was all fishy beyond words."

I knew that I should tell Eliot then that I had found the desk. I opened my mouth with the intention of doing just this thing, and closed it again because somehow the words would not be spoken. Besides, Eliot was still talking and had not noticed my incipient interruption.

"My mother swore he had some sort of a hold over Grenville."

"You make it sound like blackmail."

"Perhaps, in a modified form, it was. You know, 'Here I am, Sophia's grandson, what are you going to do for me?' And Pettifer must have known as well. Pettifer and Grenville have no secrets from each other."

"Eliot, we mustn't say that we found the picture."

He turned his head to look at me.

"You sound anxious, Rebecca. On Joss Gardner's behalf?"

"No. On Grenville's."

"But you like Joss."

"No."

165

He pretended to be amazed. "But everybody likes Joss! Everybody, it seems, has fallen under his spell of boyish charm. Grenville and Pettifer; Andrea is besotted by him, she never leaves him alone, but I think there may be something just a little physical in that attraction. I thought that you were bound to have joined the club." He frowned. "You *did* like Joss."

"Not now, Eliot."

He began to be intrigued. He shifted his position slightly, so that we half-faced each other on the sofa, his arm along its carved back, behind my shoulder.

"What happened?" he asked.

What had happened? Nothing. But I had never felt quite easy about Joss, and all the coincidences that seemed to tie our lives together. And he had stolen my mother's desk. And he was now, at this moment carrying on his clandestine affair with the unsavoury Andrea. At the very idea of this, my imagination was apt to turn and run.

Eliot was waiting for my reply. But I only shrugged and shook my head hopelessly and said, "I changed my mind."

"Could yesterday have had anything to do with it?"

"Yesterday?" I thought of sitting with Eliot on the sunbaked terrace of the little pub; of the two boys sailing their dinghy down the blue waters of the creek; and finally Eliot's arms, encircling and holding me, the feel of his kisses, and the sensation of losing control, of sliding over a cliff.

I shivered again. My hands, cold and grimy, lay in my lap. Eliot put his own over them and said, in some surprise, "You're freezing."

"I know, I've been here for hours."

"My mother told me you want to go back to London." We seemed to have dropped the subject of Joss and I was thankful for this.

"Yes, I have to go."

"When?"

"Tomorrow night."

"You never told me."

"I didn't decide until this morning."

"You seem to have changed your mind and made a lot of decisions all in one day."

"I hadn't realised how the time had flown. I've been away from work for nearly two weeks."

"Yesterday I asked you to stay."

"I have to go."

"What would make you stay?"

"Nothing. I mean . . . I can't . . ." I was stammering like a fool, but I was too cold, too dirty and too tired for such a conversation. Later, perhaps, I would be able to cope . . .

"Would you stay if I asked you to marry me?"

My head shot up. Something like horror must have shown on my face, for he put back his head and laughed.

"Don't look so shocked. There's nothing shocking about getting married."

"But we're cousins."

"That doesn't matter."

"But we don't . . . I mean . . . You don't love me."

It was an appalling thing to say, but Eliot took it in his stride.

"Rebecca, you are stammering and stuttering like a shy schoolgirl. Perhaps I do love you. Perhaps I would have loved you for a long time before asking you to marry me, but you've precipitated this situation by suddenly announcing out of the blue that you're going to go back to London. So if I'm going to say it at all, I'd better say it now. I want you to marry me. I think it would work very well."

Despite myself, I was touched. No one had ever asked me to marry them before, and I found it flattering. But even as I listened to Eliot with one part of my mind, the other part ran round in circles like a squirrel in a cage.

Because there was still Boscarva, and the land that Eliot needed to sell to Ernest Padlow.

You are not my only grandchild.

167

". . . it seems ridiculous to say goodbye and walk out of each other's lives when we've only just met each other, and there are so many good things going for us."

I said quietly, "Like Boscarva."

His smile froze slightly around the edges. He raised an eyebrow. "Boscarva?"

"Let's be honest and truthful, Eliot. For some reason you need Boscarva. And you think that Grenville might leave it to me."

He took a deep breath as though to deny this, hesitated, and then let it all out in a long sigh. His smile was rueful. He ran a hand over the top of his head.

"How cool you are. The Ice Princess all of a sudden."

"You need Boscarva so that you can sell the farm to Ernest Padlow to build his houses."

He said, carefully, "Yes." I waited. "I needed money to build the garage. Grenville wasn't interested so I approached Padlow. He agreed and the security was the Boscarva farm. Gentleman's agreement."

"But it wasn't yours."

"I was sure it would be. There was no reason why it shouldn't be. And Grenville was old and ill. The end could have come any day." He spread his hands. "Who would have imagined that three years later he'd still be with us?"

"You sound as though you want him dead."

"Old age is a terrible thing. Lonely and sad. He's had a good life. What is there for him to cling on for?"

I knew that I could not agree with Eliot. Old age, in Grenville's case, meant dignity and purpose. I had only just got to know him, but already I loved him and he was part of me; I could not bear to think of him dying.

I said, trying to stay practical, "Isn't there some other way you could pay off Mr Padlow?"

"I could sell the garage. The way things are going I might have to do that anyway."

"I thought you were doing so well."

168

"That's what everybody's meant to think."

"But if you sold the garage, what would you do then?"

"What do you suggest I should do?" He sounded amused as though I were a child with whims to be indulged. I said, "How about Mr Kemback, and the car museum in Birmingham?"

"What an uncomfortably good memory you've got."

"Would working for Mr Kemback be such a bad thing?"

"And leave Cornwall?"

"I think that's what you should do. Make a new start. Get away from Boscarva and . . ." I stopped, and then thought, *in for a penny, in for a pound*, ". . . and your mother." I finished in a rush.

"My mother?" Still that amusement, as though I were a beguiling fool.

"You know what I mean, Eliot."

There was a long pause. Then, "I think," said Eliot, "you have been talking to Grenville."

"I'm sorry."

"One thing's for certain, either Joss or I will have to go. As they say in Westerns, 'This town ain't big enough for the two of us.' But I'd rather Joss went."

"Joss is unimportant. He's not worth taking a stand over."

"If I sold the garage and went to work in Birmingham, would you come with me?"

"Oh, Eliot . . ."

I turned away from him and came face to face once more with Sophia's portrait. Her eyes met mine and it was as though Joss sat there, listening to every word we were saying, laughing at us. Then Eliot put his hand beneath my chin and jerked my head around so that once more I was forced to meet his eye.

"Listen to what I'm saying!"

"I am listening."

"We don't have to be in love with each other. You know that, don't you?"

"I always imagined it was important."

"It doesn't happen to everyone. Perhaps it won't ever happen to you."

It was a chill prospect. "Perhaps not."

"In that case," his voice was very gentle and reasonable, "would a compromise be such a bad thing? Wouldn't a compromise be better than a nine to five job for the rest of your life and an empty flat in London?"

He had touched me on the raw. I had been alone for too long, and the prospect of staying alone for the rest of my life was frightening. Grenville had said, *You were made for a man and a home and children*. And now they were all there, waiting for me. I had only to reach out my hand, to accept what Eliot was offering me.

I said his name, and he put his arms around me, and drew me very close, kissing my eyes, my cheeks, my mouth. Sophia watched us and I did not care. I told myself that she was dead, and Joss I had already put out of my life. Why should I care what either of them thought of me?

Eliot said at last, "We must go." He held me away from him. "You must have a bath and wash all those dirty marks off your face, and I must get the ice out of the fridge, and be all ready and dutiful to pour drinks for Grenville and my mother."

"Yes." I drew away from his arms, and pushed a lock of hair out of my face. I felt deathly tired. "What time is it?"

He looked at his watch, the strap that I had given him still shining and new. "Nearly half past seven. We could stay here all night, but unfortunately life has to go on."

I got wearily to my feet. Without looking at the portrait I took it up and put it back in its hidden, dusty corner, along with the cobwebs and the spiders, its face to the wall. Then I picked up other pictures, at random, and piled them around and against it. Everything, I told myself, was just as it had been before. We tidied up in a cursory fashion and covered the canvases with the fallen dust-sheet. Eliot switched off the standard lamp, and I picked up the torch. We went out of the studio, turning off the light and closing and locking the door. Eliot took the torch from me, and together, following the bobbing circle of light, we went up the garden, stumbling a little over hidden verges and tussocks of grass, mounting the shining wet steps of the terrace. Above us the house loomed, lighted rooms glowing behind drawn curtains, and all around us was the wind and the silhouettes of leafless, tormented trees.

"I've never known a storm to last so long," said Eliot, as he opened the side door and we went inside. The hall felt warm and safe, and there was the good smell of the chicken casserole that we were to have for dinner.

We parted, Eliot heading for the kitchen, and I upstairs to shed my filthy clothes, draw a bath and wallow in warm, scented steam. Relaxed at last I thought about nothing. I was too tired to think. I would fall asleep, I decided, and probably drown. For some reason the idea of this did not alarm me.

But I did not fall asleep, because as I lay there, I heard, above the noise of the wind, the sound of an approaching car. The bathroom faced over the back of the house, the drive and the front door. I had not bothered to draw the curtains and the headlights of the car flashed for a second against the dark glass. A door banged, there were voices. Thus disturbed, I climbed out of the bath, dried myself and started across the passage to my room, but stopped dead when I heard the raised voices carrying up the stairwell from the hall.

". . . found her halfway up the hill . . ." a man's voice, unrecognised.

And then Mollie, ". . . but my dear child . . ." This was interrupted by a wild cacophony of sobbing. I heard Eliot say, "For heaven's sake, girl . . ." And then Mollie again. "Come in by the fire . . . come along now, you're all right. You're safe now . . ."

I went into my room, pulled on my clothes, buttoned the neck of the brown caftan, brushed and plaited my hair, all in the space of moments. I painted on a layer of lipstick – there was no time for more – thrust my bare feet into sandals and ran downstairs, screwing on my ear-rings as I did so.

As I reached the bottom of the stairs Pettifer appeared through the kitchen door with a face like a thundercloud and bearing in his hand a glass of brandy. It was indicative of the gravity of the situation that he had omitted to put it on a silver salver.

"Pettifer, what's happened?"

"I don't know what's happened, exactly, but it sounds as though that girl's having hysterics."

"I heard a car coming. Who brought her home?"

"Morris Tatcombe. Says he was driving home from Porthkerris when he found her on the road."

I was horrified. "You mean *lying* on the road? Had she been hit by a car, or something?"

"I don't know. Probably just had a tumble."

At the far end of the hall the drawing-room door burst open and Mollie came towards us, half running.

"Oh, Pettifer, don't stand talking, hurry with the brandy." She saw me standing, quite at a loss. "Oh, my dear Rebecca, what a terrible thing, quite terrible. I'm going to ring the doctor." She was at the telephone, thumbing through the book, unable to see because she had somewhere mislaid her glasses. "Look it up for me, there's a dear. It's Doctor Trevaskis . . . we ought to have it written down somewhere, but I can't find . . ."

Pettifer had gone. I took the telephone book and started to look for the number. "What's happened to Andrea?" I asked.

"It's the most ghastly story. I can hardly believe it's true. What a mercy Morris found her. She could have been there all night. She could have died . . ."

"Here it is. Lionel Trevaskis. Porthkerris 873."

She put a hand to her cheek. "Oh, of course, I should know it off by heart." She lifted the receiver and dialled. While she waited she spoke to me, swiftly. "Go and sit by her, the men are so useless, they never know what to do."

Mystified and oddly reluctant to know the details of Andrea's unhappy experience, I nevertheless did as she asked me. I found the drawing-room in something approaching a shambles. Grenville, apparently nonplussed, stood in front of the fireplace with his hands behind his back and said nothing. The rest of them were grouped around the sofa; Eliot had given Morris a drink, and they watched while Pettifer, with commendable patience, was trying to trickle some brandy down Andrea's throat.

And Andrea . . . despite myself I was shocked and frightened by her appearance. The neat sweater and the pressed jeans in which she had set out so gaily were soaking wet and smeared with mud. Through the tear in the jeans I could see her knee, cut and bleeding, vulnerably childlike. She had lost, it seemed, a shoe. Her hair clung, like seaweed, to her skull, her face was blotched with crying, and when I said her name she turned her head to look at me from pathetic, streaming eyes; I saw with horror the great bruise on her temple, as though she had been savagely struck. The Celtic cross on its leather thong was also lost; torn off, perhaps, in some unthinkable struggle.

"Andrea!"

She gave a great wail and heaved herself over to press her face into the back of the sofa, spilling the brandy as she did so, and knocking the tumbler clean out of Pettifer's hand.

"I don't want to talk about it. I don't want to talk about it . . .!"

"But you must!"

Pettifer, exasperated, collected the glass and went from the room. I told myself that he had never liked the girl. I took his place beside her, sitting on the edge of the sofa, trying to turn her shoulders towards me.

"Did somebody do this to you?"

Andrea flung herself back at me, her body convulsed. "Yes!" She screamed at my face as though I were deaf.

173

"Joss!" And with that she dissolved once more in a welter of sobs.

I looked up at Grenville and was subjected to a stony, unblinking glare. His features might have been carved from wood. I decided there was no help to be expected from that quarter. I turned to Morris Tatcombe.

"Where did you find her?"

He shifted, one foot to another. I saw that he was dressed as though for a night on the town. A leather jacket, decorated with a rash of embroidered emblems, and spotted with rain, skin-tight jeans and boots with high heels. Even with high heels the top of his head scarcely reached to Eliot's shoulder, and his long hair hung damp and lank.

He tossed this back, a gesture both aggressive and self-conscious.

"Half-way up Porthkerris Hill. You know, where the road narrows and there isn't a pavement. She was half-way up the bank, half in the ditch. Lucky I saw her, really. Thought she'd been hit by a car, but it wasn't that. Seems she had this row with Joss Gardner."

I said, "He asked her to go to the cinema with him."

"I don't know how it all started," said Morris.

"But this, it seems . . ." said Eliot gravely ". . . is how it ends."

"But . . ." There had to be some other explanation. I was about to tell them this when Andrea let out another wail, like some aged sibyl keening at a wake, and I lost my temper.

"Oh, for goodness sake, girl, shut up!" I took her by her shoulders and gave her a little shake so that her head bobbed on the silk cushion like a badly stuffed rag-doll. "Stop making that dementing noise and tell us what happened."

Words began to spill out of her mouth, made ugly with weeping. (I thought briskly, *at least she isn't missing any teeth,* and hated myself for my own hard heart.)

"I . . . we . . . went to the cinema . . . and wh . . . when we came out, we went to a pub, and . . ."

174

"Which pub?"

"I don't know . . ."

"You must know which pub . . ."

My voice rose in impatience. Behind me, Mollie, whom I had not heard come into the room, said, "Oh, don't shout at her. Don't be unkind."

I made an effort and tried again, more gently.

"Can't you remember where you went?"

"No. It was d . . . dark . . . and I . . . couldn't see. And then . . . and then . . ."

I held her firmly, trying to calm her. "Yes. And then?"

"And Joss had a lot of whisky to drink. And he wouldn't bring me home. He wanted me to g . . . go back to his flat with him . . . and . . ."

Her mouth went square, her features dissolved into uncontrollable weeping. I let her go and stood up, backing away from her. At once Mollie took my place.

"There," she said. "There, there." She was more gentle than I, her voice as soothing as a mother's. "Now there's nothing more to worry about. The doctor's on his way, and Pettifer's putting a nice hot bottle in your bed. You don't need to tell us any more. You don't need to talk about it any more."

But, perhaps calmed by Mollie's manner, Andrea seemed anxious to make a clean breast of it, and, through interminable sobs and gasps, we were to hear the rest of the story.

"And I didn't want to go. I . . . I wanted to come home. And I . . . left him. And he came after me. And . . . I tried to run, and I tripped on the p . . . pavement, and my shoe . . . c . . . came off. And then he c . . . caught me, and he be . . . began shouting at me . . . and I screamed and he *hit* me . . ."

I looked at the faces around me, and the same horror and consternation, in varying degrees, was mirrored upon them. Only Grenville appeared coldly, deeply angry, but still he did not move, he did not say a word.

"It's all right," Mollie said again, her voice shaking

175

only a little. "Now, everything's all right. Come along, upstairs."

Somehow Andrea, wilted and bedraggled, was eased off the sofa, but her legs would not hold her weight, and she started to collapse. It was Morris who, standing nearest to her, stepped forward and caught her before she fell, swinging her up, with surprising strength, into his puny arms.

"There," said Mollie, "Morris will carry you upstairs. You'll be all right . . ." She moved towards the door. "If you'll come this way, Morris."

"OK," said Morris, who did not appear to have much option in the matter.

I watched Andrea's face. As Morris moved, her eyes opened and looked straight into mine, and our glances clashed and held. And I knew that she was lying. And she knew that I knew she was lying.

Leaning her head against Morris's chest, she began to cry again. Swiftly, she was borne from the room.

We listened as Morris's burdened footsteps went down the hall, started up the staircase. Then Eliot said, with masterly understatement, "An unsavoury business." He glanced at Grenville. "Shall I ring the police now or later?"

Grenville spoke at last. "Who said anything about ringing the police?"

"You surely don't intend to let him get away with it?" I said. "She was lying."

Both men looked at me in some surprise. Grenville's eyes narrowed and he was at his most formidable. Eliot frowned. "What did you say?"

"Some of her story may be true. Most of it probably is. But still, she was lying."

"How was she lying?"

"Because as you said yourself, she was besotted with Joss. She wouldn't leave him alone. She told me that she'd been often to his flat, and she must have been, because she described it to me and every detail was right. I don't know what happened this evening. But I do know that if Joss wanted her to go back with him, she'd have gone like a shot. No arguments."

"Then how," asked Eliot smoothly, "do you account for the bruise on her face?"

"I don't know. I said I don't know about the rest of her story. But that bit, for sure, she made up."

Grenville moved. He had been standing for a long time. Slowly, he went to his chair and lowered himself carefully into it.

"We can find out what really happened," he said at last.

"How?" Eliot's question came out like the shot of a gun.

Grenville swung his head around and fixed his gaze on Eliot.

"We can ask Joss."

Eliot let out a sound, which in old-fashioned novels would have been written as "Pshaw."

"We shall ask him. And we will be given the truth."

"He doesn't know what the truth means."

"You have no justification for making such a statement."

Eliot lost his temper. "Oh, for God's sake, does the truth have to be thrown in your face before you recognise it?"

"Don't raise your voice to me."

Eliot was silent, staring in disbelief and disgust at the old man. When at last he spoke, it was in scarcely more than a whisper. "I've had enough of Joss Gardner. I've never trusted him nor liked him. I believe he's a phoney, a thief and a liar, and I know that I'm right. And one day you too will know that I'm right. This is your house. I accept that. But what I will not accept is his right to take it over, and us with it, just because he happens to be . . ."

I had to stop him. "Eliot!" He turned to look at me. It was as though he had forgotten I was there. "Eliot, please. Don't say any more."

He looked down at his glass, finished the drink in a single

mouthful. "All right," he said at last. "For the moment, I won't say any more."

And he went to pour himself another whisky. As he did this, with Grenville and I watching him in silence, Morris Tatcombe came back into the room.

"I'll be off then," he said to the back of Eliot's head.

Eliot turned and saw him. "Is she all right?"

"Well, she's upstairs. Your mother's with her."

"Have another drink before you go."

"No, I'd better be off."

"We really can't thank you enough. What would have happened if you hadn't seen her . . ." He stopped, the unfinished sentence conjuring up visions of Andrea dying of exposure, exhaustion, loss of blood.

"Just lucky I did." He backed away, obviously anxious to be off, but not quite sure how to get there. Eliot put the stopper into the decanter, left his freshly filled glass on the table and came to his rescue.

"I'll see you to the door."

Morris ducked his head in the general direction of Grenville and myself.

"Night, all."

But Grenville had hauled himself to his feet with massive dignity. "You've handled things very sensibly, Mr Tatcombe. We're grateful to you. And we would be grateful, too, if you would keep the girl's version of what happened to yourself. At least until it has been authenticated."

Morris looked sceptical. "These things get around."

"But not, I am sure, through you."

Morris shrugged. "It's your affair."

"Exactly. Our affair. Good night, Mr Tatcombe."

Eliot led him away.

Grenville laboriously settled himself once more in his chair. He passed a hand over his eyes, and it occurred to me that such scenes could not be good for him.

"Are you all right?"

"Yes. I'm all right."

I wished that I could confide in him, tell him that I knew about Sophia, and Joss being her grandson. But I knew that if there were any telling to be done, it had to come from him.

"Would you like a drink?"

"No."

So I left him alone, busying myself in tidying the cushions on the flattened sofa.

It was some time before Eliot reappeared, but when he did he seemed quite cheerful again, the sudden row which had flared between him and Grenville now quite forgotten. He went to pick up his drink. "Good health," he said, raising his glass to his grandfather.

"I suppose we're in debt to that young man," said Grenville. "I hope one day we'll be able to settle it."

"I shouldn't worry too much about Morris," Eliot replied lightly. "I should think he's quite capable of settling it for himself. And Pettifer has asked me to tell you both that dinner is ready."

We ate alone, the three of us. Mollie stayed with Andrea, and in the middle of dinner the doctor arrived and was taken upstairs by Pettifer. Later, we heard him talking to Mollie in the hall, then she showed him out and came into the dining-room to tell us what he had said.

"Shock, of course. He's given her a sedative, and she has to stay in bed for a day or two."

Eliot had gone to pull out a chair for her, and she sank into this looking exhausted and shaken. "Imagine such a thing happening. How I'm going to tell her mother, I can't think."

"Don't think about it," said Eliot, "till tomorrow."

"But it was such an appalling story. She's only a child. She's only seventeen. What could Joss have been thinking of? He must have gone out of his mind."

"He was probably drunk," said Eliot.

"Yes, perhaps he was. Drunk and violent."

Neither Grenville nor I said anything. It was as though we had entered into some sort of an unspoken conspiracy, but this did not mean that I had forgiven Joss, nor condoned anything that he had done. Later, probably, when he had been interrogated by Grenville, the whole truth would come out. By then I would probably be back in London.

And if I was still here . . . Slowly, I ate a little bunch of grapes. This could be my last dinner at Boscarva, but I truly did not know whether I wanted it to be or not. I had reached a crossroads, and had no idea which was the way I should take. But soon I was going to have to make up my mind.

A compromise, Eliot had said, and it had sounded tepid. But after the histrionics of this evening, the very words had a solid ring to them, sensible and matter-of-fact, with their feet planted squarely on the ground.

You were made for a man and a home and children.

I reached for my wineglass and, glancing up, saw that Eliot watched me across the polished table. He smiled, as though we were conspirators. The expression on his face was both confident and triumphant. Perhaps, while I was thinking that I would probably end up by marrying him, he already knew that I would.

We were back in the drawing-room, sitting around the fire and finishing our coffee, when the telephone started to ring. I thought that Eliot would go to answer it, but he was deep in a chair with the paper and a drink, and managed to linger so long that it was Pettifer who finally took the call. We heard the kitchen door open and his old feet go so slowly across the hall. The ringing stopped. For some reason I glanced up at the clock on the mantelpiece. It was nearly a quarter to ten.

We waited. Presently the door opened and Pettifer's head came around the edge of it, his spectacles glinting in the lamplight.

"Who is it, Pettifer?" asked Mollie.

"It's for Rebecca," said Pettifer.

I was surprised. "For me?"

Eliot said, "Who's ringing you at this hour of the day?"

"I've no idea."

I got up and went out of the room. Perhaps it was Maggie, wanting to tell me something about the flat. Perhaps it was Stephen Forbes, wondering when I was going to return to work. I felt guilty, because I should have been in touch with him, letting him know what I was doing and when I planned to go back to London.

I sat on the hall chest and picked up the receiver.

"Hello?"

A small, mouse-like voice began speaking, sounding very far away.

"Oh, Miss Bayliss, we were passing, and he was lying there . . . my husband said . . . so we got him up the stairs and into the flat . . . don't know what happened. Covered in blood and he could hardly talk. Wanted to call the doctor . . . but he wouldn't let us . . . frightened leaving him there on his own . . . there ought to be somebody there . . . said he'd be all right . . ."

I must have been exceptionally slow and stupid, but it took me a little time to realise that this was Mrs Kernow, calling me from the phone box at the end of Fish Lane, to tell me that something had happened to Joss.

12

I was amazed and gratified to find myself in a state of almost total calm. It was as though I had already been prepared for this crisis, been given my orders and told what to do. There were no doubts and so no indecision. I must go to Joss. It was as simple as that.

I went up to my bedroom and got my coat, put it on, did up the buttons, came downstairs again. The key of Mollie's car lay where I had left it, on the brass tray in the middle of the table in the hall.

I picked it up, and as I did so the drawing-room door opened and Eliot came up the passage towards me. It never occurred to me that he would try to stop me going. It never occurred to me that anyone or anything could stop me going.

He saw me, bundled into my old leather coat. "Where are you off to?"

"Out."

"Who was that on the telephone?"

"Mrs Kernow."

"What does she want?"

"Joss has been hurt. She and Mr Kernow were walking home along the harbour road, they'd been visiting her sister. They found him."

"So?" His voice was cold and very quiet. I expected to be intimidated, but I was not.

"I'm going to borrow your mother's car. I'm going to him."

His thin face hardened, the skin drawn tight over the jutting bones.

"Have you gone out of your mind?"

"I don't think so."

He said nothing. I slipped the key into my pocket and made for the door, but Eliot was faster than I, and in two strides was in front of me, standing with his back to the door and with his hand on the latch.

"You're not going," he said pleasantly. "You don't really think I'd let you go?"

"He's been hurt, Eliot."

"So what? You saw what he did to Andrea. He's rotten, Rebecca. You know he's rotten. His grandmother was an Irish whore, God knows who his father was, and he's a womanising bastard."

The ugly words, which were meant to shock me, slid off my back like water from a duck. Eliot saw this and my unconcern infuriated him.

"Why do you want to go to him? What good could you do? He won't thank you for interfering, if it's thanks you're looking for. Leave him alone, he has no part of your life, he's none of your concern."

I stood watching him, hearing him, without making sense of anything he said. But I knew, all at once, that it was over, the uncertainty and the indecision, and I felt light with relief, as though a great weight had been lifted from my shoulders. I still stood at the crossroads. My life was still a confusion. But one thing had made itself abundantly clear. I could never marry Eliot.

A compromise, he had said. But, for me, it would have been a poor bargain. All right, he was weak, and probably not the most successful of businessmen. I had recognised these flaws in his character and had been prepared to accept them. But the welcome he had shown me, the hospitality, and the charm which he could turn on and off like a tap, had blinded me to his vindictiveness and the frightening strength of his jealousy.

I said, "Let me go, Eliot."

"Supposing I say that I won't let you go? Supposing I keep you here?" He put his hands on either side of my head, pressing so tightly that it felt as though my skull would crack open, like a nut. "Supposing, now, that I said I loved you?"

I was sickened by him. "You don't love anyone. Only Eliot Bayliss. There's no room for anyone else in your life."

"I thought we decided that it was you who didn't know how to love."

His grip tightened. My head began to pound and I closed my eyes, enduring the pain.

"When I do . . ." I told him through clenched teeth ". . . it won't be you."

"All right then, go . . ." He let me loose so suddenly that I nearly lost my balance. Savagely he turned the handle and flung the door open, and instantly the wind poured in, like some monstrous creature that had been waiting all evening to invade the house. Outside was the dark and the rain. Without another word, not stopping to look at Eliot, I ran past him and out into it, as though to some sanctuary.

I had still to get to the garage, to struggle with doors in the darkness, to find Mollie's little car. I was convinced that Eliot was just behind me, as frightening as an imagined bogey man, waiting to jump, to catch me, to stop me from getting away. I slammed the car door shut, and my hand shook so much I could scarcely get the ignition key fitted. The first time I turned it, the engine did not start. I heard myself whimpering as I pulled out the choke and tried again. This time the engine caught. I put the car into gear and shot forward, through the darkness and the rain, up the puddled driveway with a great spattering of gravel, and so at last out and on to the road.

Driving, I regained some of my previous calm. I had eluded Eliot, I was going to Joss. I must drive with care and good sense, not allow myself to panic, not risk a skid or a possible collision. I slowed down to a cautious thirty miles per hour. I deliberately loosened my death-like clutch on the driving wheel. The road ran downhill, black and wet with rain. The lights of Porthkerris came up towards me. I was going to Joss.

185

Now, the tide was at full ebb. As I came out on to the harbour road, I saw the lights reflected in wet sand, the boats drawn up out of the reach of the storm. Overhead tattered scraps of cloud still poured across the sky. There were people about, but not very many.

The shop was in darkness. Only a single light glowed from the top window. I parked the car by the pavement and got out and went to the door and it opened. I smelt the new wood, my feet brushed through the shavings which still lay about the place. From the light of the street lamp outside I could see the staircase. I went up it, cautiously, to the first floor.

I called up, "Joss!"

There was no reply. I went on, up into the soft light. There was no fire and it was very cold. A squall of rain swept the roof above me.

"Joss."

He was lying on his bed, roughly covered by a blanket. His forearm lay across his eyes, as though to shut out some unbearable light. When I spoke he lowered this, and raised his head slightly to see who it was. Then he dropped back on to the pillow.

"Good God," I heard him say. "Rebecca."

I went to his side. "Yes, it's me."

"I thought I heard your voice. I thought I was dreaming."

"I called up, but you didn't reply."

His face was in a terrible mess, the left side bruised and swollen, the eye half-closed. Blood had trickled and dried from a cut in his lip, and there did not seem to be any skin on the knuckles of his right hand.

"What are you doing here?" He spoke muzzily, perhaps because of the lip.

"Mrs Kernow rang me."

"I told her not to say anything."

"She was worried about you. Joss, what happened?"

"I fell amongst thieves."

"Are you hurt anywhere else?"

186

"Yes, everywhere else."

"Let me see . . ."

"The Kernows bandaged me up."

But I stooped over him, gently drawing back the blanket. As far as his rib-cage he was naked and below this tenderly swathed in what looked like strips torn from an old sheet. But the ugly bruising had spread up and on to his chest, and on his right side the red stain of blood had started to seep through the white cotton.

"Joss, who did this?"

But Joss did not answer me. Instead, with a strength surprising in one so hurt, he put up an arm and pulled me down so that I was sitting on the edge of his bed. My long, blonde plait of hair hung forward over my shoulder, and while he held me with his right arm, his left hand was occupied in slipping off the rubber band which held the ends together, and then, using his fingers like a comb, he loosened the strands, unravelling them, so that my hair hung like a silken tassel, brushing on to his naked chest.

He said, "I always wanted to do that. Ever since I first saw you looking like the head girl of . . . what was it I said?"

"The head girl of a nicely run orphanage."

"That's it. Fancy you remembering."

"What can I do? There must be something I can do?"

"Just stay. Just stay, my darling girl."

The tenderness in his voice . . . Joss, who had always been so tough . . . dissolved me. Tears sprang into my eyes and he saw these and pulled me down, so that I lay against him, and I felt his hand slip up beneath my hair and close around the back of my neck.

"Joss, I'll hurt you . . ."

"Don't talk," he said, as his seeking mouth found mine. And then, "I've always wanted to do this, too."

It was evident that none of his infirmities, his bruises, his bleeding, his cut lip, were to deter him in any way from getting exactly what he wanted.

187

And I, who had always imagined that loving was something to do with fireworks and explosions of emotion, discovered that it was not like that at all. It was warm, like sudden sunshine. It had nothing to do with my mother and the endless procession of men who had invaded her life. It was cynicism and preconceived ideas flying out of an open window. It was the last of my defences gone. It was Joss.

He said my name and he made it sound beautiful.

Much later, I lit a fire, piling on the driftwood so that the room was bright with flickering firelight. I would not let Joss move, so that he lay with his dark head propped on his arms, and I felt his eyes following every move I made.

I stood up, away from the fire. My hair fell loose on either side of my face, and my cheeks were warm from the fire. I felt soft with content.

Joss said, "We have to talk, don't we?"

"Yes."

"Get me a drink."

"What do you want?"

"Some whisky. It's in the galley, in the cupboard over the sink."

I went to find it, and two glasses. "Soda or water?"

"Soda. There's a bottle-opener hanging on a hook."

I found the opener and took the cap off the bottle. I did this clumsily and it fell to the floor, rolling in the maddening manner of such things into a dark corner. I went to retrieve it and my eye was caught by another small and shining object, lying half under the kickboard beneath the sink. I picked it up and it was Andrea's Celtic cross, the one that she had worn on a leather thong around her neck.

I kept it in my hand. I poured the drinks and took them back to Joss. I handed him one, and knelt on the floor beside him.

I said, "This was under the sink," and showed him the cross.

His swollen eye made it difficult for him to focus. He squinted at it painfully.

188

"What the hell's that?"

"It's Andrea's."

He said, "Oh, to hell." And then, "Get me some more pillows, there's a good girl. I could never drink whisky lying down."

I gathered up a couple of cushions off the floor, and propped him against them. The action of sitting up was agony for him and he let out an involuntary groan.

"Are you all right?"

"Yes, of course I'm all right. Where did you find that thing?"

"I told you. On the floor."

"She came here this evening. She said she'd been to the cinema. I was working downstairs, trying to get the shelving finished. I told her I was busy, but she just came up here, as though I'd never said a word. I followed her up and told her to go home. But she wouldn't go. She said she wanted a drink, she wanted to talk . . . you know the sort of drivel."

"She's been here before."

"Yes, once. One morning. I was sorry for her and I gave her a cup of coffee. But this evening I was busy; I had no time for her and I wasn't sorry for her. I said I didn't want a drink. I told her to go home. And then she said that she didn't want to go home, everybody hated her, nobody would talk to her, I was the only person she could talk to, I was the only person who understood."

"Perhaps you were."

"OK, so I was sorry for her. I used to let her come and get in my way when I was working at Boscarva, because there wasn't much else I could do about it, short of bodily throwing her out of the room."

"Did you do that this evening? Throw her out?"

"Not in so many words. But finally I'd had enough of her batty conversation and her totally unfounded belief that I was ready, willing and eager to jump into bed with her, and I lost my temper and told her so."

"What happened then?"

"What didn't happen? Screams, tears, accusations, routine hysteria. I was subjected to every sort of vilification. Face slapping, the lot. That was when I finally resorted to force, and I bundled her down the stairs and threw her raincoat and her beastly handbag after her."

"You didn't hurt her?"

"No, I didn't hurt her. But I think I frightened her, because she went then, like the hammers of hell. I heard her clattering down the stairs on those ghastly clogs she wears, and then I think she must have slipped because there was the most frightful thumping and bumping as she went down the last few stairs. I shouted down to make sure she was all right, but then I heard her running out of the shop and slamming the door behind her, so that I imagined she was."

"Could she have hit herself on anything? Bruised her face when she fell?"

"Yes, I suppose she could. There was a packing case full of china standing at the bottom of the stairs. She could have collided with that . . . Why do you ask anyway?"

I told him. When I had finished he let out a long, incredulous whistle. But he was angry too.

"The little bitch. I think she's a nymphomaniac, do you know that?"

"I've always thought so."

"She was always talking about some guy called Danus, going into the most gruesome of intimate details. And the bloody cheek of telling everyone that I had asked her to go to the cinema with me. I wouldn't ask her to empty a dustbin with me . . . What's happened to her now?"

"She's been put to bed. Mollie got the doctor."

"If he's worth his salt he'll have diagnosed self-induced hysteria. And he'll prescribe a good walloping and send her back to London. And that'll get her out of everybody's way."

"Poor Andrea. She's very unhappy."

As though he could not keep his hands off it, he reached

190

out to touch my hair. I turned my head and kissed the back of his hand, the lacerated knuckles.

He said, "You didn't believe her, did you?"

"Not really."

"Did anyone else?"

"Mollie and Eliot did. Eliot wanted to call the police but Grenville wouldn't let him."

"That's interesting."

"Why?"

"Who was it who brought Andrea home?"

"I thought I'd told you. Morris Tatcombe . . . you know, the boy who works for Eliot . . ."

"Morris? Well I'll be . . ." He stopped in mid-sentence, and then said again, "Morris Tatcombe."

"What about him?"

"Oh, Rebecca, come along. Pull yourself together. Use your wits. Who do you think gave me this beating?"

"Not Morris." I did not want to believe it.

"Morris and three others. I went along to The Anchor for a glass of beer and a pie for my supper, and when I was walking home, they jumped me."

"You knew it was Morris?"

"Who else would it be? He's always had this grudge going for me ever since we last crossed swords and he ended up on his backside in the gutter. I thought his putting the boot in this time was just a continuation of our running feud. But it seems that it wasn't."

Without thinking I began to say, "Eliot . . ." and then stopped, but it was too late. Joss said quietly, "What about Eliot?"

"I don't want to talk about Eliot."

"Did he tell Morris to come after me?"

"I don't know."

"He could, you know. He hates my guts. It fits."

"I . . . I think he's jealous of you. He doesn't like your being so close to Grenville. He doesn't like Grenville being so fond of you. And . . ." I looked down at my drink,

191

turning the glass in my hand, feeling suddenly nervous. "There's something else."

"From your expression one would think you'd murdered somebody. What is it?"

"It's . . . the desk. The desk downstairs in your workroom. I saw it this morning, when you were telephoning."

"I wondered why you'd suddenly gone cantering out into the rain. What about it?"

"The desk and the Chippendale chair. They came from Boscarva."

"Yes, I know."

His calmness shocked me. "You didn't *take* them, Joss?"

"*Take them?* No, I didn't take them. I bought them."

"Who from?"

"A man who runs an antique shop up beyond Fourbourne. I'd been to a sale about a month ago, and I dropped in to see him on the way back, and I saw the chair and the desk in his shop. By then I knew all Grenville's furniture and I knew they'd come from Boscarva."

"But who took them?"

"I regret to have to shatter your innocence, but it was your cousin Eliot."

"But Eliot knew nothing about them."

"Eliot most certainly did. They were in one of the attics, as far as I remember, and he probably imagined they'd never be missed."

"But why . . .?"

"This is like playing the truth game. Because Eliot, my love, my darling child, is head over heels in debt. That garage was financed by Ernest Padlow in the first place, it cost a bomb and it's been losing money steadily for the past twelve months. God knows what use fifty pounds would have been to Eliot, a mere drop in the ocean one would have thought, but perhaps he needed a little ready cash to pay a bill or put on a horse or something . . . I don't know. Between you and me, I don't think he should be running his own business. He'd be better working for some other guy, being paid a regular salary. Perhaps, one evening, when you're sitting over drinks at Boscarva, you could try and persuade him."

"Sarcasm doesn't suit you."

"I know, but Eliot makes me edgy. Always has done."

I felt, obscurely, that I must stand up for Eliot, make excuses for him.

"In a way, he thinks that Boscarva and everything in it already belong to him. Perhaps he didn't feel it was . . . stealing . . .?"

"When did they realise the things were missing?"

"A couple of days ago. You see, the desk belonged to my mother. Now it belongs to me. That's why we started to look for it."

"Unfortunate for Eliot."

"Yes."

"I suppose Eliot said I'd taken them."

"Yes," I admitted miserably.

"What did Grenville say?"

"He said that you'd never do a thing like that."

"And so there was another monumental row."

"Yes."

Joss sighed deeply. We fell silent. The room was growing cold again, the fire beginning to die down. I got up and went to put another log on it, but Joss stopped me.

"Leave it," he said.

I looked at him, surprised. He finished his drink and put the empty glass down on the floor beside him, and then pushed back the blanket and began, carefully, to get out of bed.

"Joss, you mustn't . . ."

I flew to his side, but he pushed me away, and slowly, with infinite caution, got to his feet. Once there, he grinned triumphantly down at me, a bizarre sight, bruised and battered, and dressed in bandages and a crumpled pair of jeans.

"Into battle," he said.

"Joss, what are you going to do?"

193

"If you'll find me a shirt and a pair of shoes, I'll get dressed. And then we're going to go downstairs, and get into the truck and drive back to Boscarva."

"But you can't drive like that."

"I can do anything I want," he told me, and I believed him. "Now find my clothes and stop arguing."

He would not even let me take Mollie's car. "We'll leave it there, it'll be all right. Someone can fetch it in the morning." His own little truck was parked around the corner, up a narrow alley. We got in, and he started the engine and backed out on to the road, with me giving directions because he was too stiff to turn around in the seat. We headed up through the town, along streets that had become familiar to me, over the crossroads and up the hill.

I sat, staring ahead, with my hands clasped tightly in my lap. I knew that there was still something else we had to talk about. And it had to be now, before we reached Boscarva.

For some reason, as though he were immensely pleased with life in general, Joss had started to sing.

> The first time ever I saw your face
> I thought the sun rose in your eyes
> And the moon and stars . . .

"Joss."

"What is it now?"

"There's something else."

He sounded shocked. "Not another skeleton in the cupboard?"

"Don't joke."

"I'm sorry. What is it?"

I swallowed a strange obstruction in the back of my throat.

"It's Sophia."

"What about Sophia?"

"Grenville gave me the key of the studio so that I could

194

go and choose a picture to take back to London. I found a portrait of Sophia. A proper one, with a face. And Eliot came to find me, and he saw it too."

There was a long silence. I looked at Joss but his profile was stony, intent on the road ahead. "I see," he said at last.

"She looks just like you; or you look just like her."

"Naturally enough. She was my grandmother."

"Yes, I thought that was probably it."

"So the portrait was in the studio?"

"Is . . . is that why you came to live in Porthkerris?"

"Yes. Grenville and my father fixed it between them. Grenville put up half the capital for my shop."

"Your father . . .?"

"You've met him. Tristram Nolan Gardner. He runs an antique shop, in the New Kings Road. You bought a pair of balloon-back chairs from him. Do you remember?"

"And he found from my cheque that I was called Rebecca Bayliss."

"Right. And he found out, by cunning question and answer, that you were Grenville Bayliss's granddaughter. Right. And he found out that you were catching the train to Cornwall last Monday. Right."

"So he rang you up and told you to meet the train."

"Right."

"But why?"

"Because he felt involved. Because he thought you seemed lost and vulnerable. Because he wanted me to keep an eye on you."

"I still don't understand."

"You know something?" said Joss. "I love you very much."

"Because I'm being stupid?"

"No, because you're being marvellously innocent. Sophia wasn't only Grenville's model, she was his mistress as well. My father was born at the beginning of their relationship, long before your mother arrived. Sophia married, eventually, an old friend she'd known from childhood days, but she never had any more children."

195

"So Tristram . . .?"

"Tristram is Grenville's son. And Grenville is my grandfather. And I am going to marry my half-cousin."

"Pettifer told me that Sophia meant nothing to Grenville. That she was just a girl who'd worked for him."

"If it meant protecting Grenville, Pettifer would swear that black is white."

"Yes, I suppose he would." But Grenville, in anger, had been less discreet. "'You are not my only grandchild!'"

"Did Grenville say that?"

"Yes, to Eliot. And Eliot thought he meant me."

We had reached the top of the hill. The lights of the town were far behind us. Ahead, beyond the huddled shapes of Ernest Padlow's housing estate, lay the dark coastline, pricked with the tiny lights of random farms, and beyond it the black immensity of the sea.

I said, "I don't seem to remember you asking me to marry you."

The little van bumped and lurched down the lane towards Boscarva. "I'm not very good at asking things," said Joss. He took his hand off the wheel and put it over mine. "I usually just tell people."

As once before, it was Pettifer who came out to meet us. As soon as Joss switched off the engine of the van, the light in the hall went on, and Pettifer opened the door, as though he had known instinctively we were on our way.

He saw Joss open the car door and ease himself out, in obvious discomfort and pain. He saw Joss's face . . .

"For heaven's sake, what happened to you?"

"I had a difference of opinion with our old friend Morris Tatcombe. I probably wouldn't look like this except that he had three of his chums with him."

"Are you all right?"

"Yes, I'm fine. No bones broken. Come on, let's go in."

We went indoors and Pettifer closed the door.

"I'm glad to see you, Joss, and that's the truth. We've had a proper how-do-you-do here and no mistake."

"Is Grenville all right?"

"Yes, he's all right. He's still up, in the drawing-room, waiting for Rebecca to come home."

"And Eliot?"

Pettifer looked from Joss's face to mine.

"He's gone."

Joss said, "You'd better tell us about it."

We ended up in the kitchen, around the table.

"After Rebecca had gone, Eliot went down to the studio and came back with that portrait of Sophia. The one we looked for, Joss. The one we never found."

I said, "I don't understand."

Joss explained. "Pettifer knew Sophia was my grand-mother, but no one else did. No one else remembered her. It was all too long ago. Grenville wanted it to stay that way."

"But why was there only one picture of Sophia with a face? There must have been dozens Grenville painted of her. What happened to all of them?"

There was a pause while Joss and Pettifer looked at each other. Then it was Pettifer's turn to explain, which he did with much tact.

"It was old Mrs Bayliss. She was jealous of Sophia . . . not because she had any notion of the truth . . . but because Sophia was part of the Commander's other life, the life Mrs Bayliss didn't have no time for."

"You mean his painting."

"She would never have anything to do with Sophia, more than a frosty 'good morning' if she happened to meet her in the town. And the Commander knew this, and he didn't want to upset her, so he let all the pictures of Sophia go . . . all except for the one you found. We knew it was somewhere around. Joss and I spent a day looking for it, but we never turned it up."

"What were you going to do with it if you found it?"

"Nothing. We just didn't want anyone else to find it."

"I don't see why it was so important."

Joss said, "Grenville didn't want anyone to know about what happened between him and Sophia. It wasn't that he was ashamed of it, because he'd loved her very much. And after he's dead, it won't matter any longer, he doesn't give a damn who knows then. But he's proud, and he's lived his life according to a certain set of standards. We probably think they're old-fashioned, but they're still his own. Does that make sense to you?"

"I suppose so."

"Young people now," said Pettifer heavily, "talk about a permissive society as though it were something they'd invented. But it's not new. It's been going on since the beginning of time, only in the Commander's day it was handled with a little more discretion."

We accepted this meekly. Then Joss said, "We seem to have gone off at a tangent. Pettifer was telling us about Eliot."

Pettifer collected himself. "Yes, well. So down to the drawing-room Eliot went, and stormed in, with me behind him, went straight to the mantelpiece, and dumped it up there, alongside the other picture. The Commander never said a word, just watched him. And Eliot said, 'What's that got to do with Joss Gardner?' Then the Commander told him. Told him everything. Very quiet and very dignified. And Mrs Roger was there too, and she just about threw a fit. She said all these years the Commander had deceived them, letting Eliot believe that he was his only grandson, and he'd get Boscarva when the Commander died. The Commander said he'd never said anything of the sort, that it was all surmise, that they'd simply been counting their chickens before they were hatched. Then Eliot said, very cold, 'Perhaps now we can know what your plans are?' but the Commander said that his plans were his own business, and *quite right* he was too."

This little bit of championship was accompanied by Pettifer's fist coming down with a thump on the kitchen table.

"So what did Eliot do?"

"Eliot said in that case he was going to wash his hands of the whole lot of us . . . meaning the family, of course . . . and that he had plans of his own and he was thankful to be shed of us. And with that he collected a few papers and a brief-case and put on his coat and whistled up his dog and walked out of the house. Heard his car go up the lane and that was the end of him."

"Where's he gone?"

"To High Cross, I suppose."

"And Mollie?"

"She was in tears . . . trying to stop him doing anything stupid, she said. Begging him to stay. Turning on the Commander, saying it was all his fault. But of course, there wasn't anything she could do to stop Eliot. There's nothing you can do to stop a grown man walking out of the house, not even if you do happen to be his mother."

I was torn with sorrow and sympathy for Mollie.

"Where is she now?"

"Up in her room." He added gruffly, "I made her a little tea-tray, took it up to her, found her sitting at her dressing-table like something carved out of stone."

I was glad I had not been here. It all sounded very dramatic. I stood up. Poor Mollie. "I'll go up and talk to her."

"And I . . ." said Joss ". . . will go and see Grenville."

"Tell him I'll be there in a moment or two."

Joss smiled. "We'll wait," he promised.

I found Mollie, white-faced and tear-stained, still sitting in front of her frilled dressing-table. (This was in character. Even the deepest excesses of grief would not cause Mollie to fling herself across any bed. It might crease the covers.) As I came into the room, she looked up, and her reflection was caught three times over in her triple mirror; for the first time ever, I thought that she looked her age.

I said, "Are you all right?"

She looked down, balling a sodden handkerchief in her fingers. I went to her side. "Pettifer told me. I'm so very sorry."

"It's all so desperately unfair. Grenville's always disliked Eliot, resented him in some extraordinary way. And of course, now we know why. He was always trying to run Eliot's life, come between Eliot and me. Whatever I did for Eliot was always wrong."

I knelt beside her, and put my arm around her, "I really believe ьe meant it for the best. Can't you try to believe that too?"

"I don't even know where he's gone. He wouldn't tell me. He never said goodbye."

I realised that she was a great deal more worried about Eliot's abrupt departure than she was about the evening's revelations concerning Joss. This was just as well. I could comfort her about Eliot. There was not a mortal thing I could do about Joss.

"I think," I said, "that Eliot may have gone to Birmingham."

She looked at me in horror. "*Birmingham?*"

"There was a man there who wanted to give him a job. Eliot told me. It was to do with second-hand cars. He seemed to think that it might be quite interesting."

"But I can't go and live in *Birmingham*."

"Oh, Mollie, you don't have to. Eliot can live on his own. Let him go. Give him the chance of making something of his life."

"But we've always been together."

"Then perhaps it's time to start living apart. You've got your house at High Cross, your garden up there, your friends . . ."

"I can't leave Boscarva. I can't leave Andrea. I can't leave Grenville."

"Yes, you can. And I think Andrea should go back to London, to her own parents. You've done all you can for her, and she's miserable here. That's why all this happened, because she was unhappy and lonely. And as for Grenville, I'll stay with him."

I came downstairs at last carrying the tea-tray. I took it into the kitchen and put it on the table. Pettifer, sitting there, looked up at me over the edge of his evening paper.

"How is she?" he asked.

"All right now. She's agreed that Andrea should go home, back to London. And then she's going back to High Cross."

"That's what she's always wanted. And you?"

"I'm staying here. If that's all right with you."

A chill gleam of satisfaction crossed Pettifer's face, the nearest he could get to a look of delight. There was no need for me to say more. We understood each other.

Pettifer turned his paper. "They're in the drawing-room . . ." he told me ". . . waiting for you," and he settled down to the racing page.

I went and found them, backed by the two portraits of Sophia in her white dress, Joss standing by the fire, and Grenville deep in his chair. They both looked up as I came in, the long-legged young man with his villainous black eye, and the old one, too tired to pull himself to his feet. I went towards them, the two people I loved most.

BOOK TWO

ROSAMUNDE PILCHER

ANOTHER VIEW

1

In Paris, in February, the sun was shining. At Le Bourget Airport, it gleamed coldly from an ice blue sky, and this was reflected, with much dazzle, from the runways, still wet after a night's rain. From inside, the day looked inviting, and they had been tempted out on to the terrace, only to discover that the bright sun held no real warmth and the gay breeze that blew the wind socks out at right angles had an edge to it like a knife. Defeated, they withdrew to the restaurant to wait for Emma's flight to be called, and sat now, at a small table, drinking black coffee and smoking Christopher's Gauloises cigarettes.

Unselfconscious, absorbed in each other, they nevertheless attracted a certain amount of attention. This was inevitable, for they made an arresting pair. Emma was tall and very dark. Her hair, worn back off her forehead and held in place by a tortoiseshell band, fell in a straight black tassel to below her shoulder-blades. Her face was not beautiful – it was too clearly boned and strongly built for beauty, with a straight nose, and a square and determined chin. But these features were redeemed and given much charm by large and unexpectedly grey-blue eyes, and a wide mouth, which, although it was quite capable of drooping disconsolately if she did not get her own way, could grin, from ear to ear, like a boy's, when she was happy. She was happy now. She wore, on this cold bright day, a bitter green trouser suit and a white polo-necked sweater that made her face look very brown, but her sophisticated appearance was off-set by the mass of luggage with which she was surrounded, and which appeared, to the casual passer-by, to have been salvaged from some disastrous act of God.

It was, in fact, the accumulation of six years of living abroad, but no one was to know this. Three suitcases, at enormous expense, had already been checked in. But there was still a canvas grip, a Prisunic paper carrier sprouting long French loaves, a basket bulging with books and records, a raincoat, a pair of ski-boots and an enormous straw hat.

Christopher surveyed it all, speculating, in a detached and unbothered fashion, as to how it was all going to be conveyed into the aeroplane.

"You could wear the hat and the ski-boots and the raincoat. That would make three less things to carry."

"I've already got a pair of shoes on, and the hat would blow off. And the raincoat's disgusting. I look like a displaced person in it. I can't think why I bothered to bring it at all."

"I'll tell you why. Because it will be raining in London."

"It may not be."

"It always is." He lit another Gauloise from the stub of the first. "Another good reason for staying in Paris with me."

"We've had this out a hundred times. And I'm going back to England."

He grinned without rancour. He had been teasing her. When he smiled, his yellow-flecked eyes slanted upwards at the corners, and this, combined with his lanky, idle body, gave him a curiously feline appearance. His clothes were colourful, casual, faintly Bohemian. Narrow cord trousers, battered chukka boots, a blue cotton shirt worn over a yellow sweater, and a suède jacket, very old and shiny about the elbows and the collar. He looked French, but in fact he was as English as Emma and even related to her in a tenuous way, for, years ago, when Emma was six and Christopher ten, her father, Ben Litton, had married Hester Ferris, Christopher's mother. The arrangement had lasted, with only the smallest degree of success, for eighteen months, before it finally fell apart, and now Emma remembered it as the only time in her life when she had ever known anything vaguely approaching an ordinary family life.

It was Hester who had insisted on buying the cottage at Porthkerris. Ben had owned a studio there for a number of years, since long before the war, but its conveniences were non-existent, and after one look at the squalor in which she was expected to live Hester went straight out and acquired two fisherman's cottages, which she proceeded, with taste and charm, to convert. Ben was disinterested in any such activity, so it became very much Hester's house, and it was she who insisted on a kitchen that would work, and a boiler that would heat water, and a big fireplace blazing with driftwood, a heart to their home, a focal point around which the children could gather.

Her intentions were splendid, her methods of carrying them out not so successful. She tried to make allowances for Ben. She had married a genius, and she knew his reputation and she was prepared to turn a blind eye to his love affairs, his disreputable companions and his attitude towards money. But in the end, as so often happens in quite ordinary marriages, she was defeated by the small things. By meals, forgotten and uneaten. By trivial bills left unpaid for months. By the fact that Ben preferred to drink in the local pub, rather than in a civilised fashion, at home, with her. She was defeated by his refusal to have a telephone, to own a car; by the stream of apparent derelicts whom he invited to sleep on her sofa; and finally by his total inability to show at any time any sort of affection.

She left him at last, taking Christopher with her, and sued almost immediately for a divorce. Ben was delighted to let her have it. He was delighted, too, to see the back of the small boy. The two of them had never got on. Ben was jealous of his male priority, he liked to be the only man of importance in his household, and Christopher, even at ten years old, was an individual who refused to be ignored. Despite all Hester's efforts, this antagonism endured. Even the boy's good looks, which Hester truly believed would charm Ben's painter's eye, had the very opposite effect, and when Hester tried to persuade Ben to do a portrait of him, he refused.

After their departure, life at Porthkerris slid easily back into its old seamy routine. Emma and Ben were cared for by a series of messy females, either models or student painters, who moved into and through and out of Ben Litton's life with the monotonous regularity of a well-ordered cinema queue. The only thing they had in common was an adulation of Ben, and a lofty disregard for housekeeping. They took as little notice of Emma as possible, but, in fact, she did not miss Hester as much as people thought she would. She had become weary – as Ben was – of being organised, and perpetually buttoned into clean clothes, but Christopher's going left a great void in her life which refused to be filled. For a little, she had mourned for him, tried to write him letters, but had not dared to ask Ben for his address. Once, in the desperation of loneliness, she ran away to find him. This entailed walking to the station and trying to buy a ticket to London, which seemed as good a place as any to look for him. But she had only one and ninepence in the world, and the stationmaster, who knew her, had taken her into his office which smelt of paraffin lamps and the black railway coal he burnt in his grate, and had given her a cup of tea out of an enamel pot, and walked her home. Ben was working, and had not noticed her absence. She never tried to look for Christopher again.

When Emma was thirteen, Ben was offered a teaching fellowship at the University of Texas for two years, which, without thought of Emma, he instantly accepted. There was a small hiatus while Emma's future was discussed. When taxed with the question of his daughter, he announced that he would simply take her to Texas with him, but someone – probably Marcus Bernstein – persuaded Ben that she would be better off away from him, and she was sent to a school in Switzerland. She stayed in Lausanne for three years – never returning to England, and then went to Florence to study Italian and Renaissance Art, for another year. At the end of this time, Ben was in Japan. When she suggested that she should join him, he replied by telegram. ONLY SPARE BED OCCUPIED BY CHARMING GEISHA GIRL WHY DONT YOU TRY LIVING IN PARIS.

Philosophically, for she was now seventeen and life was no longer surprising, Emma did as he suggested. She found herself a job with a family called Duprés who lived in a tall scholarly house in St Germain. The father was a professor of medicine, and the mother a teacher. Emma cared for their three well-behaved children, taught them English and Italian, and took them, in August, to the modest family villa at La Baule, and all the time waited patiently until Ben should return to live in England. He stayed in Japan for eighteen months, and when he did return it was by way of the United States, where he spent a month in New York. Marcus Bernstein flew out to meet him there, and it was typical that Emma learned the reason for this reunion, not from Ben himself, nor even from Leo, who was her usual source of information, but from a long and fully illustrated article in the French *Réalités*, which dealt with a newly built Museum of Fine Arts in Queenstown, Virginia. This museum was a memorial created by his widow, to a rich Virginian called Kenneth Ryan, and the opening of the Art Section was to be a retrospective exhibition of the paintings of Ben Litton, ranging from his pre-war landscapes, right through to his latest abstractionisms.

Such an exhibition was an honour and a tribute, but inevitably suggested a painter to be revered, a Grand Old Man of the arts. Emma, studying one of the photographs of Ben, all angles and contrasts, dark-tanned skin and jutting chin and snowy hair, wondered how he felt about such veneration. He had been a rebel all his life against convention, and she could not imagine him tamely submitting to being a Grand Old anything.

"But what a man!" said Madame Duprés, when Emma showed her the photograph. "He is very attractive."

"Yes," said Emma, and sighed, because that had always been the trouble.

With Marcus, he returned to London in January, and went straight back to Porthkerris to paint. This was confirmed by a letter from Marcus. The day the letter arrived, Emma went to Madame Duprés and gave in her notice. They tried to coax, cajole, bribe her into changing her mind, but she was adamant. She had scarcely seen her father for six years. It was time they got to know each other again. She was going back to Porthkerris, to live with him.

In the end, because they had no option, they agreed to letting her go. Her flight was booked, and she started to pack, throwing out some of the accumulated possessions of six years, and cramming the rest into a variety of battered and much-travelled suitcases. But even these were sadly inadequate, and Emma was eventually driven to going out and buying herself a basket, a huge French marketing basket that would accommodate the number of awkwardly-shaped objects that refused to go into anything else.

It was a grey and cold afternoon, two days before she was due to fly home. Madame Duprés was at home, so Emma, explaining her errand, left the children with her, and went out alone. To her surprise, she found that it was raining, lightly, in a chill drizzle. The cobbled pavements of the narrow street shone with wet, and the tall bleached houses stood quiet and closed against the murk, like faces which give nothing away. From the river a tug hooted, and a solitary gull hung, high above, in the mist, screaming dismally. The illusion of Porthkerris was suddenly more real than the reality of Paris. The resolve to return, which had for so long been in the back of her mind, was crystallised now into the impression that she was already there.

This street would lead – not to the busy Rue St Germain,

212

but out on to the harbour road, and it would be flood tide, the harbour full of grey sea and bobbing boats, and a heavy swell running out beyond the north pier, the Atlantic crested with white horses. And there would be familiar smells – fish from the market, and hot saffron buns from the baker's; and all the little summer shops would be shuttered and closed for the season. And back at the studio Ben would be working, hands mittened against the cold, the brilliance of his palette a scream of colour against the sweep of grey cloud that was framed by his towering north window.

She was going home. In two days, she would be there. The rain was wet on her face and all at once she felt that she could not wait, and this sense of happy urgency made her run, and she ran all the way to the little épicerie in the Rue St Germain, where she knew she would be able to buy the basket.

It was a tiny shop, fragrant with fresh bread and garlic-flavoured sausage meat, with onions strung like white beads from the ceiling, and jars of wine, which the local workmen bought by the litre. The baskets hung at the door, strung together and suspended by a single piece of rope. Emma did not dare untie it and choose herself a basket in case the whole lot fell to the pavement, so she went into the shop to find someone to do it for her. There was only the fat woman with the mole on her face, and she was busy with a customer, so Emma waited. The customer was a young man, fair haired, his raincoat streaked with damp. He was buying a long loaf and a pat of country butter. Emma eyed him and decided that, from the back at least, he looked attractive.

"*Combien?*" he said.

The fat woman did a sum with a stub of pencil. She told him. He felt in his pocket and paid, turned, smiled at Emma and made for the door.

And there he stopped. With his hand against the edge of the door, he swung slowly around, to take a second look. She saw the amber eyes, the slow, incredulous smile.

The face was the same, the familiar, boy's face on the unfamiliar man's body. With the illusion of Porthkerris so near and so strong, it seemed that he was simply an extension of that illusion, a figment of her own highly-stimulated imagination. This was not him. This could not be . . .

She heard herself say "Christo," and it was the most natural thing in the world to call him by the name that only she had ever used. He said, quietly, "I simply don't believe it," and then he dropped his parcels and held out his arms and Emma fell into them, pressed close against the shiny, wet front of his raincoat.

They had two days to spend together. Emma told Madame Duprés, "My brother is in Paris," and Madame, who was kind-hearted, and had, anyway, resigned herself to being without Emma, set Emma free to spend them with Christopher. They used up these two days in slowly walking the streets of the city; hanging over the bridges to watch the barges slip away below them, bound for the south and the sun; sitting in the thin sunshine and drinking coffee at the small, round iron tables, and when it rained, taking refuge in Notre Dame or the Louvre, perched on the stairs beneath the Winged Victory and always talking. They had so much to ask and so much to tell. She learned that Christopher, after a number of false starts, had decided to become an actor. This was much against his mother's wishes – after eighteen months of Ben Litton she had had enough of artistic temperaments to last her for the rest of her life – but he had stuck to his guns and even managed to get a scholarship to RADA. He had worked for two years in a repertory theatre in Scotland, had moved, unsuccessfully, to London, done a little television work, and then had been diverted by an invitation from an acquaintance, whose mother owned a house in St Tropez.

"St Tropez in the winter?" Emma could not help asking.

"It was then or never. We'd never have been offered it in the summer."

"But wasn't it cold?"

"Freezing. Never stopping raining. And when the wind blew all the shutters rattled. It was like some ghastly film."

In January he had returned to London to see his agent, and had been offered a twelve-month contract with a small repertory company in the south of England. It was not the sort of work he wanted, but it was better than nothing, and he was running out of money, and it was not too far from London. The job, however, did not start until the beginning of March, and so he had returned to France, finished up in Paris, and finally met Emma. Now, it irked him that she was returning so soon to England, and did everything he could to make her change her mind, postpone her flight, stay in Paris with him. But Emma was adamant.

"You don't understand. This is something that I have to do."

"It's not even as though the old boy asked you to go. You're just going to get in his way, and interfere with all his amorous adventures."

"I never have before – interfered, I mean." She laughed at his stubborn expression. "Anyway, there's no point my staying, if you're coming back to England next month."

He made a face. "Wish I wasn't. That lousy little theatre at Brookford. I shall get lost in the jungle of fortnightly rep. Besides, I'm not due there for two weeks. Now if you would only stay in Paris . . ."

"No, Christo."

"We could rent a tiny attic. Think of all the fun we could have. Bread and cheese every night for supper and lots of rough red wine."

"No, Christo."

"Paris in the Spring . . . blue skies and blossom and all that rot?"

"It isn't spring yet. It's still winter."

"Were you always so unco-operative?"

But still she would not agree to staying, and in the end

he admitted defeat. "Very well, if I can't persuade you to keep me company, I shall simply behave in a very well-bred and British way, and come and see you on to your plane."

"That would be perfect."

"It's very self-sacrificing of me. I hate saying goodbyes."

Emma agreed with this. Sometimes, it felt as if she had been saying goodbye to people all her life, and the sound of a train moving out of a station, gathering speed, was enough to reduce her to tears. "But this goodbye is different."

"How is it different?" he wanted to know.

"It isn't really goodbye. It's *au revoir*. A stepping stone between two hellos."

"My mother and your father are not going to approve."

"It doesn't matter if they approve or not," said Emma. "We've found each other again. For the moment, that's all that matters."

Above them, the loudspeakers gave a click, began to speak with a feminine voice.

"Ladies and gentlemen. Air France announce the departure of their flight Number 402 for London . . ."

"That's me," said Emma.

They stubbed out their cigarettes, stood up, began to gather in the baggage. Christopher took the canvas grip and the Prisunic paper carrier, and the great bulging basket. Emma slung the raincoat over her shoulder, carried her handbag, the ski-boots and the hat.

Christopher said, "I wish you'd wear the hat. It really would complete your ensemble."

"It would blow off. Not to say look funny."

They went downstairs, crossed the expanse of shining floor towards the barrier where a small queue of passengers was already forming.

"Emma, are you going down to Porthkerris today?"

"Yes, I'll get the first train I can."

"Have you got any money? Pounds, shillings and pence, I mean?"

She had not thought of this. "No. But it doesn't matter. I'll cash a cheque somewhere."

They joined the queue behind a British businessman who carried only his passport and a slim brief-case. Christopher leaned forward.

"Oh, sir, I wonder if you could help."

The man swung round, and found to his surprise Christopher's face only inches from his own. Christopher was wearing his sincere expression. "I am sorry, but we're in rather a predicament. My sister's returning to London, she's not been home for six years, and she has such a lot of hand luggage, and she's only just recovered from a serious operation . . ."

Emma remembered Ben saying that Christopher never told a small lie if he could get away with a bigger one. Looking at him as he came out with this outrageous fabrication, she decided that he had chosen his career wisely. He was a wonderful actor.

The businessman, thus approached, could make no excuse.

"Well, yes, I suppose . . ."

"It's more than kind of you . . ." The canvas grip and the carrier with the bread went under one arm, the basket in the other along with the slim brief-case. Emma felt sorry for him.

"It's just till we get on to the plane . . . it is so kind of you, and you see my brother isn't coming with me . . ."

The queue moved forward, they had reached the barrier.

"Goodbye, darling Emma," said Christopher.

"Goodbye, Christo." They kissed. A brown hand whipped away her passport, riffled the pages, stamped it.

"Goodbye."

They were divided by the barrier, by the formalities of the French government, by other travellers, surging forward.

217

"Goodbye."

She would have liked him to wait and see her safely on to the plane, but even as she waved, flapping the sun hat, he had turned, and was walking away from her, the light shining on his hair, and his hands buried deep in the pockets of his leather coat.

2

In London, in February, it was raining. It had started to rain at seven o'clock in the morning, and it had rained without ceasing ever since. By half past eleven only a handful of people had visited the exhibition, and those enthusiasts, one suspected, had simply come in order to get out of the rain. They shed wet raincoats and dripping umbrellas, and stood around, bemoaning the weather before they had even bought themselves a catalogue.

At eleven-thirty, the man came in to buy a picture. He was an American, staying at the Hilton, and he asked to see Mr Bernstein. Peggy, the receptionist, took the card which he proffered, asked him politely if he would mind waiting for a moment, and then came through to the office to speak to Robert.

"Mr Morrow, there's an American outside by the name of . . ." she glanced at the card. "Lowell Cheeke. He was here a week ago, and Mr Bernstein showed him the Ben Litton of the deer, and thought he was going to buy it, but he went off without making up his mind. Said he wanted to mull it over."

"Have you told him Mr Bernstein's in Edinburgh?"

"Yes, but he can't wait. He's going back to the States the day after tomorrow."

"I'd better see him," said Robert.

He stood up, and while Peggy went to open the door and invite the American in, did a swift spring-clean of his desk, squaring some letters, emptying the ash-tray into the wastepaper basket and shoving the basket under the desk with the toe of his shoe.

"Mr Cheeke," said Peggy, announcing the visitor like a well-trained parlourmaid.

Robert came around the desk to shake hands.

"How do you do, Mr Cheeke? I'm Robert Morrow, Mr Bernstein's partner. I am sorry, I'm afraid he's in Edinburgh today, but perhaps I could help you . . . ?"

Lowell Cheeke was a short, powerful-looking individual in a dacron raincoat and a narrow-brimmed hat. Both of these were very wet, indicating that Mr Cheeke had not arrived in a taxi. He began divesting himself, with Robert's help, from these sodden garments, and revealed an uncrushable navy blue terylene suit and a pin-striped nylon shirt. He wore rimless spectacles and behind them his eyes were cool and grey, and it was impossible to assess any sort of potential either financial or artistic.

"Thank you very much . . ." said Mr Cheeke. "What a terrible morning . . ."

"It doesn't look as though it's going to let up either . . . A cigarette, Mr Cheeke?"

"No, thank you, I no longer smoke." He coughed self-consciously. "My wife made me give it up."

They grinned at this female idiosyncrasy. The grin did not reach Mr Cheeke's eyes. He reached for a chair and settled himself into it, hitching a polished black shoe across his knee. He already looked very much at home.

"I was in here a week ago, Mr Morrow, and Mr Bernstein showed me a painting by Ben Litton – your receptionist probably told you."

"Yes, she did, the deer painting."

"I'd like to see it again if I may. I'm returning to the States the day after tomorrow, and I have to make up my mind."

"But of course . . . !"

The picture waited for Mr Cheeke's decision, resting, where Marcus had left it, against the wall of the office. Robert drew the padded easel into the centre of the room, turned it towards the light, and gently lifted the Ben Litton into position. It was a large picture, an oil of three deer

220

in a forest. Light filtered through the barely-suggested branches, and the artist had used a quantity of white which gave the work an ethereal quality. But its most interesting feature was the fact that it had been painted, not on stretched canvas, but on jute, and the coarser weave of this textile had blurred the artist's brush, like the outlines of an action photograph taken at high speed.

The American swung his chair into position, and turned the cold beam of his spectacles on to the painting. Discreetly, Robert removed himself to the back of the room so as not to obtrude in any way upon Mr Cheeke's own assessment, and his own view of the painting was obscured by the round crew-cut head of his potential customer. Personally, he liked the picture. He was not a fan of Ben Litton's. He thought his work affected and not always easy to understand – a reflection, perhaps, of the artist's own personality – but this swift sylvan impression was a thing to be looked at and lived with and never tired of.

Mr Cheeke got out of his chair, moved up to the painting, examined it minutely, backed away once more, and finished up leaning against the edge of Robert's desk.

"Why do you suppose, Mr Morrow," he said, without turning round, "that Litton was inspired to paint it on burlap?"

The word burlap made Robert want to laugh. He longed to say irreverently, *Probably had an old sack lying around* but Mr Cheeke did not look as though he would appreciate irreverence. Mr Cheeke was here to spend money – always a serious business. Robert decided then that he was buying the Litton as an investment, and he hoped it would pay him off.

He said, "I'm afraid I have no idea, Mr Cheeke, but it does give a most unusual quality to the work."

Mr Cheeke turned his head to send Robert a cold smile over his shoulder.

"You are not as well informed on such aspects as Mr Bernstein."

"No," said Robert. "I'm afraid I'm not."

Mr Cheeke relapsed once more into contemplation. The silence settled and lasted. Robert's own concentration had begun to wander. Small sounds intruded. The ticking of his own wrist-watch. A murmur of voices from the other side of the door. The thunderous rumble, like distant surf, that was Piccadilly traffic.

The American sighed gustily. He began to feel in his pockets, one by one, searching for something. A handkerchief, perhaps. Some change for his taxi ride back to the Hilton. His attention had strayed. Robert had not convinced him that the Litton was worth buying. He was going to make some excuse and go away.

But Mr Cheeke was simply searching for his pen. When he turned round, Robert saw that he already held his cheque book in the other hand.

Their business finally completed, Mr Cheeke relaxed. He became quite human and even took off his glasses and stowed them away in a tooled leather case. He accepted the offer of a drink, and he and Robert sat for a little, with two glasses of sherry, and talked about Marcus Bernstein and Ben Litton, and the two or three paintings which Mr Cheeke had purchased on his last visit to London, with which to form, with his latest acquisition, the nucleus of a small private collection. Robert told him about the retrospective Ben Litton exhibition which was being held in Queenstown, Virginia, in April, and Mr Cheeke made a note of it in his diary, and then they both stood up, and Robert helped Mr Cheeke into his raincoat, and gave him his hat, and they shook hands.

"I've enjoyed meeting you, Mr Morrow, and doing business with you."

"I hope we'll see you next time you come to London."

"Most certainly I shall pay you a visit . . ."

Robert held the door open and they moved out into the Gallery. Bernstein's were showing, that fortnight, a collection of bird and animal paintings by an obscure South American with an unpronounceable name, a man of humble origins, who had somehow, sometime, incredibly,

222

taught himself to paint. Marcus had met him last year in New York, had been instantly impressed by his work, and invited him then and there to stage a London exhibition. Now, his brilliant pictures lined the straw-green walls of the Bernstein Gallery and on this gloomy morning seemed to fill the room with the verdancy and sunshine of a more salubrious climate. The critics had loved him. Since the exhibition opened ten days ago, the Gallery had never once been empty, and within twenty-four hours there was not a picture that had not been sold.

At this moment, however, there were only three people in the Gallery. One of them was Peggy, neat and unobtrusive behind her kidney-shaped desk, busy with the proofs of a new catalogue. Another was a black-hatted man, stooped as a crow, doing a slow round of inspection. The last was a girl, who sat, facing the office door, on the circular buttoned sofa in the middle of the room. She wore a bright green trouser suit and was surrounded by luggage, and appeared to have wandered into Bernstein's under the mistaken impression that it was the waiting-room of a railway station.

Robert, with considerable self-possession, managed to behave as if she was not there. Together he and Mr Cheeke moved across the thick carpet towards the main door, Robert's head bent to catch the last of Mr Cheeke's small talk. The glass doors opened and swung shut behind them, and they were swallowed into the gloom of the dismal morning.

Emma Litton said, "Is that Mr Morrow?"

Peggy looked up. "That's right."

Emma was not used to being ignored. The single swift glance had made her feel uncomfortable. She wished that Marcus was not in Edinburgh. She crossed her legs and then uncrossed them again. From outside came the sound of the departing taxi. In a moment, the glass door opened, once more, and Robert Morrow came back into the Gallery. He did not make any comment, simply put his

223

hands in his pockets, and calmly regarded Emma and her attendant chaos.

She decided that she had never, in her life, seen a man who looked less like an art dealer. His was the sort of face that, groggy and unshaven, is helped from a small sailboat at the end of a single-handed circumnavigation; or, darkly goggled, looks down from the peak of a previously unconquered mountain. But here, in the precious and rarefied atmosphere of the Bernstein galleries, he did not fit at all. He was very tall, wide-shouldered, long-legged; all this emphasised – and yet made incongruous – by his smoothly-tailored dark grey suit. In his youth his hair might have been red, but the years had tamed it to a tawny brown, and in contrast his grey eyes seemed pale as steel. He had high cheek-bones and a long, stubborn jaw, and she was diverted by the discovery that such a collection of features could be so attractive, and then remembered that Ben always averred that the character of a man lies, not in his eyes, where emotions are fleeting and can always be masked, but in the physical shape of his mouth, and this man's mouth was wide, with a jutting lower lip, and looked now as though it was trying, hard, not to laugh.

The silence became uncomfortable. Emma tried a smile. She said "Hello!"

For enlightenment, Robert Morrow turned to Peggy. Peggy was amused. "This young lady wants to see Mr Bernstein."

He said, "I am sorry, he's in Edinburgh."

"Yes, I know, so I've been told. The thing is, I only wanted him to cash me a cheque." He looked more puzzled than ever. Emma decided it was time to explain. "I'm Emma Litton. Ben Litton's my father."

His puzzlement cleared. "But why on earth didn't you say so? I am sorry, I had no idea." He came forward. "How do you do . . ."

Emma stood up. The straw hat, which had been on her knee, floated to the carpet and lay there, adding to the confusion which she had already wrought to the elegantly designed room.

They shook hands. "I . . . there wasn't any reason why you should know who I was. And I'm terribly sorry about all this stuff, but you see I haven't been home for six years, so there's bound to be quite a lot."

"Yes, I can see that."

Emma was embarrassed. "If you can just cash me a cheque, I'll take it all out of your way again. I only want enough to get back to Porthkerris. You see, I forgot to get any sterling when I was in Paris, and I've run out of traveller's cheques."

He frowned. "But how did you get this far? From the airport, I mean?"

"Oh." She had already forgotten. "Oh, there was a kind man on the plane, he helped me to carry my stuff on, and off again at London, and he lent me a pound. I'll have to send it back. I've got his address here . . . somewhere." She felt vaguely in pockets, but could not find the man's card. "Well, anyway, I've got it somewhere." She smiled again, hoping to disarm him.

"And when are you going down to Porthkerris?"

"There's a train at twelve-thirty, I think."

He glanced at his wrist-watch. "You've missed that. When's the next?"

Emma looked blank. Peggy broke into the conversation in her usual polite and practical fashion. "I think there's one at two-thirty, Mr Morrow, but I can check."

"Yes, do that, Peggy. Would the two-thirty be all right for you?"

"Yes, of course. It doesn't matter what time I arrive."

"Is your father expecting you?"

"Well, I wrote him a letter and told him I was coming. But that doesn't mean he's *expecting* me . . ."

He smiled at this. "Yes. Well . . ." He glanced at his watch again. It was twelve-fifteen. Peggy was already on the telephone, inquiring about train times. His eyes returned to the turmoil of suitcases. In a feeble effort to improve the situation, Emma stooped and picked up her sun hat.

He said, "I think the best thing would be to get all this out of the way . . . we'll pile it up in the office, and then . . . Have you had anything to eat?"

"I had some coffee at Le Bourget."

"If you catch the two-thirty, there's time for me to give you lunch before you go."

"Oh, you don't have to bother."

"It's no bother. I have to eat anyway and you might as well eat with me. Come along now."

He picked up two of the suitcases, and led the way into the office. Emma gathered up as much as she could carry, and followed him. The deer painting was still on the stand, and she saw it at once and was diverted.

"That's one of Ben's."

"Yes, I just sold it . . ."

"To the little man in the raincoat? It's good, isn't it?" She continued to admire it, while Robert toted the remainder of her luggage. "Why did he paint it on sacking?"

"You'd better ask him when you see him tonight."

She turned and grinned at him over her shoulder. "Influenced, do you think, by the Japanese school?"

"I wish," said Robert, "I'd thought of saying that to Mr Cheeke. Now, are you ready for lunch?"

He took an enormous black umbrella out of a stand, and stood aside for Emma to go out through the door ahead of him, and they left Peggy to hold the fort, sitting in a gallery restored once more to its usual ordered calm, and they went out into the rain and walked together, beneath the black umbrella, shouldering their way through the lunch-hour jostle of Kent Street, London, W1.

He took her to Marcello's where he normally lunched if he was not expected to entertain some important expense-account customer. Marcello was an Italian who ran a small upstairs restaurant, two streets from Bernstein's, and a table was perpetually reserved for either Marcus

226

or Robert, or both of them, on the odd occasion when they were able to lunch together. It was a modest table, in a quiet corner, but today when Robert and Emma came up the stairs, Marcello took one look at her, with her long tassel of black hair, and her green trouser suit, and suggested that they might prefer to sit in the window.

Robert was amused. "Would you like to sit in the window?" he asked Emma.

"Where do you usually sit?" He indicated the small corner table. "Well, why don't we just sit there?"

Marcello was charmed by her. He led the way to the smaller table, held Emma's chair for her, gave them each an enormous menu written in dubious purple ink and went to fetch two glasses of Tio Pepe while they decided what they were going to eat.

Robert said, "My stock with Marcello will have gone up. I don't think I've ever brought a girl here for lunch."

"Who do you usually bring?"

"Just myself. Or Marcus."

"How is Marcus?" . . . her voice was warm.

"He's well. He'll be sorry to have missed you I know."

"It's my fault. I should have written and told him I was coming. But as you've probably realised, we Littons aren't very good at letting anybody know about anything."

"But you knew Ben had gone back to Porthkerris."

"Yes. Marcus wrote and told me that. And I know all about the retrospective exhibition, because I read an article on it in *Réalités*." She smiled wryly. "Being the daughter of a famous father does have some compensations. Even if he never does anything except send telegrams, you can usually read up what is happening to him in some paper or other."

"When did you last see him?"

"Oh," she shrugged. "Two years ago. I was in Florence, and he stopped off on his way to Japan."

"I didn't know you went through Florence when you went to Japan."

"You do if you happen to have a daughter living there."

She put her elbows on the table, and rested her chin in her hand. "I don't suppose you even knew Ben had a daughter."

"Yes, of course I did."

"Well, I didn't know about you. I mean, I didn't know Marcus had a partner. He was still on his own when Ben went to Texas and I was bundled off to Switzerland."

"It was about that time that I joined Bernstein's."

"I . . . I never knew anyone who looked less like an art dealer. Than you, I mean."

"Perhaps that's just because I'm not an art dealer."

"But . . . you just sold that man Ben's painting."

"No," he corrected her. "I simply accepted the cheque. Marcus had already sold it to him a week ago, but even Mr Cheeke didn't realise that."

"But you must know something about painting."

"Now, I do. One couldn't work with Marcus for all these years and not have some of his boundless knowledge rub off. But I'm basically a businessman, and that's why Marcus asked me to join him."

"But Marcus is the most successful businessman I know."

"Exactly, and so successful that the whole venture of the Gallery grew too big for him to handle on his own."

Emma continued to regard him, a slight frown between her thickly-marked brows.

"Any more questions?"

She was not disconcerted. "Were you always a very close friend of Marcus?"

"What you really mean is, why did he take me into the firm? And the answer is that Marcus is not only my partner, but my brother-in-law as well. He married my older sister."

"You mean Helen Bernstein is your sister?"

"You remember Helen?"

"But of course. And little David. How are they? You'll send them my love, won't you? You know I used to go and stay with them when Ben came up to London and

228

there wasn't anyone to leave me with at Porthkerris. And when I went to Switzerland, it was Marcus and Helen who put me on to the plane, because Ben had already gone to Texas. Will you tell Helen I'm home, and that you gave me lunch?"

"Yes, of course I will."

"Do they still have that little flat in the Brompton Road?"

"No, as a matter of fact, when my father died, they moved in with me. We all live in our old family house, in Kensington."

"You mean you all live together?"

"Together and apart. Marcus and Helen and David live on the first two floors, and my father's old housekeeper lives in the basement, and I roost in the attics."

"Aren't you married?"

Momentarily, he looked put out. "Well, no, I'm not."

"I was sure you'd be married. You have a very married look about you."

"I don't quite know how to take that."

"Oh, it wasn't meant in a derogatory fashion at all. It's really quite a compliment. I only wish Ben had that look about him. It would make life so much easier for all concerned. Especially me."

"Don't you want to go back and live with him?"

"Yes, of course I do, more than anything. But I don't want it to be a failure. I was never very good at coping with Ben, and I don't suppose I'll be any better now."

"Then why are you going?"

"Well . . ." Under Robert Morrow's cool grey regard, it was difficult to be coherent. She picked up a fork and began to make patterns with it on the white damask cloth. "I don't know. You only have one family. If people belong to each other, they should at least be able to live together. I want to have something to remember. When I'm old I want to be able to remember that once, even if it was only for a few weeks on end, my father and I were making some sort of a life together. Does that sound crazy?"

229

"No, it doesn't sound crazy, but it sounds as if you might be disappointed."

"I learned all about being disappointed when I was a little girl. It's a luxury I can well do without. Besides, I only plan to stay until it becomes painfully obvious that we cannot stand each other's company for another hour."

"Or," said Robert gently, "until he prefers some other person's company."

Emma's head came up, her eyes a sudden furious blaze of blue. She was, in that instant, her father at his most unscrupulous, when there was no retort too cruel or too cutting to be made. But her anger provoked no reaction, and after a cold pause, she looked down again, and continued to draw patterns on the tablecloth, and only said, "All right. Until then."

The small tension was broken by the return of Marcello bringing their sherry and ready to take the order. Emma chose a dozen oysters and fried chicken; Robert, more conservatively, a consommé and a steak. Then, taking advantage of the interruption, he tactfully changed the subject.

"Tell me about Paris. How was it looking?"

"Wet. Wet and cold and sunny all at once. Does that convey anything to you?"

"Everything."

"You know Paris?"

"I go over on business. I was there last month."

"On business?"

"No, on my way back from Austria. I had three weeks' splendid ski-ing."

"Where did you go?"

"Obergurgl."

"So that's why you're so brown. That's one of the reasons you don't look like an art dealer."

"Perhaps, when my tan fades, I shall look more authentic and be able to command higher prices. How long did you spend in Paris?"

"Two years. I shall miss it. It's so beautiful, and doubly

230

so now all the buildings have been cleaned. And somehow, at this time of the year, there's that special feeling in Paris. That the winter's nearly over and the sun's just a day or so away and it's going to be spring again . . ."

And buds unfolding, and the scream of gulls, swooping over the chopped brown waters of the Seine. And barges, strung like necklaces, slipping away beneath the bridges, and the smell of the Metro, and garlic, and Gauloises. And being with Christopher.

All at once it became important to talk about him, to speak his name, to reassure herself of his existence. She said, casually, "You never met Hester, did you? My stepmother? At least for eighteen months she was my stepmother."

"I know about her."

"And about Christopher? Her son? Do you know about Christopher? Because, quite by chance, Christopher and I met up again in Paris. Just two days ago. And he came, this very morning, and saw me off at Le Bourget."

"You mean . . . you just bumped into each other . . . ?"

"Yes, we really did . . . in a grocer's shop. It could only happen in Paris."

"What was he doing there?"

"Oh, filling in time. He'd been to St Tropez, but he comes back to England in March to join some repertory theatre or other."

"He's an actor?"

"Yes. Didn't I tell you that? There is just one thing . . . I'm not going to say anything to Ben. You see, Ben never liked Christopher, and I don't think Christopher lost any love over him. To be truthful, I expect they were a little jealous of each other. But there were other things as well, and Ben and Hester didn't exactly part company on the best of terms. I don't want to start off by having a row with Ben about Christopher, so I'm not going to say anything. At least not right away."

"I see."

Emma sighed. "You've got a very stuffy expression

231

on your face. You obviously think I'm being under-hand."

"I don't think anything of the sort. And when you've finished making patterns on the table-cloth, your oysters have arrived."

By the time they had finished lunch and drunk their coffee, and Robert had paid the bill, it was half past one. They got up from the table, and said goodbye to Marcello, and collected the big black umbrella and went downstairs. They walked back to Bernstein's, asked the doorman to get Emma a taxi.

"I'd come with you and put you on to the train, but Peggy has to go out and get herself some lunch."

"I'll be all right."

He took her into the office and unlocked the safe.

"Will twenty pounds be enough?"

She had already forgotten her reason for coming to the Gallery in the first place. "What? Oh, yes, of course . . ." She began to feel for her cheque book, but Robert stopped her.

"Don't bother. Your father has a sort of petty cash account with us. He's always running out of small change when he's in London. We'll put your twenty pounds down to that."

"Well, if you're sure . . ."

"Sure I'm sure. And, Emma, there is one other thing. The man who lent you the pound. Somewhere you have his address. If you find it and give it to me now, I'll see he gets the pound back again."

Emma was amused. Searching for the card, finding it at last, entangled with a French bus ticket and a book of matches, she began to laugh, and when Robert asked her what was so funny, she simply said, "How well you know my father!"

3

It stopped raining at tea-time. There was a subtle lifting of the atmosphere, a freshness in the air. An errant shaft of sunlight even found its way into the Gallery, and by five-thirty, when Robert locked up his office, and went out to join the rush hour torrent of home-going humanity, he found that a small breeze had got up and blown the clouds away, leaving the city to sparkle beneath a pale, pellucid blue sky.

It was somehow more than he could bear to plunge into the subterranean stuffiness of the tube, so he walked as far as Knightsbridge, and then got on a bus and rode the rest of the way home.

His house, in Milton Gardens, was separated from the busy artery of the Kensington High Street by a maze of small streets and squares, a pleasant neighbourhood of miniature, early-Victorian houses, cream-painted, and with bright front doors and small gardens that in summer bloomed with lilac and magnolia. The streets had wide pavements where nannies pushed prams and small, well-dressed children walked to their expensive schools and the local dogs were rigorously exercised. After this, Milton Gardens came as something of a let down. It was a terrace of large and shabby houses, and Number Twenty-three, which was Robert's – the centre house, and crowned with the main pediment of the terrace – quite often looked the shabbiest. It had a black front door, and two dried-up bay trees in tubs, and a brass letter-box that Helen always meant to polish, but quite often forgot. The household cars were parked at the pavement's edge – a big dark-green Alvis coupé which was Robert's, and a dusty red Mini which was Helen's. Marcus did not own a car because he had never found time to learn how to drive.

Robert went up the steps, feeling in his pocket for his latchkey, and let himself in. The hall was large and spacious, a surprisingly wide and shallow staircase curved up to the first floor. Beyond the staircase, the hall continued in a narrow passage, which led to a glassed door, and the garden. This beguiling vista of distant grass and sun-touched chestnut trees gave the immediate impression of being in the country, and was one of the most endearing aspects of the house.

The front door slammed shut behind him. From the kitchen, his sister Helen called his name.

"Robert."

"Hello!"

He chucked his hat on to the hall table, and went in through the door at the right of the hall. In the old days this room, facing out over the street, had been the family dining-room, but when Robert's father had died, and Marcus and Helen and David had moved in, Helen had converted it into a kitchen dining-room, with a scrubbed country table, and a pine dresser, crammed with patterned china and a counter, like a bar, behind which she could work. There were also a great many plants in pots, straggling geraniums, and herbs, and bowls of bulbs. Bunches of onions and marketing baskets hung from hooks, and there were recipe books, and racks of wooden spoons, and the cheerfulness of bright rugs and cushions.

Helen was behind her counter now, in a blue and white butcher's apron, peeling mushrooms. The air was filled with fragrant smells – of baking and lemons, and warm butter and the lightest suggestion of garlic. She was an exceptional cook.

She said, "Marcus called from Edinburgh. He's coming home tonight. Did you know?"

"What time?"

"There's a plane at a quarter past five. He was going to

234

try and get a seat on that. It gets in to the terminal at half past seven."

Robert pulled a high stool up to the counter, and perched on it, like a man sitting at a bar.

"Does he want to be met at the airport?"

"No, he'll get the bus in. I thought one of us would go and pick him up. Are you in or out for dinner tonight?"

"It smells so good, I think I'm in."

She smiled. Facing each other across the counter, the family resemblance between them was very marked. Helen was a big woman, tall and heavy-boned, but when she smiled her face and her eyes lit up like a girl's. Her hair, like Robert's, was reddish, but softened by streaks of grey, and she wore it drawn tightly back into a knot, to reveal a small and unexpectedly neat pair of ears. She was proud of her pretty ears, and always wore ear-rings. She had a whole boxful of them in her dressing-table drawer, and if you didn't know what to give her for a present, you simply bought a pair of ear-rings. This evening they were green, some sort of semi-precious stone, set in a narrow rope of woven gold, and their colour brought out the green lights in her indeterminate, speckled eyes.

She was forty-two, six years older than Robert, and she had been married to Marcus Bernstein for ten years. Before that she had worked for him, as secretary, receptionist, book-keeper, and – on occasions when finances were shaky – as office cleaner as well, and it was as much due to her efforts and faith in Marcus that the Gallery had not merely survived the initial lean patches, but had grown to achieve its present international reputation.

Robert said, "Did Marcus tell you anything . . . about how he got on . . . ?"

"Not much, there wasn't time. But the old Lord of the Glens, whoever he is, has three Raeburns, a Constable and a Turner. So that should give you all something to think about."

"Does he want to sell them?"

"Apparently. He says that at the current price of whisky,

235

he can no longer afford to keep them hanging on the wall. Anyway, we'll hear all about it when Marcus gets back. How about you . . . what have you been doing today . . . ?"

"Nothing much. An American called Lowell Cheeke came in and wrote a cheque for a Ben Litton . . ."

"That's fine . . ."

"And . . ." he watched his sister's face ". . . Emma Litton's home."

Helen had started to slice the mushrooms. Now, swiftly, she looked up and her hands were still.

"Emma. You mean Ben's Emma?"

"Flew back from Paris today. Came into the Gallery to collect enough money to get her back to Porthkerris."

"Did Marcus know she was coming back?"

"No, I don't think so. I don't think she wrote to anyone except her father."

"And of course Ben wouldn't say a word." Helen made an exasperated face. "Sometimes I could just strangle that man."

Robert was amused. "What would you have done if you'd known she was coming?"

"Well, met her at the airport. Given her lunch. Anything."

"If it's any comfort to you, I gave her lunch."

"Well, good for you." She sliced another mushroom, considering this. "What does she look like now?"

"Attractive, in a rather unusual way."

"Unusual," Helen repeated dryly. "Tell me she's unusual and you tell me nothing I don't already know."

Robert picked up a slice of raw mushroom and ate it, experimentally. "Do you know about her mother?"

"Of course I do." Helen rescued her mushrooms, whisking them out of his reach, and taking them to her cooker, where a pan simmered with warm butter. With another deft movement, she spilled the mushrooms into the butter, and there were faint sizzling sounds and a delicious smell. She stood there, moving the mushrooms around with a wooden spatula, her strong features profiled.

236

"Who was she?"

"Oh, a little art student, half Ben's age. She was very pretty."

"Was he married to her?"

"Yes, he did marry her. I think, in his way, he was very fond of her. But she was simply a child."

"Did she leave him?"

"No, she died, having Emma."

"And then, later on, he married someone called Hester."

Helen turned to look at him, her eyes narrowed. "How do you know about that?"

"Emma told me today at lunch."

"Well, I never did! Yes, Hester Ferris. That was years ago."

"But there was a boy. A son. Called Christopher?"

"Don't say he's turned up again."

"Why do you sound so alarmed?"

"You'd sound alarmed, too, if you'd lived through those eighteen months when Ben Litton was married to Hester . . ."

"Tell me."

"Oh, they were murder. For Marcus, for Ben . . . I suppose for Hester, and certainly for me. If Marcus wasn't being roped in to referee some sordid domestic fracas, then he was being showered with ridiculous little bills which Hester said Ben refused to pay. And then, you know how Ben has this phobia about telephones, and Hester put one into her house and Ben tore it out by the roots. And then Ben ran into some sort of mental block and couldn't do any work, and spent all his time in the local pub, and Hester would get hold of Marcus and say that Marcus must come because he was the only person who could do anything with him, and so on, and so on. Marcus aged, visibly, before my eyes. Can you believe that?"

"Yes. But I don't see what it has to do with the boy."

"The boy was one of the bones of contention. Ben couldn't bear him."

"Emma said he was jealous."

"She said that? She was always a perceptive child. I suppose in a way Ben was jealous of Christopher, but Christopher was a devil. He looked like a saint, but his mother spoiled him rotten." She drew her pan of mushrooms away from the heat, and came back to lean her elbows on the counter. "What did Emma say about Christopher?"

"Just that they'd met in Paris."

"What was he doing there?"

"I don't know. I suppose having a holiday. He's an actor. Did you know that?"

"No, but I can well believe it. Was she looking very starry-eyed about him?"

"I should say so, yes. Unless it was the thought of going back to live with her father."

"That's the last thing in the world for her to be starry-eyed about."

"I know that. But when I started to say as much, I near as dammit got my head bitten off."

"Yes, you would. They're as loyal as thieves to each other." She patted his hand. "Don't get involved, Robert; I couldn't bear the strain."

"I'm not involved, simply intrigued."

"Well, for your own peace of mind, take my advice and keep it that way. And while we're on the subject of involvements, Jane Marshall called at lunch-time, and she wants you to ring her up."

"What about, do you know?"

"She didn't say. Just said she'd be in any time after six o'clock. You won't forget, will you?"

"No, I won't forget. But don't you forget, either, that Jane is not an involvement."

"What you're jibbing at, I cannot imagine," said Helen, who had never, with her brother at any rate, bothered to mince words. "She is charming, attractive and efficient."

Robert made no comment on this, and exasperated by his silence, she went on, justifying herself. "You have everything in common, interests, friends, a way of life.

238

Besides, a man of your age should be married. There's nothing so pathetic as an elderly bachelor."

She stopped. There was a pause. Robert said politely, "Have you finished?"

Helen sighed deeply. It was hopeless. She knew, had always known, that no words would provoke Robert into any action that he did not choose to make. He had never been talked into anything in his life. Her outburst had been a waste of breath and she already regretted it.

"Yes, of course I've finished. And I apologise. It's none of my business and I have no right to interfere. It's just that I like Jane, and I want you to be happy. I don't know, Robert. I can't work out what it is you're looking for."

"I don't know either," said Robert. He smiled at his sister, and ran a hand over his head and down the back of his neck, a familiar gesture made when he was either confused or tired. "But I think it has something to do with what exists between you and Marcus."

"Well, I just hope you find it before you drop dead of old age."

He left her to her cooking, collected his hat and the evening paper and a handful of letters, and went upstairs to his own flat. His sitting-room, which looked out over the big garden and the chestnut tree had once been the nursery. It was low-ceilinged, close-carpeted, lined with books, and furnished with as much of his father's stuff as he had been able to get up the staircase. He dropped his hat and the paper and the letters on a chair, and went to the antique bombé cupboard where he kept his drink, and poured himself a whisky and soda. Then he took a cigarette from the box on the coffee table, lit it, and, cradling his glass, went to sit at the desk, to lift the telephone receiver and dial Jane Marshall's number.

She took some time to answer. While he waited, he doodled on the blotting paper with a pencil, and glanced at his watch and decided that he would have a bath, and change before he went to pick Marcus up at the Cromwell Road terminal. And, as a peace offering to Helen, he would take a bottle of wine downstairs and they would have it with their dinner, the three of them, sitting round the scrubbed table in Helen's kitchen and, inevitably, talking shop. He discovered that he was very tired, and the prospect of such an evening was comforting.

The double burr stopped. A cold voice said, "Jane Marshall here."

She always answered the telephone in this manner, and Robert still found it chilling, although he knew the reason for it. At twenty-six, Jane, with a broken marriage and a divorce behind her, had been forced to start earning her own living, and had ended up with a modest interior decorating business which she ran from her own house. Thus, a single telephone number had to do double duty, and she had long since decided it was prudent to treat an incoming call as potential business until it proved to be otherwise. She had explained this to Robert when he complained about her frigid manner.

"You don't understand. It might be a client ringing up. What's he going to think if I sound all sexy and treacle-voiced?"

"You don't need to sound sexy. Just friendly and pleasant. Why don't you try it? You'd be ripping out walls and running up curtains and loose covers before you knew where you were."

"That's what you think. More likely to be fending him off with a curved upholstery needle."

Now he said, "Jane . . . ?"

"Oh, Robert." Her voice was at once its normal self, warm and obviously pleased to hear him. "I am sorry, did Helen give you my message?"

"She asked me to call you."

"It's just that I wondered . . . Look, I've been given two tickets for the ballet on Friday. It's La Fille Mal Gardée and I thought you might like to come. Unless you're going away or something."

He looked down at his own hand, drawing boxes, in perfect perspective, on the blotting pad. He heard Helen's

240

voice. *You have everything in common. Interests, friends, a way of life.*

"Robert?"

"Yes. Sorry. No, I'm not going away. I'd love to come."

"Shall we eat here first?"

"No, we'll go out. I'll book a table."

"I'm glad you can make it." He could tell that she was smiling. "Is Marcus back yet?"

"No, I'm just going to meet him."

"Send him and Helen my love."

"I will."

"See you Friday, then. Goodbye."

"Goodbye, Jane."

After he had replaced the receiver, he did not get up from his desk, but sat there, his chin in his hand, putting the final touches to the last box. When it was finished, he laid down the pencil and reached for his drink, and sat, looking at what he had drawn, and wondered why it should make him think of a long line of suitcases.

Marcus Bernstein came through the glass doors of the terminal building looking, as he always looked, like a refugee or a street musician. His overcoat sagged, his old-fashioned black hat had somehow got turned up in the front, his long, lined face was sallow with tiredness. He carried his bulging brief-case, but his grip had travelled from the airport in the luggage compartment of the bus, and when Robert found him, he was standing, patiently, by the circular conveyor-belt, awaiting its arrival.

He managed to look both humble and dejected, and the casual passer-by would have found it hard to believe that this modest and unassuming man was, in fact, a powerful influence in the art world on both sides of the Atlantic. An Austrian, he had left his native Vienna in 1937, and after the horrors of an alien's war, had burst upon the post-war art world like a bright flame. His obvious knowledge and perception quickly drew attention, and his backing of young artists showed an example which other dealers were quick to follow. But his real impact upon the lay public was made in 1949, when he opened his own gallery in Kent Street with an exhibition of abstracts by Ben Litton. Ben, already famous for his pre-war landscapes and portraits, had been moving for some time towards this new medium, and the 1949 exhibition was the beginning of a working friendship which rode all personal storms and quarrels. It also marked the end of Marcus's initial struggles, and the start of a long, slow haul to success.

"Marcus!"

He gave a small start, and turned and saw Robert coming towards him, and looked surprised, as though he had not expected to be met.

"Hello, Robert. This is very kind of you."

After thirty years in England, his accent was still strongly marked, but Robert no longer noticed it.

"I would have come to the airport, but we weren't sure if you'd get on the plane. Did you have a good flight?"

"It was snowing in Edinburgh."

"It's been raining here all day. Look, there's your bag." He whipped it off the conveyor-belt. "Come on, now . . ."

In the car, waiting for the lights in the Cromwell Road to change, he told Marcus about Mr Lowell Cheeke returning to Bernstein's to buy the Litton of the deer. Marcus acknowledged this with a grunt, giving the impression that he had known all along that the sale was simply a matter of time. The lights went from red to yellow to green and the car moved forward and Robert said, "And Emma Litton is home from Paris. She flew in this morning. Didn't have any sterling, so she came to the gallery to get you to cash her a cheque. I gave her lunch and twenty pounds and sent her on her way."

"On her way to where?"

"Porthkerris, and Ben."

"I suppose he is there."

"She seemed to think he would be. For the time being, at any rate."

"Poor child," said Marcus.

Robert made no answer to this, and they drove home in silence, each busy with his own thoughts. Back at Milton Gardens, Marcus got out of the car, and went up the steps, feeling for his latchkey, but before he could run it to earth, the door was opened by Helen, and Marcus, in his sagging coat and comic's hat, was silhouetted against the hall light.

She said, "Well, how lovely!" and because he was so much smaller than she, stooped to embrace him, and Robert, extracting Marcus's grip from the boot of the Alvis, tried to work out why it was that they never looked ridiculous.

It seemed to have been dark for a long time. But when the London express came to the junction where she had to change for Porthkerris, and Emma got out of the train, she found that it was not really dark at all. The sky was bright with stars, and the night blown through with a buffeting wind that smelt of the sea. When she had unloaded all her luggage, she stood waiting on the platform for the express to pull out, and above her the tattered leaves of a palm tree rattled incongruously in this restless wind.

The train moved on, and she saw the single porter on the opposite platform, occupied, in a leisurely fashion, with a barrow-load of parcels. When at last he noticed her, he set down the handles of his barrow, and called, across the lines, "Want some help, do you?"

"Yes please."

He jumped down on to the tracks and walked across to her side, and somehow gathered all her belongings into his two arms, and then Emma followed him back across the tracks, and he gave her a hand up on to the other platform.

"Where are you going?"

"Porthkerris."

"Taking the train?"

"Yes."

The smaller train waited on the single line branch track that ran round the coast to Porthkerris. Emma appeared to be the only passenger. She thanked the porter and tipped him and collapsed into a seat. Exhaustion consumed her. Never had a day seemed so long. After a little she was joined by a country-woman in a brown hat like a pot. Perhaps she had been shopping, for she carried a bulging, checked leather bag. Minutes passed, the only sound the wind thudding at the closed windows of the train. At last, the engine gave a single whistle and they were off.

It was impossible not to feel excited as familiar landmarks loomed up through the darkness, and were recognised, and then fled past. There were only two small halts before Porthkerris and then, at last, the steep cutting which in spring was quilted in primroses, and then the tunnel, and then the sea was below them, dark as ink, the tide out, the wet sands like satin. Porthkerris was a nest of lights, the curve of the harbour seemed strung with a necklace, and the riding lights of fishing boats were reflected in a maze of shimmering black and gold water.

They had begun to lose speed. The platform slid alongside. The name PORTHKERRIS passed and fell behind. They finally stopped alongside a shiny tin advertisement for boot polish which had been there ever since Emma could remember. Her companion, who had spoken not a word the entire journey, now stood up, opened the door, and stepped sedately out, disappearing into the night. Emma stood in the open door, looking for a porter, but the only visible official was up at the other end of the train, unnecessarily shouting, "Porthkerris! Porthkerris!" She saw him stop to chat to the driver, pushing his cap back off his forehead, and standing with his hands on his hips.

There was an empty barrow by the boot polish advertisement, so she loaded her luggage on to this, and then abandoned it, carrying only a small overnight bag. She began to walk up the platform. In the stationmaster's office, the lights were on, they shone out in warm yellow patches, and a man sat on a bench, reading a newspaper.

Emma walked by him, her footsteps ringing on the stone flags, but as she passed, he put down the newspaper and said her name.

Emma stopped, and slowly turned. He folded the newspaper and stood up, and the light seemed to turn his white hair into a halo.

"I thought you were never going to arrive."

"Hello, Ben," said Emma.

"Is the train late, or did I get the times all wrong?"

"I don't think we're late. Perhaps we were late starting from the junction. We seemed to wait there a long time. How did you know what train I'd be on?"

"I had a telegram from Bernstein's." *Robert Morrow*, thought Emma. *How kind.* Ben glanced at her bag. "You haven't much luggage."

"I have a barrow-load at the other end of the platform."

He turned to vaguely peer in the direction that Emma indicated. "Never mind. We'll fetch it some other time. Come on, let's get back."

"But someone might take it," Emma protested. "Or it might rain. We'd better tell the porter."

The porter had by now finished his social chat with the engine driver. Ben attracted his attention, told him about Emma's luggage. "Put it somewhere, would you, we'll collect it tomorrow." He gave him five shillings. The porter said, "Yes, Mr Litton, don't worry, I'll do that," and went off down the platform whistling, tucking the money in the pocket of his waistcoat.

"Well," said Ben again, "what are we waiting for? Come on, let's get moving."

There was no suggestion of a car or a taxi, they were simply going to walk home. They did this by way of a series of narrow short-cuts, steep flights of stone steps, tiny sloping alleys, always leading downhill, until finally they emerged on to the brightly lighted harbour road.

Emma, trudging beside her father, still carrying the overnight bag which he had not thought to carry for her, took a long sideways look at Ben. It was the first time she had seen him for nearly two years, and she thought that no man changed as little as he. He was no fatter, no thinner. His hair, which had been snow-white as long as Emma could remember, was neither thinning nor receding. His face, weathered by years of working in the sun, in the outdoors, by the sea, was darkly tanned and netted with fine lines which could never be described as anything so prosaic as wrinkles. From him, Emma had inherited her strong cheek-bones, and her square chin, but her pale eyes must have come from her mother, for Ben's were deep-set beneath craggy brows, and of so dark a brown that in certain lights they looked black.

Even his clothes did not seem to have changed. The sagging corduroy jacket, the narrowly cut trousers, the suède shoes of immense elegance and age – they could have belonged to no one else. Tonight his shirt was a faded orange wool, a paisley cotton handkerchief did duty as a necktie. He had never owned a waistcoat.

They came to his pub, the Sliding Tackle, and Emma half expected him to suggest that they should go in for a drink. She did not want a drink, but she was ravenously hungry. She wondered if there was any food in the cottage. She wondered, in fact, if they were actually going to the cottage. It was quite within the bounds of possibility that Ben had been living in his studio, and would expect Emma to shake down there with him.

She said, tentatively, "I don't even know where we're heading for."

"The cottage, of course. Where did you imagine?"

"I didn't know." They were safely past the pub. "I thought perhaps you might have been living at the studio."

"No, I've been staying at the Sliding Tackle. This is the first time I've been to the cottage."

"Oh," said Emma, glumly.

He caught the inflexion in her voice and reassured her. "It's all right. When they knew at the Sliding Tackle that you were turning up there was a positive deputation of eager ladies all wanting to get the place ready for you. In the end Daniel's wife saw to it for me." Daniel was the barman. "She seemed to think that after all these years everything would be covered in blue mould, like Gorgonzola cheese."

"And was it?"

"No, of course it wasn't. A bit cobwebby, perhaps, but perfectly habitable."

"That was kind of her . . . I must thank her."

"Yes, she'd like that."

The cobbled road climbed steeply away from the harbour. Emma's tired legs ached. Suddenly, and with no word of explanation, Ben removed her bag from her grasp.

"What the hell have you got in this?"

"A toothbrush."

"It weighs like pig-iron. When did you leave Paris, Emma?"

"This morning." It seemed a lifetime ago.

"And how did Bernstein's know about you?"

"I had to go there to get some money. Some sterling. I was given twenty pounds out of your petty cash account. I hope you don't mind."

"I don't give a damn."

They passed his studio, shuttered and dark. "Have you started painting yet?" asked Emma.

"Of course I have. That's what I came back for."

"And the work you did in Japan?"

"I left it in America for the exhibition."

Now, the air was full of the sound of surf, of breakers rolling up on to the beach. The big beach. Their beach. And then the uneven roof of their cottage came into view, illuminated by the street lamp which stood by the blue gate. As they approached it, Ben felt in his jacket pocket for the key, and he went ahead of Emma, through the gate and down the steps, unlocking the door, and letting himself in, switching on the lights as he went, so that in a moment every window was blazing.

247

Emma followed more slowly. She saw at once the bright flicker of firelight and the almost inhuman cleanliness and order which Daniel's wife had somehow created out of neglect. Everything shone, was scrubbed and whitewashed and polished to within an inch of its life. Cushions had been plumped and placed with geometrical precision. There were no flowers, but the house was pervaded with a strong smell of carbolic.

Ben sniffed and made a face. "Like a bloody hospital," he said. He had put down Emma's bag, and now disappeared in the direction of the kitchen. Emma crossed the room and stood at the fireplace, warming her hands at the blaze. Cautiously, she was beginning to feel more hopeful. She had been afraid that there would be no welcome. But Ben had met her train and there was a fire in the fireplace. No human being could ask for much more.

Over the mantelshelf was the room's only picture, the painting that Ben had done of Emma when she was six years old. It was the first time in her life – and, it transpired, the last – that she had been the centre of his attention, and, for this reason alone she had borne uncomplaining the long hours of sitting, the boredom, the cramps, and his unleashed fury if she moved. For the picture, she had worn a wreath of marguerite daisies, and each day had brought the recurring pleasure of watching Ben's clever hands make a fresh wreath, and then the pride of having him place it on her head, solemnly, as though he were crowning a queen.

He came back into the room. "She's a good woman, that wife of Daniel's. I shall tell him so. I told her to stock up with a few supplies." Emma turned, and saw that he had found himself a bottle of Haig and a tumbler. "Get me a jug of water, would you, Emma?" A thought occurred to him. "And I suppose another glass, if you want a drink."

"I don't want a drink. But I'm hungry."

"I don't know if she laid in *those* sort of supplies."

"I'll look."

The kitchen, too, had been scoured and scrubbed and swept. She opened the fridge and found eggs and bacon and a bottle of milk, and there was bread in the bin. She took a jug off a hook on the dresser and filled it with cold water, and carried it back into the sitting-room. Ben was wandering about, fiddling with the lamps, trying to find something wrong. He had always hated this house.

She said, "Do you want me to cook you some scrambled eggs?"

"What? Oh, no, I don't want anything. You know, it's odd being back here. I keep feeling Hester's going to appear and tell us to start doing something we don't want to."

Emma thought of Christopher. She said, "Oh, poor Hester."

"Poor nothing. Interfering bitch."

She went back to the kitchen, found a saucepan, a bowl, some butter. From the living-room, she could hear the continued sounds of Ben's restlessness. He opened and shut doors, drew a curtain, kicked a log back on to the fire. Presently, he appeared in the kitchen doorway, a cigarette in one hand, his glass cradled in the other. He watched Emma, stirring eggs. He said, "You've grown up, haven't you?"

"I'm nineteen. Whether I've grown up or not, I really wouldn't know."

"It's odd, your not being a little girl any longer."

"You'll get used to it."

"Yes, I suppose so. How long are you going to stay?"

"Let's say I've made no plans for going away again."

"You mean, you want to live here?"

"For the time being."

"With me?"

Emma glanced at him, over her shoulder. "Would that be so painful?"

"I don't know," said Ben. "I've never tried it."

"That's why I came back. I thought perhaps it was time you did."

"You couldn't, by any chance, be reproaching me?"

"Why should I reproach you?"

"Because I abandoned you, and went off to teach in Texas. Because I never came to see you in Switzerland. Because I wouldn't let you come to Japan."

"If I really minded about those things, I shouldn't have wanted to come back."

"And supposing I decide to go away again?"

"Are you going to go?"

"No." He looked down at his drink. "Not for the moment. At the moment I'm tired. I've come back for a bit of peace." He looked up again. "But I shan't stay here for ever."

"I shan't stay here for ever, either," said Emma. She put the toast on a plate, the egg on the toast, opened a drawer to find a knife and fork.

Ben watched all this with some agitation. "You aren't going to be an efficient little housewife, are you? Another Hester? If so, I shall throw you out."

"I couldn't be efficient if I tried. If it's any comfort to you, I miss trains, burn food, lose money, drop things. I had a sun hat, this morning, in Paris, but by the time I'd got to Porthkerris, it had gone. How could anyone lose a sun hat in this country, in February?"

But he was still not convinced. "Won't you want to be driving around in a car all the time?"

"I don't know how to drive a car."

"And television and telephones and all that rubbish?"

"They've never figured largely in my life."

He laughed then, and Emma wondered if there was something wrong in thinking your own father so attractive.

He said, "You know, I wasn't sure how well this was going to work. But under such favourable circumstances, I can only say I'm glad you came back. Welcome home."

And he raised his glass to Emma and finished his drink, and then went back to the sitting-room to retrieve the bottle and pour himself the other half.

4

The bar of the Sliding Tackle was small and snug, blackly panelled, very old. It boasted only one tiny window, which looked out over the harbour, so that a visitor's first impression, as he came in from the glaring outside light, was one of utter darkness. Later, when his eyes became accustomed to the gloom, other peculiarities became evident, the most prominent being that there were not two parallel lines in the place, for over the centuries the little pub had settled into its foundations, like a deep sleeper in a comfortable bed, and various irregularities, like optical illusions, were apt to make potential customers feel intoxicated before they had even downed their first drink. The flagged floor sank in one direction, displaying a sinister gap between stone and wainscoting. The blackened beam, which formed the framework of the bar itself, sloped in another. And the whitewashed ceiling had such a lethal tilt to it that the landlord had been driven to put up notices saying "Watch That Beam" and "Mind Your Head".

Over the years the Sliding Tackle had remained, stubbornly, itself. Set in the old and unfashionable part of Porthkerris, slap on the harbour, with no space for chi-chi terraces or tea gardens, it had managed to resist the spate of summer tourism which engulfed the rest of the town. It had its regulars, who came to drink, and talk in comfortable, undemanding grunts, and play shove-ha'penny. It had a dart board and a small blackened grate where, winter and summer, a fire always burned. It had Daniel, the barman, and Fred, turnip-faced and squint-eyed, who was employed in the summer cleaning trash from the beaches and hiring out deckchairs, and spent the rest of the year blissfully drinking his takings.

And it had Ben Litton.

"It's a matter of priorities," said Marcus, as he and Robert set forth in the Alvis to run Ben Litton to earth. It was so fine that Robert had put the hood down, and so Marcus wore, with his habitual black overcoat, a tweed cap like a mushroom that looked as though it had been bought for some other person. "Priorities and timing. At mid-day on a Sunday, the first place to look is the Sliding Tackle. And if he isn't there, which I very much doubt, we'll go on to the studio, and then try the cottage."

"Or maybe, on such a wonderful morning, just out and about?"

"I don't think so. This is his drinking time, and as far as that is concerned, he has always been a creature of habit."

Still only March, it was indeed a freak day of unbelievable beauty. The sky was cloudless. The sea, driven obliquely into the curve of the bay by a buffeting north-west wind, lay streaked before them in every shade of blue, from deep indigo to palest turquoise. From the top of the hill, the view stretched to infinity, distant headlands merging into a haze that suggested the full heat of midsummer. And below, down the twisting road, the town dropped steeply, a jumble of narrow cobbled lanes, and whitewashed houses, and bleached, crooked roofs, clustered around the harbour.

Each year, during the three months of summer, Porthkerris became a small hell on earth. Its inadequate streets were jammed with cars, its pavements overflowed with underdressed humanity, its shops spilled over with postcards, sun hats, sand-shoes, shrimping-nets, surfboards and inflatable plastic cushions. On the big beach the tents and the bathing huts went up, and the cafés opened, their terraces crammed with round iron tables, speared by umbrellas. Orange banners flapped in the wind, advertising Raspberry Sticks, and Frozen Chocolate-Coated Clusters and other horrors, and if these were not sustenance enough, there were Cornish splits for sale, and pasties, filled with soggy grey potato.

And around Whitsun, the amusement arcade opened up, with pin-ball machines and juke boxes blaring, and perhaps another cluster of ramshackle but picturesque houses would go down before the bulldozers, to clear the space for yet another car park, and the residents, and the people who loved the town, and the artists, would be horrified witnesses to this rape and say, *It's worse than ever. It is ruined. We can stay no longer*. But each autumn, once the last train had borne away the last peeling-nosed invader, Porthkerris settled back, miraculously, in its normal tempo. The shops put up their shutters. The tents came down, and the beaches were washed clean by the winter storms. The only flags which flew were lines of washing, flapping from house to house, like pastel-coloured bunting, or propped high over the greenswards where the fishermen spread their nets to dry.

And it was then that the old magic reasserted itself, and it became easy to understand why a man like Ben Litton should return time and time again, like a homing pigeon, for refreshment, and the security of familiar things, to be caught up once more in the painter's obsession with colour and light.

The Sliding Tackle was at the far end of the harbour road. Robert drew up outside its crooked porch and killed the engine. It was very warm and quiet. The tide was out, the harbour full of clean sand and seaweed and screaming gulls. Some children, coaxed out by the sunshine, played with buckets and spades, watched over by a couple of knitting grannies in pinafores and hairnets, and a scrawny black cat sat on the cobbles and washed its ears.

Marcus got out of the car. "I'll go and see if he's inside. You wait here."

Robert took a cigarette from the packet on the dashboard and lit it, and watched the cat. Above his head the inn sign creaked in the wind, and a gull came and sat on it and eyed Robert with malevolence, screaming defiance. Two men came down the road, walking with the slow righteous gait of a restful Methodist Sunday. They wore navy blue guernseys and white cloth caps.

"'Morning," they said as they passed.

"Lovely day," said Robert.

"Yes. Lovely."

After a little, Marcus appeared once more. "All right, I've found him."

"What about Emma?"

"He says she's back at the studio. Whitewashing."

"Want me to go and get her?"

"If you would. It's . . ." he glanced at his watch, "twelve-fifteen. Suppose you're back here at one. I said we'd lunch at one-thirty."

"Right. I'll walk. It's not worth taking the car."

"Can you remember the way?"

"Of course." He had been before, twice, to Porthkerris, chasing up Ben Litton for some reason or other when Marcus had not been available to do it for himself. Ben's phobia about telephones and cars and all forms of communication, presented, from time to time, the most hideous complications, and Marcus had long since accepted the fact that it was quicker to make the journey from London to Cornwall and beard the lion in his den than to wait for an answer to the most impassioned of reply-paid telegrams.

He got out of the car and slammed the door shut. "Do you want me to tell her what it's all about, or shall I leave that pleasant task to you?"

Marcus grinned. "You tell her."

Robert pulled off his narrow tweed cap and dropped it on to the driving seat. He said, amiably, "You bastard."

He had had a letter from Emma, a week or two after she passed through London.

> Dear Robert,
> If I call Marcus Marcus, I can't possibly call you Mr Morrow, can I? No, of course I can't,

not possibly. I should have written at once to thank you so very much for the lunch and for letting me have the money, and for letting Ben know that I was on the train. He actually came to meet me at the station. Everything is going wonderfully well, so far we haven't had a row, and Ben is working like a fiend on four canvases at once.

I didn't lose any of my luggage except the sun hat, which I'm sure someone stole.

My love to Marcus. And you.
Emma.

Now, he made his way through the baffling maze of narrow streets and tightly-packed houses that led to the north shore of the town. Here, there was another beach, a bleak and unprotected bay only esteemed for the long surfing rollers which poured in, straight from the Atlantic. Ben Litton's studio faced out over this beach. Once, long ago, it had been a net store and its only access was a cobbled ramp which sloped down from the street to a double, black-tarred door. There was a printed sign with his name, and an immense iron knocker, and Robert took hold of this and banged it, and called "Emma."

There was no reply. He opened the door, and it was immediately almost torn from his hand by a gust of wind which poured, like a torrent of water, through the open window on the far side of the studio. Once the door had slammed shut again behind him, the draught subsided. The studio was empty and bitterly cold. There was no sign of Emma, but a step ladder and whitewash brush and bucket bore witness to her recent occupation. She had finished the whole of one wall, but when he went to touch it with his hand, he found that it was still cold and damp.

From the middle of this wall protruded an ugly old-fashioned stove, empty now and unlit, and beside it a gas ring, a battered kettle, and an upturned orange box containing blue and white striped mugs and a jar of sugar lumps. On the opposite side of the room stood Ben's work table, littered with drawings and papers, tubes of paint, and hundreds of pencils and brushes all contained on sheets of corrugated cardboard. The wall above this table was dark and dirty with age, and smeared with the scrapings of countless palette knives, that had built up, over the years, into a crustaceous shell of colour. At the top of the desk was a narrow level shelf, and on this ranged a selection of *objets trouvés* which at some time or another had caught Ben's eye. A stone from the shore, a fossilised starfish. A blue jug of dried grasses. A postcard reproduction of a Picasso; a piece of bleached driftwood, carved by sea and wind to abstract sculpture. There were photographs, a fan of curling snapshots, arranged in an old silver menu-holder; an invitation to a private view that had taken place six years ago, and, finally, a heavy, old-fashioned pair of binoculars.

At floor level, the walls were stacked with leaning canvases, and in the middle of the room the current work stood, easeled and shrouded with a faded pink cloth. Turned towards the empty stove was a sagging sofa, draped in what looked like the remains of an Arabic rug. There was also an old kitchen table, with its legs cut short, and on this a tin of cigarettes, and an overflowing ash-tray, a pile of *Studios*, and a green glass bowl, full of painted china eggs.

The north wall was all glass, squared off by narrow wooden partitions and designed so that its lower portions would slide aside. Along the foot of this was a long seat, piled with cushions, and from beneath this protruded further ill-assorted flotsam. The spars of a boat, a stack of surfboards, and a crate of empty bottles, and, in the middle, beneath the open window, two iron hooks had been screwed into the floor, and on to those were looped the spliced ends of a rope ladder. This disappeared out of the window, and Robert, going to investigate, saw that it dropped straight down to the sand, twenty feet below.

The beach appeared to be empty. The ebb tide had left

it a sweep of hard clean sand, divided from the sky by a narrow line of frothing white breakers. Further inshore, there was a stratum of rock, crusted with shellfish and seaweed, and over this the seagulls hovered, occasionally pouncing to fight and scream over some prize. Robert sat on the window-seat, and lit himself a cigarette. When he looked up again, a figure had appeared on the horizon, right on the edge of the sea. It wore a long white gown, like an Arab's, and as it walked back towards the studio, appeared to be wrestling with some large and unidentifiable red package.

He remembered the binoculars on Ben's table and went to fetch them. Focused, the figure sprang into relief, and revealed itself as Emma Litton, long hair blowing, dressed in a huge white towelling robe and lugging, with some difficulty, for the wind kept catching it broadside and jerking it out of her grasp, a scarlet surfboard.

"You surely haven't been swimming?"

Emma, struggling with the surfboard, had not seen him at the window. Now, with a hand on the rope ladder, she nearly jumped out of her skin at the sound of his voice. She looked up, trailing the surfboard in the sand, her wet black hair ripped to ribbons by the wind.

"Yes, I have, and what a fright you gave me. How long have you been there?"

"About ten minutes. How are you going to get the surfboard up the ladder?"

"I was wondering that, but now you've turned up all my problems are solved. There's a rope under the seat. If you chuck one end down, I'll tie it on, and you can pull it up for me."

This was duly accomplished. Robert hauled the board through the open window, and hard on its heels came Emma herself, her face and hands and feet crusted with dry sand, and her black lashes spiked like starfish.

She knelt on the window-seat, and laughed at him. "Now, wasn't that the luckiest thing! What would I have done? I could hardly get it over the beach, let alone up the ladder."

Beneath the sand, her face looked blue with cold. He said, "Come along in, and get the window shut . . . that wind's freezing. How could you bear to go and swim? You'll die of pneumonia."

"No I won't." She stepped down on to the floor, and watched him furl the ladder in and slide the window shut. It did not fit properly and there was still a draught like the edge of a knife. "Anyway, I'm used to it. We always used to swim in April when we were children."

"This isn't April. It's March. It's winter. What would your father say?"

"Oh, he wouldn't say anything. And it's such an utterly gorgeous day and I was sick of whitewashing . . . have you seen my lovely clean wall? The only thing is, it makes the rest of the studio look like a slum. Besides, I wasn't swimming, I was surfing, and the breakers kept me warm." And then, without any noticeable change of expression, "Have you come to see Ben? He's down at the Sliding Tackle."

"Yes, I know."

"How do you know?"

"Because I left Marcus there with him."

"Marcus." She raised her strongly-marked eyebrows, considering this. "Has Marcus come too? My goodness, it must be important business!"

She shivered slightly.

Robert said, "Do get some clothes on."

"Oh, I'm all right." She went to take a cigarette from the table, and lit it, and then collapsed on to the old sofa, flat on her back, with her feet propped on the arm.

"Did you get my letter?"

"Yes, I did." With Emma taking up all the sofa, there was nowhere to sit, apart from the window-seat, but on the table, so he eased the pile of magazines on to the floor, and sat there. "I was sorry about your sun hat."

Emma laughed. "But glad about Ben?"

"Of course."

"It's amazing how well it's working. Unbelievable. And he really likes having me around."

"I never imagined for a moment that he wouldn't."

"Oh, don't start being gallant. You know you did. At lunch that day, you were all quizzical eyebrows and scepticism. But you see, it really is the perfect arrangement. Ben doesn't have to pay me to keep house for him, or be bothered with tedious details like days off and insurance stamps, nor does he have to become emotionally involved. He never knew that life could be so simple."

"Have you heard from Christopher?"

Emma turned her head sideways to look at him. "How do you know about Christopher?"

"You told me yourself. At Marcello's. Remember?"

"So I did. No, I haven't heard. But he'll be at Brookford by now, in the thick of rehearsals. He won't have had time to write. Anyway, there's been such a lot to do here, getting the cottage organised and cooking and things. Don't believe people when they say that artists never eat. Ben's inner man is quite insatiable."

"Have you told him you met up with Christopher again?"

"Good heavens, no! And spoil the even tenor of our life? I haven't even mentioned his name. You know, you look much nicer in those tweedy sort of clothes than you do in the London kind. I thought when I first saw you that you weren't the type to spend his days buttoned up in a charcoal grey suit. When did you get down here?"

"We drove yesterday afternoon. We spent last night at The Castle."

Emma made a face. "In with all the potted palms and the cashmere cardigans. Ugh!"

"It's very comfortable."

"The central heating gives me hay fever. I can't even breathe."

She stubbed her half-smoked cigarette out in the over-flowing ash-tray, and swung her feet off the sofa, and

259

stood up and walked away from him, towards the window, untying the sash of the robe as she went. She took a pile of clothes from beneath a cushion, and with her back to him, started to dress. She said, "Why did you and Marcus come together?"

"Marcus doesn't drive."

"There are trains. And that wasn't what I meant."

"No, I know." He picked up one of the painted china eggs and began to play with it as an Arab handles a string of worry beads. "We've come to try and persuade Ben to go back to the United States."

There was a sudden great squall of wind. It broke over the glass window of the studio like a wave, poured, roaring over the roof above them, with the thunder of a passing train. A cluster of gulls rose screaming from the rocks, were flung across the sky. And then, as suddenly, it was over.

Emma said, "Why does he have to go back?"

"This retrospective exhibition."

She dropped the white towelling robe, and stood silhouetted, in jeans, pulling a navy blue sweater over her head.

"But I thought he and Marcus fixed all that when they were in New York in January."

"We thought so too. But you see, this exhibition is being sponsored by a private individual."

"I know," said Emma, turning, and flipping her dark hair free of the turtle-neck of the sweater. "I read all about it in _Réalités_. Mrs Kenneth Ryan. The widow of the wealthy man whose memorial is the Queenstown Museum of Fine Arts. You see how well informed I am. I hope you're impressed."

"And Mrs Kenneth Ryan wants a private view."

"Then why didn't she say so?"

"Because she wasn't in New York. She was sunning it in Nassau or the Bahamas or Palm Beach or somewhere. They never met her. They only saw the curator of the museum."

"And now Mrs Ryan wants Ben Litton to go back, so that she can throw a nice little champagne party and show

260

him off, like a trophy, to all her influential friends. It makes me sick."

"She's done more than decide, Emma. She's come to persuade him."

"You mean come to England?"

"I mean come to England, come to Bernstein's, come to Porthkerris. She drove down with Marcus and me yesterday and at this very moment, is sitting in the bar of The Castle Hotel, drinking very cold martinis and waiting for us all to go and have lunch with her."

"Well, I for one am not going."

"You have to. We're all expected." He glanced at his wrist-watch. "And we're running late. Do hurry up."

"Does Ben know about the private view?"

"He will by now. Marcus will have told him."

She picked up a brown sailcloth smock off the floor and pulled it on over her sweater. As her head came through the neck, she said, "Ben may not want to go."

"You mean you don't want him to go?"

"I mean that he's settled down here again. He's not prowling, he's not restless, he's not even drinking very much. He's working like a young man, and what he's doing is fresh and new and better than ever. Ben is sixty, you know. Looking at him, it's hard to believe, but he's nearly sixty. Isn't it possible that all this hopping about all over the world may no longer stimulate him, but simply wear him out?" She came back to the sofa to sit down, facing Robert, her earnest face on a level with his own. "Please. If he doesn't want to go, don't try to persuade him."

Robert still held the china egg. He looked at it intently as though its convolutions of blue and green would miraculously provide the answer to every problem. Then, with care, he laid it back in the glass dish, along with its fellows.

He said, "You talk as though this were something important, as though he were returning to the States to teach again, as though he weren't going to come back for years. But it isn't. It's simply a party. He needn't be away for more than a few days." She opened her mouth with a fresh protest, but he talked her down. "And you mustn't forget that this exhibition is a great tribute to Ben. A lot of money's been ploughed into it, and a great deal of organisation, and perhaps the least he can do . . ."

Furiously, Emma interrupted. "The least he can do is go and parade up and down like a pet monkey for some fat old American. And what makes it so awful is that he likes that sort of thing. That's what I hate, that he likes it."

"So he likes it. So, if he wants to, he'll go."

She was silenced. She sat, eyes downcast, her mouth sulky as a child's. Robert finished his cigarette and stubbed it out, and stood up and said, more gently, "Now, do come on or we're going to be late. Have you got a coat?"

"No."

"Some shoes then, you must have some shoes."

She felt under the sofa and produced a pair of thong sandals, and stood up, thrusting her bare feet into them. Her feet were still covered in sand, and the sailcloth smock spotted in whitewash.

She said, "I can't go to The Castle, for lunch, looking like this."

"Nonsense." He tried to sound bracing. "You'll give the residents something to talk about. Brighten their dull lives no end."

"Isn't there time to go back to the cottage? I haven't even got a comb."

"There'll be a comb at the hotel."

"But . . ."

"There simply isn't time. We're late already. Now come along . . ."

They went together, out of the studio and up the ramp, and into the sunlit street, and began to walk back towards the harbour. After the chill of the studio the air felt warm, and the brightness of the sea was reflected from the whitewashed walls of houses, and assailed the eye like the glare of snow.

5

Emma did not want to go into the Sliding Tackle.

"I'll wait here. You go and prise them out."

"All right."

He went across the cobbles, and she noticed how he had to duck his tall head to get in under the porch. The door of the pub swung shut behind him. She wandered over to his car and inspected it with interest, because it belonged to him, and should therefore provide further clues to his character, as a shelf of book-titles will do, or the pictures that a man hangs on his walls. But, apart from the fact that it was dark-green, had fog lights and wire wheels and a couple of car-club badges, the Alvis gave little away. Inside on the driving-seat was a tweed cap; cigarettes in the dashboard cupboard, a book of maps. On the back seat, neatly folded, a thick, expensive-looking tartan rug. She decided that he was either trusting, or careless, but also lucky, for the rug had not been stolen.

A gust of wind blew in from the sea and Emma shivered. After the swim and the session in the draughty studio, she still was very cold. Her hands had gone numb, quite colourless, the fingernails tinged with blue. But the metal of the car was warm, and, for comfort, she leaned against it, spreadeagled across the bonnet, with her hands splayed like starfish.

The pub door opened and Robert Morrow emerged once more, ducking cautiously. He was alone.

"Aren't they there?"

"No. We're late, and they got fed up with waiting, so they got a lift back to the hotel." He opened the driving-seat door, picked up his cap and pulled it on, jerked down over his nose, to add yet another sharp angle to his formidable profile. "Come on . . ." And he leaned over and opened the other door, and Emma unpeeled herself from the bonnet, and slid in beside him.

They left the harbour behind and below them, roared up through the town, up the steep narrow streets, up between terraces of prim houses, and the signs which said Bed and Breakfast, and front gardens where sad palm trees tossed their heads in the alien wind. They came out on to the main road, still climbing, turned into the drive of The Castle Hotel; climbed on, between banks of hydrangeas, and landward-leaning elm trees, and at last came out at the very top of the hill, into an open space of tennis courts, and lawns, and a miniature golf course. The hotel had once been a country house, and prided itself on its authentic atmosphere. A white post and chain fence kept cars away from the gravel sweep in front of the hotel, and here, in deckchairs, sat a handful of hardy residents, scarved, gloved and swaddled in rugs, like the passengers of some trans-Atlantic liner. They read books or newspapers, but when the Alvis roared up the drive and drew up with a massive scrunch of gravel, these were lowered, and in some cases, spectacles were removed, and Robert and Emma's progress observed and noted as though they were visitors from another planet.

Robert said, "We're probably the first exciting thing to happen since the manager fell into the swimming-pool."

Once inside the revolving doors, the heat of the place struck like a newly-opened oven. Emma professed to despise such comfort, but today it was blissfully welcome.

She said, "I expect they'll be in the bar. You go, I'll be there in a moment. I must try and get rid of some of this sand."

In the Ladies', she washed her hands and her face, and rubbed the sand off her feet on to the back of her jeans, like a schoolboy trying to polish his shoes. There was a pretentious set of brushes and combs on a beruffled dressing-table, and she used the comb on the snarls of her hair, breaking half the teeth, but reducing the tangled mass into some sort of order. As she turned back for the door, she caught sight of herself in the long mirror. No make-up, faded jeans, whitewash stains. She pulled off the offending smock, and then was infuriated with herself for minding about anything so trivial as her own personal appearance, and pulled it on again. They would think she was a beatnik art student. A model. Ben Litton's mistress. Let them. As Robert Morrow had so rightly said, it would give them something to talk about.

But as she emerged from the Ladies' and went down the long, carpeted hall, she was grateful to see that Robert Morrow had not abandoned her and gone to join the others, as she had told him to, but was waiting for her by the porter's desk, reading a Sunday paper which had been left on a chair. When he saw her coming, he folded the paper and tossed it down again, and gave her a grin of encouragement.

"You've done splendidly," he said.

"I've ruined the hotel comb. Ever so nice it was, too, one of a matching set. You didn't need to wait. I've been before and I know the way . . ."

"Come along, then."

It was a quarter to two, and the busy Sunday lunchtime session was over. Only a few serious drinkers still sat at the bar, cradling their gin and tonics and beginning to look a bit red in the face. Ben Litton, Marcus Bernstein and Mrs Kenneth Ryan were over on the other side of the room, grouped in the bay formed by a huge picture window. Mrs Ryan was on the window-seat, against a backdrop like a travel agent's poster – a shout of blue sea, a sweep of sky, and the green undulations of the miniature golf course. The two men, Ben in his French workman's *bleus*, and Marcus in his dark suit, were talking, turned slightly towards her, so that it was Mrs Ryan who first saw Emma and Robert.

"Well, look who's here . . ." she said.

They turned. Ben remained sitting, but Marcus stood up and came to greet Emma, his arms outstretched, his pleasure at seeing her both genuine and demonstrative and very un-British. He could on occasion be almost embarrassingly Austrian.

"Emma, my darling child. Here you are at last." He put his hands to her shoulders and kissed her, formally, on both cheeks. "What a pleasure to see you again, after this very long time. How long is it? Five years? Six years? What a lot we have to talk about. Come along, and meet Mrs Ryan." He took her hand to lead her over. ". . . But your hand is like a block of ice. What have you been doing?"

"Nothing," said Emma, catching Robert's eyes, and daring him to say more.

"And your bare feet . . . how can you stand it? Mrs Ryan, this is Ben's daughter, Emma, but don't shake hands with her, or you will die of shock."

"I can think of worse ways to die," said Mrs Ryan, and held out her hand. "How do you do?"

They shook hands. "I must say, you are very cold."

On an insane impulse, Emma said, "I was swimming. That's why we're late. And why I'm so untidy. There wasn't time to go back to change."

"Oh, but you don't look untidy, you look charming. Sit down . . . we have time for another drink, don't we? The dining-room isn't going to shut down on us or anything like that. Robert, would you be a darling, and order another round for us. What would you like, Emma?"

"I . . . I don't really want anything." Ben gave a small cough. "Well . . . a glass of sherry."

"And we're all drinking martinis, Robert. If you want one too?" Emma lowered herself carefully on to the chair that Marcus had vacated, aware of her father watching her from the other side of the table.

"I simply don't believe," said Mrs Ryan, "that you really have been swimming."

"Not really. I just went in and out again. There were huge waves."

"But won't you get the most terrible chill? It can't be good for you." She turned to Ben. "You don't approve, surely, of swimming when it's as cold as this? Haven't you got any influence on your daughter?"

Her voice was gay and teasing. Ben made some reply, and she went on, telling him that he should be ashamed of himself . . . that she could see he was an outrageous father . . .

Emma did not listen. She was far too busy looking. For Mrs Ryan was not old and fat, but young and beautiful and very attractive, and from the top of her smoothly-coiffed golden blonde head to the tips of her shining crocodile pumps there was no single detail that did not give active pleasure. Her eyes were enormous and blue as violets, her mouth full and sweet-tempered, and when she smiled, as she did now, revealed two perfect rows of even, white, American teeth. She wore a most becoming suit of rose-pink tweed, the collar and cuffs edged with starched white pique. Diamonds sparkled from her ears, her lapel, her neatly-manicured hands. There was nothing vulgar about her, nothing brash. Even her scent was flower-like.

". . . The fact that she has been away from you for six years is all the more reason for you to take care of her now."

"I don't take care of her . . . she takes care of me . . ."

"Now there is a real man talking . . ." Her soft, southern voice made the words sound like a caress.

Emma's eyes moved round to her father. His attitude was a characteristic one, legs crossed, right elbow resting on his knee, his chin supported by his thumb, a cigarette between his fingers, its smoke rising before his eyes. The eyes were dark as black coffee, deeply shadowed, and they watched Mrs Ryan as though she were a fascinating new specimen, caught between the glass plates of a laboratory slide.

"Emma, your drink."

It was Marcus. She dragged her eyes from Ben and Mrs Ryan and turned to him in relief.

"Oh, thank you . . ."

He sat beside her. "Robert has told you about the private view?"

267

"Yes, he told me."

"Are you angry with us?"

"No." And this was true. You could not be angry with such an honest man who came so instantly to the point.

"But you don't want him to go?"

"Did Robert say that?"

"No, he didn't say. But I know you very well. And I know how long you've waited to be with Ben. But it's only for a little while."

"Yes." She looked down at her drink. "He really is going, then?"

"Yes, he really is going. But not until the end of the month."

"I see."

Marcus said, gently, ". . . if you wanted to go with him . . ."

"No. No, I don't want to go to America."

"Do you mind being alone?"

"No. It doesn't bother me. And, as you say, it won't be for long."

"You could come to London, and stay with Helen and myself. You could have David's room."

"Where would David sleep?"

"It is so sad, he is away at boarding school. It broke my heart, but I am now an Englishman and my son was torn from me at eight years old. Come and stay, Emma. In London, there is a lot to see. The Tate Gallery has been re-hung, and it is a masterpiece . . ."

Despite herself Emma began to smile.

"What are you laughing about, you horrible child?"

"I'm laughing at your shamelessness. You take my father away with one hand, and offer me the Tate Gallery with the other. And," she added, dropping her voice, "nobody bothered to tell me that Mrs Kenneth Ryan was the Beauty Queen of Southern Virginia."

"We didn't know," said Marcus. "We had never seen her. She flew to England on an impulse, she walked into the Bernstein Galleries the day before yesterday and said she wanted to see Ben Litton, and that was the first time I had ever set eyes on her."

"Well, she's certainly worth setting eyes on."

"Yes," said Marcus. He looked across at Mrs Ryan with his sad, hound's eyes. He looked at Ben. He looked back into his martini, and touched the sliver of lemon peel with his forefinger. "Yes," he said again.

Their arrival, late, in the dining-room caused something of a stir. The best table had been reserved for them, the round one in the window, and it was necessary to cross the length of the floor to get there. Mrs Ryan led the way, aware of adulation from every eye in the room, and apparently unconcerned. She was quite used to it. Behind her came Marcus, shabby, but oddly distinguished and obviously interesting. Then Robert and Emma, and finally Ben. Ben fell behind to stub out his cigarette and made what amounted to a star entrance, stopping for a moment in the doorway to speak to the head waiter, so that by the time he did move forward into the room, he was the sole centre of attraction.

Ben Litton . . . There's Ben Litton, the whispers went up, as he walked between the tables, magnificent in his blue French overalls, the red and white scarf knotted at his throat, his white hair thick as a young man's, a quiff like a comma falling across his forehead.

Ben Litton . . . you know, the painter.

It was exciting. Everybody knew that Ben Litton had a studio in Porthkerris, but if you were determined to actually see him, you had to make your way down to the town, and find a fisherman's pub called the Sliding Tackle, and there sit, in the stuffy gloom, making a glass of warm beer last as long as possible, and wait for him to come. It was rather like a strange form of bird-watching.

But today, Ben Litton had abandoned his usual haunts, and was here, at The Castle Hotel, about to eat Sunday lunch, like any other ordinary human being. The mountain had come to Mahomet. An elderly lady stared openly at him through her lorgnette, and a visiting Texan was heard mourning the fact that he had left his flash camera in the bedroom.

Emma caught Robert Morrow's eye, and just managed to suppress a snort of laughter.

Ben reached the table at last, settled himself in the place of honour at Mrs Ryan's right, picked up a menu, and suggested, simply by raising a finger, that the wine waiter should be fetched. Gradually, the excitement in the dining-room died down, but it was obvious that for the rest of the meal they would be the object of all attention.

Emma said to Robert, "I know I shouldn't approve – I should be ashamed of such blatant exhibitionism, but somehow, he gets away with it every time."

"Well, at least it's made you laugh, and you've stopped looking all pinched and nervous."

"You might have told me Mrs Ryan was young and beautiful."

"She's certainly beautiful. But I don't think she's as young as she appears. Well-preserved more like it."

"That's the sort of bitchy remark a woman would make."

"I'm sorry. It was meant with the best will in the world."

"You still should have told me."

"You never asked."

"No, but I made some remark about fat old Americans, and even then you didn't put me right."

"Perhaps I didn't realise that it was so important to you."

"A beautiful woman and Ben Litton, and you didn't realise it was important? It's more than that; it's lethal. One thing, you and Marcus won't have to do any persuading. Ben is going to America. One sweep of those lashes, and he was already mid-Atlantic."

"I don't think you're being entirely fair. The longest lashes in the world wouldn't sweep him into anything he didn't want to do."

"No, but he could never resist a challenge."

Her voice was cold.

Robert said, "Emma."

She turned to look at him. "What?"

"Your resentment is showing." He measured between his forefinger and thumb. "Just the very smallest amount."

"Yes . . . well . . ." She decided to change the subject. "When do you go back to London?"

"This very afternoon." He glanced at his watch. "We're running late, as it is. We'll need to leave, as soon as I can coax Little Miss Millions away."

But Mrs Ryan was not to be hurried. The luncheon wore on through four courses, through wine and brandy and coffee, served in the now-empty dining-room, because she did not want to move from their table. At last, taking advantage of a pause in the conversation, Robert cleared his throat, and said, "Marcus, I am sorry to interrupt, but I really think we should make a start, we've got a three hundred mile drive."

Mrs Ryan seemed astonished. "But whatever time is it?"

"Nearly four o'clock."

She laughed. "Already! It's like being in Spain. I once went to a lunch party in Spain, and we didn't get up from the table until half-past seven in the evening. Why does time have to go so fast when you're really enjoying yourself?"

"Cause and effect," said Ben.

Across the table, she smiled at Robert. "You don't want to leave right away, do you?"

"Well . . . as soon as possible."

"But I wanted to see the studio. I can't come all the way across the Atlantic, and all the way down to Porthkerris and not see Ben's studio. Couldn't we drop in just for a moment, on the way back to London?"

This light-hearted suggestion was received in silence. Robert and Marcus both looked momentarily confused; Robert, because he did not want to put off any more time, and Marcus, because he knew that of all things, Ben hated to have his studio inspected. Emma also experienced

271

a sinking of the heart. The studio was in chaos – not Ben's chaos which was of no account, but her own chaos. She thought of the step ladder, and the whitewash bucket, the wet towelling coat, and the bathing-suit which she had left abandoned on the floor, the brimming ashtrays, and the sagging sofa, and the sand everywhere. She looked at Ben, praying for him to refuse. They all looked at Ben, waiting like puppets, to see which way he would jerk the strings.

But for once he did not let them down.

"My dear Mrs Ryan, despite the pleasure it would give me to show you my studio, I think I should point out that it is not on the way to London."

They all looked at her, to see how she would take this. But she merely pouted, and they laughed in relief, and Mrs Ryan laughed too, with good grace.

"All right, I know when I'm beaten." She began to collect her bag and gloves. "But there is just one thing. You've all been so sweet to me, and I don't want to feel like a stranger any longer. My name's Melissa. Do you-all think you could manage to call me that?"

And later, when the men were loading the car, she got Emma to herself.

"You've been specially sweet," she said. "Marcus told me that you'd come back from Paris to be with your father, and here I am, taking him away from you again."

Emma, who knew that she had not been specially sweet, felt guilty. "The exhibition has to come first . . ."

"I'll take good care of him," Melissa Ryan promised.

Yes, thought Emma, *I'm sure you will*. And yet, despite herself, she liked the American woman. And there was something about the set of her chin and the clarity of her violet-blue eyes that made Emma wonder if perhaps, this time, Ben would not enjoy his usual walkover. And if things did not go his way from the very beginning he was apt to become discouraged. She smiled at Mrs Ryan. She said, "I don't suppose it'll be long before he's home again." And she picked up the honey-coloured mink which lay across the back of a chair and helped Mrs Ryan into it. They went out of the hotel together. It was colder now. The warmth of the sun had left the sky and a chill, like frost, swept up from the sea. Robert had put up the hood of the Alvis, and Melissa, wrapped in the mink, went to say goodbye to Ben.

"But it isn't goodbye," he told her, holding her hand, and gazing darkly down at her. "It's au revoir."

"Of course. And if you let me know when your flight arrives at Kennedy Airport, I'll arrange to have you met."

Marcus said, "I will do that. Ben has never in living memory let anybody know anything, least of all his time of arrival. Goodbye, Emma, my darling child, and don't forget that I have invited you to stay with us for as long as you like when Ben is in America."

"Bless you, Marcus. You never know. I might come."

They kissed. He got into the back of the car, and Melissa Ryan into the front, her elegant legs wrapped in Robert's car rug. Ben shut the door, then stooped to continue his conversation with her through the open window.

"Emma." It was Robert.

She turned. "Oh, goodbye, Robert."

To her surprise he took off his cap and bent to kiss her. "You'll be all right?"

She was touched. "Yes, of course."

"If you want anything, give me a ring, at Bernstein's."

"What could I want?"

"I don't know. Just a thought. Goodbye, Emma."

They stood, she and Ben, watching until the car had disappeared down the tunnel of trees. After it had gone, neither of them spoke, and then Ben cleared his throat, and said, portentously, as though he were giving a lecture, "What an interesting head that young man has. The narrow skull and the strong facial bones. I should like to see him with a beard. He would make a good saint – or perhaps, a sinner. Do you like him, Emma?"

She shrugged. "I suppose so. I scarcely know him."

He turned to move off, and caught sight of the small

gathering of hotel guests, who, setting off for walks, or coming in from golf, or aimlessly snatching at the smallest straw of entertainment, had stayed to witness Melissa's departure. As Ben fixed them with his dark eyes, they became discomfited, turned away and moved on as though they had been caught doing something shameful.

He shook his head in amazement. "I think," he said, "I have had enough of being stared at as though I were a two-headed chimpanzee. Come along, we'll go home."

6

Ben Litton left for America at the end of March, travelling from Porthkerris to London via British Railways and from London to New York on a BOAC Boeing. At the last moment Marcus Bernstein decided to go with him, and the evening papers carried photographs of their departure, Ben with his white hair a coxcomb in the breeze, and Marcus almost obliterated by his black hat. Both looked faintly self-conscious.

It was from Marcus that Emma received the airmail bundle of American newspapers, carrying in their columns the comments of every worthwhile art critic in the country. They were unanimous in their praise of the whole concept of the Queenstown Museum of Fine Arts, acclaiming it as a perfect example of architecture, lighting, and immaculate display. And the Ben Litton exhibition was on no account to be missed. Never again would the artist's work be available to the public in its entirety, and the two or three pre-war portraits, lent by private individuals, were alone worth a visit, if only to see how a single man could be painter, psychiatrist and absolving priest at one and the same time.

"Ben Litton uses his brush as a surgeon's scalpel, first laying bare the hidden sickness, then treating it with the utmost compassion."

The word compassion was used again for his war-time drawings, the shelter groups, the fire-fighters, and a handful of sketches salvaged from the time of the Allied advance in Italy. And of his post-war work they said, "Other painters abstract from nature. Litton abstracts from imagination, and an imagination so lively that it

275

is difficult to believe that these vital paintings were not turned out by a man of half his age."

Emma read these and allowed herself to feel proud. The private view took place on the 3rd of April, and by the tenth there was still no word of Ben's return, but she filled in the days with time-consuming household chores, and eventually moved back to the studio to finish the whitewashing. This took little mental concentration, and her mind wandered aimlessly into the future, indulging in the sort of day dreams that, a month ago, she would never have allowed herself. But now, she truly felt that things had changed. When she had gone to the station to put Ben on to the London train, he had kissed her goodbye – absentmindedly to be sure, as though he had forgotten for the moment who she was, but still, he had kissed her and that surely marked a milestone. And when he did eventually tear himself away from the adulation of the American public and return to Porthkerris, she saw herself meeting the train, cool and composed, the perfect social secretary. And, maybe the next time he took off for some far-flung, but obviously colourful, corner of the globe, he would take Emma with him, and she would book flights, and see that he caught connections, and keep Marcus informed as to his movements.

And then, a day or two later, there was a letter from Marcus, postmarked London. She opened it hopefully, thinking that it would tell her that Ben was coming back, but, in fact, it was simply to say that Marcus had returned to London alone, and Ben had stayed in Queenstown.

> The Ryan Memorial Museum is fascinating, and if I had been able, I should have stayed as well. It embraces all forms of art, has a small theatre and concert hall and a collection of Russian jewellery which has to be seen to be believed. Queenstown itself is charming, full of red brick Georgian houses, set in green lawns and veiled in flowering dogwood . . . they all

276

look as though they have been there since the days of William and Mary, but in fact, I saw one in the process of being built, the mature lawn being laid in turves, and the dogwoods planted, fully grown. What it is to have a warm and temperate climate, to be sure.

Redlands (the Ryan homestead) is a great white house with a pillared "porch" where Ben sits in a long chair and gets brought mint juleps by a coloured butler called Henry. Henry comes to work each day in a lilac Chevrolet, and hopes, in the not-too-distant future, to become a lawyer. He is a bright young man and should achieve his ambition. There are also a couple of tennis courts – a paddock (corral) full of spirited horses, and the inevitable swimming-pool. Ben, as you can imagine, neither rides nor plays tennis, but spends long hours, when he isn't adding a little local colour to the retrospective exhibition, floating around the pool on a rubber mattress. I am sorry that he has stayed away from you for so long, but honestly believe that he needs this rest. He has been working hard for the last few years, and a little harmless relaxation will do him no harm. If you are lonely, our invitation still stands. Come and stay with us. We should so love to have you.

Always your loving Marcus.

The whitewashing was finished, the studio floor scrubbed. Ben's drawings had been stacked and stowed in numbered folios. His pens and brushes graded and various tubes of solidified oil paint, used once, and then abandoned, had been discreetly shovelled into the dustbin.

There was nothing left to do.

He had been gone two weeks when the postcard came from Christopher. Emma was in the kitchen of the cottage, making coffee and squeezing orange juice, still wrapped in her dressing-gown and with her hair tied back in a pony tail, when the postman, who was a cheeky young man in an open-necked shirt, put his head round the door and said, "Well, and how are you this morning, my handsome?"

"Splendid, thank you," said Emma, who had been putting up with this camaraderie ever since she returned from Paris.

He flapped a bundle of letters at her. "All for your old man. But . . . here . . . is a postcard for you." He inspected the picture before Emma snatched it from him. "So vulgar those things are; I don't know how decent folks can buy them."

"No, you wouldn't," said Emma rudely, scarcely glancing at the bulging lady in the bikini before turning the card over to see who it was from. The postmark was Brookford.

> Emma darling, when are you coming to see me? I can't come and see you, because we're up to the ears in rehearsals for *Dead on Time*. Phone number Brookford 678, best about ten in the morning before we start work. Producer nice chap, stage manager bloody, all girls have spots, and not as pretty as you. Love Love Love Christo.

The nearest phone box was a mile away, so Emma went down the street to the ramshackle grocer's where she bought cigarettes and tins of food and soap flakes, and used the telephone there.

It was an old-fashioned one, in two separate bits, and with a hook that you jiggled to get the operator. She sat on a beer crate and waited while the call was put through and a grey and white cat, fat as a cushion, came and lay exhaustedly across her knee.

The phone was answered at last by a cross-sounding female.

"Brookfield Theatre."

"Can I speak to Christopher Ferris?"

"I don't know if he's in yet."

"Could you go and look?"

"Oh, I suppose so. Who shall I say it is?"

"Say Emma."

The cross female departed. Various voices could be heard, chattering. A man in the distance shouted, "*Here I said, you clot, not there.*" And then there were footsteps and a voice, and it was Christo.

"Emma."

"You are there. They didn't know if you were in."

"Yes, of course I'm in . . . we're rehearsing in five minutes . . . Did you get my postcard?"

"This morning."

"Did Ben read it?" (He obviously hoped that he had.)

"Ben isn't here. He's in America. I thought you'd know."

"How should I know?"

"It's been in all the papers."

"Actors don't read papers and if they do it's always the *Stage*. But if the old boy's in America, why didn't you let me know and come and stay with me?"

"For a hundred reasons."

"Name two."

"Well, he only meant to go for a week at the most; and I didn't know where you were."

"I told you. Brookford."

"I don't even know where Brookford is."

"Thirty-five minutes from London, trains run every half hour. Look, do come. Come and stay. I've been moved into a sinister basement flat. It smells of dry rot and old cats, but it's ever so cosy."

"Christo, I can't. I must be here. Ben'll be home any day now, and . . ."

"Did you tell him about meeting me again?"

"No, I didn't."

"Why not?"

"The subject never came up."

"You mean you were scared?"

"I was nothing of the sort. It was simply – irrelevant . . ."

"Nobody's ever called me irrelevant and got away with it. Oh, do come, ducky. My little basement nest needs the touch of a woman's hand. You know, scrubbing and all that jazz."

"I can't come till Ben's home. Then I'll try."

"It'll be too late by then. I'll have got it clean. Please. I'll get you a free ticket for the show. Or two tickets and you can bring a friend. Or three tickets and you can bring them all."

His voice dissolved into amusement. He had always laughed at his own jokes.

"Oh, very funny," said Emma, but she was laughing too.

"You're just playing hard to get. You wouldn't stay with me in Paris, and you won't come and keep house in the wilds of Surrey. What have I got to do to win your heart?"

"You won it years ago and you've had it ever since. Truthfully, I'm longing to see you. But I can't come. I simply can't come till Ben gets back."

Christo said a rude word.

The telephone went pip-pip-pip.

"That's it, then," said Christo. "Let me know when you make up your mind. Goodbye."

"Goodbye, Christo." But he had already hung up. Smiling foolishly, going back over every word he had said, she put the receiver back on to the hook. The cat on her knee purred momentously, and Emma realised it was about to produce a family at any moment. An old man came into the shop to buy two ounces of plug, and when he had gone Emma picked up the cat and placed her gently on the floor, and felt in her pocket for loose change to pay for the call.

"When are the kittens due?" she asked.

The old woman behind the counter was called Gertie, and wore, indoors and out, an enormous brown beret pulled down over her eyebrows.

"Only time can tell, my dear." She put Emma's money into her till, which was an old tin box, and gave her her change. "Only time can tell."

"Thank you for letting me use your phone."

"It's a pleasure," said Gertie, who always listened, shamelessly, and relayed every word she heard.

In March it had been like midsummer. Now, in May, it was cold as November, and pouring with rain. He had never imagined Porthkerris in the rain; had always pictured it painted in the bright blues of summer, gay with the white wings of gulls and yachts, everything dazzling in a glaring sunlight. But now squalls, borne in on a cutting east wind, were flung against the windows of the hotel, sounding like fistfuls of pebbles. The gusts rattled the casements and then whined away beneath doors, down chimneys, blowing curtains, chilly and inescapable.

It was a Saturday, and Robert, flat on his bed, had been asleep. He looked at his watch and saw that it was five to three, so he reached for a cigarette, and lit it, and lay, watching the leaden sky race across the window, and waiting for the telephone to ring.

It did, at precisely three o'clock. He lifted the receiver.

"Three o'clock, sir," said the hall porter.

"Thank you very much."

"Sure you're awake, sir?"

"Yes. I'm awake."

He finished the cigarette, and stubbed it out, and got up, pulling on his white towel robe and heading for the bathroom for a hot shower. He hated sleeping in the afternoon, hated waking with the feeling that his teeth were itching, and that he was on the verge of a splitting headache, but after driving all through the night from London it had been impossible to stay awake. He had had an early lunch, and left word with the porter to call him. But the wind, blown up while he slept, had wakened him first.

He dressed, put on a clean shirt, tied his tie, picked up

281

the jacket of his suit, and then changed his mind, and pulled on a polo-necked sweater instead. He combed his hair, slid his belongings from the top of the dressing-table into his trouser pockets, took a raincoat from the back of the door and went downstairs.

The lounge was thick with the silence of mid-afternoon. Elderly residents snoozed, snoring lightly in dry heated air. Frustrated golfers watched the rain, rattling loose change in the pockets of their tweed knickerbockers, wondering if the weather was going to let up, if there would be time for nine holes before it got dark.

The hall porter took Robert's key and hung it up.

"Going out now, sir?"

"Yes, and perhaps you can help me. I want to get to the Society of Artists Gallery. I believe it's an old chapel, converted. Have you any idea where it is?"

"That's down the old part of the town. Know your way round, do you?"

"I know the Sliding Tackle," said Robert, and the hall porter grinned. He liked a man who used pubs as landmarks.

"Well . . . say you're going to the Sliding Tackle, but turn up the street before you get there. Up, away from the harbour. Narrow little road, very steep, and there's a square at the head of it. Gallery's on the other side of the square. You can't miss it. Got great posters up outside . . . not that any living soul can make head nor tail of them . . ."

"Well, we'll have to see. Thank you very much."

"You're welcome." The porter swung the revolving door, and Robert was ejected into the bitter cold. Rain hammered at his unprotected head, he hunched himself into his raincoat, and picked his way across the gravel, trying to avoid the worst of the puddles. Inside, his car smelt damp and musty, an alien smell over the usual one of leather and cigarettes. He switched on the engine and the heater began to hum. A leaf was stuck in the blade of the windscreen-wiper, but when he turned it

282

on, the leaf was dislodged and torn from the wet glass by the wind.

He drove down to the town, and it was all deserted, abandoned, the inhabitants in a state of siege from the weather. Only a drenched policeman stood at point duty at the foot of the hill, and an old lady fought with an umbrella. The narrow streets acted as chimneys for the wind, which funnelled up them, cold and ferocious as a torrent of water, and when he came out on to the harbour road, he saw that the tide was full, and the harbour itself grey and choppy, fleeced with white-capped waves.

He found the street the porter had described. It climbed away from the harbour between crowded cottages, the cobbles wet and shining like the scales of a newly-caught fish. It crested the hill, and opened out into a picturesque square, and he saw the old chapel, a solid, gloomy building, quite at odds with the poster at its door.

PORTHKERRIS SOCIETY OF ARTISTS
SPRING EXHIBITION
Admission 5/-

Beneath this was a strange motif in purple – the suggestion of a staring eye, a six-fingered hand. Robert decided that he could see the hall porter's point of view.

He parked the car, and went up the streaming steps, and through the door, and was immediately assailed by the smell of a paraffin stove. He saw that the old chapel had been whitewashed, the walls soared to high private windows, and liberally hung with every sort and size of painting.

Just inside the door, her knees covered with a rug, sat a lady in a felt hat. On one side of her was a wooden table, with catalogues and a bowl for money, on the other was the paraffin heater, at which she was trying to warm a pair of purple-knuckled hands.

"Oh, close the door, close the door," she implored as Robert blew in on a gust of wind. He leaned against the door, shutting it, and feeling in his trouser pocket for two half-crowns. "What a freezing day," she went on, "and this is meant to be summer. You're my first visitor this afternoon. You are a visitor, aren't you? I haven't seen your face around the place."

"No, I haven't been here before."

"We've got a most interesting collection, you'll have a catalogue, of course. Another half-crown, please. But I think you'll agree, well worth it."

"Thank you," said Robert, feebly.

He took the catalogue, decorated with the same purple hand-and-eye motif as the poster outside, and opened it casually, running his eye down the list of artists for the name he wanted. ". . . er . . . any particular artist?" The woman at the desk managed to sound diffident, but she had an inquisitive gleam in her eye.

"No . . . not really."

"Just generally interested, I expect. Are you staying in Porthkerris?"

"Yes . . ." he began to move away from her. "For the moment I am."

He took it slowly, pacing down the long room, feigning interest in every picture. He had found the name, Pat Farnaby. Number 24. The Journey, by Pat Farnaby. He stayed a long time at number 23, then moved on again.

The colour pounced at him. There was a sensation of great height, a dizzying sensation, like vertigo. And yet with it, a sense of elation, as though he were above the clouds, caught, suspended, between the blue and the white.

You must go, Marcus had said. *I want you to form an opinion of your own. You can't remain the man who keeps the books for the rest of your life. Besides, I'd like to see your reaction.*

And this was it. This pure, high note of simple colour.

After a little, he went back to the persistent lady. He was aware that all the time she had been watching him.

284

Now, he thought, she was bright-eyed as a greedy robin, waiting for a bread crumb.

"Is that Pat Farnaby's only exhibit?"

"I'm afraid so. It was all we could persuade him to let us have."

"He lives around here, doesn't he?"

"Oh, yes. Out at Gollan."

"Gollan?"

"That's about six miles away, out on the moor road. It's a farm."

"You mean he's a farmer?"

"Oh, no." She laughed. *Merrily*, thought Robert, as though she were following the directions in an old-fashioned play. "He lives in the loft over the barn. Here," she drew a scrap of paper towards her, wrote an address. "If you want to see him, I'm sure you'll find him here."

He took the paper. "Thank you very much." He started for the door.

"But don't you want to look at the rest of our exhibition?"

"Another time, perhaps."

"It's so *interesting*." She sounded as though her heart would break if he did not look at some more pictures.

"Yes, I'm sure. But another time." It was at this moment that he thought of Emma Litton. His hand on the doorknob, he turned back. "By the way, if I wanted to find Ben Litton's house . . . is it near here? The house, I mean, not the studio?"

"Well, of course, it's just round the corner. About a hundred yards down the road. It's got a blue gate. You can't miss it. But you do know that Mr Litton's not at home?"

"Yes, I know."

"He's in America."

"Yes, I know that, too."

It was still streaming with rain. He got back into the car,

285

and started the engine, and nosed it forward down a street as narrow as a burrow. At the blue gate he left it, parked, completely filling the road, and went through the gate, and down a flight of steps which led to a flagged courtyard where tubs stood, filled with drowned-looking plants, and a painted wooden seat disintegrating slowly in the damp. The house itself was long and low, single-storied, but the uneven roofs and ill-matched chimney pots indicated that it had once been two small cottages, or even three. The front door was painted blue to match the gate, and had a copper dolphin as a knocker.

Robert knocked. From above a stream of water poured down upon him from a faulty gutter. He stepped back and looked up to see where it came from, and as he did so, the door was opened.

He said, "Good afternoon. Your gutter's leaking."

"Where on *earth* have you sprung from?"

"London. You should get it mended or it'll rust away."

"Have you come all the way from London to tell me that?"

"No, of course I haven't. Can I come in?"

"Of course . . ." She stood back, holding the door open for him. "But you are the most disconcerting man. You keep just turning up, with no notice at all."

"How can we give you notice if you aren't on the telephone? And there wasn't time to write a letter."

"Is it about Ben?"

Robert went into the house, ducking his head beneath the lintel of the door, unbuttoning his wet raincoat.

"No. Should it be?"

"I thought he might be home."

"As far as I know he's still basking in that balmy Virginia sunshine."

"Well, then?"

He turned to face her. It occurred to him then that in an odd way she was unpredictable as the weather itself. Each time he met up with her, she seemed a different person. Today she wore a dress in red and orange stripes, and long black stockings. Her hair had been caught back on the nape of her neck with a tortoise-shell slide, and her fringe had grown. It was too long, it would get into her eyes, give her a squint. As he watched her, she pushed it back, off her face, with the heel of her hand. It was a gesture both defensive and disarming and it made her seem very young.

He took the scrap of paper out of his pocket and handed it across to her. Emma read it aloud.

"Pat Farnaby, Gollan Home Farm." She looked up at him. "But where did you get this?"

"From the female at the Art Gallery."

"Pat Farnaby?"

"Marcus is interested."

"Why didn't he come himself?"

"He wanted a second opinion. Mine."

"Have you formed one?"

"It's difficult to say after seeing only a single painting. I thought I might be able to see some more."

Emma said warningly, "He's a very odd young man."

"I should expect him to be. Do you know where Gollan is?"

"Of course. It belongs to Mr and Mrs Stevens. We used to go out in summer for picnics on the cliffs. But I haven't been since I got back this time."

"Will you come with me now? Show me the way?"

"How do we get there?"

"The car's outside. I drove down from London last night."

"You must be exhausted."

"No, I've had a sleep."

"Where are you staying?"

"At the hotel. Can you come? Now?"

"Of course."

"You'll need a coat."

Emma smiled at him. "If you can spare thirty seconds, I'll get one."

When she had gone, her footsteps clattering away down an uncarpeted passage, Robert lit a cigarette and stood,

287

looking about him, intrigued not only by the oddly-shaped little house, but also because it represented the unfamiliar, domestic side of Ben Litton's stormy personality.

The blue front door had led them straight into the living-room, low ceilinged and darkly beamed. There was a huge window with a view of the sea, its deep sill crowded with indoor plants – geraniums and ivy and a Victorian jug full of pink roses. The floor was flagged with slate and scattered with bright rugs, and there were books and magazines everywhere, and a great deal of blue and white Spanish pottery. In a granite hearth, flush with the floor, a log fire smouldered, flanked by baskets of weathered driftwood, and over this hung the only picture in the room.

His professional eye had noticed this as soon as he came into the house, but now Robert went over to inspect it more closely. It was a large oil of a child on a donkey. She wore a red dress, carried a bunch of white daisies, wore a garland of them on her dark head. The donkey stood knee-deep in the lush grass of summer, and, far beyond, the sea and the sky were suffused by a haze of fine weather. The child's dangling feet were bare, her eyes pale in the brown bloom of her face.

Emma Litton, by her father. Robert wondered when it had been painted.

The wind rose, with a sudden witch's shriek, and flung a torrent of rain at the window. It was an eerie sound and he realised that this could be a lonely place to live, and wondered what Emma found to do on such a day. When she came back, carrying her coat and a pair of gumboots, which she proceeded to pull on, he asked her about this.

"Oh, I clean the house, and I cook things and I go and shop. It all takes quite a long time."

"And this afternoon? What were you doing this afternoon when I knocked on the door?"

Emma tugged at the gumboot. "I was ironing."

"And what about evenings? What do you do in the evenings?"

"I usually go out. I go for walks and things. I watch the gulls and the cormorants. I look at the sunset, pick up driftwood for the fire."

"Alone? Haven't you got any friends?"

"Oh, yes, but the children who lived here when I was little have all grown up and gone away."

It sounded bleak. On an impulse, Robert said, "You could come back to London with me. Helen would love to have you."

"Yes, I know she would, but it's hardly worth it, is it? After all, Ben'll be back any day now. It's only a matter of days."

She began to pull on her coat. It was navy blue and, with her black stockings and gumboots, made her look like a schoolgirl.

"Have you had any word from Ben?" Robert asked.

"From Ben? You must be joking."

"I'm beginning to wish we'd never suggested he went back to America."

"Why?"

"Because it doesn't seem fair on you."

"Oh, heavens, I'm all right." She smiled. "Shall we go?"

The Stevens's farm lay in a grey stretch of moor that swept down to the cliffs. Grey, lichened, sunk like a boulder into the land, it might have been simply another larger outcrop of granite. The lane which led down from the road wound deep between tall stone hedges, crowned with hawthorn and brambles. The car bumped and jolted down the track, crossed a small bridge, came to the first cottages, a flock of white geese, and finally the farmyard, shrill with the voice of a screaming cockerel.

Robert stopped the car and switched off the engine. The wind was dying, the rain seemed to have congealed into a sea-mist, thick as smoke. There were various farm sounds; cows lowing, hens clucking, the distant churning of a tractor.

"Now," said Robert, "how do I find this man?"

"He lives in the loft of that barn . . . you go up the stone steps to his door." The stone steps were already occupied by a number of wet hens, pecking for scraps of grain, and a bored-looking tabby cat. Below them, in the mud of the yard, a huge sow was rootling about. There was a strong smell of manure. Robert sighed. "The things I am expected to do, and all in the name of Art." He opened the door of the car and began to get out. "Do you want to come?"

"I think I'd be more use out of the way."

"I'll try not to be too long."

She watched him pick his way across the sodden farmyard, toe the pig aside, cautiously climb the steps. He knocked on the door, and then, when there was no reply, opened it and stepped inside. The door shut behind him. Almost at once another door opened, in the farmhouse this time, and the farmer's wife emerged, in boots and a raincoat to her ankles, and a black sou'wester. She carried a stout stick and came down the garden path, peering through the rain to see who was in the big green car.

Emma rolled down the window. "Hello, Mrs Stevens. It's me."

"Who?"

"Emma Litton."

Mrs Stevens broke into a cackle of delighted astonishment, slapped her side, put her hand over her heart. "Emma! Well, what a surprise you gave me. I haven't seen you since goodness knows how long. What are you doing here?"

"I came out with a man who wants to see Pat Farnaby. He's up there now."

"Is your father home yet?"

"No, he's still in America."

"On your own, are you?"

"That's right. How's Ernie?" Ernie was Mr Stevens.

"He's lovely, but had to go into town today to see the dentist about his plate. Agony, it gives him, he can scarcely bear to keep it in his mouth. That's why I'm getting the cows in for him . . ."

290

On an impulse Emma said, "I'll come with you . . ."

"Too wet for you."

"I've got boots . . . besides, I'd like the walk." She liked Mrs Stevens, too, a woman who remained unquenchably cheerful under all circumstances. They climbed a stile and started out over the sodden fields. "You've been abroad, haven't you?" said Mrs Stevens. "Yes, I thought you had. I never knew you were home. Pity your Daddy had to go off like this. Still, can't be helped, I suppose, him being the sort of man he is . . ."

The interview with Pat Farnaby was a difficult one, to say the least of it. He was an intense young man, very pale and undernourished, with a shock of carroty hair and a beard to match. His eyes were green and suspicious as a hungry cat's, and he appeared to be very dirty. His abode was also dirty, but this Robert had expected and, accordingly, ignored.

What he had not expected, though, was such antagonism. Pat Farnaby did not like strangers walking in, uninvited and unannounced, when he was working. Robert apologised and explained that he had come on business, whereupon the young man simply asked Robert what he was trying to sell.

Beating down his irritation, Robert tried another tack. With some ceremony, he produced Marcus Bernstein's card. "Mr Bernstein asked me to come and see you, perhaps to look at your work, find out what your plans are . . ."

"I haven't any plans," said the artist. "I never make plans." He treated the card as though it were contaminated and must not be touched, so that Robert was forced to put it down on the corner of a littered table.

"I saw your picture at the gallery in Porthkerris, but it is only one picture."

"So what?"

Robert cleared his throat. Marcus was infinitely better at dealing with this sort of thing, and Marcus never lost his temper. It took time to cultivate such patience, Robert knew. His own was slipping away, like greasy rope between his fingers. He took a firm grip of it.

"I'd like to see some more of your work."

Pat Farnaby's pale eyes narrowed. "How did you find me?" he asked, sounding like a cornered criminal.

"They gave me your address at the gallery. Emma Litton came with me to show me the way. Perhaps you know Emma."

"I've seen her around."

They seemed to be getting nowhere. In the silence that followed Robert let his eyes travel over the unsavoury studio. There were only the most sordid signs of human habitation; a bed like a disintegrating nest, a dirty frying pan, some nasty socks soaking in a bucket, an opened tin of beans, the jagged edge of the lid sticking up. But there were also many canvasses, stacked, scattered, propped on chairs, against walls. A potential treasure trove. Anxious beyond belief to inspect them, he dragged his eyes back to meet the cold unwinking stare of the artist.

He said at last, gently, "Mr Farnaby, I haven't all the time in the world."

Put to the test, Pat Farnaby's resistance cracked. He seemed, all at once, unsure of himself. Arrogance and rudeness were his only defences against the whims of a more sophisticated world. He scratched his head, frowned, made a face of resignation, and at last went to lift a random canvas and turn it to face the light.

"There's this," he said uncertainly, and backed away from it to stand by Robert. As he did so, Robert took a new packet of cigarettes from his pocket and handed them across to the young man. In the silence that followed, Pat Farnaby cautiously slit the cellophane wrapper, took out a cigarette and lit it, and then, with the stealthy movements of a man who does not wish to be observed, slid the packet into his own trouser pocket.

An hour later Robert returned to the car. Emma, waiting for him, saw him come down the steps of the barn, pick his way across the farmyard. She leaned across to open the door for him, and as he got in beside her, asked, "How did you get on?"

"I think all right." He sounded cautious, but excited.

"Did he show you his work?"

"Most of it."

"And it's good?"

"I think so. We may be on the verge of something enormously important, but it's all in such an appalling mess that it's hard to be sure. Nothing's framed, there's no sequence or order . . ."

"I was right, wasn't I? He's a real oddball?"

"Crazy," said Robert. He grinned at her. "But a genius."

He turned the car in the yard and headed back up the lane towards the road. He was whistling tunelessly through his teeth and Emma sensed, beneath his excitement, the satisfaction of a job well done.

She said, "You'll want to speak to Marcus now."

"I said I'd telephone right away." He eased his cuff from the face of his watch, checked on the time. "A quarter past six. He said he'd wait in the Gallery till seven and then go home."

"If you like, you can drop me at the crossroads and I'll walk home."

"Now, why should I do that?"

"I haven't got a telephone, and you'll want to hurry back to the hotel."

He smiled. "It's not as urgent as all that. And if it hadn't been for you, I'd probably still be looking for Pat Farnaby. The least I can do is to take you home."

They were on the moor now, high above the sea. The wind had eased off considerably, veering round to the west, and ahead the sky seemed to be opening and breaking up, and there were unexpected scraps of blue, growing larger every moment, and watery fingers of sunlight. Emma said, "It's going to be a lovely evening," and as she spoke was conscious that she did not want Robert to go back to the hotel and leave her to spend it on her own. He had blown, unexpectedly, into the gloomy day, given it shape and purpose, filled with companionship of a shared venture, and now she did not want it to end.

She said, "When are you going back to London?"

"Tomorrow morning. Sunday. Back in the Gallery Monday morning. It's been a full weekend."

So there was only this evening. She imagined him telephoning Marcus from the phone by his bed. Then he would have a bath, perhaps a drink, go down for dinner. On Saturday evenings The Castle Hotel held little dinner dances; there was a band in white mess jackets and a patch of floor cleared for dancing. Deeply influenced by Ben, Emma had been brought up to regard such functions as unbearably genteel and boring, but tonight she felt that it would be fun to let Ben's rigid opinions go to the devil. She yearned for the starched white table-cloths, the last year's hit tunes, the ritual of the wine list, the souped-up glamour of pink-shaded lights.

Beside her Robert spoke unexpectedly, interrupting her train of thought.

"When did your father paint the picture of you on the donkey?"

"Why did you suddenly ask that?"

"I was thinking about it. It's enchanting. You look so solemn and important."

"That's the way I felt, solemn and important. I was six, and it was the only painting he ever did of me. The donkey was called Mokey. He used to carry us up and down to the beach along with all the picnic baskets and things."

"Have you always lived in the cottage?"

"Not always. Just since Ben married Hester. Before that we used to stay anywhere – in boarding-houses, or with friends. Sometimes we just camped in the studio. It was rather fun. But Hester said she had no intention of living like a gipsy, so she bought the cottages and converted them."

"She did a good job."

"Yes, she was clever. But Ben has never thought of that house as home. His home is his studio and when he's in Porthkerris, he spends as little time as possible in the cottage. I think its associations with Hester slightly get him down. He's always expecting her to walk in and tell him that he's late for something, or that he's tracking mud on to the floor, or he's putting paint on the sofa cushions . . ."

"The creative instinct seems to thrive in disorder."

Emma laughed. "Do you suppose, that when you and Marcus have made Pat Farnaby rich and famous, he will still want to roost with Mrs Stevens's chickens?"

"That remains to be seen. But if he does come to London, there's no doubt that somebody will have to scrub him down and comb the dust of ages out of that scrofulous beard. Still . . ." He stretched luxuriously, arching his back against the leather seat. "It'll be worth it."

They had crested the hill and were now running down the long road that led to Porthkerris. The sea, in the calm evening light, had turned the translucent blue of butterfly wings; the tide was out, and the great bay an arc of newly-washed sand. The rain had left everything sparkling and fresh, and as the moors and the fields fell behind them, and they drove down through the narrow streets, Emma saw windows flung open to the fresh evening air, and caught, from tiny stamp-sized gardens, the heady smells of roses and lilac.

And there were other smells, too. Saturday evening smells, of fish frying and cheap scent. And there were people strolling the pavements in their best clothes, a smattering of early summer visitors, and boys and girls, hand in hand, headed for the cinema and the little cafés that lined the harbour road.

Stopped at the crossroads by the point-duty policeman, Robert observed them.

"What does young love do in Porthkerris on Saturday night, Emma?"

"It depends on the weather."

The policeman waved them on.

"What are we going to do?" asked Robert.

"We?"

"Yes. You and I. Do you want to be taken out for dinner?"

For a mad moment Emma wondered if she had been yearning aloud. "Well . . . I . . . you don't have to feel you have to . . ."

"I don't feel I have to. I want to. I'd like to. Where shall we go? My hotel? Or would you hate that?"

"No . . . of course . . . I wouldn't hate it . . ."

"Perhaps you've got some amusing little Italian place you like better."

"There aren't any amusing little Italian places in Porthkerris."

"No, I was afraid there wouldn't be. So it'll have to be the palm court and the central heating."

"There's a band too," said Emma, feeling she should warn him. "On Saturday nights. And people dance."

"You make it sound indecent."

"I thought perhaps you disliked that sort of thing. Ben does."

"I don't dislike it at all. Like most things, it can be quite fun if you do it with the right person."

"I never thought of it that way."

Robert laughed and looked again at his watch. "Half past six. I'll take you home, then go back to the hotel and change, and speak to Marcus, and then come back for you. Would half past seven be time enough?"

"I'll give you a drink," said Emma. "There's a bottle of Uncle Remus's Genuine Ole Rye Whisky that Ben was given ten years ago, and it's still not been opened. I've always longed to see what was inside."

But Robert was unenthusiastic. "Perhaps I'd better just make a martini."

At the hotel he collected his key, and three messages with it.

"When did these come?"

296

"The times are noted, sir. Three forty-five, five o'clock, half past five. A Mr Bernstein, telephoning from London. He says to call him the moment you come in."

"I was going to do that anyway, but thanks."

Frowning a little, for such impatience was foreign to Marcus, Robert went upstairs to his room. The copious telephone calls were disturbing. He wondered if Marcus had heard rumours that some other Gallery was after the young artist. Or perhaps he had had second thoughts about Farnaby's work, and wanted to cancel the whole thing.

In his room, the curtains had been drawn, the bed turned down, the fire turned on. He sat on the bed, and picked up the receiver and gave the number of the Gallery. He took the three telephone messages out of his pocket and put them in a neat row on top of the bedside table. *Mr Bernstein would like you to call him. Mr Bernstein called, will ring later. Mr Bernstein . . .*

"Kent 3778. Bernstein Galleries."

"Marcus . . ."

"Robert, thank God I've got you at last. Did you get my message?"

"Three of them. But I said I would call you about Farnaby."

"This isn't about Farnaby. This is much more important. This is about Ben Litton."

There was a dress, seen in Paris, wildly expensive, coveted, and finally bought. It was black, sleeveless, very plain. "But when will you wear such a dress?" Madame Duprés had asked, and Emma, basking in the luxury of possession, had replied, "Oh, some time. Some special time."

There had never been such an occasion until tonight. Now, with her hair coiled high and pearl earstuds set in her ears, Emma drew the black dress carefully over her head, zipped it up and fastened the tiny belt, and her reflection in the mirror reassured her that all those thousands of francs had been well spent.

When Robert came, she was in the kitchen, struggling

297

with a trayful of ice-cubes for the martinis that he had promised to make. She heard his car, the slam of the door, the gate open and shut and his footsteps as he ran down the steps, and in a panic, she tumbled the ice into a glass dish and went to let him in, and found that the sullen day had turned into a clear and perfect night, jewel-blue and scattered with stars.

In surprise, she said, "What a beautiful night."

"Amazing, isn't it? After all that wind and rain Porthkerris is looking like Positano." He came into the house and Emma closed the door behind him. "There's even a moon rising over the sea to complete the illusion. All we need now is a guitar and a tenor singing 'Santa Lucia'."

"Perhaps we'll find one."

He had changed into a dark grey suit, a starched shirt with an impeccable collar and a gleam of white cuff, linked with gold, showing at his wrist. His tawny hair was once more tamed and smoothly brushed, and he brought with him the crisp, lemony smell of aftershave.

"Do you still want to make a martini? I've got everything ready, I was just trying to get the ice . . ." She went back to the kitchen, raising her voice to talk through the open door. "The gin and the Martini are on the table and a lemon. Oh, and you'll need a knife to cut the lemon with."

She opened a drawer and found one, pointed and very sharp, and she carried the knife and the bowl of ice back into the living-room. "What a pity Ben isn't here. He adores martinis, only he can never remember the right proportions and he always drowns them with lemon . . ."

Robert made no reply to this. It occurred then to Emma that he had made no effort to make himself at home. He had done nothing about their drinks, he had not even lit himself a cigarette, and this in itself was unusual, for he was normally the most relaxed and composed of men. But now there was a definite constraint about him, and with a sinking heart, Emma wondered if he was already regretting the evening they were to spend together.

She went to put the lemon down beside the empty glasses, told herself she was imagining things, turned to swiftly smile at him. "Now, what else do you need?"

"Not another thing," said Robert, and put his hands into his trouser pockets. *Not the gesture of a man who is about to make a martini*. In the fire a burning log settled and broke, sending up a shower of sparks.

Perhaps it was the telephone call that had upset him. "Did you speak to Marcus?"

"Yes, I did. As a matter of fact, he'd been trying to get me on the telephone most of the afternoon."

"And of course you were out. Was he pleased when you told him about Pat Farnaby?"

"He wasn't calling about Farnaby."

"He wasn't?" Suddenly she was afraid. "Is it bad news?"

"No, of course not, but you may not be very pleased. It's about your father. You see, he called Marcus this morning, from the States. He wanted Marcus to tell you that yesterday, in Queenstown, he and Melissa Ryan were married."

Emma realised that she was still holding the knife, that it was very sharp and that she might cut herself with it, so she set it down, very carefully alongside the lemon . . .

Married. The word conjured up a hysterical image of a wedding; of Ben with a white flower in the button-hole of his sagging corduroy jacket; of Melissa Ryan in her pink wool suit, misted in white veiling and paper confetti; of demented church bells jangling their message out across the verdant Virginia countryside that Emma had never seen. It was like a nightmare.

She realised that Robert Morrow was still talking, his voice even and calm. ". . . Marcus feels that in some obscure way, he is to blame. Because he thought the private view was a good idea, and because he was with them in Queenstown – he saw them together all the time, and he never had the faintest inkling that this was going to happen."

Emma remembered Marcus's description of the beautiful house, saw Ben caged by Melissa's money, a pacing tiger with all his creative impulses smothered by luxury; and she realised that she had underestimated Melissa Ryan in imagining that Ben would be put off by having to fight for what he wanted. She had not appreciated how much he would want it.

Suddenly, she was angry. "He should never have gone back to America. There was no need. He simply wanted to be left alone and to get on with his painting."

"Emma, nobody made him go."

"It isn't as though the marriage will last. Ben's never stayed faithful to a woman longer than six months, and I can't see Melissa Ryan standing for that."

Robert said mildly, "Perhaps this time it will work, and it will last."

"But you saw them together that day they met. They couldn't keep their eyes off each other. If she had been old and ugly, nothing would have dragged him away from Porthkerris."

"But she wasn't old and ugly. She's very beautiful, and highly intelligent and very rich. And if it hadn't been Melissa Ryan, very soon it would have been somebody else, and what is more . . ." he went on, swiftly, before Emma could interrupt, ". . . you know as well as I do that that is true."

She said bitterly, "But at least we would have had more than a month together."

Hopelessly, Robert shook his head. "Oh, Emma, let him go."

His tone infuriated her. "He's my father. What's wrong in wanting to be with him?"

"He's not a father, any more than he's a husband or a lover or a friend. He's an artist. As that dedicated maniac we went to see this afternoon is an artist. They have no time for our values or standards. Everything, and everybody else, has to take second place."

"*Second* place? I wouldn't mind taking second place, or

third, or fourth. But I've always come at the bottom of a long list of priorities. His painting, his love affairs, his perpetual shunting about all over the world; even Marcus, and you. You're all more important to Ben than ever I was."

"Then leave him alone. Think about something else for a change. Chuck all this, leave it behind. Get yourself a job."

"I've done all those things. I've been doing them for the past two years."

"Then come back to London with me tomorrow and stay with Marcus and Helen. It'll get you away from Porthkerris, give you time to get used to the idea of Ben being married again, decide what you want to do next."

"Perhaps I've already decided."

It was there, in the back of her mind. Like watching the revolving stage from the darkened auditorium of a theatre. One set moves out of sight and as it does the new scenery comes slowly on to the stage. A different set. Another room, perhaps. Another view from another window. "But I don't want to come to London."

"And this evening?"

Emma frowned. She had forgotten. "This evening?"

"We're having dinner together."

She felt that she could not bear it. "I really would rather not . . ."

"It'll do you good . . ."

"No it won't. And I've got a headache . . ." It was an excuse, made-up, and it was with astonishment that she realised it was true. A pain that felt like the start of a migraine, with her eyeballs dragged by wires into the back of her head; the thought of food, chicken in gravy, ice-cream, was nauseous. "I couldn't come. I couldn't."

Robert said gently, "It isn't the end of the world," and the old, comforting cliché was somehow more than Emma could take. To her horror, she began to cry. She covered her face with her hands pressing her fingertips into her thudding scalp, trying to stop, knowing that crying would make it worse, that she would be blinded with pain, that she would be sick . . .

She heard him say her name, and in two strides he had covered the space between them, and he put his arms around her, cradling her, letting her cry all over the immaculate grey lapels of his good suit. And Emma did not try to move away, but stayed still, tightly clenched against her own grief, rigid and unresponsive and hating him for what he had done to her.

7

Jane Marshall, her hand curved round a half full tumbler of Scotch-on-the-rocks, said, ". . . so what happened then?"

"Nothing happened. She didn't want to come out to dinner, and she looked as though she was going to have a bilious attack, so I put her to bed, and gave her a hot drink and an aspirin, and then I went back to the hotel and had dinner on my own. Then, the next morning, the Sunday, I went down to the cottage to say goodbye before I drove back to London. She was up and about, rather pale, but she seemed to be all right."

"Did you try again to make her come back with you?"

"Yes, I did, but she was adamant. So we said goodbye, and I left her. And since then there has been no word."

"But you can surely find out where she is?"

"There is no way of finding out. There's no telephone, never has been. Marcus wrote, of course, but Emma seems to have inherited Ben's built-in aversion to answering letters. There hasn't been another word."

"But this is crazy. In this day and age . . . there must be someone who can tell you . . ."

"There's no one. No one Emma ever talked to. There was no daily woman, coming in to clean, she did it all herself. That was the big reason for going back to Porthkerris in the first place, so that she could keep house for Ben. Of course, after two weeks of frigid silence, Marcus could stand it no longer, and put through a telephone call to the landlord of the Sliding Tackle, which was the pub Ben used to frequent, but Ben had been gone for six weeks, anyway, and Emma never went near the place."

"Then you'll have to go down to Porthkerris and ask around."

"Marcus isn't prepared to do that."

"Why not?"

"For reasons. Emma isn't a child. She's been hurt, and Marcus respects the fact that if she wants to be left alone, he has no right to interfere. He's asked her to come to London and live with Helen and himself . . . anyway until she's found her feet again. He can scarcely do more. And there's another reason, too."

"I know," said Jane. "It's Helen, isn't it?"

"Yes, it is," said Robert, hating to admit it. "Helen has always resented the hold Ben has over Marcus. There have been times when she would gladly have seen Ben at the bottom of the ocean. But she's accepted it because she had to, because wet-nursing Ben's career is part of Marcus's job, and without Marcus to keep him, more or less on the rails, God knows what would have happened to Ben Litton."

"And now she doesn't want him to start killing himself over Emma."

"Precisely."

Jane rocked her glass, letting the ice clink against its side. She said, "And you?"

He looked up. "What about me?"

"Do you feel involved?"

"Why do you ask that?"

"You sound involved."

"I scarcely know the girl."

"But you're worried about her."

He considered this. "Yes," he said at last. "Yes, I suppose I am. God knows why."

His glass was empty. Jane laid down her own drink, and got up to take his glass and pour him another whisky. From behind him, busy with ice, she said, "Why don't *you* go down to Porthkerris and find out?"

"Because she isn't there."

"She isn't . . . ? You know? But you never told me that."

304

"After the abortive telephone call to the Sliding Tackle, Marcus got the wind up. He rang the local police, and they found out a few facts and called us back. Cottage closed up, studio closed up, Post Office told to keep all mail until further notice." He reached up to take the fresh drink that Jane handed him over the back of the sofa. "Thanks."

"And her father . . . ? Does he know?"

"Yes, Marcus wrote and told him. But you can't expect Ben to get unduly excited. After all, he's still in the throes of what is virtually a honeymoon, and Emma's been sculling round Europe on her own since she was fourteen. Don't forget, that this is not a normal father-daughter relationship."

Jane sighed. "It most certainly isn't."

Robert grinned at her. She was a comfortingly down-to-earth person and it was for this reason that, on an impulse, he had dropped in this evening for a drink on his way home from work. Usually, the double life he led with Marcus Bernstein, working with him at the Gallery, as well as living in the same house, offered no strain at all. But just now, things were difficult. Robert had come back from a business trip to Paris, to find Marcus on edge, and unable to concentrate for very long on anything but the problem of Emma Litton. After discussing it with him, Robert realised that Marcus blamed himself for what had happened, and refused to be talked out of his guilt. Helen, on the other hand, was unsympathetic, and determined that he should not get himself more deeply involved in the whole sorry business, and for the moment the tensions had got on top of them, and split the ménage at Milton Gardens from top to bottom.

The situation was not improved by the weather. After a cool spring, London had suddenly been caught up in the throes of a veritable heatwave. The early mornings broke in a pearl-like mist which gradually dissolved into day after day of baking sun. Girls went to work in sleeveless dresses, men shed their jackets and sat at their desks in shirt-sleeves. The parks at lunch-time were filled with recumbent picnickers; shops and restaurants sprouted striped awnings, windows were flung open to the smallest breeze, and in the streets, parked cars frizzled and pavements glared, and melted tar stuck to the soles of shoes.

The heat, like some monstrous epidemic, had invaded even the quiet, pond-green recesses of the Bernstein Gallery. All day long there had been an endless stream of visitors and prospective clients, for the trans-Atlantic tourist season had started, and this was apt to be their busiest time. And at the end of it all, Robert, driving home, had found himself longing for a new face, a cool drink, and some conversation that had nothing to do with Artists, be they Renaissance, Impressionist or Pop.

Jane Marshall sprang immediately to mind.

Her little house was in a narrow mews between Sloane Square and Pimlico Road. As he turned the car into the street, and eased down over the cobbles, he gave a double toot on the horn, and she appeared at the open upstairs window, her hands on the sill, her fair hair falling over her face as she leaned out to see who it was.

"Robert! I thought you were still in Paris."

"I was till two days ago. Have you got such a thing as a long, cool, alcoholic drink for an exhausted working man?"

"Of course I have. Hold on. I'll come down and let you in."

Her tiny house had always charmed him. Originally a coachman's cottage, it had a steep, narrow staircase, which led straight up to the first floor. Here there was an open hall-way, a sitting-room, and a kitchen, and upstairs again, in the slope-roofed loft, her bedroom and bathroom. As such it was inadequate enough, but since she had started her interior decorating business, it had become a joke. The sitting-room she had turned into a workroom, but still the bales of fabric, the fringing and the cushions, and the small bits of bric-à-brac she so cleverly picked up, overflowed into every available

306

corner of space, rendering it all as gay and colourful as a patchwork quilt.

She was delighted to see him. She had spent the morning with a tiresome woman who wanted her entire house in St John's Wood done up in cream, which she called "Redecorating in Magnolia." And then there had been a session with a young and rising actress who demanded something startling for her new flat.

"She sat here for hours, showing me pictures of the sort of thing she had in mind. I tried to tell her she should get a bulldozer in, not an interior decorator, but she wouldn't listen. These people never do. Whisky?"

"That," said Robert, collapsing on the sofa in front of the open window, "is the nicest thing anybody has said to me all day."

She poured two drinks, made sure he was supplied with cigarettes and an ash-tray, and then settled herself composedly down to face him. She was a very pretty girl. Her blonde hair was straight and thick, cut in a curve to her chin. Her eyes were green, her nose tip-tilted, her mouth sweet, but implacable. Her broken marriage had left certain scars upon her character and she was not always the most tolerant of people, but there was a directness about her that he found as refreshing as a drink of cold water, and she always looked delicious.

Now he said, "I came here with the express purpose of not talking shop. How did we get on to the subject of Ben Litton anyway?"

"I brought it up. I was intrigued. Every time I saw Helen, she kept dropping maddening hints and then refusing to say more. She feels strongly about this, doesn't she?"

"Only because, in his day, Ben Litton has run poor Marcus ragged."

"Does she know Emma?"

"She hasn't seen her since she went to Switzerland six years ago."

"It's difficult," said Jane, "to be fair about people if you don't know them very well."

307

"It's sometimes difficult to be fair even if you do. And now . . ." He leaned forward to stub out his cigarette. "Let's drop the subject and make a tacit agreement not to mention it again. Are you doing anything this evening?"

"Not a thing."

"Then why don't we go and find somewhere with a roof garden or a terrace, and have a quiet dinner together?"

"I'd like that," said Jane.

"I'll call Helen and tell her I'm not coming back . . ."

"In that case . . ." She stood up. "I shall go and have a shower and change. I shan't be long."

"There isn't any hurry."

"Make yourself at home . . . get yourself another drink. There are cigarettes here, and an evening paper somewhere if you care to look for it . . ."

She went up the stairs. He heard her moving about, high heels tapping on the polished floor. She sang under her breath, slightly out of tune. He put down his glass and went into her living-room, and ran her telephone to earth at last, beneath a bundle of flowered chintzes, and called Helen to say he would not be home for dinner. Then he went back to pour the third drink of the evening, and loosened his tie, and flopped once more on the sofa.

The whisky had revived him slightly, and beneath its clean cold bite, his tiredness had changed from end-of-the-day fatigue to a pleasant lassitude. The paper protruded from beneath a cushion, and he pulled it out, and then saw that it was not the *Evening Standard*, but the *Stage*.

"Jane."

"Hello!"

"I didn't know you took the *Stage*."

"I don't."

"Well it's here."

"Is it?" She didn't sound particularly interested. "Dinah Burnett must have left it behind. You know she's the actress who needs the bulldozer."

He opened it aimlessly. "Wanted One All Round Girl Dancer. Why does she have to be all round? Why can't she be all square?"

"Search me."

He turned to the Repertory page. They were doing Shakespeare at Birmingham, a Restoration revival at Manchester, and at Brookford, staging the première of a new play . . .

Brookford.

The name leapt at him from the page like a bullet. Brookford. He sat up, slapped the paper into shape, and read the whole item.

> Brookford Rep's summer season opens this week with the world première of *Daisies on the Grass*, a comedy in three acts by local writer Phyllis Jason. This light but well-knit play stars actress Charmian Vaughan in the lead role of Stella. Other parts are supplementary, but John Rigger, Sophie Lambart and Christopher Ferris all help to bring the mirthful suspense to its climax, and Sara Rutherford is charmingly natural as the bride. Tommy Childers' production is fast and furious, and the set, by scenic artist Brian Dare, evoked a spontaneous applause from the enthusiastic first-night audience.

Christopher Ferris.

He laid the paper carefully down, and reached for a cigarette, and lit it. Christopher Ferris. He had forgotten Christopher.

But now, out of a jumble of memories, he heard Emma's voice again, that first day, when he had given her lunch at Marcello's.

Did you know about Christopher? Quite by chance Christopher and I met up again in Paris. And he came this very morning and saw me off at Le Bourget.

And he remembered – facing her across the table – being suddenly wise, and knowing the reason for her smile and the bloom of her skin and the brightness of her eyes.

And later, in the draughty studio at Porthkerris, the subject of Christopher had, fleetingly, come up again, sandwiched between other more important items of discussion. *He'll be at Brookford by now*, Emma had said. *In the thick of rehearsals*.

He stood up and went to the foot of the stairs.

"Jane."

"Hello!"

"How nearly ready are you?"

"I'm just doing my face."

"Where's Brookford?"

"In Surrey."

"How long will it take us to get there?"

"Brookford? Oh, about forty-five, fifty minutes."

He glanced at his watch. "If we leave right away, or as near as we can . . . we shouldn't be too late."

Jane appeared at the head of the stairs, with a mirror in one hand and an eyeliner brush in the other.

"Late for what?"

"We're going to the theatre."

"I thought we were going out for dinner."

"Later, perhaps we will. But first we're going to Brookford, to see a well-knit comedy called *Daisies on the Grass* . . ."

"Have you gone out of your mind?"

". . . by local writer Phyllis Jason."

"You have gone out of your mind."

"I'll explain on the way down. Be a darling and hurry."

As they roared down the M4 Jane said, "You mean that nobody knows about this young man except you."

"Emma didn't tell Ben, because he'd never liked Christopher anyway – Helen says he was jealous of the boy."

"And Emma didn't tell Marcus Bernstein."

"I don't think so."

"But she told you."

"Yes, she told me. She told me that very first day. And why the devil I didn't think of him before I cannot imagine."

"Is she in love with him?"

"I wouldn't know. She's certainly very fond of him."

"Do you think we'll find her at Brookford?"

"If we don't, then I'll bet even money that Christopher Ferris will know where she is." Jane did not reply. After a little, he added, his eyes still fixed on the speeding road, "I'm sorry about this. I promised the subject wasn't to be raised again, and here I am whisking you off to the wilds of darkest Surrey."

"Why," asked Jane, "are you so anxious to find Emma?"

"Because of Marcus. I should like to set Marcus's mind at rest."

"I see."

"Because if Marcus's mind is at rest, then Helen will relax and life will be a great deal more comfortable for all of us."

"Well, that's fair enough . . . Look, I think we should turn off here."

The Brookford Repertory Theatre took some finding. They cruised up and down the High Street, then asked directions from a tired-looking policeman in shirt-sleeves. He sent them a half a mile from the centre of town, and, off a back street, up a cul-de-sac, they found the large brick edifice, looking more like a mission hall than anything else, but for the word THEATRE written above the door in neon letters, deadened by the hot evening light.

Outside, by the pavement, were parked a couple of cars, and alongside them, with their feet in the gutter, sat two small girls playing with a broken perambulator.

There were posters.

311

DAISIES ON THE GRASS
by PHYLLIS JASON
A comedy in Three Acts
Produced by
TOMMY CHILDERS

Jane stood, taking in this inauspicious façade. "So much for the living theatre."

Robert put his hand under her elbow. "Come along now."

They went up a flight of stone steps, and into a small foyer, with a cigarette kiosk on one side, and a box office on the other. In the box office a girl sat knitting.

"I'm afraid the show's started," she said, as Robert and Jane appeared on the other side of the glass.

"Yes, we thought it would have. But we'll have a couple of tickets anyway."

"What price?"

"Oh . . . well – stalls."

"That's fifteen shillings. But you'll have to wait till the second act."

"Is there anywhere we could get a drink?"

"The bar's upstairs."

"Thank you very much." He took the tickets and his change. "I expect you know all the people who work here."

"Well, yes . . ."

"Christopher Ferris . . ."

"Oh, is he a friend of yours?"

"Well, a friend of a friend. The thing is, I wondered if he has his sister here . . . at least, she's his step-sister. Emma Litton."

"Emma's working here."

"She's *working* here? In the theatre?"

"That's right. As ASM – Assistant Stage Manager. Our last girl suddenly went off ill with an appendix, and Emma said she'd come and help out. Of course," her voice became

312

professional ". . . Mr Childers usually likes someone in the job who's had a bit of stage training, you know, RADA, or a bit of experience somewhere, so that they double up in small parts. But as she was here, and didn't have anything to do, he let her have the job. Just until the regular girl's better."

"I see. Do you think we'd be able to see her?"

"Well, after the show, yes. But Mr Childers won't have anyone back stage until it's over."

"That's all right. We can wait. Thank you very much."

"Not at all. It's a pleasure."

They went upstairs to a second, larger foyer with a bar in the corner, and sat there, drinking lager and talking to the barman until a light spatter of applause announced the end of the first act. The lights went up, the doors opened, and a small stream of people emerged for refreshment. Jane and Robert waited until the first curtain bell, and then went into the auditorium themselves, buying a couple of programmes on their way, and being shown to their seats by an eager young girl in a nylon overall. Attendance that night was certainly sparse, and Jane and Robert were the only two people sitting in the third row. Jane looked about her with a professional eye.

"I think it was once a mission hall," she decided. "Nobody would have built anything so ugly as a theatre. But I must say, they have done it up quite imaginatively, and the lighting and the colours are good. What a shame they don't get better audiences . . ."

The curtain at last went up on the second act. "The lounge hall of Mrs Edbury's house in Gloucestershire" said the programme note, and there it was, complete with french windows, staircase, settee, table with drinks, table with telephone, low table with magazines (for leading lady to pick up and idly flick through in moments when she did not know what to do with her hands?) and three doors.

"Draughty house," murmured Jane.

"It's better when they shut the french windows."

313

But the french windows had to be open, for in bounced the *ingénue* (*Sara Rutherford is charmingly natural as the bride*), flung herself on the settee and burst into tears. Jane's profile was alert with delighted disbelief. Robert settled more deeply into his seat.

It was a terrible play. Even if they had seen the first act, and so been able to unravel the tangled skein of the plot, it would still have been a terrible play. It bristled with clichés, with stock characters (there was even a comic charlady), with contrived exits and entrances, and with telephone calls. There were eight of these in the course of the second act alone.

When the curtain came down, Robert said, "Let's go and have another drink. I could do with a double brandy after that."

"I'm not going to move," said Jane. "I'm not going to break the spell. I haven't seen a play like this since I was seven. And the set makes me positively nostalgic. But there's one thing, Robert, that sticks out like a sore thumb."

"What's that?"

"Christopher Ferris is very, very good . . ."

He was, too. When he had shambled on stage, as the vague young university student who was eventually to win the heroine from her stockbroker fiancé, *Daisies on the Grass* showed its first, faint spark of life. His lines were not better than anyone else's, but his timing was impeccable, and he managed to make them funny or sad, or wryly charming. For the part he wore corduroys, a sagging sweater and horn-rimmed spectacles, but even these could not disguise his elegance and his good looks and the natural long-legged grace with which he moved.

". . . and he's not merely very good, he's very attractive," Jane went on. "I can see why his step-sister was so pleased to bump into him again in Paris. I wouldn't mind bumping into him myself."

The third act had the same set, but now it was night. Blue moonlight shone through the open window, and down the stairs came the little bride, carrying a suitcase, tiptoeing, all ready to run away or elope or whatever it was she'd spent the last hour in deciding to do. Robert couldn't remember. He was waiting for Christopher to come back on stage. When he did, Robert simply watched him the entire time, detachedly, absorbed and full of admiration. By now, he had the audience, small as it was, in the palm of his hand. As Robert watched, so they watched. Christopher scratched the back of his head and they laughed. He took off his spectacles to kiss the girl, and they laughed again. He put them back on to say goodbye for ever, and there was silence, and then people began to blow their noses. And when it was all over, and the cast lined up for the curtain call, the applause was long, and real, and it was all for Christopher.

"What do we do now?" asked Jane.

"It's not closing time for another ten minutes. Let's go and find a drink."

They went back to the bar. The barman said, "Well, how did you enjoy the show, sir?"

"Well, I don't know . . . I . . ."

Jane was braver. "We thought it was terrible," she said, but quite politely. "And I've fallen in love with Christopher Ferris."

The barman grinned. "Quite something, isn't he? Pity you had to come tonight, when the audience was so thin on the ground as it were. Mr Childers did hope, Miss Jason being local and all that jazz, that this play would bring them in. But you can't fight a heatwave."

"Do you usually have good houses?" Jane wanted to know.

"They go up and down. Now, last show we did was *Present Laughter* . . . that fairly filled the place up."

"It's a good play," said Robert.

"What part did Christopher Ferris have?" asked Jane.

"Now, let me see. Oh, I know, he was the young playwright. You know, the one that bounces round on the chairs and eats biscuits. Ronald Maule he's called in

315

the play. Oh, very funny, Christopher Ferris was in that part. Brought the house down, he did . . ." Wiping away at his tumblers, he glanced up at the clock. "I'm afraid I'll have to ask you to drink up, sir . . . closing time . . ."

"Yes, of course. By the way, how do we get back stage? We want to see Emma Litton."

"You can just go down the auditorium, sir, go through the door at the right of the stage. But watch out for Mr Collins the Stage Manager. He doesn't exactly relish visitors."

"Thanks," said Robert. "And good night."

They went back into the theatre. The curtains had been drawn back, and the stage was revealed once more, but without footlights the set looked less inspiring than ever. On stage a young boy was struggling with the sofa, trying to heave it to one side, and someone, somewhere, had left a door open, so that the whole theatre was swept with a stuffy draught of used-up air. The programme girl was going round, slapping up the empty seats and collecting empty chocolate boxes and cigarette cartons in a trash can.

"There is nothing," said Jane, "so depressing as an empty theatre."

They started to walk down towards the stage. As they approached, Robert realised that it was not a boy who struggled, single-handed with the heavy sofa, but a girl, dressed in an old blue sweater and jeans.

When he was close enough, he said, "I wonder if you can help me . . . ?"

She turned to look at him, and Robert, with the shock of sheer disbelief, found himself face to face with Emma Litton.

8

After a second's gaping silence, Emma stopped trying to move the sofa, and straightened up. He thought that she seemed much taller and thinner, the cold stage light was not flattering, her wrists hung like sticks from her rolled-up sleeves. But the worst thing was her hair. She had cut off her hair, and now her head seemed small and vulnerable, furred like the pelt of an animal.

There was the animal feel of watchfulness about her, too. A scarey look as though she waited for him to make the first move, to say the first word, before she knew which way to jump. He slid his hands into his pockets, in a deliberate attempt to both look and feel casual, and he said, "Hello, Emma."

She gave the ghost of a smile. She said, "This sofa feels as though it's been stuffed with lead and lost its castors in the process."

"Isn't there anyone who can help you?" He came forward to the edge of his side of the stage, so that he was looking up at her. "It looks very heavy."

"Yes, there'll be someone in a moment." She did not seem to know what to do with her hands. She rubbed them on the seat of her jeans as though they were dirty, and then folded her arms. It was a curiously defensive movement, and made her shoulder-bones jut forward beneath the thin cotton of her shirt. "What are you doing here?"

"We came down to see *Daisies on the Grass* . . . We drove down from town. This is Jane Marshall. Jane, this is Emma."

They smiled, nodded at each other, murmured how do

you do? Emma turned back to Robert. "Did . . . did you know I was here?"

"No, but I knew Christopher was, and I thought you might be."

"I've been working for a couple of weeks. It gives me something to do."

Robert made no comment on this, and, perhaps disconcerted by his silence, Emma suddenly sat down on the sofa that she was meant to be shifting. Her hands hung listlessly between her knees. After a little, she said, "Did Marcus send you?"

"No. We just came to call. Make sure you're all right . . ."

"I'm all right."

"What time are you finished here . . . ?"

"I'll be about half an hour. I have to clear the stage for rehearsal tomorrow morning. Why?"

"I thought we might have all gone to some hotel or other, for a sandwich and a drink. Jane and I haven't had any dinner . . ."

"Oh, how kind!" She did not sound enthusiastic. "Well . . . the thing is . . . that I usually leave something in the oven at the flat . . . a casserole or something. Johnny and Christo never eat anything otherwise. We'll have to go back or it'll burn."

"Johnny?"

"Johnny Rigger. He was the fiancé. You know, the other man. He lives with Christo . . . and me."

"I see."

There was another silence. Emma, discomfited, struggled with her more hospitable instincts. "I would ask you to come back, if you'd like to, but there's nothing but a few cans of beer . . ."

"We like beer," said Robert promptly.

"And the flat's in a dreadful mess. There never seems to be time to clean it properly. Not now that I'm working, I mean."

"We don't mind. How do we get there?"

"Well . . . have you got a car?"

"Yes. It's outside."

"Yes . . . well. If you go out and wait, Christo and I will join you later. If that's all right. And then we can show you where it is."

"Splendid. How about Johnny?"

"Oh, he'll be along later."

"We'll wait for you."

He took his hands out of his pockets and turned, and he and Jane walked back up the slight slope of the auditorium. As they reached the double doors, and Robert held one half open for Jane to go through, all hell seemed to break loose on stage.

"Where the devil is that Litton girl?" Robert was in time to see Emma scramble off the sofa as though someone had set off a firework, and try once more to move the cumbersome thing. A small man with a black beard shot on stage, looking like the worst-tempered sort of pirate. "Look, ducky, I asked you to move the bloody sofa, not to go to sleep on it. God, I'll be thankful to see that other girl back and you safely out of this place . . ." One either had to go and knock him down, or withdraw. For Emma's sake Robert withdrew.

The door swung shut behind him, but as they crossed the foyer, the voice could still be heard ". . . She's a moron, we all know, but no one could be as crassly stupid as you . . ."

"Charming," said Jane, as they went down the stairs. Robert did not reply, because, until the white-hot blaze of anger with which he had been suddenly consumed, died down, he was not capable of saying anything. "That must be Mr Collins, the stage manager. Not a very nice man to work for."

They reached the street door, and went down the steps and crossed the pavement and got into the car. It was dark now, a soft, bloomy dusk had descended upon the town, but the heat of the day still lingered, held by the narrow confines of the street, by sunbaked stone and paving. Above them the Theatre sign shone brightly, but as they got into the car, someone from inside the building turned it off. The evening's entertainment was over. Robert reached for his cigarettes, gave Jane one and lit it, and then took one for himself. After a moment he felt a little calmer.

He said, "She's cut off all her hair."

"Has she? What was it like before?"

"Long and silky and dark."

"She doesn't want us to go tonight. You know that, don't you?"

"Yes, I know that. But we must. We don't need to stay long."

"And I hate beer."

"I'm sorry. Perhaps someone will make you some coffee."

". . . It isn't even as though it's a job that requires any sort of brain. The most idiotic creature straight out of RADA could do it more competently than you."

Collins was letting fly, unloading the day's tensions and frustrations in a flood of invective that was directed solely at Emma. He hated her. It had something to do with Christopher; with the fact that her father was both successful and famous. At first, she had tried sticking up for herself, but now she knew better than to try and stem this venomous flood. With Collins, you couldn't win. She simply listened, got on with her work, tried not to let him see how deeply he could upset her.

". . . you got this job because I have to have someone to help me . . . God help me. You didn't get it because Chris shoved his oar in, and you didn't get it because some fool is willing to pay twenty thousand for a Ben Litton of red spots on a blue background. I've got more sense than that, as by now you have no doubt found out. So don't start thinking you can loll around entertaining your toffee-nosed friends . . . and the next time they condescend to visit our humble little show, tell them to bloody well wait till we've finished,

320

will you? Now come on, get that sofa out of the bloody way . . ."

It was nearly eleven before at last he let her go, and then she found Christo waiting for her in Tommy Childers' office. The door was open and she heard them talking, and she knocked and put her head in and said, "I'm ready now. I'm sorry I was so long."

Christo stood up. "That's all right." He stubbed out his cigarette. "Good night, Tommy."

" 'Night, Chris."

"Thanks for everything."

"That's OK, old chap . . ."

They went downstairs towards the stage door. He put his arm around her as they went. Their warm bodies touched, it was too hot for such contact, but she found it comforting. Outside, in the little alley that led down to the street, he stopped by the dustbins to light another cigarette.

He said, "You were long enough. Collins playing up?"

"He was furious because Robert Morrow's here."

"Robert Morrow?"

"He's in Bernstein's, with Marcus. He's Marcus's brother-in-law. I told you. He came down to see the show . . . He's brought a girl with him."

Christo stood looking down at her. "To see the show or to see you?"

"I think to see us both."

"He can't try to take you back. Say you're under age or anything?"

"Of course not."

"Then that's all right."

"Yes, I suppose it is. But, you see, like a fool, I asked them back to the flat. At least, I didn't mean to ask them, but somehow I did, and they're coming. They're waiting for us now, in the car. Oh, Christo, I am sorry."

He laughed. "*I* don't mind."

"They won't stay long."

"I don't mind if they stay all night. Don't look so tragic."

321

He took her in his arms, and kissed her cheek. She thought that if only the evening, the day, the endless day, could end right here and now, she would be well content. She was afraid of Robert. She was too tired to fence with him, to answer questions, to try and evade those watchful grey eyes. She was too tired to compete with his friend, who was blonde and pretty and almost indecently cool-looking in her sleeveless navy-blue dress. She was too tired to tidy the flat for them, to shovel clothes and scripts and empty glasses out of sight, to open beer cans, and make coffee, and get Christo's dinner out of the oven.

Christo rubbed his chin against her cheek. "What's wrong?" he asked gently.

"Nothing." He did not like her to say she was tired. He was never tired. He did not know what the word meant.

He said, in her ear, "It's been a good day, hasn't it?"

"Yes, of course." She drew away from him. "A good day." With their arms entwined, they went down the alley towards the street. Robert heard their voices, and got out of the car to meet them. They came towards him, in and out of the patches of light flung by the street lamps. They walked like lovers, Emma trailing a sweater, Christo with a bulky script under one arm and a cigarette between his fingers. When they reached the car, they stopped. "Hello," said Christopher, smiling.

"Christo, this is Robert Morrow, and Miss Marshall . . ."

"Mrs Marshall," Jane corrected sweetly, leaning over the back of the front seat. "Hello, Christopher."

"Sorry we've been so long," said Christo ". . . Emma's only just told me you were here. And she was having her nightly set-to with Collins, so we've all been fairly occupied. I believe you're coming back to have a can of beer, or something. I'm afraid we've got nothing stronger."

"That's OK," said Robert. "If you can tell us the way . . ."

"Of course."

The flat was in the basement of a row of daunting Victorian

houses that had once seen better days. They were much gabled, and decorated with fancy brick work and stained windows, but the street itself was dismal, and the curtains of bow-windowed front rooms sagged sadly and were not always very clean. Worn stone steps led down to an area where there were dustbins and one or two dead geraniums in pots, and, as they descended, there was a scream of fury from a frustrated cat, and a black, rat-like form shot up the stairs between their legs. Jane let out a small scream of fright.

"It's all right," said Emma. "It's only a cat."

Christo opened the door, and went ahead, turning on cold overhead lights, for the flat was a furnished one, and not supplied with lamps. Johnny had started making a couple out of Chianti bottles but had got no further than buying adaptors and a pair of fancy shades. The rooms of the flat had been sketchily converted, and it was still sadly obvious that their original intentions had been kitchens, larders, and wash-houses. An old range had been torn from the wall, and the resultant void filled with shelves, which no one had ever bothered to paint, and which acted as a catch-all for books, shoes, scripts, cigarettes, letters and a pile of old magazines. There was a divan which had been covered with an orange curtain and piled with thinly-filled cushions, but remained stubbornly a bed. There were one or two rickety kitchen chairs and a folding table, and the flagged floor was sparsely covered by an elderly carpet which had long since lost all colour and most of its pile. The walls had been whitewashed, but there were oozing damp stains like maps, and the corners of a bull-fighting poster, stuck to the bricks, was already beginning to curl. There was the smell of mice and dry rot, and, even on this hot summer evening, the very airlessness was clammy, like the inside of a cave.

Christo dropped his script on a table and went to open the window which was protected with iron bars, like a prison.

"Let's have some air. We have to keep the place shut up because of the cats, they get in anywhere. What would you like to drink? . . . There is beer, if Johnny hasn't drunk it all . . . or perhaps you'd like coffee. Have we got any coffee, Emma . . . ?"

"There's some instant coffee. I don't get the other sort, because there's nothing to make it in. Do sit down . . . sit on the bed. Sit anywhere. There are some cigarettes . . ." She found them, a box of fifty, handed them round, searched for an ash-tray while Robert lit them. There was no ash-tray, so she went down the flagged passage to the kitchen for a couple of saucers. The sink was full of dirty dishes, and for a moment she could not think when they had used them, when she had last been here, from what back-log of history they dated. Pinned down, remembered, the morning seemed three weeks away. No day had ever lasted for longer. And now, it was past eleven o'clock at night, and still it was not over. Still, the boys had to be given their supper, the kettle boiled for coffee, the can-opener found.

She found two clean saucers and took them back to the others. Christo had put on a record. He could do nothing, not even talk, without perpetual background music. It was Ella Fitzgerald and Cole Porter.

> Every time we say good-bye
> I die a little.

They were talking about *Daisies on the Grass*. ". . . if you can breathe life into a script like that," Jane was saying to Christopher, ". . . I'm sure you're going to go far." She was laughing. Emma put down the ash-tray, and Jane looked up. "Thank you . . . is there anything I can do?"

"No, nothing. I'll just go and get some glasses. Would you like beer, or would you rather have coffee?"

"Would coffee be too much trouble?"

"No, not at all . . . I'd like coffee too . . ."

Back in the kitchen, she closed the door, so that they would not hear her clattering dishes, and tied on an apron, and put a kettle on to boil. When she lit the gas, it always

324

backfired and frightened her out of her wits. She found a tray and cups and saucers, the tin of coffee, sugar, the cans of beer in a box beneath the sink. There were black beetles on the floor and Johnny had not emptied the trash can. She picked it up to take it out to the dustbin, but as she did so the door behind her opened, and she turned to face Robert Morrow.

He looked at the bucket. "Where are you taking that?"
"Nowhere," said Emma, furious at being caught. She turned to sling it back under the sink again, but he caught her arm and took it from her, looking with distaste at the mixture of old tea-leaves and of opened tins, and wet paperbags.

"Where does this go?"
Defeated, Emma told him. "In the dustbin. By the door. Where we came in."

He bore it off, down the passage, looking ridiculous, and Emma went back to the sink, and wished that he had not come. He didn't belong in Brookford; at the theatre; here, in the flat. She didn't want him to be sorry for her. For after all, there was nothing to be sorry about. She was happy, wasn't she? She was with Christo, and that was all that mattered, and how they managed their affairs had nothing whatever to do with Robert.

She prayed that he and his immaculate friend would be gone by the time Johnny Rigger returned.

When he came back with the empty bucket, she was clattering dishes, trying to give the impression that she was being busy. She half-turned over her shoulder and said coolly, "Thank you. I shan't be a moment," hoping that he would take the hint and leave her alone.

But it was no good. He shut the door, put the trash can down on the floor, and taking Emma by the shoulders, turned her round to face him. He wore an unrumpled and cool-looking suit, a blue shirt, and a dark tie, and Emma had the dish-mop in one hand and a plate in the other, and had to make herself look up and meet those probing grey eyes.

325

She said, "I wish you hadn't come. Why did you come?"

"Marcus has been worried about you." He took the dish-mop and the plate from her and leaned over to tip them back into the cluttered sink. "Perhaps you should have let him know where you were."

"Well, now you can tell him, can't you? And, Robert, I've got a lot to do, and there's just not room for two people in this kitchen . . ."

"Isn't there?" He was smiling. He settled himself on the edge of the table, and now his face was on a level with hers. He said, "You know, this evening, when I first saw you in the theatre I didn't know it was you. Why did you cut your hair?"

He could be very disarming. Emma put up a hand to stroke the stubbly nape of her neck. "When I started working at the theatre, it was such a nuisance. It got in the way, and then it was so hot, and it was always being splashed with paint when I was doing scenery. And there's nowhere here to wash it, and even if I did wash it, it took hours to dry." She hated talking about her hair. She missed it; missed its weight and familiarity and the soothing therapy of brushing it each night. "So one of the girls in the theatre cut it off for me." It had lain on the Green Room carpet like skeins of brown silk and Emma had felt like a murderer.

"Do you like working in the theatre?"

She thought of Collins. "Not much."

"Do you have to . . . ?"

"No, of course not. But Christo's there all day, you see, and there's nothing much to do here, on my own. Brookford's terribly dull. I didn't know such dull places even existed. So when this other girl went ill with appendicitis, Christo fixed it for me to go and help out."

"What will you do when she comes back?"

"I don't know. I haven't thought."

Behind her, the kettle boiled over. Emma turned swiftly to put out the gas, and lift the kettle on to the tray, but Robert said, "Not just yet."

She frowned. "I was going to make coffee."

"Coffee can wait. Let's get everything sorted out first."

Emma's face closed up. "There's nothing to sort out."

"Yes, of course there is. And I want to be able to tell Marcus what happened. For instance, how did you get hold of Christopher?"

"I rang him up – early that Sunday morning. I went to the call box and rang him up. They were having a dress rehearsal, so he was at the theatre. You see, he'd already asked me to come to Brookford and be with him, but I couldn't, because of Ben."

"You'd already spoken to him that morning, when I came to say goodbye?"

"Yes."

"And you never told me?"

"No, I didn't tell you. I wanted to start something quite new, a whole new life, without anybody knowing."

"I see. So you rang Christopher . . ."

"Yes, and that night he borrowed Johnny Rigger's car, and he came down to Porthkerris and brought me back here. We closed up the cottage together, and we left the key of the studio at the Sliding Tackle."

"The landlord didn't know where you were."

"I didn't tell him where I was going."

"Marcus phoned him."

"Marcus shouldn't have. Marcus isn't responsible for me any more. I'm not a little girl now."

"What Marcus feels is not simply responsibility, Emma, but a real fondness and you should realise that. Have you heard from Ben?"

"Yes, I had a letter on that Monday morning, before I left Porthkerris. And one from Melissa, too . . . asking me to go out and visit them."

"And did you write back?"

Emma shook her head. "No." She was ashamed of this, and swiftly looked down, to fiddle with a jagged thumbnail.

"Why not?"

She shrugged. "I don't know. I suppose I thought I'd be in the way."

"I should have thought that even being in the way was preferable to this . . ." His gesture embraced the littered kitchen, the whole seedy flat.

It was not the most fortunate of remarks. "What's wrong with it?"

"It's not just this place, it's that crumby theatre, the lunatic with a beard who was yelling at you to move the sofa . . ."

"Well, you told me to get a job."

"Not this kind of a job. You have a good brain, you speak three languages, and you appear to be moderately intelligent. What sort of a job is it pushing furniture around a third class re . . . ?"

"My real job is being with Christo!"

After this outburst, there was a terrible silence. A car passed in the street outside. Christopher's voice came up the stone passage, backed by the soft-playing record. A cat started yowling.

Robert spoke at last. "Do you want me to tell your father that?"

Emma blazed once more into the attack. "I supposed that's why you came. Spying for Ben."

"I simply came to find out where you were and how you were."

"Be sure to give him all the ghoulish details. It doesn't matter to us, and he won't take any notice, anyway."

"Emma . . ."

"Don't forget, he is no ordinary, run-of-the-mill parent, as you are only too fond of telling me."

"Emma, will you listen . . . !"

The last word was scarcely out of his mouth, when the door behind him burst open and a slurred and cheerful voice broke in. "Well, what a nice little chat you two are having!"

Robert wheeled. In the open doorway stood the young man who had played the part of the stuffy stockbroker in

328

Daisies on the Grass. Only now he was stuffy no longer, but quite simply very drunk, and to steady himself hung on to the top of the doorway, like a monkey swinging on a trapeze. His legs, buckling slightly, did nothing to dispel this impression.

"Hello, darling," he said to Emma. He let go of the door and weaved into the tiny kitchen, rendering it unbearably crowded. With the palms of his hands flat on the table, he leaned forward to kiss Emma. The kiss was loud and smacking, but did not come within six inches of her face.

"We've got callers," he observed. "And a bloody great car parked outside. It adds great tone to the neighbourhood." His legs buckled again, and for a second his weight was supported solely by his arms. He smiled expansively at Robert. "What's your name?"

"He's called Robert Morrow," said Emma shortly, "and I'll make you some coffee."

"I don't want coffee. I do not want coffee." He raised his fist to the words, and once more his legs let him down. This time Robert caught him, and hauled him upright.

"Thanks, old boy. Very civil of you. Emma, how about a little sustenance? Feed the inner man; you know the routine. I do hope you've asked this nice chap Robert to stay for dinner. There's also a toothsome blonde in the other room, chatting Christopher up to no mean tune. Know anything about her?"

Nobody bothered to answer him. Emma turned back to the cooker, took the lid off the kettle and put it on again. Johnny Rigger stared at her back and then at Robert, apparently waiting for life, with all its confusions, to be explained to him.

Robert could not trust himself to speak. He yearned to pick up this shambling drunk by the scruff of his neck and chuck him somewhere; preferably in the dustbin, where he had just dumped the unsavoury contents of the trash can. Then he would come back to deal with Emma in the same way, flinging her into the back of his car, driving her to London, to Porthkerris, to Paris – anywhere, away from this terrible basement, from the theatre, from the depressing suburban town.

He stared at her stubborn back view, willing her to turn round and face up to him. But she did not move, and her thin neck, and her shorn head, and the droop of her shoulders, all of which, he knew, should touch on his sympathy, did nothing but infuriate him.

He said, at last, formally, "This is simply a waste of everybody's time. I think Jane and I should go."

Emma accepted this in silence, but Johnny was full of protests. "Oh, you must stay, old chap. Stay and have something to eat . . ."

But Robert had pushed past him and was already halfway down the flagged passage. He found the other two deep in conversation, and quite unaware of any sort of drama. Christopher was saying, "Yes, it's a wonderful play. And what a part! You can build on to it, yet never overload it, never interfere in any way with production . . ."

(And he remembered bitterly the old crack about actors. "Now, let's talk about *you*, my friend. What did *you* think of my performance?")

"I trust you're not discussing *Daisies on the Grass*."

Christopher looked round. "Good God, no! *Present Laughter*. What's Emma doing?"

"Your friend has just arrived back."

"Johnny? Yes, we just saw him tottering by."

"He's drunk."

"He quite often is. We fill him up with black coffee and shovel him into his bed. He's right as rain in the morning. Most unfair, really."

"Is there any particular reason why he should have to be here with you and Emma?"

Christopher raised his eyebrows. "Every reason." His voice was cool. "It's his flat. He got here first. I was second. Emma made a very cosy third."

There was a pause in the conversation. Jane, sensing the worst sort of conflict, broke tactfully in.

"Robert, it is getting late . . ." She picked up her bag

330

and her gloves, and got up off the divan. ". . . Perhaps we should be going."

"But you haven't had your coffee. Or beer, or anything. What is Emma doing?"

"Doing her best to prop up Mr Rigger," Robert told him. "I suggest you go and help her. His legs don't seem to be at their most reliable."

Christopher, shrugging, acknowledged this. He uncurled his length from the low chair in which he had been sitting, and stood up. "Well, if you really feel you have to go . . ."

"I think we should. Thank you for . . ."

The words died out. There was nothing to thank him for. Christopher looked amused and Jane once again came to Robert's rescue.

". . . thank you for your wonderful performance this evening. We won't forget it." She held out her hand. "Goodbye."

"Goodbye. And goodbye, Robert."

"Goodbye, Christopher." And then he had to make himself say it. "Look after Emma."

They drove with unlawful speed back to London. On the motorway the needle of the speedometer crept up and up. Eighty, ninety, a hundred . . .

Jane said, "You're going to get into trouble."

"I already am," said Robert shortly.

"Did you have a row with Emma?"

"Yes."

"I thought you were looking a little fraught. What was it about?"

"Snooping. And moralising. And interfering. And trying to make a basically intelligent girl see the smallest glimmer of sense. She looked awful, too. She looked ill."

"She'll be all right."

"Last time I saw her, she was brown as a gipsy, with hair to her waist and a sort of bloom about her, like a delicious ripe fruit." He remembered the pleasure of kissing her goodbye. "Why do people have to do such dreadful things to themselves?"

"I don't know," said Jane. "Perhaps because of Christopher."

"How did you get on with him? I mean, apart from falling in love with him."

She ignored this. "He is clever. He is single-minded. He is ambitious. I think he will go far. But alone."

"You mean, without Emma."

"I'd say that."

Even at one in the morning London was alive with lights and traffic. They turned down into Sloane Street, circled Sloane Square, took the narrow road that led to Jane's mews. Outside her little house, he killed the engine of the Alvis, and it was very quiet. Street lamps shone on to the cobbles, on to the gleaming bonnet of the car, on to Jane's blonde and shining head. Robert was suddenly very tired. He began to reach for a cigarette, but Jane was there first. She put the cigarette into his mouth and lit it for him. In that instant her eyes became large and mysteriously shadowed, and there was a small and beguiling shadow, like a smudge, below the curve of her lower lip.

She snapped out the lighter. He said, "It's been a bloody awful evening. And I'm sorry."

"It always makes a change. It was interesting."

He pulled off his cap and dropped it on to the back seat. "Do you suppose," he said, "that they're living together?"

"Darling, I wouldn't know."

"But she's in love with him."

"I would say so."

For a little they were silent. Then Robert stretched, flexing himself after the long drive. He said, "We never got any dinner, did we? I don't know about you, but I'm hungry."

"If you want, I'll cook you scrambled eggs. And pour you a big cold Scotch-on-the-rocks."

"You're twisting my arm . . ."

332

They laughed, quietly. Night time laughter, he thought Pillow laughter. He put his left hand up and around her neck, slid his fingers up into her hair, and leaned forward to kiss her mouth. She tasted sweet and fresh and cool. Her lips parted, and he threw his cigarette away, and pulled her tightly and closely into his arms.

After a little, he took his mouth from hers. "What are we waiting for, Jane?"

"One thing."

He smiled. "What's that?"

"Me. I don't want to start something that isn't ever going to be finished. I don't want to be hurt again. Even for you, Robert, and God knows how fond I am of you."

He said, "I won't hurt you," and meant it, and kissed the shadow under her mouth.

"And please," she said, "no more Littons."

He kissed her eyes, and the end of her short nose. "It's a promise. No more Littons."

He let her go then, and they got out of the car, and closed the doors as quietly as they had laughed together. And Jane found her key, and Robert took it from her and opened the door, and they went in, and Jane turned on the light, and started up the narrow stairs, and Robert closed the door, gently, behind them.

9

One of the delights of the big old house in Milton Gardens was living there in the summer. At the end of a warm and stuffy June day, and after the frustrations of a snail's-pace, petrol-laden journey back down the Kensington High Street, it was a positive physical pleasure to come in through the front door and slam it with happy finality behind you. The house always felt cool. It smelt of flowers and wax-polish, and in June the chestnut trees were out and so thick with leaves and pink and white blossom that the surrounding terraces of houses were shrouded from sight, sounds of all traffic were muffled, and only the occasional aeroplane, passing overhead, broke the evening calm.

Today was a classic example of this particular relief. There was thunder about, and since morning the temperature had steadily risen as the storm clouds gathered. Beneath this doom-like atmosphere, the city sweltered. By now the parks were dusty and the trampled grass turning brown, and the air about as refreshing as a draught of used bath-water. But here, at home, Helen had the sprinklers working on the lawn, and a gust of sweet, damp air swept through the open door at the end of the hall, and greeted Robert as he came indoors.

He dropped his hat on the hall chair, picked up his letters, called "Helen?"

She wasn't in the kitchen. He went down the hall and out of the door and down the steps to the terrace and found her there, with a tea-tray and a book – unread – and a basket of mending. She wore a sleeveless cotton dress and a faded pair of espadrilles, and the sun had brought freckles out, big as paint spots, across her nose.

335

He came across the grass towards her, shedding the jacket of his suit.

She said, "You have caught me, doing nothing."

"And very nice too." He slung the jacket over the back of a painted wrought-iron chair, and collapsed beside her. "What a day! Anything left in that teapot?"

"No, but I can make you some more."

"Why don't I?" said Robert automatically, but without notable enthusiasm.

She did not reply to this hypothetical question, simply got up and took the teapot indoors. There was a plate of biscuits, and he took one and began to eat it, pulling his tie loose with the other hand. Beneath the sprinklers the lawn lay thick and green. It needed cutting again. He leaned back and shut his eyes.

It was now six weeks since he had been to Brookford to find Emma Litton, and in all that time there had been no word from her. After some discussion with Marcus and Helen he had written to Ben, telling him that Emma was staying with Christopher Ferris, whom she had re-met in Paris. That she was working in the Repertory Theatre in Brookford. That she was well. He could not, in truth, say more. Surprisingly, Ben had acknowledged this, not directly, to Robert, but as a scribbled footnote to a letter to Marcus. The purpose of the letter itself was purely business, typewritten on the impressive engraved paper of the Ryan Memorial Museum of Fine Arts. The retrospective Litton Exhibition was now over. In every way it had been a resounding success. Now, the new exhibition – a posthumous collection of drawings of a Puerto Rican genius who had lately died in dismal circumstances in a Greenwich Village garret, was well under way, and he and Melissa were taking the opportunity of a trip to Mexico. He intended to start painting again. He did not know when he would be returning to London. He remained, always, Marcus's Ben. And then, under the signature, and in Ben's own indecipherable scrawl:

336

Had a letter from R. Morrow Please thank him.
Emma always fond of Christopher. Only hope
his manners have improved.

Marcus showed this to Robert. "I don't know what
you expected," he said, dryly, "but this is what you
have got."

So it was over. For the first time Robert found himself
in whole-hearted agreement with his sister Helen. The
Littons were brilliant, unpredictable and charming. But
they refused to conform to any pre-set behaviour pattern and they would not help themselves. So they were
impossible.

To his surprise, he found that Emma was easy to forget.
He could put her out of his mind as ruthlessly as an old
trunkful of junk, relegated to the darkest recesses of some
distant, dusty attic. And his life immediately became so full
that the void left by her going was, almost at once, filled by
more worthwhile pursuits.

At the Gallery, they were furiously busy. His days
were a round of prospective clients, foreign visitors, and
eager young artists carrying folios which bulged with
their unsalubrious paintings. Would Bernstein mount an
exhibition for them? Would Bernstein back this flame of
new talent? The answer was usually, No, Bernstein's would
not, but Marcus was a kindly man, and it was a house rule
that no young man was returned to Glasgow or Bristol or
Newcastle, or wherever it was he lived, without a good meal
in his stomach, and the price of his return fare in the pocket
of genuinely work-stained jeans.

Robert found that his vitality leapt to meet these
demands, and, running at full speed, his energy could
not – or would not – slow down. He could not bear to find
himself doing nothing, and deliberately filled his leisure
time with extraneous diversions, and a surprising number
of them were involved with Jane Marshall.

The fact that their working hours did not always coincide
put him off not at all. Sometimes he would call in for a drink

337

at her little house, on the way home from the Gallery, and find her still in an apron, sewing braid on to yards of curtain, or working out the intricacies of a scalloped pelmet on graph paper. Sometimes she was out of town, and then he would fill the evening with furious physical labour, digging the garden or mowing the lawn.

One weekend he and Jane went down to Bosham, where Jane's brother had a small cottage, and kept a catamaran moored out on the choppy waters of the Hard. They sailed all Sunday and there was a stiff breeze and a bright, burning sun, and at the end of the day, sleepy with all the fresh air, they sat in the village pub and drank draught bitter and played shove ha'penny, and drove back to London very late, with the roof of the Alvis down, and wind blowing scraps of cloud across the face of the stars.

Once more Helen started saying, "I think you should marry her."

Robert ignored the nudging suspicion that he was behaving badly, and only said, "Perhaps I will."

"But when? What are you waiting for?"

He did not answer because he did not know. He only knew that this was not the time to plan; or assess; or to start to analyse the feelings that he had for Jane.

Now, he was disturbed, by Helen, returning with his tea-tray. She set it down, and the iron table grated on the pavings as she pulled it towards him. She said, "Marcus phoned at lunch-time."

Marcus had had to return to Scotland. The whisky-loving Scottish baronet, who had been so anxious to part with his art treasures, was being balked by his son, who would presumably inherit the heirlooms and did not want them sold out of hand. Or, if they were to be sold, he wanted three times as much for them as his thirsty father was prepared to ask. After a great deal of expensive telephoning, Marcus had reluctantly decided that another visit must be paid north of the border. Business must always come before personal comforts and preferences, and if, to lay his hands

338

on those pictures, he had to sleep in damp beds and icy rooms and eat appallingly-cooked food, then he was ready to do so.

"How is he getting on?"

"He was reserved. No doubt speaking from some soaring baronial hall, with the old Laird listening from one end of the room, and the young Laird listening from the other."

"Has he got the pictures?"

"No, but he will. If not all, then some of them . . ." She went away from him, across the grass, to move the sprinkler. "The Raeburn he is determined on," she said, over her shoulder. "He'll go to any price."

Robert poured his tea, and began to read the evening paper. When Helen came back, he handed it to her open at a middle page.

"What's this?" she asked.

"That girl. Dinah Burnett . . ."

"Who is she?"

"You should know her face by now. She's a young actress with an efficient publicity agent. Every time you open a paper or a magazine, there's a picture of her perched on a piano, or cuddling a kitten or something equally obnoxious."

Helen made a comic face at the thrusting, sexy photograph, and read the caption aloud.

> Dinah Burnett, the red-head who made such an impact on the TV series *Detective*, is in rehearsal now for the new Amos Monihan play *The Glass Door*, her first serious stake in legitimate theatre. "I'm scared," she told our special reporter. "But so very proud to have been chosen for this wonderful play." Miss Burnett is twenty-two and comes from Barnsley.

"I didn't know there was a new Amos Monihan play on the stocks. Who's producing?"

339

"Mayo Thomas."

"Then she must be good. Extraordinary, what talent can lurk behind really very stupid faces. But why did you suddenly show this to me?"

"No reason, really. Just that Jane's doing up a flat for her. At first it was going to be a pretty modest affair, but as soon as she got this part, she reckoned she'd moved in with the big-time spenders; you know, mirror bathrooms and white mink bedcovers."

"Very nice," said Helen. She tossed the paper back into his lap but he was too hot and lazy to catch it, so it slipped from his knee and fell to the ground. After a little, Helen began, in a desultory fashion, to gather the tea things together. She picked up the tray and started indoors.

"How about dinner?" she asked. "You going to Jane's or are you staying here?"

"I'm going to Jane's."

"That's fine. I'll eat a piece of cheese. It's too hot to cook, anyway."

When she had gone, he lit a cigarette and sat, listening to the pigeons, and watching the shadows lengthen over the grass. The cool and the quiet were like a benediction. The cigarette finished, he got up and went back into the house, and upstairs to his own flat, where he showered and shaved, and changed into jeans and a cool shirt. As he was pouring the first drink of the evening, the telephone rang. He filled the tumbler halfway up with soda, and went to his desk to answer it. It was Jane.

"Robert?"

"Yes."

"Darling, it's me. Look I just wanted to warn you, don't get here till about eight . . ."

"Why, are you entertaining a lover?"

"Wish I were. No, it's Dinah Burnett, she's had a new idea for her bathroom, God rot her soul, and she wants to come along after rehearsals and talk about it."

"For a girl who is so proud about being in the blasted play, her mind does harp on material things, doesn't it?"

340

"So you've been reading the evening paper. That blurb makes me ill."

"I can't think why she didn't bother to mention that she was doing up a flat, and had chosen well-known interior decorator, twenty-seven-year-old Jane Marshall, 34, 26, 36, to help her. Were you expecting to be taken out for dinner, because I'm not dressed accordingly."

"Of course not, it's much too hot. I've got some cold chicken; I thought I'd make a salad."

"And I shall subscribe a frosty bottle of wine."

"Delicious."

"Till eight, then."

"Yes, eight." He was on the point of putting down the receiver when she said again, "Don't come before," and than rang off. Mildly puzzled, he put down the receiver and then decided that he must have imagined a certain urgency in her voice. He went to find ice for his drink.

Deliberately, he was a little late, but even so, when he drew up outside Jane's house, there was a small blue Fiat still parked by her door. He gave his double toot on the horn and got out of the car, carrying the bottle of wine, and almost at once the front door opened and Jane stood there, in a faded pair of pink cotton trousers and a sleeveless top. Her hair fell across her cheek and she looked, for Jane, mildly distraught, making flapping gestures with her hand, and pointing upstairs.

He was amused. He came to kiss her. "What is it?"

She took the bottle of wine from him. "She's still here. She won't go. She won't stop talking. And now you've come, nothing's going to shift her."

"We'll say we're going out, and that we're late already."

"I suppose it's worth a try." They had been talking in whispers. Now she said in clear and social tones, "I wasn't sure if it was you or not. Come along up."

He followed her up the narrow, steep stairs. "Dinah, this is Robert Morrow . . ." Casually she introduced them, before going into the kitchen with the wine. He heard the big fridge door open and shut as she put it away.

341

Dinah Burnett sat on Jane's big sofa by the open window, with her legs curled up beneath her, looking as though she was expecting a photographer, or an interviewer, or a prospective lover. She was a beautiful girl, ripe and colourful, and it occurred to Robert that no photograph could do her full justice. She had auburn hair and pale green eyes, and skin like an apricot, and was built on proportions that are normally described as "lavish". She wore a short shift dress in a green to match her eyes, and it might have been designed to display as much as possible of her smooth, well-rounded arms and endless legs. Her feet were thrust into wooden sandals, her wrists jangled with gold bracelets and in her ears, gleaming through the profusion of hair, were enormous gold hoop ear-rings. Her teeth were white and even, and her black lashes long and black as soot, and it was hard to believe that she had started life in Barnsley.

"How do you do," said Robert. They shook hands. "I've just been reading all about you in the evening paper."

"Wasn't it a dreadful photograph?" She still had an endearing trace of a Yorkshire accent. "I look like a broken-down barmaid. But still, I suppose it's better than nothing."

She smiled at him, all her feminine charm rising to the bait of a new and attractive man, and Robert, flattered and warmed by her friendliness, settled himself at the other end of the sofa. She went on, "I shouldn't really be here at all, but Jane's doing up this new flat for me, and today I found this American magazine with a fabulous bathroom and I just had to bring it along, after rehearsals, and show it to her."

"How's the play going?"

"Oh, it's most exciting."

"What's it about?"

"Well, it's . . ."

At this juncture Jane reappeared from the kitchen and briskly interrupted. "How about a drink? Dinah, Robert and I are actually going out, but there's just time for a drink before you go."

"Oh, that's sweet of you. If you're sure. I'd love a glass of beer."

"How about you, Robert?"

"Sounds very nice, let me get it . . ."

"No, that's all right. I'm up." She snapped the top off a beer bottle, and poured a glass expertly, with no head to it. "Dinah, Robert's an art dealer, he works in Bernstein's in Kent Street."

"Oh, are you really?" said Miss Burnett, looking wide-eyed and interested, but not very much wiser. "Do you sell pictures and stuff. . . ?"

"Well, yes . . ."

Jane brought Dinah's beer across, pulled up a small table and set the glass down.

"Robert is a very high-powered man," she said. "He's always dashing off to Paris or Rome, to pull off enormous deals, aren't you, Robert?" She went back to her drink tray. "Dinah, you should get him to look out for a picture for the new flat. You need something modern over that fireplace and you never know, it might be an investment. Something to sell when they run out of good parts for you."

"Don't talk about running out. I've only just started. Besides, wouldn't it be very expensive?"

"Not as expensive as that American bathroom."

Dinah smiled engagingly. "But, I always feel a bathroom's terribly important."

Jane had poured two more drinks, now she brought them over, and handed one to Robert. Then settled herself in the chair opposite the sofa, and faced them both across the low table.

"Well, it's your flat, ducky," she said.

Her voice was a little acid. Robert said quickly, "You still haven't told me about the new play . . . *The Glass Door*. When are you opening?"

"Wednesday. This Wednesday as ever is. At the Regent Theatre."

"We must try and get seats, Jane."

"Yes, of course," said Jane.

"The thought of a first night makes me sick with nerves. You see, it's my first shot at the living theatre, as it were, and if it wasn't for Mayo being such a fabulous producer I'd have dropped out weeks ago. . . ."

"You still haven't told us what it's about."

"Well, it's . . . oh, I don't know. It's about this young man, from an ordinary, working-class family. And he writes a book and it's a best seller, and he becomes a sort of celebrity – you know, on television and such. And then he gets mixed up with the film people, and all the time, he's getting richer, and nastier, and he's drinking and having affairs, and generally living it up. And then, of course, in the end, the whole racket falls round his ears like a pack of cards and he finishes up, right where he started, in his mother's house, in the kitchen, with his old typewriter and a blank sheet of paper. It sounds corny, I know, but it's moving and real and the dialogue is out of this world."

"Do you think it's going to go?"

"I don't see how it can fail. But then I'm prejudiced."

"What part do you play?"

"Oh, I'm just one of the many girls. But I'm different, because I get pregnant."

"Charming," murmured Jane.

"But it isn't sordid, not a bit," Dinah assured her. "When I first read the script I didn't know whether to laugh or cry. Real life, I suppose."

"Yes." Jane finished her drink, and put down the empty glass and looked at her watch. She said, pointedly, "Robert, I'm going up to change. We mustn't be late. We'll keep everybody waiting." She stood up. "You'll excuse me, Dinah, won't you?"

"Of course I will, and thank you for being so sweet about the bathroom. I'll ring you up and let you know what I've decided."

"Yes, you do that."

When she had gone upstairs, Dinah smiled once more,

confidingly, at Robert. "I hope I'm not keeping you. I will go when I've finished my drink, but I live in such a dump just now, it's depressing. And it's so hot, isn't it? I wish it would thunder. It would be so much cooler if only it would thunder."

"It will this evening, I'm sure. Tell me, how did you get this part?"

"Well, Amos Monihan, you know, he wrote the play – he'd seen me on TV in *Detective*, and he rang Mayo Thomas and said he thought I'd be right for the part. So I had an audition. That's all really."

"And who plays the lead? The young man. The writer?"

"This is the gamble. The backers wanted a big name, somebody famous. But Mayo had found this new boy – he'd seen him in some provincial rep, and somehow, he convinced the man with the money to give him a try."

"So you have an unknown in the lead?"

"That's about it," said Dinah. "But, believe me, he's good."

She finished her drink. Upstairs Jane was moving about in her bedroom, going to and fro, opening and shutting drawers. Robert got up to retrieve the empty glass. "Would you like the other half?"

"No, really, I won't. I mustn't keep you any longer . . ." She stood up, pulling down her dress, and tossing her long hair away from her neck. She called up the stairs. "I'm off. Goodbye, Jane!"

"Oh, goodbye." Jane sounded more friendly now that her visitor was actually on her way out.

Dinah started downstairs, and Robert followed her, intending to politely see her off the premises. Over her bright head, he leaned forward to unsnib the latch of Jane's front door. Outside, the mews slumbered in the hot airless evening.

He said, "I'll keep my fingers crossed for Wednesday."

"Bless you."

They went out into the street. He opened the door of the Fiat for her. He said, "What's he called, this young actor?"

345

Dinah slid into the driving-seat, revealing more leg than was good for anybody's blood pressure.

She said, "Christopher Ferris."

He thought, *So that's why Jane didn't want me to meet you.*

"Christopher Ferris? I know him."

"Do you? How funny."

"At least . . . I knew his sister."

"I don't know anything about his family."

"He's never mentioned her? Emma?"

"Never a word. But then, chaps don't usually talk about their sisters, do they?"

She laughed, and slammed the car door shut, but the window was down, and Robert leaned his elbow on it, like a salesman with a foot in the door.

He said, "I'd like to wish him luck."

"I'll give him a message for you tomorrow."

"Could I ring him up?"

"Well, I suppose you could, but calls aren't exactly welcome when we're working." And then she had a bright idea. "Tell you what, I've got his home number somewhere. I had to ring up for Mayo, once, and leave a message."

She picked her bag off the other seat, and started to delve. She brought out a script, a purse, a scarf, a bottle of sun oil, a diary. She leafed through the diary. "Here it is, Flaxman 8881. Do you want me to write it down for you?"

"No. I'll remember."

"He might be there now . . . I don't know what he does in his spare time." She smiled again. "Fancy you knowing him. It's a small world, isn't it?"

"Yes. It's a small world."

She started up her engine. "Well, it's been fun meeting you. Cheerio."

He stood back. "Goodbye."

The little car roared away down the mews, and he watched it go. At the junction at the end of the narrow street it paused for a moment, then shot away, turned left and was gone, the sound of its engine swallowed into the anonymous grumble that was London traffic.

He went back into the house, closed the door, went upstairs. There was no sound from the bedroom.

"Jane."

She began immediately to move about, as though occupied.

"Jane."

"What is it?"

"Come here."

"But I'm not . . ."

"Come down here."

After a moment, she appeared at the head of the stairs, wrapped in a thin dressing-gown. "What is it?"

"It's Christopher Ferris," said Robert.

She stared down at him, her expression closed and suddenly implacable.

"What about him?"

"You knew he was in this play. That he's been in London all this time."

She came down the stairs towards him. When her face was on a level with his, she said coolly, "Yes, I knew."

"But you never told me. Why not?"

"Perhaps because I don't believe in stirring up muddy ponds. Besides, you promised. No more Littons."

"This has nothing to do with that promise."

"Then what are you getting so hot and bothered about? Look, Robert, I think I feel about this business much the same way as your sister Helen. Bernstein's act, in a professional capacity, for Ben Litton, and after that, their commitments to the family should end. I know about Emma and the sort of life she's led and I'm sorry for her. I went to Brookford with you, and I saw that creepy little theatre and that dreadful flat. But she is adult, and, as you said yourself, highly intelligent . . . What if Christopher is in London? That doesn't mean Emma has been abandoned. It's a part of his job, and she'll accept it as such, I'm sure."

"That still doesn't explain why you never told me."

"Perhaps because I knew all along that you'd start running round in circles like a demented sheepdog. Imagining the worst, nagged by responsibility, simply because the wretched girl is Ben Litton's daughter. Robert, you *saw* her. She doesn't want to be helped. And if you try, you'll just be interfering . . ."

He said slowly, "I don't know if you're trying to convince me, or yourself."

"You fool, I'm trying to make you see the truth."

"The truth is that, as far as we know, Emma Litton is alone, living in a damp basement with a paralytic drunk."

"Isn't that what she chose to do?"

She flung the question at him, and then, before he could reply, pushed past him and went to the trolley and began fiddling about with empty glasses and beer-bottle tops in a feeble pretence at tidying up. He watched, with a great sadness, her back view, the smooth bell of hair, the tiny waist, the small, capable hands. She was unrelenting.

He said gently, "Dinah Burnett gave me Christopher's number. Perhaps it would be better if I rang him from here."

"Do whatever you like." She carried the glasses through to the kitchen. Robert picked up her phone and dialled the remembered number. Jane came back to collect up the empty bottles.

"Hello." It was Christopher.

"Christopher, this is Robert Morrow speaking. You remember, I came down to Brookford . . ."

"To see Emma. Yes, of course. How splendid! How did you know where to find me?"

"Dinah Burnett gave me your number. She also told me about *The Glass Door*. Congratulations."

"You can save them till we see what the critics have to say."

"Still, it's a great effort. Look, I was wondering about Emma."

Christopher's voice turned cautious. "Yes?"

Jane had come back from the kitchen and now stood by the window, her arms folded, looking down into the street.

"Where is she?"

"In Brookford."

"In the flat. With your friend?"

"My friend? Oh, Johnny Rigger? No, he left. He came to rehearsals drunk one morning and the producer slung him out. Emma's on her own."

Carefully controlling his temper, Robert said, "You never thought of ringing up Marcus Bernstein or myself and telling us this?"

"Well, I would have, but before I left Brookford, Emma made me promise not to. So, you see, I couldn't." While Robert, in seething silence, tried to accept this excuse, Christopher went on, sounding suddenly much younger and not so sure of himself. "I tell you what I did do, though. I felt a bit of a heel leaving her like that . . . so I wrote to Ben."

"You wrote to *who*?"

"Her father."

"But what the hell could he do? He's in America . . . he's in Mexico . . ."

"I didn't know he was in Mexico, but I wrote to him care of Bernstein's, and put please forward on the envelope. You see, I felt *someone* should know what had happened."

"And Emma? Is she still working in the theatre?"

"She was when I left. You see, there was really no point her coming up to London with me. I rehearse dawn to dusk as it is, and we'd never have seen each other. Besides, if *The Glass Door* folds up after a week, then I'll need my old Brookford job back again. Tommy Childers is very kindly keeping it open for me. So we decided it would be better if Emma stayed down there."

"And if *The Glass Door* runs for two years?"

"I don't know what would happen then. But right now, I'll be honest with you, things are a bit tricky. This house I'm living in – it belongs to my mother. I'm living with my mother. You can see, what with things being the way they are, it is a bit tricky."

"Yes," said Robert. "Yes, I can see . . . as you say, it's tricky."

He put down the receiver. Jane, not turning from the window, said, "What's so tricky?"

"He's living with Hester, his mother. And she's obviously refusing to let a Litton darken her door. Silly old bitch. And the drunk flatmate has had the sack, so Emma's on her own. And, to ease his conscience, Christopher has written to Ben Litton to tell him what has happened. And I should like to tie the lot of them together with one great big millstone, and consign them all to a bottomless lake."

"I knew this would happen," said Jane. She turned, then, to face him, her arms still rigidly folded, and he saw that she was not only angry, but deeply upset. "It could be good, this thing between us . . . you know that, don't you, as well as I do. And that's why I didn't tell you about Christopher, because I knew, that if you knew, it would be the end of everything."

He wished he could say *It doesn't have to be the end*, but it was impossible.

"In a way, Robert, all this time, you did keep your promise. You never mentioned Emma. But she was never out of the back of your mind."

Now that it was said, and out in the open, he saw that this was true. He said, hopelessly, "Only because in some extraordinary way, I am involved with her."

"If you are involved with her, it's because you want to be. And it's not good enough, Robert. Not for me. I won't settle for second best. I'd rather go without. I hoped I'd made that clear. With me, it has to be all or nothing at all. I can't go through it all again."

350

He understood. But could only say that he was sorry.

"I think . . . perhaps, you'd better go."

Her arms were still folded, a barrier against him. There was no way to say goodbye. He could not kiss her. He could not lightly say, "It's been fun" in the best traditions of drawing-room comedy. And he could never forgive her for trying to keep him from Emma.

He said, "I'll go now."

"Yes, do that." But as he started downstairs, she remembered something. "You left the wine."

"Forget about the wine," said Robert.

10

The song was over. The lights were dimmed. Charmian as
Oberon moved forward for her final speech. The taped
Mendelssohn music – for the meagre proportions of the
Brookford Rep did not allow space for an orchestra – stole
out across the dark cave of the auditorium and evoked for
Emma, sitting at the prompt desk – all the distilled magic
of a summer night.

> Now until the break of day
> Through this house each fairy stray . . .

It was the end of the first week of *A Midsummer Night's
Dream*. The financial fiasco of *Daisies on the Grass* had
driven the management to a production of Shakespeare
which, although it entailed double the work for everybody,
ensured an Arts Council grant and full houses, composed
mostly of school children and students.

By now Emma was no longer working for Collins, the
stage manager. There was a new ASM, a young girl
fresh from drama school, dedicated, tough and seemingly
immune to Collins' barbed tongue. She was on-stage now,
in the grey velvet tunic and silvered wings of Cobweb,
the fairy, for the huge cast of *The Dream* demanded that
every member of the company should be called in and
given a part.

Because of this, Tommy Childers had asked Emma to
come back and lend a hand with the back-stage activ-
ities. During the past fortnight she had coped with a
number of jobs; helping in the wardrobe, working in
the scenery store; typing scripts, and all the time nipping

out for sandwiches and cigarettes, and making endless pots of tea.

Tonight, she had been given the job of prompter, and had spent the evening with her eyes glued to the prompt copy, terrified of losing her place, of missing a cue, of letting somebody down. But now, as the play drew to its close, and, knowing the rest of it by heart, she allowed her concentration to relax a little, and indulged in the luxury of watching the stage.

Charmian wore a crown of emerald leaves, a silver tabard and silver tights on her long, slim legs. The audience, caught by the old magic of the words, stayed breathless, spellbound.

> Trip away; make no stay;
> Meet me all by break of day.

To eke out the cramped wing space on either side of the stage, Tommy Childers had had built a ramp which led down from the stage and into the centre aisle of the auditorium. Now Oberon and Titania, hand-in-hand, and followed by a retinue of fairies, made their exit down this ramp, running, with the draperies flying like exuberant wings, off the lighted stage, and down into the darkness; swift and quiet; up the aisle and out of the double doors at the back with such an airy suddenness that they were gone almost without a sound, without a trace.

And then it was left to Sara Rutherford, playing Puck, as a tilt-eared teenager, with the stage to herself and a single spotlight.

> If we shadows have offended,
> Think but this, and all is mended.

She had a little pipe. When she got to "So good night unto you all," she played on it the single thread of notes that was the theme of the Mendelssohn music.

Then, triumphant, "Give me your hands, if we be friends, and Robin shall restore amends." And darkness, and curtain, and applause.

All over. Emma let out a sigh of relief that nothing had gone wrong, shut the prompt copy and sat back in her chair. The cast were surging back on stage for the first curtain call. As he went past her, the boy who played Nick Bottom leant over to whisper,

"Tommy asked me to tell you – there's some chap waiting to see you. He's been sitting in the Green Room for half an hour, but Tommy's put him in his office. Thought it might be a bit more private for you. Better go and see what it's all about."

"To see me? But who is it?"

But Bottom was already on stage. The curtain swept up, there was a fresh burst of applause, and smiles and bows and curtsys . . .

Emma's first thought was that it was Christo. But if it was Christo, why hadn't he said? She went down the wooden steps and along the cat-walk that led to the landing at the head of the stage door stairs. Ahead, down a short passage, the Green Room door stood ajar, showing a glimpse of sagging velvet sofa, the old playbills framed on the walls. Tommy Childers's office led off this passage. The door was shut.

Behind her, the applause died down, and then rose again for the second curtain call.

She opened the door.

It was a tiny room, scarcely bigger than a cupboard; scarcely big enough to contain the desk, and a couple of chairs and a filing cabinet. He sat behind the desk, in Tommy's chair, behind Tommy's personal and private chaos of scripts and letters and programme proofs and production notes. The wall behind him was thumb-tacked with stage photographs. Someone had made him a cup of tea, but he had not deigned to drink it, and it stood before him, horribly cold, untouched. He wore pearly-grey trousers, a russet corduroy jacket, a dark blue cotton shirt and a chrome yellow tie, loosely tied, so that his top button showed. He was browner than ever, and he looked about ten years younger, and almost indecently attractive.

He was smoking an American king-size cigarette, and an ash-tray full of butts was indicative of the length of time he had been waiting for Emma. When she came through the door, he turned his head to look at her, resting his elbow on the desk, his chin on his thumb. His eyes, through the veil of cigarette smoke, remained dark and shadowed and quite unreadable.

He said, sounding mildly irritated, "What have you been doing?" and Emma was too stunned to do anything but tell him.

"Prompting."

"Well, come along in and shut the door."

She did as she was told. The applause from the auditorium was closed away. She found that her heart was thudding, but whether this was due to shock, or pleasure, or a certain apprehension it was impossible to know. She said at last, feebly, "I thought you were in America."

"I was, this morning. Flew back today. And yesterday . . . at least I suppose it was yesterday, these International date lines and clocks being changed complicate life to an alarming degree . . . I was in Mexico. Yes; yesterday. Acapulco."

Emma felt for a chair, lowered herself gently on to it before her legs gave way.

"Acapulco?"

"Do you know that the aeroplanes that fly to Acapulco are all painted different colours? And as you go south, the air hostesses do a sort of uniform strip tease. Fascinating." He continued to survey her. "Emma, there's something different about you. That's it, you've cut your hair. What a good idea! Turn around and let me see the back." She did so, swivelling her head cautiously, and watching him out of the corner of her eye. "Much better. Never knew you had such a good shape to your head. Have a cigarette."

He pushed the packet across the desk. Emma took one,

and he lit it for her, leaning forward, cupping the flame with his familiar and beautiful hands. As he shook out the match he said, casually, "A great many letters have been winging their way across the Atlantic. None of them written by you."

It was a rebuke. "No. I know."

"Difficult to understand. Not that I minded in particular – though I must say, as it was about the first letter I'd ever written you, it would have been pleasant to get a reply. But with Melissa it was different. She wanted you to come out to the States, and be with us, if only for a short visit. You've always been rather good about these things. What happened?"

"I don't know. I suppose I was . . . disappointed because you didn't come home. And the idea of your being married took a bit of time to get used to. And then, by the time I got round to accepting it . . . it had become too late to answer your letters. And every day that passed made it worse; made it more impossible. I never knew that if you did something you weren't particularly proud of . . . it became progressively more difficult to undo it again." He did not comment on this. Simply continued to smoke, to watch her. "You said a great many letters. Who did you hear from?"

"Well, I heard from Marcus, of course. That was business. And then a rather stilted, formal affair from Robert Morrow. Saying that he'd been here to see some play or other, and had had a drink with you and Christopher. I couldn't gather, however, whether he had come specifically to see the play or to see you."

"Yes. Well . . ."

"As soon as we realised that you were still alive and apparently occupied and with no intention of visiting us, Melissa and I set off in our coloured aeroplane for Mexico where we stayed with a mad old film star who lives in a house full of parakeets. Then, yesterday, we flew back to Queenstown, and what should I find waiting for me but yet another letter."

"From Robert?"

"No. From Christopher."

She could not help it. "From *Christopher*?"

"He must be an exceptionally talented young man. A London production, so soon, with so little experience. Of course, I always knew that he'd make a flagrant success of his life. Either that or end up in prison . . ."

But even this provocation could not divert her. "You mean *Christopher*? Wrote to *you*?"

"Said in that tone of voice, it sounds insulting."

"But why?"

"One can only imagine that he felt mildly responsible."

"But . . ." An idea was forming. A suspicion so wonderful that, if it was not true, then it must be scotched immediately. "But you didn't come home because of that letter? You came home to paint. To go back to Porthkerris and paint again?"

"Well, of course, taking the long view, I have. Mexico was inspiring. They have an extraordinary pink that keeps recurring in their buildings, and their pictures, and their very clothes . . ."

"Perhaps you'd had enough of Queenstown, and America," she persisted. "You've never been much good at staying in any one place for more than a couple of months. And, of course, you'll have to see Marcus. And start thinking about a new exhibition."

He stared at her blankly. "Why this catalogue of motives?"

"Well, there has to be some reason."

"I've just told you. I came to see you."

She did not want the cigarette he had given her. She leaned forward and stubbed it out, and then clasped her hands in her lap, the palms pressed tight together, the fingers interlaced. Misinterpreting her silence, Ben looked aggrieved. "I don't think, Emma, that you quite understand the situation. I literally flew in from Mexico, read Christopher's letter, kissed Melissa goodbye and flew out again. Didn't even have time to change my shirt. I then

358

subjected myself to another twelve hours of flying, the tedium broken only by a series of uneatable meals, all of which tasted like plastic. Do you think I endure such tortures simply to talk to Marcus Bernstein about another exhibition?"

"But Ben . . ."

He was, however, well away, and in no mood to be interrupted.

"And, once arrived, do I go to Claridges, where Melissa has thoughtfully cabled in advance and reserved me a room? Do I indulge in a bath, or a drink, or a decent meal? No. I climb into the slowest taxi-cab this side of the Atlantic, and drive, through unspeakable rain, to Brookford" (he said the word as though it were something distasteful), "where, after interminable incorrect directions, I eventually run the repertory theatre to earth. The taxi is at this moment outside, ticking up a monumental fare. And if you don't believe me, you can go and look."

"I believe you," said Emma, quickly.

"And then, when you do deign to appear, all you can talk about is Marcus Bernstein and some hypothetical exhibition. Do you know something? You're an ungrateful brat. A typical example of the modern generation. You don't deserve to have a father."

She said, "But I've been alone before. For years I've been alone. In Switzerland and Florence and Paris. You never came to see me then."

"You didn't need me then," said Ben flatly. "And I knew what you were doing, and who you were with. This time, when I read that letter from Christopher, I knew the first, faint stirrings of concern. Perhaps because Christopher, of all people, would never have written if he hadn't been concerned himself. Why didn't you tell me you'd met him in Paris?"

"I thought you wouldn't be pleased."

"It depends on what sort of a person he's turned into. Has he changed very much from the small boy who lived with us at Porthkerris?"

"He looks the same . . . but he's tall . . . he's a man now. Single-minded and ambitious and, perhaps, a little self-centred. And with all the charm in the world." Talking about him, to Ben, was like having a weight lifted from her shoulders. Emma smiled. She said, "And I adore him."

Ben, accepting this, returned the smile. "You sound like Melissa, talking about Ben Litton. It seems that young Christopher and I have, after all, much in common. It's ironic that we should have wasted so many years in detesting each other. Perhaps I should make his acquaintance again. This time, we might get on a little better."

"Yes, I think you might."

"Melissa is joining me in a week or two. Coming down to Porthkerris."

"Living at the cottage?" said Emma, unbelieving.

Ben was amused. "Melissa? At the cottage? You must be joking. A suite has already been reserved at The Castle Hotel. I shall lead the life of a goldfish in a bowl, but perhaps, as I get older, the sybaritic existence is beginning to reveal its charms."

"But didn't she mind? Your coming home like that? Kissing her and leaving her without even taking time to change your shirt?"

"Emma, Melissa is a clever woman. She doesn't try to pin a man down or to possess him. She knows that the best way to hold on to someone you love is to . . . very gently . . . let him go. Women take a long time to learn this. Hester never did. How about you?"

"I'm learning," said Emma.

"The extraordinary thing is, I believe you are."

By now, darkness had fallen. This had happened, unheeded, while they talked, the dusk deepening imperceptibly until Ben's face, across the tiny distance that separated them, was simply a blur, his hair a wing of white. There was a lamp on the desk, but neither of them reached out to turn it on. The twilight enclosed them, the shut door kept the rest of the world out. They were the Littons; a family; together.

As they talked, the backstage shell of the theatre had rung with routine sounds. The last curtain call. Voices; Collins swearing at some unfortunate electrician. Hurrying feet, running upstairs to the dressing-rooms, anxious to be away, to be free of costumes and make-up, to catch buses, to go home, to cook food and wash stockings and, perhaps, to make love. Footsteps passed to and fro, in and out of the Green Room, *Darling, have you got a cigarette? Where's Delia? Has anybody seen Delia? There wasn't a phone call for me, was there?*

The sounds thinned out, as in twos and threes they left the theatre. Down the stone stairs, out of the banging door, into the narrow alley. A car started up. Somewhere a man started to whistle.

Behind Emma the door was abruptly opened, and the soft darkness split with an oblong of yellow light.

"Sorry to interrupt you . . ." It was Tommy Childers . . . "Wouldn't you like some illumination?" He snapped on the switch, and Ben and Emma were transfixed, blinking, like a couple of sleepy owls. "I just wanted something off my desk, before I go home."

Emma stood up, pulling her chair out of the way.

"Tommy, did you know this was my father?"

"I wasn't sure," said Tommy, smiling at Ben. "I thought you were in America."

"Everybody thought I was in America. Even my wife did until I said goodbye to her. I hope we haven't inconvenienced you, sitting here for so long in your office."

"Not at all. The only thing is the night-watchman's getting a bit edgy about the stage door. I'll tell him you'll shut it, Emma."

"Yes, of course."

"Well . . . Good night, Mr Litton . . ."

Ben heaved himself to his feet. "I had thought of taking Emma to London with me tonight. You wouldn't have any objections to that?"

"None at all," said Tommy. "She's been working like a

361

slave for the past two weeks. Do her good to have a few days off."

Emma said, "I don't know why you ask Tommy, when you haven't even asked me."

"I don't ask you things," Ben said. "I tell you."

Tommy laughed. He said, "In that case, I expect you'll be going to the first night."

Ben remained vague. "First night?"

Dryly, Emma enlightened him. "He means Christopher's private view. On Wednesday."

"So soon? I shall probably be back in Porthkerris by then. We shall have to see."

"You should try and make it," said Tommy. They shook hands. "It's been splendid meeting you. And Emma . . . I'll see you sometime . . ."

"Maybe next week if *The Glass Door* folds up . . ."

"It won't," said Tommy. "If what Chris did to *Daisies on the Grass* is anything to go by, it'll run as long as *The Mousetrap*. Don't forget to shut the door."

He went away, downstairs; they heard his footsteps fade down the alley below the window, out into the street. Emma sighed. She said, "I think we should go. The nightwatchman gets traumas if he thinks the place isn't properly locked up. And that taxi driver of yours will either give up hope of ever seeing you again, or else die of old age."

But Ben had once more settled himself into Tommy's chair. "In a moment," he said. "There's just one more thing." He tapped a fresh cigarette from the American packet. "I wanted to ask you about Robert Morrow."

He had the most disconcertingly calm voice. It never changed or varied its inflections so that you were continuously being taken unawares. Every nerve in Emma's body leapt in warning, but she only said, casually enough, "What about him?"

"I always had a . . . strong feeling about that young man."

She tried being flippant. "You mean, apart from admiring the shape of his head."

He ignored this. "I asked you once if you liked him, and you said, 'I suppose so. I scarcely know him.'"

"What of it?"

"Do you know him any better now?"

"Well, yes, I suppose I do."

"When he came to Brookford that time, he wasn't simply visiting the theatre, was he? He came to see you."

"He came to find me. That isn't quite the same thing."

"But he took the trouble to find you. I wonder why."

"Perhaps he was prompted by the famous Bernstein sense of responsibility."

"Stop fencing."

"What do you want me to say?"

"I want you to tell me the truth. And to be honest with yourself."

"What makes you think I haven't?"

"Because a light has gone out of your eyes. Because I left you at Porthkerris, blooming and brown as a gipsy. Because of the way you sit, the way you talk, the way you look." He lit the cigarette then, broke the match, and dropped it meticulously into the ash-tray. "Perhaps you forget I've been watching people, dissecting their personalities, painting them, for more years than you've been alive. And it's not Christopher who's made you unhappy. You've as good as told me that yourself."

"Perhaps it was you."

"Rubbish? A father? Angry, maybe. Hurt and resentful. Never heart-broken. Tell me about Robert Morrow. What went wrong?"

The little room was suddenly unbearably stuffy. Emma got up and went to the window, and opened it wide, leaning her elbow on the sill, and breathing in great draughts of cool, rain-washed air.

She said, "I suppose I never bothered to understand what sort of a person he really was."

"I don't understand."

"Well . . . meeting him, for the first time, the way I did. That started everything off on the wrong foot. I never thought of him as a person with a private life, and a private existence, and likes and dislikes . . . and lovers. He was just part of Bernstein's, as Marcus is part of Bernstein's. Simply there to look after us. To arrange exhibitions, and cash cheques and reserve hotel accommodation, and make sure that life, for the Littons, at least, runs on oiled wheels." She turned to frown at her father, puzzled by her own revelation. "How *could* I have been so moronic?"

"You probably inherited it from me. What put an end to this happy illusion?"

"Oh, I don't know. Things. He came down to Porthkerris to look at Pat Farnaby's pictures, and he asked me to go out to Gollan with him, because he didn't know the way. And it was raining, and very stormy, and he had a big thick sweater on, and we laughed about things. I don't know, but it was nice. And we were going to have dinner together, but he . . . well . . . anyway, I had a headache, so I didn't go after all. And then I came to Brookford to be with Christo, and I didn't think about Robert Morrow any more until that evening when he came to the theatre. I was clearing the stage, and suddenly he spoke, just behind me, and I turned round and he was there. And he had this girl with him. She's called Jane Marshall, and she's an interior decorator, or something very talented. She's pretty, and successful, and they seemed so much a couple. Do you know what I mean? Contained and self-sufficient and . . . together. And I felt as though someone had slammed a door in my face and left me out in the cold."

She turned from the window then, and came back to the desk and sat on it, with her back to her father, and picked up a rubber band and began to play with it, snapping it like a catapult through her fingers.

"And they came back to the flat, for a beer or a coffee or something, and everything was hideous, and Robert and I had a horrible row, and he just walked out without saying goodbye and took Jane Marshall with him. And drove back to London, and, one imagines . . ." she tried desperately to keep her voice light,

". . . lived happily ever after. Anyway, I haven't seen him since."

"Is that why you wouldn't let Christopher tell him that you were on your own?"

"Yes."

"Is he in love with this girl?"

"Christo thought he was. Christo thought she was gorgeous. He said that if Robert didn't marry her, he ought to have his head examined."

"And what was the row about?"

Emma could scarcely remember. In retrospect, it jarred as painfully as a gramophone record, played backwards, at full pitch. An exchange of shouted words, meaningless, hurtful, regretted.

"Oh, everything. You. And not answering your letter. And Christo. I think he imagines Christo and I are madly in love, but by the time we'd got round to that I was so angry I didn't bother to disillusion him."

"Perhaps that was a mistake."

"Yes, perhaps it was."

"Do you want to stay here, at Brookford?"

"There's nowhere else to go."

"There's Porthkerris."

Emma turned to smile down at him. "With you? At the cottage?"

"Why not?"

"A thousand reasons. Running home to Daddy never solved anything. Besides, you can't run away from the inside of your own head."

He was on his way at last, and the self-delusion and the restlessness of the past six weeks were over. The Alvis – like a home-bound hunter – streamed west, out over the Hammersmith fly-over and on to the M4. Robert settled her permanently in the fast outer lane, and kept her speedometer prudently, carefully down to seventy, for the frustration, at this stage, of being stopped by a police patrol would be almost more than he could bear.

As he approached Heathrow Airport, the first rumble of thunder broke the heavy, quiet air, and he stopped in at the first lay-by and put up the hood. He was only just in time. As he moved out into the road again, the sullen evening erupted like a volcano. The wind, with staggering abruptness, swept up from the west, bearing towering black thunderheads before it, and when the rain came it was a positive explosion of water, sheets of it, like a monsoon downpour, against which the windscreen-wipers could scarcely compete. In seconds, the surface of the road was awash, reflecting the livid streaks of forked lightning which split the sky.

It occurred to him that perhaps it would be wise to stop, and wait until the worst of the storm was over, but by now his sense of relief at doing what he had for weeks been subconsciously wanting to do, was stronger than any ideas of caution. So he went on, and the huge cambered curve of the motorway pouted up towards him, and roared beneath his wheels, and was flung away in a wave of water; already a thing of the past; rejected and forgotten, along with his own feeble uncertainties.

He found the theatre closed. By the light of the street lamp, he was able to read the posters. A MIDSUMMER NIGHT'S DREAM. Unlit, deserted, the place looked gloomy as the mission hall it had once been. The door was barred and bolted; all the windows dark.

He got out of the car. It was cooler now, and he reached into the back seat and took out a sweater that had been lying there since the Bosham weekend, and pulled it on over his shirt. He slammed the door shut, and then saw the solitary taxi, waiting at the pavement's edge, the driver slumped over his wheel. He might have been dead.

"Is there anyone in there?"

"Must be, Guv-nor. I'm waiting for a fare."

Robert walked down the pavement, as far as the narrow lane, down which, so long ago, Emma and Christopher had come, walking like lovers, with their arms about each other. On this side of the sombre building a first-floor window blazed with uncurtained light. He went down the shadowed alley, tripped over a dustbin, found an open door. Inside, a flight of stone stairs led upwards, illuminated palely from a light which burned on the first-floor landing. He was assailed by the stale theatre smell of grease-paint, oil-paint, musty velvet. From above came the murmur of voices and he went upstairs, towards it, and found the short passage, and the door marked Producer's Office, ajar, and edged with bright light.

He pushed the door open and the voices ceased abruptly, and he found himself on the threshold of a tiny, crowded office, looking down into the astonished faces of Ben and Emma Litton.

Emma sat on the desk, with her back to her father, facing Robert. She wore a short dress, cut simply as an overall, and her long legs were bare and brown. The room was so small that as he stood there in the doorway, he was only an arm's length from her. If he wanted he could reach out and touch her. He thought that she had never looked so beautiful.

His relief and pleasure at seeing Emma was so great that the unexpectedness of Ben Litton's appearance became insignificant. Ben himself simply raised his dark eyebrows and said:

"Well, bless my soul, see who's turned up now."

Robert put his hands in his pockets, and said, "I thought . . ."

Ben held up a hand. "I know. You thought I was in America. Well, I'm not; I'm in Brookford. And the sooner I get out of the place and back to London, the better."

"But when did you . . . ?"

But Ben was stubbing out his cigarette, standing up, ruthlessly interrupting. "You didn't by any chance notice a taxi-cab at the front of the theatre, did you?"

"Yes, I did. The driver looked as though he had become fossilised to the wheel."

"Poor fellow. I must go and put his mind at rest."

"I've got my car," said Robert. "If you like I'll drive you back to London."

367

"Even better. I can pay the man off." Emma had not moved. Now, Ben edged his way around the desk, and Robert stood aside to let him out of the door.

"By the way, Robert, Emma's coming too. Will you have room for her?"

"But of course." In the doorway, they eyed each other. Then Ben gave a satisfied nod. "Splendid," he said. "I'll wait outside for you both."

"Did you know he was coming?"

Emma shook her head.

"Did it have anything to do with the letter Christopher wrote to him?"

Emma nodded.

"He flew back, today, from the States, to make sure you were all right?"

Emma nodded again, her eyes shining. "He'd been in Mexico with Melissa. But he came straight here. Even Marcus doesn't know he's in the country. He didn't even go to London. He took a taxi from the airport to Brookford. And he wasn't angry about Christopher, and he says if I want I can go back to Porthkerris with him."

"And are you?"

"Oh, Robert, I can't go on, all my life, making the same mistakes. And it was Hester's mistake, too. We both wanted Ben to conform to our ideas of a nice reliable husband, and a kind domestic father. And it was as realistic as trying to cage a panther. And when you come to think of it, how dull caged panthers are! Besides, Ben isn't my problem any longer. He's Melissa's."

Robert said, "So what price now, coming at the bottom of a long list of priorities?"

Emma made a face at him. "You know, Ben once said that you had a noble head, and that you should grow a beard and then he would paint you. But if I tried to paint you it would be with a great big balloon coming out of your mouth with I TOLD YOU SO written on it."

"I never said that to anyone in the whole of my life. And

I certainly didn't come all the way down here tonight to say it."

"What did you come to say?"

"That if I'd known you were on your own, I'd have been here weeks ago. That if I can get two seats for Chris's first night, I want you to come with me. That I'm sorry about shouting at you, that last time I was here."

"I shouted too."

"I hate having rows with you, but in some extraordinary way, being away from you is a thousand times worse. I kept telling myself that it was simply something that was over, and best forgotten. But all the time you were never out of the back of my mind. Jane knew. She told me this evening, she'd known all along."

"Jane . . . ?"

"I'm ashamed to say I've been running Jane round in demented circles trying to keep myself from squaring up to the horrible truth."

"But it was because of Jane that I made Christopher promise not to ring you up. I thought . . ."

"And it was because of Christopher that I didn't come back to Brookford."

"You thought we were having an affair, didn't you?"

"Wasn't that what I was meant to think?"

"But you silly man, Christopher's my brother."

Robert took her head between his hands, and put his thumbs beneath her chin and turned her face up to his. Just before he kissed her, he said, "And how the hell was I supposed to know that?"

When they got back to the car, there was no sign of Ben, but he had left a message for them, tucked between the windscreen-wiper and the wind-shield. "Like a parking ticket," said Emma.

It was an unconventional letter, written on a sheet of cartridge paper torn from Ben's sketch book, and headed by two thumbnail sketches – two profiles turned to face each other. There was no mistaking her own determined chin and Robert's formidable nose.

"It's us. It's for both of us. Read it aloud."

Robert did so. *"The cabby seemed morose at the thought of returning to London on his own, so I decided to accompany him. I shall be at Claridges, but would prefer not to be disturbed before noon tomorrow."*

"But if I'm not to go to Claridges before noon, where am I meant to go?"

"You're meant to come home with me. To Milton Gardens."

"But I haven't any things. I haven't even got a toothbrush."

"I will buy you a toothbrush," said Robert, and kissed her, and then went on reading the letter. *"By then I should have caught up on my sleep and had time to cool the champagne, and will be ready to celebrate anything you may have to tell me."*

"The wily old brute! He knew, all along."

"My love, and God bless you both. Ben."

After a little while, Emma said, "Is that all?"

"Not quite." He handed her the letter and Emma saw, beneath Ben's signature, a third little drawing. A wing of white hair, a brown face, a pair of dark and cruelly observant eyes.

"Self-portrait," said Robert. "Ben Litton by Ben Litton. It must be unique. One day, we might sell it for thousands of pounds."

My love and God bless you both.

"I shan't ever want to sell it," said Emma.

"Nor I. Come on, my darling, it's time to go home."

BOOK THREE

ROSAMUNDE PILCHER

SLEEPING TIGER

1

The wedding dress was creamy-white with a suggestion of pink behind it, like the inside of a shell. It was made of very stiff, thin silk, and it swept the red carpet as Selina moved forward, and when she turned, the hem stayed where it was, so that she felt as if the dress were wrapping her up in a luxurious parcel.

Miss Stebbings said, in a high ladylike voice, "Oh, yes, you couldn't choose one prettier than that. It suits you down to the ground." She pronounced it *syuits*. "Now, what about the length?"

"I don't know – what do you think?"

"Let's pin it a little. . . . Mrs Bellows." Mrs Bellows moved forward from the corner where she had been standing waiting to be needed. Miss Stebbings wore draped crêpe, but Mrs Bellows was in a black nylon overall and shoes that looked suspiciously like bedroom slippers. She had a velvet pincushion held to her wrist by a piece of elastic, and knelt down and pinned up a portion of the hem. Selina watched in the mirror. She was not sure if she agreed with Miss Stebbings that the dress *syuited* her down to the ground. It made her look much too thin (surely she had not lost yet more weight!) and the warm colour only emphasised her pallor. Her lipstick had come off and her ears were showing. She tried to shake her hair over her ears and only succeeded in dislodging the small coronet of satin which Miss Stebbings had placed on the top of her head, and when she reached up to push it straight again, she spoiled the set of the skirt, and Mrs Bellows drew her breath in through her teeth, as though some terrible catastrophe was about to take place.

375

"Sorry," said Selina.

Miss Stebbings smiled quickly to show it didn't matter, and said conversationally, "And when is the happy day?"

"We thought about a month . . . I think."

"You won't be having a big wedding . . .?"

"No."

"Of course not . . . under the circumstances."

"I don't really want to have a proper wedding dress. But Rodney . . . Mr Ackland . . ." She hesitated again, and then said it: "My fiancé . . ." Miss Stebbings beamed with nauseous sweetness. "He thought I ought to. He said my grandmother would have wanted me to be married in white. . . ."

"Of course she would. How right he is! And I always think a very small, quiet wedding, with the bride in white, has a special charm all of its own. No bridesmaids?"

Selina shook her head.

"Charming. Just the two of you. Finished, Mrs Bellows? Now. How does that strike you? Just take a step or two." Selina paced obediently. "That's better. We can't have you tripping."

Selina wriggled slightly inside the rustling taffeta. "It seems awfully loose."

"I think you're getting thinner," said Miss Stebbings, plucking at the material to make it fit.

"Perhaps I'll get fat again before the wedding."

"I doubt it. Better make a tiny alteration, just to be sure."

Mrs Bellows hauled herself off her knees and inserted a few pins at the waistline. Selina turned and walked some more, and finally the dress was unzipped, levered delicately off, over her head, and borne away on the arm of Mrs Bellows.

"When will it be ready?" she asked, pulling her sweater over her head.

"Two weeks, I think," said Miss Stebbings. "And you've decided on this little coronet?"

"Yes, I suppose so. It's quite plain."

"I'll let you have it a few days before, so that you can show it to your hairdresser. It would be rather sweet to have your hair swept up, and through the coronet . . ."

Selina had an obsession about her ears, which she considered large and ugly, but she said weakly, "Yes," and reached for her skirt.

"And you'll see about the shoes, Miss Bruce?"

"Yes, I'll buy some white ones. Thank you so much, Miss Stebbings."

"Not at all." Miss Stebbings held out the jacket of Selina's suit and helped her into it. She noticed that Selina was wearing her grandmother's pearls, two rows fastened with a sapphire-and-diamond clasp. She noticed, too, the engagement ring, a huge star sapphire, set alternately in pearls and diamonds. She longed to remark on it, but didn't want to be thought inquisitive or vulgar. Instead, in a ladylike silence, she watched Selina pick up her gloves, then held aside the brocade curtain of the fitting-room, and saw her out.

"Goodbye, Miss Bruce. It really has been a pleasure."

"Thank you. Goodbye, Miss Stebbings."

She went downstairs in the lift, walked through various departments, and finally out of the revolving doors and into the street. After the overheated interior of the store, the March day felt nippy. Above, the sky was blue, patterned with racing white clouds, and as Selina moved to the edge of the pavement to call a taxi, the wind caught at her, blew her hair all over her face, her skirt up, dust into her eye.

"Where to?" said the driver, a young man in a sporty checked cap. He looked as though he might race greyhounds in his spare time.

"The Bradley, please."

"Rightey ho!"

The taxi smelt of scented disinfectant with an undertone of stale cigars. Selina got the bit of dust out of her eye, and then rolled down the window. There were daffodils blowing in the park, and a girl on a brown horse, and all the trees were misted with green, the leaves as yet untouched by soot or the dirt of the city. It was not a day for London. It was a day to be in the country, to climb a hill, run down to the sea. The streets and the pavements were crowded with lunch-hour traffic, businessmen, and shopping ladies, and typists, and beatniks and Indians, and lovers, hands entwined, laughing at the wind. A woman sold violets from a barrow by the pavement, and even the old derelict who paced the gutter between a pair of sandwich boards wore a daffodil, perkily, in the lapel of his sagging overcoat.

The taxi turned into Bradley Street, and stopped in front of the hotel. The doorman came to open the door, and let Selina out. He knew her, because he had known her grandmother, old Mrs Bruce. Selina had been coming to the Bradley for lunch with her grandmother since she was quite a little girl. Now Mrs Bruce was dead and Selina arrived on her own, but the doorman still knew her, and called her by her name.

"Morning, Miss Bruce."

"Good morning." She opened her bag to find some change.

"It's a lovely day."

"Frightfully windy." She paid the driver, and thanked him, and turned towards the door. "Has Mr Ackland come yet?"

"Yes, about five minutes ago."

"Oh, bother, I'm late!"

"Doesn't do any harm to keep them waiting."

He spun the door for her, and Selina was injected into the warm, expensive interior of the hotel. There was the smell of fresh cigars, of warm delicious food, of flowers and scent. Elegant little parties of people sat about in groups, and Selina felt windblown and untidy. She was about to sidle in the direction of the Ladies' Room, when the man who sat by himself near the bar saw her, stood up, and came over towards her. He was tall and good-looking, in his middle thirties, dressed in the businessman's uniform of dark grey suit, lightly striped shirt, inoffensive regimental tie. His face was unlined, well-featured, his ears flat against his head, his brown hair thick and smooth, coming down, at the back, to meet the shining edge of his collar. Across his well-cut waistcoat hung a gold watch-chain, and his cuff-links and his watch were also gold. He looked what he was: well-to-do, well-groomed, well-bred, and slightly pompous.

He said, "Selina."

Her flight to the Ladies' abruptly halted, Selina turned and saw him.

"Oh, Rodney . . ."

She hesitated. He kissed her, and said, "You're late."

"I know. I'm sorry. There's so much traffic."

His eyes, though quite kind, conveyed that he thought she looked a mess. She was just about to say, "I must go and powder my nose," when Rodney said, "You go and powder your nose." This, she found maddening. She hesitated for a second, wondering whether to explain that she had been on the point of going to the Ladies' when he had interrupted her, but it hardly seemed worth the trouble. Instead, she smiled, and Rodney smiled back, and, apparently in complete accord, they momentarily parted.

When she returned, her fawn-coloured hair straight and combed, her nose powdered, her lipstick fresh, he was sitting on a small curved satin sofa, waiting for her. In front of him was a small table on which stood his martini and the glass of pale dry sherry which he always ordered for Selina. She went to sit beside him. He said, "Darling, before we talk about anything else, I must tell you this afternoon's off. I've got a client coming to see me at two, rather an important chap. You don't mind, do you? I can make it tomorrow."

Their plan had been to go to the new flat which Rodney had leased, and in which they intended starting their married life. It had recently been re-painted and the plumbing and electrical work was completed, and now all they had to do was to measure and choose carpets, and curtains, and decide on colour schemes.

Selina told him that of course she didn't mind. Tomorrow was as convenient as today. Secretly, she was grateful for twenty-four hours' grace before she was compelled to make up her mind about the colour of the sitting-room carpet, and the alternative merits of chintz and velvet.

Rodney smiled again, warmed by her acquiescence. He took her hand, moved the engagement ring a little so that the sapphire lay dead centre on her narrow finger, and said:

"And what have you been doing this morning?"

To such a straightforward question Selina had an essentially romantic answer.

"I've been buying my wedding dress."

"Darling!" He was delighted. "Where did you go?"

She told him. "It sounds very unimaginative, I know, but Miss Stebbings – she's in charge of the model gown department and my grandmother always went there, and I thought I'd rather go to someone I knew. Otherwise I'd probably make the most frightful bloomer and buy something desperate."

"Now why should you do that?"

"Oh, you know how feeble I am with shops; they make me buy anything."

"What's the dress like?"

"Well, it's white, sort of pinky-creamy white. I can't describe it. . . ."

"Long sleeves?"

"Oh, yes."

"And is it short or long?"

Short or long! Selina turned to stare at Rodney. "Short or long? But it's long, of course! Oh, Rodney, do you think I should have got a short one? I never thought of buying a short wedding dress. I didn't even know you could get them."

"Darling, don't look so worried."

380

"Perhaps I should have got a short one. As it's going to be such a quiet wedding, a long one's going to look ridiculous, isn't it?"

"You could change it."

"No, I can't. It's being altered."

"Well then . . ." Rodney was soothing.

"In that case it doesn't matter."

"You don't think I'll look a fool?"

"Of course not."

"It's very pretty. Really."

"I'm sure it is. And now I have news for you. I spoke to Mr Arthurstone, and he has agreed to give you away."

"Oh!"

Mr Arthurstone was Rodney's senior partner, an elderly bachelor, very set in his ways. He suffered from arthritis in his knees, and the thought of coming up the aisle – supporting, rather than being supported by, Mr Arthurstone – was daunting.

Rodney went on, with raised brows, "Darling, sound a little more pleased than that."

"Oh, I am. It's so nice of him to say he'll do it. But, really, does anybody have to give me away? Can't we just go to the church together, and you and I walk up the aisle and then get married?"

"That really wouldn't do at all."

"But I hardly know Mr Arthurstone."

"Of course you know him. He's looked after your grandmother's business affairs for years."

"But that isn't the same as knowing him."

"You only have to walk up the aisle with him. Somebody has to give you away."

"I don't see why."

"Darling, this is the way things are conducted. And there is no one else. You know that."

And of course, Selina did know that. No father, no grandfather, no uncle, no brother. Nobody. Only Mr Arthurstone.

She sighed deeply.

"I suppose so."

Rodney patted her hand again.

"That's my girl! Now, I've got a surprise for you. A present."

"A present?" She was intrigued. Was it possible that Rodney, too, had been affected by the springlike gaiety of this bright March day? Had he, while walking to the Bradley for his lunch date with Selina, been induced into some charming boutique, bought her some useless frivolity to bring a little romance into her day? "Have you, Rodney? Where is it?"

(In his pocket? Expensive presents come in small parcels.)

Rodney reached behind him and produced a package wrapped in stationer's paper and string, which obviously contained a book.

"Here," he said.

Selina tried not to let her disappointment show on her face. It was a book. She hoped that it was a funny one.

"Oh, a book!"

It felt heavy, and hope that it might make her laugh died. It would be an instructive, thought-provoking volume, touching intelligently on various social problems of the day. Or maybe a travel book, with eye-witness accounts of the garish customs of some Central African tribe. Rodney was a great one for improving Selina's mind, and it distressed him deeply that she showed such a marked partiality to magazines, paperbacks and detective stories.

It was the same in other fields of culture. Selina loved the theatre, but could not enjoy a four-hour endurance test about two people living in dustbins. Likewise she was devoted to ballet, but preferred her ballerinas to wear tutus, and waltz to Tchaikovsky, and her musical appreciation did not include solo violin concerts which invariably left her teeth feeling as though she had lately bitten on a sloe.

"Yes," said Rodney, "I've read it myself, but I was so impressed by it that I bought you a copy of your own."

"How very kind." She weighed the parcel up. "What's it about?"

"It's about an island in the Mediterranean."

"That sounds nice."

"It's a sort of autobiography, I suppose. This chap went to live there about six or seven years ago. Converted a house, became very much involved with the local people. His comments on the Spanish way of life struck me as being very balanced, very sane. You'll enjoy it, Selina."

Selina said, "Yes, I'm sure I shall," and laid the parcel down on the sofa beside her. "Thank you very much, Rodney, for buying it for me."

After lunch, they said goodbye on the pavement, standing facing each other, Rodney with his bowler tipped forward over his nose, and Selina carrying the new parcel and with her hair blowing over her face.

He said, "What are you going to do with yourself this afternoon?"

"Oh, I don't know."

"Why not toddle along to Woollands and try to make up your mind about those curtains? If you could get hold of some patterns, we could take them along to the flat when we go tomorrow afternoon."

"Yes." It seemed a sound idea. "That's a good idea."

He smiled at her encouragingly. Selina smiled back. He said, "Well, goodbye then." He did not kiss her in the street.

"Goodbye, Rodney. Thank you for lunch. And the present," she remembered to add.

He made a small gesture with his hand, indicating that neither the lunch nor the present were of any account. Then, with a final smile, he turned and walked away from her, using his umbrella like a walking-stick, and edging swiftly and in a practised fashion between the crowds on the pavement. She waited, half-expecting him to turn for a final wave, but he did not.

Selina, alone, sighed. The day was warmer than ever. All the clouds had been blown away, and she could not bear the thought of sitting in a stuffy shop trying to choose patterns for sitting-room curtains. She walked aimlessly down into Piccadilly, crossed the road, at peril of her life, and turned into the park. The trees were at their prettiest, and grass beginning to be new and green, not brown and dingy with winter any longer. When she walked on the grass it smelt bruised and fresh, like a summer lawn. There were spreading carpets of yellow and purple crocuses, and chairs, in pairs, under the trees.

She went and sat in one of the chairs, leaned back with her legs sprawled and her face turned up to the sun. Soon her skin began to prickle with its warmth. She sat up, and shucked off the jacket of her suit and pushed up the sleeves of her sweater, and thought, I can just as easily go to Woollands tomorrow morning.

A child passed, on a tricycle, with her father walking behind, and a little dog. The child had on red tights and a blue dress and a black band on her hair. The father was quite young, in a polo-necked sweater and a tweed jacket. When the child stopped her tricycle and went over the grass to smell the crocuses he made no attempt to stop her, but watched, holding the tricycle so that it wouldn't roll away, smiling as the little girl bent over, revealing a charming expanse of red tights. The little girl said, "They haven't got a smell."

"I could have told you that," said her father.

"Why haven't they got a smell?"

"I haven't any idea."

"I thought all flowers had a smell."

"Most of them do. Come along now."

"Can I pick them?"

"I shouldn't."

"Why not?"

"The park men don't like it."

"Why not?"

"It's a rule."

"Why?"

"Well, other people like to look at them. Come along now."

The little girl came, clambered back on to her trike and pedalled off down the path, her father behind her.

Selina watched this small scene, torn between pleasure and wistfulness. All her life she had listened in on the lives and conversations of other families, other children, other parents. Their attitudes towards each other caused her endless speculation. As a child, taken to the park by Agnes, her Nanny, she had always hung shyly about at the edge of other people's games, longing to be invited to join in, but too timid to ask. It was not very often that she was invited. Her clothes were always too tidy, and Agnes, sitting knitting on a nearby bench, could look very forbidding. If she thought there was a danger of Selina becoming embroiled with a set of children whom old Mrs Bruce would obviously consider "unsuitable," then Agnes would roll up her ball of wool, spear it with needles, and announce that it was time to walk back to Queen's Gate.

Here, they were a household of women – a small feminine world, ruled by Mrs Bruce. Agnes, who had once been her maid, and Mrs Hopkins, the cook, and Selina, were all her obedient subjects, and a man, unless it was Mr Arthurstone, Grandmother's lawyer, or, in more recent years, Rodney Ackland, representing Mr Arthurstone, had scarcely ever entered the house. When one did – to mend a pipe, do a bit of painting, or read the meter – Selina was invariably found in his company, asking questions. Was he married? Did he have children? What were the children called? Where did they go for their holidays? It was one of the few things that made Agnes cross.

"What on earth would your grandmother say if she could hear you at it – keeping the man from his work?"

"I wasn't." On occasions Selina could be stubborn.

"What do you want to talk to *him* for?"

She could not answer because she did not understand why it was so important. But nobody would talk about

385

her father. His name was never mentioned. Selina did not even know what he had been called, for Mrs Bruce was her mother's mother and Selina had taken her name.

Once, indignant on some score, she had asked outright, "I want to know where my father is. Why haven't I got one? Everybody else has."

She had been told, coldly, but quite kindly, that he was dead.

Selina was taken regularly to Sunday school. "Do you mean he's gone to heaven?"

Mrs Bruce had tugged at a tiresome knot in her tapestry wool. The idea of That Man consorting with the angels she found hard to swallow, but her religious discipline was strong and it would be wrong to disillusion the child.

"Yes," she said.

"What happened to him?"

"He was killed in the war."

"How killed? How was he killed?" (She could imagine nothing more horrifying than being run over by a bus.)

"We never knew, Selina. We really can't tell you. Now —" Mrs Bruce glanced at her watch with an air that indicated the conversation was closed. "Go and tell Agnes it's time for your walk."

Agnes, when tackled, proved a little more forthcoming.

"Agnes, my father's dead."

"Yes," said Agnes. "I know."

"How long has he been dead?"

"Since the war. Since nineteen forty-five."

"Did he ever see me?"

"No. He died before you were born."

This was discouraging.

"Did *you* ever see him, Agnes?"

"Yes," said Agnes reluctantly. "When your mother was engaged to him."

"What was his name, Agnes?"

"Now that, I cannot tell you. I promised your grandmother. She doesn't want you to know."

"Well, was he nice? Was he good looking? What colour was his hair? How old was he? Did you like him?"

Agnes, who was also highly-principled, answered the one question that she could answer truthfully.

"He was very good-looking. Now, I think that's enough. Hurry along, Selina, and don't drag your feet; you'll scuff the toes of your new shoes."

"I'd like to have a father," said Selina, and later that afternoon spent half an hour or more standing watching a father and son sail their model yacht on the Round Pond, edging nearer and nearer all the time in the hope of listening in to their conversation.

She found the photograph when she was fifteen. It was a depressing, wet London Wednesday. There was nothing to do. Agnes had her day off, Mrs Hopkins was sitting with her arthritic legs on a footstool, immersed in the *People's Friend*. Grandmother had a bridge party. Muted voices and the smell of expensive cigarettes stole from behind the closed drawing-room doors. Nothing to do! Selina, prowling restlessly, came into the spare bedroom, looked at the view from the window, made a few film-star faces into the triple mirror, and was just on the way out when she noticed the books in the small cupboard between the two beds. It occurred to her that she might perhaps find a book she had never read, and with this idea in mind she went to kneel between the beds and run her forefinger along the titles.

It stayed still at *Rebecca*. A yellow-jacketed war-time edition. She took it out and opened it, and a photograph fell from the closely-printed pages. A photograph of a man. Selina picked it up. A man in uniform. Very dark-haired, with a cleft in his chin, his eyebrows irregular, his black eyes glinting with laughter although his face was set in suitable solemn lines. He was a soldier, tailored and well-buttoned, with a glimpse of gleaming Sam Browne across one shoulder.

There was the beginning of a wonderful suspicion.

Somewhere, behind the dark amused face, was a suggestion of Selina's own. She took the photograph to the mirror, trying to find resemblances in the planes of her face, the way her hair grew, the squared-off corners of her chin. There wasn't much to go on. He was very handsome, and Selina was plain. His ears lay neatly against his head, and Selina's stuck out like jug-handles.

She turned the photograph over. On the back was written:

> *Harriet, darling,*
> *from G.*

and a couple of crosses for kisses.

Harriet had been her mother's name, and Selina knew then that the photograph was of her father.

She never told anybody about it. She slid *Rebecca* back into the shelf, and took the photograph into her room. After that, she carried it everywhere with her, wrapped in thin paper to keep it clean and crisp. She felt now that she had, at least, a root, however tenuous, but it still didn't fill her need, and she still watched other families, and still listened in to other people's conversations . . .

A child's voice penetrated her thoughts. Selina had been dreaming in the sun. Now, awakened, she was aware of the endless roar of Piccadilly traffic, car horns, and the high-pitched chatter of a baby girl, sitting in a pushchair. The other little girl on the tricycle and her father had long since disappeared. Other groups had taken their place, and a loving couple lay, entwined with complete abandon, only a few yards from where Selina sat.

The wooden chair had grown uncomfortable. Selina shifted her position slightly, and the parcel that Rodney had given her slid off her lap and fell on to the grass. Stooping, she picked it up, and aimlessly, without a thought, began to undo it. The dust-jacket of the book was in glossy-white with the lettering in red:

Selina turned down the corners of her mouth. The book seemed very heavy. She riffled its pages and then closed it, as though she had already finished reading it, with the back of the book lying upwards on her knee.

The face leapt at her, as a name does, suddenly out of a column of newspaper print. It was a casual photograph, blown up to fill the space on the back of the jacket. George Dyer. He wore a white open-necked shirt, and his skin, in contrast, was dark as leather. His face was seamed with lines, they splayed from the corners of his eyes, drew deep channels from nose to mouth, furrowed his brow.

But still, it was the same face. He hadn't changed so much. The cleft was there in the chin. The neat ears, the light in his eye, as though he and the photographer were sharing some outrageous joke.

George Dyer. The author. The man lived on an island in the Mediterranean and wrote about the inhabitants with such balance and sanity. That was his name. George Dyer. Selina picked up her bag, took out the photograph of her father, and, with hands that trembled, held the two photographs alongside each other.

George Dyer. And he had published a book. And he was alive.

2

She took a taxi back to Queen's Gate, ran up the stairs, burst into the flat and called for Agnes.

"I'm here, in the kitchen," Agnes replied.

She was making tea. As Selina appeared in the open kitchen door, Agnes, spooning tea into the pot, looked up. She was a small, ageless person, her slightly sour expression a defence against the tragedies of life, for she had the kindest heart in the world, and she could scarcely bear to hear of hardship or sadness which she was unable to relieve. "Those poor Algerians," she would say, putting on a hat in order to go out and buy a postal order, probably for more than she could afford, and during the Freedom from Hunger campaign she had done without lunch for seven days on end, and suffered cruelly from the resultant tiredness and indigestion.

The lease of the Queen's Gate flat had already been sold, and when Rodney and Selina were married and moved into their new house, Agnes was going with them. It had taken some time to make her agree to this. Surely Selina wouldn't want old Agnes under her feet . . . she would want a fresh start on her own. Selina had managed to assure Agnes that nothing was further from her mind. Well, Mr Ackland, then, Agnes argued; heavens, it would be like having his mother-in-law come to live! Rodney, primed by Selina, talked Agnes out of this one. Then she said she didn't like the idea of moving, she was too old to move, so they took her to see the new flat, and she was charmed, as they had known she would be, by the brightness and convenience of it all, the American kitchen filled with sunlight, and the small sitting-room which would be Agnes's own, with a view of the park, and her own telly. After all, she told herself stoutly, she was going with them to help. She was going to work. And, in time, no doubt she would become a Nanny again, with a new nursery to rule, and another generation of babies, an idea that stirred anew all her latent mothering instincts.

Now she said, "You're back early. I thought you were going to go and measure the floors." Selina stood in the door, pink-cheeked from running upstairs, and her blue eyes bright as glass. Agnes frowned. "Is anything wrong, dear?"

Selina stepped forward and laid a book on the scrubbed table between them. She said, looking Agnes straight in the eye, "Have you ever seen that man before?"

Agnes, alarmed, let her gaze slowly drop to the book on the table. Her reaction was more than satisfactory. She gave a small gasp, dropped the caddy spoon, and sat down suddenly on a blue painted chair. Selina half-expected her to place a hand over her heart. She leaned forward across the table. "Have you, Agnes?"

"Oh," said Agnes. "Oh, what a turn you gave me!"

Selina was relentless. "You have seen him before, haven't you?"

"Oh, Selina . . . where did you . . . How did you know . . . When did you . . ." She was incapable of framing a single question or finishing a single sentence. Selina pulled up a second chair and sat facing her across the table.

"It's my father, isn't it?" Agnes looked as though she was about to cry. "Is that his name? George Dyer? Was that my father's name?"

Agnes pulled herself together. "No," she said. "No, it wasn't."

Selina looked rebuffed. "Well, what was it?"

"It was Gerry . . . Dawson."

"Gerry Dawson. G. D. The same initials. The same face. It's a pen-name. It's obvious; it's a pen-name."

"But, Selina . . . your father was killed."

"When?"

"Just after D-day. Just after the invasion of France."

"How do we know he was killed? Was he blown up in front of an eye-witness? Did he die in somebody's arms? Do we *know* he's dead?"

Agnes ran her tongue over her lips. "He was missing. Presumed killed."

Hope leapt anew. "Then we don't *know*."

"We waited three years, and then he was presumed killed. They let your grandmother know, because Harriet . . . well, you know. She died when you were born."

"Didn't my father have any family?"

"None that we knew of. That was one of the things your grandmother objected to. She said he was without background. Harriet met him at a party; she was never properly introduced, the way your grandmother would have liked."

"For heaven's sake, Agnes, there was a war on! It had been going on for five years. Hadn't Grandmother noticed?"

"Well, maybe, but she had her standards and her principles and she stuck by them. There's nothing wrong in that."

"Never mind about it. My mother fell in love with him."

"Hopelessly," said Agnes.

"And they got married."

"Without Mrs Bruce's consent."

"And did she forgive Harriet?"

"Oh, yes, she was never one to hold a grudge. And, anyway, Harriet came back to live here. You see, your father was sent . . . well, in those days they called it Somewhere in England. But he was sent to France . . . on D-Day-plus two, it was. He was killed soon after. We never saw him again."

"So they were married for . . ."

"Three weeks." Agnes swallowed the lump in her throat. "But they had a honeymoon, and they were together for a little while."

"And my mother was pregnant," said Selina. Agnes looked at her in a shocked silence. She still did not expect Selina to use such words, or even to know about such things.

"Well, yes." The face on the back of the dust-jacket caught her eye, and she straightened the book neatly, watching the wicked light in the dark eyes. Brown, they'd been. Gerry Dawson. Was it really Gerry Dawson? It certainly looked like him, or at least the way he would look now if he hadn't been killed, like that, so young and so handsome.

Memories came nudging back and they were not all of them bad. He had given Harriet a glow and a vitality that Agnes had not known she could possess. With Agnes he had flirted mildly, slid her a pound note when nobody was looking. Nothing for Agnes to be proud of to be sure, but it had been a bit of fun, just the same. A bit of fun when life was singularly unfunny. A masculine wind blowing through the house of women. Only Mrs Bruce had held out against his charm.

"He's a waster," she had announced. "You can tell. Who is he? What is he? Take away the uniform and you're left with a handsome drifter. No sense of responsibility. No thought for the future. What sort of a life can he offer Harriet?"

Of course, in a way, she was jealous. She liked to order people's lives, to keep a tight rein on the way they behaved, and the money they spent. She had meant to choose, herself, a husband for Harriet. But Gerry Dawson, for all his charm, had a personality and a determination to match her own, and he had won the battle.

Afterwards, after he was dead, after Harriet, not wanting to live, had died, Mrs Bruce said to Agnes, "I am going to change the baby's name from Dawson to Bruce. I've already spoken to Mr Arthurstone about it. It seems the obvious thing to do."

Agnes did not agree. But she had never been one to argue with Mrs Bruce. "Yes, madam," she had said.

"And, Agnes, I would rather she grew up not knowing about her father. It can do her no good, and it might make her feel very insecure. I trust you, Agnes, not to let me down." She held the baby on her knee, and she had raised her eyes, and the two women had watched each other over the fluffy head of the baby.

After a little pause, Agnes had said, again, "Yes, madam," and was rewarded with a brief, cold smile. Mrs Bruce lifted Selina and placed her in Agnes's arms. "I feel much happier now," she said. "Thank you, Agnes."

Selina said, "You think it's my father, don't you?"

"I don't know for sure, Selina, and that's the truth."

"Why wouldn't you ever tell me what his name was?"

"I promised your grandmother that I wouldn't. Now, I've broken my promise."

"You didn't have any choice."

A thought struck Agnes. "How do you *know* what he looked like?"

"I found a photograph, ages ago. I never told any of you."

"You're not going to do – do anything." Agnes's voice trembled at the very thought.

"I could find him," said Selina.

"What good would it do? Even if it was your father."

"I know it's my father. I just know it is. Everything points that way. Everything you've told me. Everything you've said. . . ."

"If it is, then why didn't he come back to Harriet, after the war?"

"How do we know? Perhaps he was wounded, lost his memory. These things happened, you know." Agnes was silent. "Perhaps my grandmother was so horrid to him . . ."

"No," said Agnes. "That would never have made any difference. Not to Mr Dawson."

"He'd want to know he had a daughter. That he had me. And I want to know about him. I want to know what

395

he's like and how he talks and what he thinks and does. I want to feel I belong to someone. You don't know how it is, never really belonging to anybody."

But Agnes understood, because she had always known Selina's hunger for what it was. She hesitated and then made the only suggestion she could think of.

"Why don't you talk it over," she said, "with Mr Ackland?"

The publisher's office was at the top of the building, at the end of an uncertain upward journey by small trembling lifts, short flights of stairs, narrow passages and again, more stairs. Out of breath, and feeling as if she were about to emerge on the roof, Selina found herself in front of a door marked "Mr A. G. Rutland."

She knocked. There was no reply, only the sound of a typewriter. Selina opened the door and looked in. The girl who was typing glanced up, stopped for a second and said, "Yes?"

"I wanted to see Mr Rutland."

"Have you an appointment?"

"I called this morning on the telephone. I'm Miss Bruce. He said that if I came about half past ten . . ." She looked at the clock. It was twenty past. The typist said, "Well, he's got someone in with him now. You'd better sit down and wait."

She went on typing. Selina came into the room, shut the door and sat down on a small, hard chair. From the inner office came the murmur of male voices. After twenty minutes or so, the murmur became more animated, and there was the sound of a chair being pushed back, and footsteps. The door to the inner office opened, a man came out, pulling on his overcoat and dropping a folder of papers.

"Oh, careless of me. . . ." He stooped to scoop them up. "Thank you, Mr Rutland, for everything. . . ."

"Not at all; come back when you've got some fresh ideas about the dénouement."

"Yes, of course."

They said goodbye. The publisher began to return to his office, and Selina had to stand up and say his name. He turned and looked at her.

"Yes?" He was older than she had imagined, very bald, with the sort of spectacles you can either look through or over. He was looking over them now, like an old-fashioned schoolmaster.

"I . . . I think I have an appointment."

"You do?"

"Yes. I'm Selina Bruce. I called this morning."

"I am very busy . . ."

"It won't take more than five minutes."

"Are you a writer?"

"No, it's nothing like that. I just wanted you to help me . . . to answer some questions."

He sighed. "Oh, very well."

He stood aside and let Selina walk past him and into his office. There was a turkey-red carpet and a littered desk, and shelves and shelves of books, and books and manuscripts piled on the tables, and on the chairs and even on the floor.

He did not apologise for any of this. He obviously saw no need . . . and indeed there was none. He pushed forward a chair for Selina and went to settle himself behind his desk. Before he was even thus installed, she had begun to explain.

"Mr Rutland, I really am sorry to bother you and I won't take a moment more than I have to. But it's about that book you published, *Fiesta at Cala Fuerte*."

"Oh, yes. George Dyer."

"Yes. Do – do you know anything about him?"

This blurted question was met with an unnerving silence and an even more unnerving glance over the top of Mr Rutland's spectacles.

"Why?" said Mr Rutland at last. "Do you?"

"Yes. At least I think I do. He was a . . . friend of my grandmother's. She died about six weeks ago, and I . . . well, I wanted to be able to let him know."

397

"I can always forward a letter for you."

Selina took a deep breath and proceeded to attack on another flank.

"Do you know very much about him?"

"I should think as much as you. I presume you've read the book."

"I mean . . . you've never met him?"

"No," said Mr Rutland, "I haven't. He lives at Cala Fuerte on the island of San Antonio. He has lived there, I believe, for the last six or seven years."

"He never came to London? Even for the publication of the book?" Mr Rutland shook his bald head so that the light from the window gleamed upon it. "Do . . . do you know if he's married?"

"He wasn't at the time. He may be by now."

"And how old is he?"

"I haven't any idea how old he is." He began to sound a little impatient. "My dear young lady, this is wasting my time."

"I know. I am sorry, I just thought you could help me. I thought there was the chance that he might have been in London, now, and I could have seen him."

"No, I'm afraid not." Firmly, Mr Rutland stood up, indicating that the interview was over. Selina stood up too, and he went to the door and opened it for her. "But if you do want to get in touch, we will be pleased to forward any correspondence on to Mr Dyer."

"Thank you. I'm sorry to have wasted your time."

"Not at all. Good morning."

"Goodbye."

But as she went through the door and crossed the outer office, she looked so despondent that Mr Rutland's heart, despite himself, was touched. He frowned a little, removed his glasses, and said, "Miss Bruce."

Selina turned.

"We send all his letters to the Yacht Club in San Antonio, but his house is called the Casa Barco, Cala Fuerte. It might save time if you wrote to him direct.

And if you are writing, remind him that I'm still waiting for the synopsis of that second book. I've written him a dozen letters, but he seems to have a built-in aversion to answering them."

Selina smiled, and the publisher was amazed at the transformation it wrought to her whole appearance. She said, "Oh, thank you. I am grateful."

"Not at all," said Mr Rutland.

The empty flat was not the most suitable place for a discussion of such importance, but there was no other.

Selina cut short Rodney's observations on the relative merits of plain and patterned carpets, and said, "Rodney, I must talk to you."

Interrupted, he looked down at her in mild annoyance. He had thought, all through lunch, and the subsequent taxi ride, that she did not seem herself. She had eaten scarcely anything, and had seemed preoccupied and vague. Furthermore, she was wearing a blouse which did not seem to go with her fawn coat and skirt, and he had spied a ladder in her right stocking. Selina was normally as well-groomed and co-ordinated as a Siamese cat, and these small irregularities worried him.

He said, "Is anything wrong?"

Selina tried to meet his eye, to take a deep breath and be entirely calm, but her heart was thumping like a sledge-hammer, and her stomach felt as though she had just ascended in a too-fast lift, leaving most of her innards in the basement.

"No, there's nothing wrong, but I simply have to talk to you."

He frowned. "Won't it keep till this evening? This is the only chance we'll get to measure the . . ."

"Oh, Rodney, please help me and listen."

He hesitated, and then with a resigned expression, laid down the book of carpet samples and folded his foot-rule and slid it into his pocket.

"Well? I'm listening."

Selina licked her lips. The empty flat unnerved her. Their voices echoed, and there was no furniture, and no ornament with which to fiddle, no cushion to plump into shape. She felt as if she had been put on to a large, empty stage, with no props and no cues, and she had forgotten her lines.

She took a deep breath and said, "It's about my father."

Rodney's expression scarcely changed. He was a good lawyer, and he enjoyed a game of poker. He knew all about Gerry Dawson, for Mrs Bruce and Mr Arthurstone had long since deemed it necessary to keep him informed on such facts. And he knew that Selina didn't know anything about her father. And he knew that he was not going to be the one to tell her.

"What about your father?" he said, quite kindly.

"Well . . . I think he's alive."

In relief, Rodney took his hands out of his pockets and gave a small snort of incredulous laughter. "Selina. . . ."

"No, don't say it. Don't say he's dead. Just listen, for a moment. You know that book you gave me yesterday? *Fiesta at Cala Fuerte*. And you know it had on the back a photograph of the author, George Dyer?"

Rodney nodded.

"Well, the thing is . . . he looks exactly like my father."

Rodney digested this, and then said, "How do you know what your father looked like?"

"I know, because I found a photograph of him, ages ago, in a book. And I think it's the same person."

"You mean George Dyer is . . ." He stopped just in time.

"Gerry Dawson," Selina finished, triumphantly, for him.

Rodney began to feel as if a carpet was being pulled from beneath his feet.

"How did you know his name? You were never meant to know his name."

"Agnes told me yesterday."

"But, Agnes has no business . . ."

"Oh, Rodney, try to understand! You can't blame her. I caught her unawares. I put the face of George Dyer like *that*, flat down on the table in front of her, and she practically fainted away."

"Selina, you do realise that your father is dead?"

"But Rodney, don't you see, he was missing? Missing, presumed killed. Anything might have happened."

"Then why didn't he come back after the war?"

"Perhaps he was ill. Perhaps he lost his memory. Perhaps he heard that my mother had died."

"And what's he been doing all this time?"

"I don't know. But for the last six years he's been living on San Antonio." She realised that Rodney was going to ask her how she had found that out, and she added quickly, "It tells you all about this in the book you gave me," because she didn't want him to know that she had been to see Mr Rutland.

"Have you got the photograph of your father with you?"

"Not the book one."

"I didn't mean that. I meant the other."

Selina hesitated. "Yes, I have."

"Let me see it."

"You'll . . . give it back . . .?"

A slight tinge of irritation crept into Rodney's voice. "My dear child, what do you take me for?"

She was immediately ashamed, for Rodney would never stoop to an underhand action. She went for her bag, took out the precious photograph, and handed it across to Rodney. He carried it to the light of the window and Selina followed to stand beside him.

"You probably won't remember the photograph on the back of the book, but it is the same person, I'd swear to it. Everything is the same. The cleft in the chin. And the eyes . . . and the way the ears are set."

"What did Agnes say?"

401

"She wouldn't commit herself, but I'm sure she thinks it's my father."

Rodney did not reply. Frowning down at the dark, amused face in the photograph he was visited by a number of anxieties. The first was the possibility of losing Selina. A painfully honest man, Rodney had never deluded himself that he was in love with her, but she had become, almost without his realising it, a pleasant part of his life. Her appearance, with her satin, fawn-coloured hair and skin and her sapphire-blue eyes, he found beguiling, and although her interests were not perhaps as esoteric as Rodney's own, she showed a charming willingness to learn.

And then, there was the question of her business affairs. Since her grandmother's death Selina was a girl of some property, a ripe fruit, if ever there was one, to fall into the hands of a possibly unscrupulous man. At the moment, Rodney and Mr Arthurstone, in complete accord, were handling her stocks and trusts, and in another six months Selina would be twenty-one, and after that any final decisions would be her own. The thought of the control of all that money passing out of his hands gave Rodney the shivers.

He looked down, over his shoulder, and met Selina's eyes. He had never known any girl with such blue whites to her eyes. Like detergent advertisements. She smelt vaguely of fresh lemons . . . verbena. Out of the past he seemed to hear Mrs Bruce's voice, and some of the biting things she had had to say about Gerry Dawson. *Shiftless* was the word that stuck in Rodney's mind. Further epithets presented themselves to him. Irresponsible. Unreliable. Financially unsound.

He held the photograph by the corner and tapped it into the palm of his left hand. He said, at last, in a small burst of annoyance, finding it necessary to blame somebody for the situation in which he found himself, "Of course, it's all your grandmother's fault. She should never have kept you in the dark about your father. This web of secrecy, never mentioning his name . . . was a ridiculous mistake."

"Why?" asked Selina, interested.

"Because it's given you an obsession about him!" Rodney shot at her. Selina stared, obviously deeply hurt, her mouth hanging slightly open like an astounded child's. Rodney plunged ruthlessly on.

"You have an obsession about fathers, and families and family life in general. The fact that you found this photograph, and kept it – hidden – is a typical symptom."

"You talk as if I had measles."

"I'm trying to make you understand that you have a complex about your dead father."

"Perhaps he isn't dead," said Selina. "And if I have got a complex about him, you've just admitted that it isn't my fault. What's so wrong about having a complex? It isn't like a squint, or a wall eye. It doesn't show."

"Selina, this isn't funny."

"I don't think it's funny either."

She was regarding him with a bright gaze that he told himself could be described as a glare. They were quarrelling. They had never quarrelled, and this was surely not the time to start. He said, quickly, "Darling, I'm sorry," and bent to kiss her mouth, but she turned her face aside and he caught her cheek. "Don't you see, I'm only thinking of you. I don't want you to get caught up with some man, go chasing him to the ends of the earth, and then find you've made a foolish mistake."

"But, supposing," said Selina, "Just supposing it really *was* my father. Alive, and living in San Antonio. Writing books and sailing his little yacht and making friends with all the local Spanish people. You'd want me to get to know him, wouldn't you? You'd want to have a proper father-in-law of your own."

It was the very last thing Rodney wanted. He said gently, "We mustn't just think of ourselves. We must consider him, too – George Dyer – whether he's your father or not."

"I don't understand."

"By now, after all these years, he's made a fine life for himself. It's a life he chose of his own free will. If he'd wanted a family and the ties of a wife and sons . . . and daughters . . . he'd have got them for himself by now. . . ."

"You mean he wouldn't want me? He wouldn't want me to go and find him?"

Rodney was shocked. "You aren't considering such a step?"

"It's so important to me. We could fly to San Antonio."

"We?"

"I want you to come with me. Please."

"It's out of the question. Besides I have to go to Bournemouth, I told you, and I'll be away for three or four days."

"Can't Mrs Westman wait?"

"Of course she can't wait."

"It's just that I want you to be with me. Help me, Rodney."

Rodney misunderstood this plea. He thought she meant "Help me" in the practical sense. Help me buy an air ticket, help me get to the right aeroplane, help me through the Customs, find me the taxis and the porters. She had never travelled any distance on her own in her life, and he was quietly confident that now she would never try.

He parried her plea with a small spurt of charm, smiled, and took her hand and said, placatingly, "Now, what's all this rush about? Be patient. I know this must be exciting for you, to suddenly suspect that your father is alive. I realise, too, that there's always been something of a void in your life. I hoped I was going to be able to fill it."

He sounded noble. Selina said, "It isn't that, Rodney. . . ."

"But, you see, we don't know anything about George Dyer. Oughtn't we to make a few quiet investigations before we take any steps we might regret?" He was talking like Royalty.

"I was born after he was reported missing. He doesn't even know I exist."

"Exactly!" Rodney risked a more forceful tone. "You know, Selina, there's an old saying and a very true one: Never wake a sleeping tiger."

"I don't think of him as a tiger. I just think that maybe he's alive and he's the one person I've wanted, more than anybody, all my life."

Rodney vacillated between being offended and being angry.

"You're talking like a child."

"It's like a penny. A penny's got two sides, heads and tails. I have two sides as well. A Bruce side and a Dawson side. Selina Dawson. That's what I'm really called. That's who I really am." She smiled at Rodney, and he thought, in his distress, that it was a smile he had never seen before. "Do you love Selina Dawson as much as you love Selina Bruce?" He was still holding the photograph of her father. She took it from him and went to return it to her bag.

Rodney said, only a little late on cue, "Yes, of course I do."

Selina closed her bag, and laid it down. "Now," she said, smoothing down the front of her skirt as though she were about to start a recitation, "isn't it time we measured this floor?"

3

Barcelona Airport, in the first pale light of dawn, was deep in puddles from the storm which had chased the aircraft across the Pyrenees. There was a thin wind, blowing down from the mountains, the airport officials all smelt of garlic, and in the lounge the benches and chairs were sunk with still-sleeping figures, tumbled in coats and rugs, bag-eyed and blue-chinned from hours of waiting. It had been a bad night. Flights from Rome and Palma had been cancelled. Flights from Madrid were late.

Selina, still queasy from her flight, came in through the swinging plate-glass doors, and wondered what to do next. She had a through ticket to San Antonio, but needed another boarding pass. At a counter a tired-looking official was weighing some luggage, so she went and stood hopefully in front of him, and presently he looked up and she said, "Do you speak English?"

"*Sí.*"

"I have a ticket for San Antonio."

Without expression, he held out a hand for it, ripped the relevant page from the ticket book, made out a boarding pass, slid the pass back into the ticket, and returned it to her.

"Thank you. What time does the plane go?"

"Half past seven."

"And my luggage?"

"It is marked through to San Antonio."

"And the Customs?"

"Customs at San Antonio."

"I see. Thank you so much." But her ingratiating efforts to raise a smile were not successful. The man

407

had had a hard night and he was in no mood to be pleasant.

She went and sat down. She ached with exhaustion, but she was too nervous to feel sleepy. The plane had left London Airport at two in the morning, and she had sat staring into darkness and telling herself briskly to take things one at a time. Barcelona. San Antonio. Customs and passports and things. Then a taxi. It would be quite easy to find a taxi. And then Cala Fuerte. Cala Fuerte would not be large. Where does the Englishman, George Dyer, live? she would ask, and they would be able to direct her to the Casa Barco, and there she would find him.

The storm hit them as they came over the Pyrenees. The captain had had warning of it, and they were all woken and buckled into their safety belts. The plane lurched and wobbled, climbed higher and lurched some more. Some passengers were sick. Selina, closing her eyes, willed herself not to be, but it had been a close shave.

As they came down into Barcelona, the lightning attacked them, seeming to fly like banners from the wing tips. Once through the clouds they were lashed by rain, and when they landed at Barcelona, rocketing down through a cross wind, the runway was waterlogged, and shimmering with reflected lights. As the wheels brushed the tarmac, they sent up great wings of water, and there was an audible sigh of relief from everybody when at last the plane trundled to a standstill and the engines were stilled.

It was strange not having anyone to meet her. There should be a driver, a chauffeur in a uniform, with a large warm car. Or Agnes, fussing with rugs. There should be someone to find her suitcase, and deal with officialdom. But there was no one. This was Spain; Barcelona at six o'clock on a March morning, and there was no one but Selina.

When the hands of the clock had crept round to seven o'clock, she went into the bar and bought a cup of coffee, paying for it with some pesetas that the thoughtful man in the bank had insisted she bring with her. It was not very good coffee, but comfortingly hot, and she sat drinking it and watching her own reflection in the mirror that backed the bar. She wore a brown jersey dress and a coat the colour of porridge, and a silk headscarf, slipping now off the back of her hair. *Travelling-clothes* Mrs Bruce called them. She had set ideas about travelling-clothes. Jersey is comfortable and doesn't crease, and the coat must go over everything. Shoes must be light, but sturdy enough for long walks over windswept airports, the handbag large and capacious. Automatically, even in moments of drama, Selina followed this excellent and unvarying advice. Not that it helped. She still looked a mess and felt exhausted. She was afraid of flying, and dressing like a knowledgeable traveller didn't make you one, nor dispel the conviction that you would either die in an air crash or lose your passport.

The plane to San Antonio seemed very small, and looked as unreliable as a toy. Oh, no, thought Selina as she walked out towards it, with the wind blowing gusts of petrol fumes into her face and the puddles splashing over the tops of her shoes. There were only a few passengers and they filed glumly into the aircraft as though they shared her convictions. Once strapped in, Selina was given a glucose sweet, and began to eat it as though it were a new miracle cure for sheer funk. It wasn't, but the plane did not crash.

The bad weather, however, was still about, and they did not see San Antonio until they came in to land. There was nothing but cloud, lumps of grey cotton wool at the windows. Then there was rain, and then, unexpectedly, fields and the tops of houses and a windmill and a bunch of pines and earth the colour of brick, and everything glistening in the rain. The airport had only just been built, the landing-strip bulldozed out of the soil, and now the runway was a sea of red mud. After they had landed, two mechanics manhandled a gangway up to the side of the aircraft. They wore yellow slickers and were spattered in mud up to their knees. For once nobody seemed over-anxious to leave the aircraft. When they did, they went cautiously, picking their way between the puddles.

San Antonio smelled of pines. Wet, resinous pines. The rain, miraculously, seemed to have stopped. It was warmer, with no bite to the wind. There were no snow-topped mountains here, only the warm, surrounding sea. This was San Antonio. The flying was over and she was still alive. Selina pulled off her headscarf and let her hair blow in the wind.

There was a queue for immigration. Members of the Guardia Civil stood about as though they were expecting an influx of criminals. They wore guns, and not for orna-mental reasons. The immigration official worked slowly. He was holding a conversation with a colleague. It was long and involved, an argument of sorts, and he only stopped short at intervals in order to inspect painstakingly, page by page, any alien passport. Selina was the third and she had been waiting ten minutes before he eventually stamped ENTRADA, and handed it back to her.

She said tentatively, "My luggage . . .?" He did not understand, or did not want to, but waved her on. She put her passport back into her sensible bag, and went on searching on her own. For a small airport, San Antonio in the early morning seemed unusually crowded, but at nine-thirty the Barcelona plane returned to Spain, and this was a popular flight. Families gathered, children cried, mothers entreated them loudly to stop. Fathers argued with porters, queued for tickets and boarding passes. Lovers stood about hand-in-hand, waiting to say goodbye, and getting in everybody's way. The noise, in the high-ceilinged building, was deafening.

"Excuse me," Selina kept saying, trying to work her way through the throng. "I am sorry . . . excuse me . . ." Some of her fellow-passengers were already gathered beneath a sign which said ADUANA, and she struggled to join them. "I am sorry" – she tripped over a bulging basket, and nearly knocked down a fat baby in a knitted yellow coat. "Excuse me, please."

The luggage was already arriving, man-handled on to the makeshift counter, claimed, examined, sometimes opened, finally passed by the Customs officer, and removed.

Selina's suitcase never appeared. It was a blue one with a white stripe and easy to identify, and after an eternity of waiting she realised that there was no more luggage to come, the other passengers had, one by one, filtered away, and Selina was alone.

The Customs officer, who had, up to now, successfully managed to ignore her, hitched hands on his hips and raised his black eyebrows at her.

"My suitcase . . ." Selina said. "It's . . ."

"*No hablo Inglese.*"

"My suitcase . . . Do you speak English?"

A second man moved forward. "He says 'No.'"

"Can *you* speak English?"

He shrugged elaborately, suggesting that maybe, under desperate circumstances, he might possibly manage a word or two.

"My case. My luggage." She broke desperately into French. "*Mon bagage.*"

"Not here?"

"No."

"Where you come from?" He rolled all his r's with a great flourish. "Wherre you come frrom?"

"Barcelona. And London."

"Oh!" He made it sound as though she had imparted grave news. He turned to his colleague and they began to speak, a liquid rattle of Spanish that might have been a private conversation. Selina wondered desperately if they were exchanging family news. Then the English-speaking man shrugged again, and turned back to Selina. "I will find out," he said.

He disappeared. Selina waited. The first man began

411

to pick his teeth. Somewhere a child wailed. The loud-speaker, to add to the misery, burst into the sort of music normally associated with bullfights. After ten minutes or more the helpful man came back, with one of the stewards from the aircraft.

The steward said, smiling as though he were imparting a charming favour, "Your suitcase is lost."

"*Lost!*" It was a despairing wail.

"Your case is, we think, in Madrid."

"*Madrid!* What's it doing in Madrid?"

"Unfortunately, at Barcelona, it has been put on the wrong truck . . . we think. At Barcelona there is also a plane going to Madrid. We think that your luggage is in Madrid."

"'But it was labelled to San Antonio. It was labelled in London."

At the word "London" the Customs man made his hopeless sound again. Selina felt she could hit him.

"I am sorry," said the steward. "I will have a message sent through to Madrid, to return the case to San Antonio."

"How long will that take?"

"I did not say it was in Madrid," said the steward, determined not to commit himself. "We must find out."

"Well, how long will it take to find out?"

"I do not know. Maybe three, four hours."

Three or four hours! If she was not angry, then she would cry. "I can't wait here three or four hours."

"Then perrhaps you can come back. Tomorrow, maybe, to see if the suitcase is here. From Madrid."

"But can't I call you? Ring you? On the telephone?"

This was apparently a joke. Through smiles, she was told, "Señorita, there are few telephones."

"Then I have to come back here tomorrow, to see if you have found my case?"

"Or the next day," said the steward, with the air of a man full of bright ideas.

Selina made a final appeal. "But everything I have is in my case."

"I am sorry."

He continued to stand smiling at her. She felt at that moment as though she were drowning. She looked from one face to another, and slowly realised that nobody was going to help her. Nobody could help her. She was alone and she had to help herself. She said at last in a voice that shook only a little, "Is it possible for me to find a taxi?"

"But of course. Outside. There are many taxis."

There were, in fact, four. Beginning to be oppressed by the warmth of the porridge-coloured travelling-coat, Selina went in search of them. As soon as she appeared, the drivers all blew their horns, waved, called "Señorita," leapt from their cars and rushed for her custom, each trying to channel Selina towards his own vehicle.

She said, loudly, "Can any of you speak English?"

"Sí. Sí. Sí."

"I want to go to Cala Fuerte."

"Cala Fuerte, sí."

"Do you know Cala Fuerte?"

"Sí. Sí," they all said.

"Oh, can't anybody speak English . . .?"

"Yes," said a voice. "I can."

It was the driver of the fourth taxi. While his colleagues had tried to beguile Selina, he waited, placidly finishing his cigar. Now he dropped the odorous stub, stepped on it, and moved forward. His appearance was not reassuring. He was an enormous man, very tall and equally fat. He wore a blue shirt, open-necked and revealing a black, furry chest. His trousers were slung by an intricately worked leather belt, and on the back of his head was an incongruous straw hat, of the variety that tourists bring back from holiday. He wore, at this early, cloudy hour, sunglasses, and narrow black moustaches suggesting unknown Don Juan qualities. He looked so villainous that Selina reeled.

"I speak English," he said, with a strong American

413

accent. "I work in Spain, on a U.S. Army air base. I speak English."

"Oh. Well . . ." Surely any of the other three taxi-drivers was preferable to this ruffian, English or not!

He ignored her hesitation. "Where d'you want to go?"

"To . . . Cala Fuerte. But I'm sure . . ."

"I'll take you. Six hundred pesetas."

"Oh. Well . . ." She looked hopefully at the other taxi-drivers, but already they seemed discouraged. One had even returned to his car and was rubbing on the windscreen with an old rag.

She turned back to the large man in the straw hat. He smiled, a broken-toothed leer. She swallowed, and said, "All right. Six hundred pesetas."

"Where is your luggage?"

"It is lost. It was lost in Barcelona."

"That's bad."

"Yes, it got put on the wrong plane. They're going to find out, and I'll get it tomorrow or the next day. I have to go to Cala Fuerte now, you see, and . . ."

Something in the big man's expression made her stop. He was gazing down at Selina's handbag. Selina followed his gaze, and saw that, indeed, something strange had happened. Although the two sturdy straps were still over her arm, the bag hung open like a gaping mouth. The front straps had been neatly cut, as if with a razor blade. And her wallet was missing!

The taxi-driver was called Toni. He introduced himself formally, and then he acted as her interpreter during the long and tedious interview with the Guardia Civil.

Yes, the señorita had been robbed. In the crowd at the airport this morning, had been a thief with a razor blade. She had been robbed of everything. Everything she owned.

Her passport?

Not her passport. But her money, her pesetas, her British money, her traveller's cheques, her return ticket to London.

The Guardia Civil, with concentration, examined Selina's bag.

Had the Señorita felt nothing?

But nothing. Pushing through the crowds, how could she feel anything?

The bag looked as if it had been cut by a razor.

That was it. A razor. A thief with a razor blade.

What was the Señorita's name?

It was Miss Selina Bruce, of London, travelling on a British passport.

And where was Miss Bruce's place of residence, in San Antonio?

It was . . . Selina hesitated here, but events had gone beyond hesitation. *Casa Barco, Cala Fuerte.*

What colour was the wallet? How much money, exactly? Were the traveller's cheques signed?

Wearily she answered the questions. The clock crawled round to ten, to half past ten and beyond. The worst of her apprehensions had more than been fulfilled. She had lost her suitcase and she had lost her money. And she still had to get to Cala Fuerte.

At last it was over. The Guardia Civil squared off his papers and stood up. Selina thanked him, and shook hands. He looked surprised, but still did not smile.

Together, Selina and Toni crossed the now empty airport building, went out through the glass doors, and stopped, facing each other. Selina held her coat over her arm, for it had begun to get uncomfortably warm, and watched him, waiting for him to make the first move.

He took off his dark glasses.

She said, "I still have to get to Cala Fuerte."

"You have no money."

"But you'll get paid, I promise you. When we get to Cala Fuerte . . . my . . . father will pay your fare."

Toni frowned enormously. "Your father? You have a father here? Why didn't you say?"

"It wouldn't have made any difference. We . . . we couldn't get in touch with him. Could we?"

"Your father *lives* in Cala Fuerte?"

"Yes. At a house called the Casa Barco. I am sure he will be there, and will pay you." Toni watched her, suspicious and unbelieving. "And you can't just leave me here. I haven't even got my plane ticket back to London."

He stared into space for a bit, then decided to light a cigarette. He was giving nothing away, and refusing to commit himself.

"You said you'd take me," Selina went on. "And I'll see that you're paid. I promise."

His cigarette was lighted. He blew a cloud of smoke into the air, and his black eyes swivelled back to Selina's face. She looked anxious and pale, but also, undoubtedly, well-to-do. The ruined handbag was alligator, and the good shoes matched. The scarf was silk, and both the dress and the coat of expensive wool. Sometimes, as she moved, Toni glimpsed the gold of a thin chain around her neck, and she wore a gold watch. There was, undoubtedly, money around – if not in the handbag, then somewhere. It was only March and there were not yet so many taxi fares that he could afford to turn down a good one. And this girl, this young *Inglesa*, did not look capable of tricking anybody.

He made up his mind. "All right," he said at last. "We go."

4

Made beneficent by his own kindness, Toni talked expansively.

"San Antonio, until five years ago, was a very poor island. The communications with Spain were lousy, only a small boat twice a week. But now we have the airport, so that visitors come and in the summer there are a lot of people, and things are getting O.K."

Selina thought that the first thing that needed to get O.K. was the surface of the roads. The one they were on was unsurfaced and rutted with car tracks, on which the aged Oldsmobile, which was Toni's taxi, rocked and bucketed like a ship at sea. It wound, between low, dry-stone walls, through a countryside squared off into little farmsteads. The ground looked stony and unpromising, the squat buildings had been bleached by the fierce sun to the colour of pale sand. The women, who worked in the fields, wore black skirts to their ankles and black scarves about their heads. The men were in faded blue, ploughing the unresponsive earth, or jolting, in wooden carts, behind a pair of mules. There were flocks of goats, and scrawny chickens, and every mile or so a well, circled by a patient, blinkered horse, and a water-wheel, spilling brimming buckets into the irrigation ditches.

Selina noticed this, and said, "But you had rain last night."

"That was the first rain for months. We are always short of water. There are no rivers, only springs. The sun is already hot, and the ground dries very fast."

"We flew through a storm last night, over the Pyrenees."

"The bad weather has been in the Mediterranean for days."

"Is it always like this in March?"

"No, it can be warm in March." And, as if to substantiate his words the sun, at that moment, chose to filter through a gap in the clouds and paint everything in a thin golden light. "Over there," Toni went on, "that is the town of San Antonio. The cathedral on the top of the hill is very old, a fortified cathedral."

"Fortified?"

"Against attack. From the Phoenicians, and pirates, and Moors. For centuries the Moors occupied San Antonio."

The town lay like a frieze against the backdrop of the sea. A hill of white houses, topped by the soaring towers and spires of the cathedral.

"We're not going through San Antonio?"

"No, we are on the road to Cala Fuerte." After a little, he added, "You've never been to the island? And yet your father lives here?"

Selina watched the slow-moving sails of a windmill. "No. No, I've never been."

"You will like Cala Fuerte. It is small, but very beautiful. A lot of yachtsmen go there."

"My father is a yachtsman." She said it without thinking, but the words caught at her, as though to say a thing, to speak it aloud, made it real, and true. *My father lives at Cala Fuerte. At a house called the Casa Barco. He is a yachtsman.*

The clouds continued to spread and part and the sun drove between them and at last they began to roll out to sea where they lay, sullenly, on the edge of the horizon. The island was bathed in warmth. Selina pushed up the sleeves of her sensible jersey dress and rolled down the window and let the scented dusty wind tear at her hair. They passed through little villages, and gold stone towns, shuttered and quiet. Doors of houses stood open, hung with curtains of chain, and on the pavement old ladies sat, upright in kitchen chairs, talking or watching their little

418

grandchildren, their worn hands busy with embroidery and lace-making.

They came to Curamayor, a sleepy town of creamy houses and narrow streets, and Toni rubbed the back of his hand across his mouth and announced that he was feeling thirsty.

Selina, not quite sure what was expected of her, said nothing.

"Some beer would be good," Toni went on.

"I . . . I would buy you a beer, but I haven't any money."

"I will buy a beer," said Toni. The narrow street opened into a large cobbled square, with a tall church, and shady trees, and some shops. He cruised gently round until he saw a café which met with his approval. "This will do."

"I . . . I'll wait for you."

"You should have something too. Driving is hot and dry. I will give you a drink." She began to protest, but he only added, "Your father will pay me back."

She sat in the sunshine at a small iron table. Behind her, inside the bar, Toni was talking to the proprietor. A small gang of children, fresh from school, approached. They were delicious, in blue cotton pinafores and spotless white socks. They all seemed beautiful – the little girls pin-neat with braided dark hair and gold rings in their ears, their limbs olive-gold and perfectly formed, and when they smiled, their teeth showed pointed and white.

They saw Selina watching them, and were convulsed with giggles. Two of the little girls, more forward than the others, stopped in front of her, their grape-dark eyes dancing with fun. She longed to make friends, and on an impulse, opened her bag and took out a propelling pencil, never liked, about three inches long and with a tassel of yellow and blue. She held it out, inviting one of them to take it. At first they were too shy, and then the little one with plaits, tentatively, as though it might bite, removed it from Selina's palm. The other, with a gesture wholly disarming, laid her own hand in Selina's, as though she

419

were bestowing a gift. The hand was chubby and smooth and wore a little gold ring.

Toni came back through the chain curtains with his beer and an orange drink for Selina, and the children took fright, and scattered like pigeons, running and taking the tasselled pencil with them. Enchanted, she watched them go, and Toni said, "The little ones . . ." with as much pride and affection in his voice as if the children had been his own.

Their journey continued. The character of the island had, by now, completely changed, and the road ran along the base of a range of mountains, while to seaward the fields sloped down in a shallow curve towards a distant misty horizon. They had been on the road nearly three hours when Selina saw the cross, high on a mountain ahead of them, silhouetted against the sky.

"Where is that?" she asked.

"That is the Cross of San Estaban."

"Just a cross? On top of a mountain?"

"No, there is a very big monastery. A closed order."

The village of San Estaban lay at the foot of the mountain, in the shadow of the monastery. At the crossroads in the centre of the town a sign pointed, at last, to Cala Fuerte, the first that Selina had seen. Toni swung the car down to the right, and the road sloped before them, running downhill through fields of cactus and olive groves and clusters of scented eucalyptus trees. Ahead the coast seemed thickly wooded with pine, but as they drew near, Selina glimpsed the white of scattered houses, and the bright pinks and blues and scarlets of the flower-filled gardens.

"Is this Cala Fuerte?"

"*Sí.*"

"It doesn't look like the other villages."

"No, it is a resort. For visitors. Many people have villas here, for the summer, you know? They come in the hot weather from Madrid and Barcelona."

"I see."

The pines closed about them, cool shadows and the smell of resin. They passed a farmyard, noisy with chickens, a house or two, a little wine shop, and then the road opened out into a small square, built around a single spreading pine. On one side was a shop, with vegetables piled at the door, and the window filled with rope-soled shoes, camera films, straw hats and postcards. On the other, whitewashed to blinding brightness, was a house of Moorish curves and shadows, fronted by a paved terrace, furnished with tables and chairs. Over the door swung a sign, "Cala Fuerte Hotel."

Toni stopped the taxi beneath the shade of the tree and switched off the engine. Dust settled and it was very quiet.

"We are here," he said. "This is Cala Fuerte."

They got out of the car, and the coolness of the sea-breeze was welcome. There were few people about. A woman came out of the shop to gather potatoes out of a basket and put them in a paper bag. Some children played with a dog. A couple of visitors, wearing home-knitted cardigans, and obviously English, sat on the terrace of the hotel and wrote postcards. They looked up and saw Selina, recognised her as a fellow-countrywoman, and hastily averted their eyes.

They went into the hotel, Toni leading the way. Beyond the chain curtain was a bar, very fresh and clean and cool, whitewashed, with rugs on the stone floors and a rustic wooden stairway leading to an upper floor. Beneath the stairway another door led to the back of the hotel. A dark girl with a broom was placidly shifting dust from one side of the floor to the other.

She looked up and smiled, *"Buenos días."*

"Dónde está el proprietario?"

The girl laid down her broom. *"Momento,"* she said and disappeared, soft-footed through the door under the stairway. It swung shut behind her. Toni went to hitch himself up on to one of the tall stools at the bar. After a little the door opened again and a man came in. He was small, quite young, bearded, with eyes like a friendly frog. He wore a white shirt and dark, belted trousers and a pair of blue espadrilles.

"*Buenos días,*" he said, looking from Toni to Selina, and back again.

She said quickly, "Do you speak English?"

"*Sí,* señorita."

"I am sorry to bother you, but I'm looking for someone. For Mr George Dyer."

"Yes?"

"You know him?"

He smiled and spread his hands. "Of course. You are looking for George? Does he know you are looking for him?"

"No. Should he?"

"Not unless you have told him you are coming."

Selina said, "It's a surprise," trying to make it sound like fun.

He seemed intrigued. "Where have you come from?"

"From London. Today from the airport at San Antonio." She indicated Toni, who was listening to all this with a sullen expression as if he did not like the command of the situation being taken from his hands. "The taxi-driver brought me."

"I have not seen George since yesterday. He was on his way to San Antonio."

"But, I said, we've just come from there."

"He is probably home by now. I am not certain. I have not seen him return." He grinned. "We are never sure if his car will make the long journey."

Toni cleared his throat and leaned forward. "Where can we find him?" he said.

The bearded man shrugged. "If he is in Cala Fuerte he will be at the Casa Barco."

"How can we find the Casa Barco?" The other frowned, and Toni, sensing his mild disapproval, explained. "We must find Señor Dyer, because otherwise I do not get my taxi fare paid. The Señorita has no money. . . ."

422

Selina swallowed. "Yes . . . yes, I'm afraid this is true. Do you think you could direct us to the Casa Barco?"

"It is too difficult. You would never find it. But," he added, "I can find someone to take you there."

"That is kind of you. Thank you so much, Mr . . . I'm afraid I don't know your name."

"Rudolfo. Not Mr anything. Just Rudolfo. If you wait here for a moment, I will see what I can arrange."

He went out through the curtains, across the square and into the shop opposite. Toni slumped on his stool, his bulk sagging on either side of the inadequate seat, and his mood obviously darkening. Selina began to be nervous. She said, trying to placate him, "It's annoying to be delayed, when you've been so kind. . . ."

"We do not know that Señor Dyer will be at the Casa Barco. They have not seen him return from San Antonio yet."

"Well, if he isn't, we can always wait a little. . . ."

It was the wrong thing to say. "I cannot wait. I am a working man. Time is money to me."

"Yes, of course. I do understand."

He made a sound as if to indicate that she could not possibly understand, and half turned his back to her like any overgrown and sulky schoolboy. It was a relief when Rudolfo returned. He had arranged for the son of the woman who ran the grocery store to take them to Casa Barco. The boy had a large order for Señor Dyer, which he was about to deliver on his bicycle. If they liked they could follow the bicycle in the taxi.

"Yes, of course, that will be splendid." Selina turned to Toni, and said, with a brightness she did not feel, "And he will pay your fare, and then you will be able to go straight back to San Antonio."

Toni did not look convinced, but he heaved himself off the bar stool, and followed Selina out into the square. By the taxi, a skinny boy waited by his bicycle. The handle-bars were slung with two enormous baskets, of the type used by all Spanish peasants. Badly-wrapped parcels of all shapes and sizes protruded from these baskets. Long loaves of bread, a bundle of onions, the neck of a bottle.

Rudolfo said, "This is Tomeu, the son of Maria. He will show you the way."

Like a little pilot fish, Tomeu weaved ahead, down the white-rutted road that wound with the convolutions of the coast. The island was pierced with inlets of peacock-blue water, and above the rocks could be glimpsed delectable white villas, small gardens spilling with flowers, sunbathing terraces and diving-boards.

Selina said, "I wouldn't mind living here," but Toni's mood was rapidly worsening and he would make no reply. The road was a road no longer, merely a lane winding between the chrysanthemum-covered walls of other people's gardens. It crested a slight rise, then sloped towards a final and much larger inlet, where a tiny harbour sheltered a few fishing-boats, and quite big yachts were moored out in deep water.

The lane ran down to the backs of houses. Tomeu, ahead of them, waited. When he saw the taxi edge over the crest of the hill, he got off his bicycle, laid it against a wall, and began to unload the baskets.

Selina said, "That must be the house."

It did not look large. The back wall was whitewashed and blank, except for a tiny slit of a window and a shuttered door, shaded by a thick, black pine. Behind the house the road branched, and ran to left and to right, along the backs of other houses. Here and there a narrow alley of stairs sliced down between the buildings towards the sea. There was a pleasantly haphazard look about it all, with washing flapping on lines and some nets put out to dry, and one or two skinny cats sitting in the sun and washing themselves.

Toni's taxi bumped and slithered the last few yards, Toni complaining meanwhile that there would be nowhere to turn, his taxi was not meant for such bad roads, he would put in a claim if any of his paintwork was scratched.

Selina scarcely listened. Tomeu had opened the green

424

shutter door and disappeared into the house, lugging his heavy baskets. The taxi lurched to a halt and Selina scrambled out.

Toni said, "I will go and turn and come back for the money."

"Yes," said Selina absently, watching the open door. "Yes, you do that."

He accelerated so swiftly that she had to step back into the gutter to avoid having her toes run over, but when he had gone, she crossed the lane, and went, under the shade of the pine, cautiously in through the open door of the Casa Barco.

She had thought it would be a little house, but instead found herself in one large high-ceilinged room. The shutters were all closed, and it was dark and cool. There was no kitchen, but a small counter enclosed a galley, like a little bar, from the main living-space, and behind this she found Tomeu, on his knees, stacking the provisions into a refrigerator.

He looked up and smiled as she leaned over the counter. She said, "Señor Dyer?"

He shook his head. "No *aquí*."

No *aquí*. Not here. Her heart sank. He wasn't back from San Antonio, and somehow she was going to have to fob Toni off with excuses, and suggestions that he be patient, when neither of them had any idea for how long they would have to wait.

Tomeu said something. Selina stared uncomprehending. To show what he meant, he came out from the little galley and went over to the far wall and began to undo the shutters and fling them wide. A blast of light and sunshine invaded the house and everything sprang into colour. The south wall, that faced out over the harbour, was almost all window, but louvred double doors opened out on to a terrace, shaded by a split-cane awning. There was a low wall, and a few battered crocks and urns, containing geraniums, and beyond the wall, the shimmering blue of the sea.

The house itself was divided in a novel way. There were no interior walls, but the roof of the galley formed a little gallery with a wooden railing and this was reached by an open flight of steps like a ship's ladder. Beneath the ship's ladder another door led into a minuscule wash-room. A hole high in the wall provided light and ventilation, and there was a sink and a lavatory and a primitive-looking shower, and a shelf with bottles and toothpaste and stuff, and a mirror, and on the floor a round washing-basket.

The rest of the space was a lofty living-room of singular charm, whitewashed, and with a stone floor, scattered with bright rugs. In one corner of the room was a wide triangular fireplace, filled with fragrant wood ashes, which looked as though they needed only the lightest puff of air to bring them back to burning life. The hearth was perhaps eighteen inches from the floor, just the right height for a comfortable seat, and this continued along the wall in a sort of shelf which was scattered with cushions and rugs, piles of books, a lamp, a piece of rope in the process of being spliced, a pile of papers and magazines and a box of empty bottles.

In front of the fireplace, with its back to the terrace and the sea, was an enormous sagging couch, with room for six and no trouble at all. It was loose-covered in fading blue linen, and draped in a red-and-white-striped blanket. On the other side of the room, at right angles to the light, stood a cheap knee-hole desk, laden with more paper, a typewriter, an open box of what looked like unopened letters, and a pair of binoculars. There was a sheet of paper in the typewriter and Selina could not resist a peep.

"George Dyer's New Novel," she read. "The lazy fox jumped over the something or other hound."

And then a row of asterisks and an exclamation mark.

She turned down the corners of her mouth. So much for Mr Rutland's hopes!

Between the galley and the door was a well, with a wrought-iron hook for the bucket and a wide shelf on which stood a half-empty bottle of wine and a cactus

426

plant. Selina looked down and saw the dark gleam of water, and smelt it, sweet and good, and wondered if it was fit to drink; but Grandmother had always said you must never drink water abroad unless it was boiled, and this was no time to risk getting gastroenteritis.

She left the well and came to stand in the middle of the room, looking up at the gallery. The temptation to investigate proved irresistible, and she climbed the ladder, and found a beguiling slope-ceilinged bedroom with an immense carved double bedstead (how had they ever got it up here?) placed, in state, beneath the high pitch of the gable. There was little room for more furniture, but a pair of sea-chests had been fitted in against the low walls, and a bulging curtain did duty as a wardrobe. There was an upended orange box for a bedside table, its shelves filled with books, and a lamp and a transistor radio, and a ship's chronometer.

From the terrace Tomeu called "Señorita!" and Selina went down the ladder to join him. He was sitting on the wall, in the company of an enormous white Persian cat. He turned to smile at Selina, gathering up the cat in his arms as though to give it to her.

"Señor Dyer," he said, indicating the cat, which mewed pathetically, and after a struggle, leapt lightly away, stalking into a sunny corner to settle itself in dignity, wrapping its tail around its front paws.

"It is very big," said Selina. Tomeu frowned. "Big," she said again, indicating with her arms a cat the size of a tiger. "Big."

Tomeu laughed. "*Sí. Muy grande.*"

"It's Señor Dyer's cat?"

"*Sí.* Señor Dyer."

She went to join him, leaning out over the wall. There was a little triangle of rocky garden with a gnarled olive tree or two, and Selina realised that, like any house built on a steep slope, the Casa Barco went in stages and the terrace was, in fact, the roof of a boathouse, with slipways which ran down to the water. A flight of steps led from the terrace to the lower level, and directly below them two men squatted, cleaning fish. Their knives sliced precisely, the blades glinting in the sunlight. They rinsed the fish in the sea, stirring up the still, jade water. Tomeu stooped to pick up a chip of stone, and threw it down at the men, and the two faces turned up to see who it was, and saw Tomeu and smiled.

"*Hombre*, Tomeu!"

He replied with some impudent backchat, for they laughed and then went back to their work. Beneath Selina's hands the stone wall was warm, and some of the whitewash had smudged off on to the front of her dress, like chalk from a blackboard. She turned to sit on the wall, with her back to the sea, and saw the washing-line, slung between two hooks, with a row of bone-dry wrinkled clothes. A faded blue work-shirt, a pair of bathing-trunks, some white ducks with patches on the knees, and a pair of old tennis shoes worn to a shred and tied over the line by their laces. The terrace also sported a few articles of furniture, but not the *House & Garden* type. A ratty old cane chair and a wooden paint-chipped table and the sort of booby-trap deckchair that collapses when you sit in it. She wished that she could speak Spanish and talk to the friendly Tomeu. She wanted to ask about Señor Dyer. What sort of a man was he? Which of the yachts was his? When did Tomeu think he would be back from San Antonio? But before she could start up any sort of communication with him, the sound of Toni's returning taxi came like a knell of doom. It stopped by the door and in a moment Toni came into the house, looking ill-tempered and more villainous than ever. Selina had to tell herself that he couldn't eat her. She said, firmly, "Señor Dyer is not back."

Toni received this information in frigid silence. Then he produced a toothpick and delved about at a troublesome back molar. He wiped the toothpick on the seat of his pants, put it back into his pocket and said, "What the hell we do now?"

"I shall wait here. He can't be long, Rudolfo said that he wouldn't be long. And you can either wait here too, or you can leave me your name and address and return to San Antonio. Either way I shall see that you get paid."

Unconsciously she spoke in her grandmother's voice, and to her own surprise, it worked. Toni resigned himself to the situation. He sucked his teeth for a moment or two more and than announced his decision.

"I shall wait too. But not here. At the hotel."

There was cognac at the hotel and he could have a siesta in the taxi, beneath the shade of the tree. It was half past two already and he did not enjoy being awake at half past two. "When Señor Dyer is here, you can come and tell me."

Selina could have hugged him in relief, but she only said, "Very well, I'll certainly do that." And then added, because he looked so despondent, "I am sorry this has happened, but it will be all right."

He shrugged hugely, sighing, and went back to his car. They heard him start up and drive back over the hill towards the Cala Fuerte hotel. Selina had time to think "Poor Rudolfo," and then she went back to Tomeu.

"I stay here," she told him.

He frowned. *"Usted aquí."*

"Yes. Here." She pointed to the ground. Tomeu grinned his comprehension and went to collect his empty baskets.

"Goodbye, Tomeu, and thank you."

"Adiós, Señorita."

He was gone, and Selina was alone. She went out on to the terrace and told herself that she was waiting for her father, but it was still not quite believable. She wondered if he would know, without being told, who she was. And if he did not know, she wondered how she would tell him.

It was very hot. The sun beat down on to the sheltered terrace, and she could not remember ever having been so hot. Her nylon stockings and her leather shoes and her woollen dress became, all at once, unbearable. They

429

were no longer sensible, but unsuitable to a degree that was lunatic.

But Grandmother couldn't stand bare legs, even with a summer dress, and gloves she considered essential. *You can tell a lady by her gloves. Such an untidy-looking gel, going about without a hat.*

But Grandmother was dead. Loved, mourned, but undoubtedly dead. The voice was stilled, the dogmatic opinions would never be uttered again, and Selina was on her own, to do what she wanted, in her father's house and a world away from Queen's Gate. She went into the house, and stripped off her stockings and her shoes, and then, feeling cool and delightfully free, went in search of food. There was butter in the refrigerator, and she put some on a slice of bread, and took a tomato and a bottle of cold soda water. This picnic she ate on the terrace, perched on the wall, and watching the boats in the harbour. Afterwards, she began to be sleepy, but she did not want to be found asleep. There was something very unguarded about being found asleep. She would have to sit somewhere hard and uncomfortable and stay awake.

In the end, she climbed the ladder to the gallery and settled herself, in a certain amount of discomfort, on the top step. After a little, the huge white cat came in out of the sun, and climbed up to settle himself, with an inordinate amount of purring and treading paws, on Selina's knee.

The hands of her watch went slowly round.

5

Frances Dongen said, "I can't think why you have to go."

"I've told you; I have to feed Pearl."

"Pearl can feed herself. There are enough dead fish around that house of yours to feed an army of cats. Stay another night, darling."

"It isn't just Pearl; it's *Eclipse* as well . . ."

"But she's ridden out one storm . . ."

"I don't know that she has ridden it out, and the bad weather's coming back . . ."

"Oh, well," said Frances, and reached for another cigarette. "If that's how you feel, you'd better go."

Her mother had told her, years ago, when she was a girl in Cincinnati, Ohio, that the best way to keep a man was to give him the impression, at least, of being free. Not that she had yet reached the stage of keeping George Dyer, because she hadn't even got him yet, but she was an old hand at this fascinating game of stalk and counter-stalk, and she was prepared to take her time.

She was sitting, on the small terrace of her house, high in the old town of San Antonio. Above, only a few hundred yards or so separated her from the cathedral, and below, a maze of winding cobbled streets, tall, narrow houses, and endless strings of washing, spilled to the wall of the old fortifications. Beyond the wall lay the new town, wide streets and tree-lined squares leading to the harbour, filled with island schooners and white, tall-masted yachts, and the steamer, which had just arrived on its weekly trip from Barcelona.

For two years she had lived in this delectable spot, ever

since she had arrived in the cruising yacht of some wealthy American friends. After six weeks of their company, Frances was bored stiff, and when they all came ashore for a party, she never left again. After a three-day binge, she had woken to a monumental hangover and a strange bed, and the realisation that the cruising yacht and all its occupants had left without her.

This troubled Frances not in the least. She already seemed to have made a lot of new friends, she was rich, twice-married, without roots. San Antonio suited her down to the ground. It was filled with painters, expatriates, writers and beatniks, and Frances, who had once lived for several months with an unsuccessful artist in Greenwich Village, felt entirely at home. Before long she had found this house, and when the initial occupations of settling-in were over, cast about for some way of filling in her time. She decided upon an art gallery. In a place where you had both resident painters and visiting tourists, an art gallery was surely a blue-chip investment. She bought up a disused fish-market on the harbour, converted it, and managed the business with an acumen she had inherited not only from her father, but from her two ex-husbands as well.

She was nearly forty, but everything about her belied the passing of years. Tall, very thin, tanned like a boy, with her blonde head a tangle of artless curls, she wore, and got away with, the sort of clothes normally reserved for teenagers. Tight pants, and men's shirts, and bikinis that were no more than a couple of knotted handkerchiefs. She chain-smoked, and she knew she was drinking too much, but most of the time, and this morning in particular, life was just as good as she'd always meant it to be.

The party last night, thrown in honour of Olaf Svensen's first exhibition, had been particularly successful. Olaf was the dirtiest young man ever seen, even by San Antonio standards, with a scrofulous beard and toenails that scarcely bore looking at, but his pop-art sculpture was guaranteed to open eyes, and Frances took a certain mild

432

pleasure in shocking the public. George Dyer had certainly been asked to the party – since the publication of his book he had become something of a celebrity – but that was no guarantee that he would come, and Frances's spirits had soared in pleasure when she saw him come through the door and start to thread his way towards her through the crowded smoke-filled room. He told her that he was in San Antonio to pick up a spare part for his boat, and after hearing his comments on Olaf's work, she knew that he had only come to the party for the free drink, but what did it matter provided he was there, and what was more, had stayed, right to the end of the party, and then afterwards, with Frances. She had known him, now, for about a year. Last spring, she had driven over to Cala Fuerte to look at the work of a young French painter who lived there. She had wound up, inevitably, in Rudolfo's bar, standing the painter a string of martinis, but when George Dyer walked in, she had abandoned the Frenchman, who went to sleep with his head on the table, and started to talk to George instead, and they ended up having lunch together, and were still drinking coffee at six o'clock in the evening, when it was time to switch back to brandy again.

He usually came to San Antonio about once a week, to pick up his mail from the Yacht Club, and go to the bank, and stock up on supplies for his boat, and on these occasions he nearly always looked Frances up, and they would have dinner, or attach themselves to some party already in full swing in one of the waterside bars. She was enormously attracted by him – more so, she knew, than he was to her, but this only served to make him all the more desirable. It made her jealous, too, of his other interests, of anything that kept him away from her. His writing, his yacht, but most of all the self-contained existence he led at Cala Fuerte. She would have liked him to need her, but he seemed to need nothing. He was unimpressed by her money, but delighted in her coarse and very masculine sense of humour. Watching him now, she thought, with satisfaction, that he was the first real man she had met in years.

He was getting ready to go, packing the things he had bought into a basket. Just watching his brown hands perform this homely task made Frances ache with physical desire. She said, against her better judgment, but hoping to make him stay a little longer, "You've had nothing to eat."

"I'll get something at home."

At home. She wished this were his home. She said, "A drink?"

He laughed, and looked up at her, distinctly bloodshot and amused as hell. "Look, ducky, I have a three-hour drive."

"A drink wouldn't kill you." She wanted one herself.

"No, but a ruddy great truck might, after I'd gone to sleep."

The basket was packed. He stood up and said, "I must go."

Frances stood too, stooped to stub out her cigarette and went to help him with his things. He lifted the heavy crate with the spare propeller, and Frances carried the basket, and led the way down the stone stairs to her enclosed courtyard, where the lemon tree grew by the well. She opened the heavy double doors that led to the narrow street, and stepped out in the sunshine. Here, on the crazy slope of the hill, George's ridiculous car was parked, an ancient Morris Cowley, with yellow wheels and a hood like a perambulator. They loaded it up, and George turned to say goodbye.

"It's been fun," he said.

"That's because we didn't plan it, darling. What's the word? Spontaneous." She kissed his mouth. She was so tall that she did not have to reach up to do it, merely leaned forward and caught him unawares. She wore a bright, thick lipstick that came off on his mouth and tasted sweet, and when she drew away, he wiped the stain away on the back of his hand.

He got into the car

"Good-bye, darling."

"'Bye, Frances."

"'Bye."

She removed the stone which, last night, feeble with laughter, they had jammed beneath the front wheel, and George took off the brake and the car free-wheeled away, gathering terrifying speed as it went, and taking the corners of the narrow, steep street like a helter-skelter at the fair, scattering cats and chickens and causing the Guardia Civil, posted at the gate of the old wall, to suck their teeth in violent disapproval.

He bowled back to Cala Fuerte, down the dusty roads, through the neatly-tended fields, past the windmills, and the patient horses turning the water-wheels. He came to the winding road beneath the mountains, and the cross of San Estaban towered above him. He squinted out to sea for signs of the returning storm, and he thought about Frances. He thought of going to live in San Antonio with Frances, if only for the satisfaction of writing to Rutland, the publisher, and telling him to go to hell, he wasn't going to write any more books, he was going to become a beachcomber, a lotus-eater, he was going to be kept by a rich American.

At San Estaban, the siesta was over, the shutters had been thrown wide and a few peaceful customers sat outside the cafés. As George passed, tooting the horn of the car, they called "*Hombre!*" and waved, because they all knew him, if not by name, then by sight, because he was the mad Englishman in the little car with yellow wheels, who drove around the island wearing a yachting cap and sometimes wrote books.

As he came free-wheeling down the last stretch of road that led to Cala Fuerte, he had a small debate with himself as to whether or not he would call in at Rudolfo's for a drink. In the end, rather to his own surprise, he decided against it. He would undoubtedly meet friends, would stay longer than he intended, would drink more than was good for him. He did not trust the weather, and Pearl would be hungry; so instead, he compromised with a friendly toot on his horn as he came through the square, and a genial wave to anybody who might be sitting on the terrace of the Cala Fuerte. There was no sign of Rudolfo, but one or two startled drinkers waved back, and there was the good feeling of coming home, and George began to whistle.

He was whistling when he came into the house. Selina, still sitting on the ladder, heard the car come over the hill, and down the slope, and stop, with a great screeching of ancient brakes, outside the Casa Barco. She sat motionless, the white cat, a great, heavy weight, asleep in her lap. The car engine was switched off, and it was then that she heard the whistling. A door opened and was slammed shut. The whistling continued, grew louder. The door of the Casa Barco was pushed open, and a man came in.

He carried a basket in one hand, a cardboard box under the other arm, and a roll of newspapers in his teeth. He shut the door with the seat of his trousers, put the basket down on the floor, took the papers out of his mouth and dropped them into the basket, and then carried the box to the table by the typewriter and set it carefully down. She couldn't see his face, because it was obscured by the peak of his battered, faintly sea-going cap, but he opened the top of the box, and checked, amongst paper shavings, on the contents. Seemingly content, he then picked up the binoculars and disappeared out on to the terrace. Selina sat still, where she was, but the cat began to wake up. She stroked it, partly out of nervousness, and partly because she didn't want it to move. After a little, he came back into the house again, laid down the binoculars and took off his cap and threw it down on the table. He had dark hair, very thick and just beginning to be run through with grey. His shirt was the faded blue one of any farmer, his trousers washed-out khaki denim, his shoes a pair of dusty espadrilles. Still whistling, he went back to collect the basket and take it into the galley, disappearing once more from Selina's view. She heard him open and shut the refrigerator door, there was the sound of a bottle being opened, the chink of glass, the pouring of a drink. When he appeared once more he was carrying a tumbler of what looked like soda water. He went back out on to the terrace and called "Pearl!" The cat began to stretch its legs. "Pearl! Pearley!" He made seductive kissing noises. The cat mewed. He came back into the house. "Pearl."

Selina ran a tongue over her lips, took a deep breath, and said, "Are you looking for the cat?"

George Dyer stopped dead in his tracks and looked up and saw the girl, sitting at the top of the steps. She had long bare legs and bare feet, and Pearl, like a huge white fur cushion, lay on her knee.

He frowned slightly, trying to remember. He said, "Were you there just now, when I came through?"

"Yes."

"I never saw you."

"No, I know you didn't." He told himself that her voice was very well modulated, very nicely brought up. She went on, "Is Pearl the name of your cat?"

"Yes, I came back to feed her."

"She's been sitting on my knee all afternoon."

"All after— . . . How long have you been here?"

"Since half past two."

"Half past two?" He glanced at his watch. "But it's past five o'clock."

"Yes I know."

Pearl now took a hand in the conversation by sitting up, stretching, uttering another plaintive mew, and springing lightly out of the girl's lap and down the steps. Purring like a kettle, she wrapped herself around George's legs, but for once was ignored.

"Are you here for any particular reason?"

"Oh, yes, I came to see you."

"Well, wouldn't it be a good idea to come down off that ladder?"

She did so. She stood up, obviously very stiff, and descended a step at a time, trying to push her hair back from her face. After Frances Dongen, and all the other suntanned young ladies at San Antonio, she looked very pale, with straight fawn-coloured hair that hung to her shoulders and a fringe to her eyebrows. Her eyes were blue, but shadowed with tiredness. He thought that she was too young even to be pretty.

He said, "I don't even know you . . . do I?"

"No. No, you don't. I hope you don't mind my just walking into your house."

"Not at all."

"The door wasn't bolted."

"It doesn't have any bolts."

Selina smiled, thinking perhaps this was a joke, but it apparently wasn't, so she stopped smiling, and tried to think what to say next. Subconsciously, she had been waiting for him to recognise her, to say "Who do you remind me of?" or "But, of course, I've met you before, some time, somewhere." But none of these remarks was forthcoming, and she found his appearance disconcerting, with no suggestion of the bright-eyed, clean-cut young officer who had been her father. She had expected him to be very brown, but she had not realised that his face would be so lined, or his dark eyes so bloodshot. The fact that he needed a shave not only hid the clean line of his jaw and the cleft of his chin, but added to his villainous appearance. Furthermore he did not seem in the least pleased to see her.

She swallowed, "I . . . expect you're wondering why I'm here."

"Well, yes, I am, but I've no doubt that in time you'll tell me."

"I flew here, from London . . . this morning, last night. No, this morning."

He was visited with a horrible suspicion. "Did Rutland send you?"

"Who? Oh, Mr Rutland the publisher. No, he didn't,

438

but he did say that he wished you'd answer his letters."

"The devil he did." Another thought occurred to him. "But you do know him?"

"Oh, yes, I went to see him and ask him how I could find you."

"But who are you?"

"My name's Selina Bruce."

"I'm George Dyer, but I imagine you know that."

"Yes, I know. . . ."

There was another silence. George, despite himself began to be intrigued. "You couldn't be a fan? You couldn't be the Organising Secretary of the George Dyer Fan Club." Selina shook her head. "Then you're staying at the Cala Fuerte Hotel and you've read my book?" She shook her head again. "This is like Twenty Questions, isn't it? Are you famous? Are you an actress? Do you sing?"

"No, but I had to see you, because . . ." Her courage left her. "Because," she finished, "I have to ask you to lend me six hundred pesetas."

George Dyer felt his own jaw sag with astonishment, and hastily laid down the glass of soda water before he should drop it.

"What did you say?"

"Do you have," said Selina, sounding very clear and highly pitched, as though she were talking to someone suffering from deafness, "six hundred pesetas you could lend me?"

"Six hundred!" He laughed. He laughed without mirth. "You must be joking."

"I only wish I were."

"Six hundred pesetas! I don't have that much!"

"But I must have six hundred, to pay the taxi-driver."

George looked around him. "Where does the taxi-driver come into it?"

"I had to get a taxi from the Aeropuerto to Cala Fuerte. I told the taxi-driver that you would pay him because I hadn't got any money. My wallet was stolen at the

Aeropuerto, while I was waiting to see if they could find my luggage. . . . Look. . . ." She went to pick up her handbag, and show him the two clear-cut edges of the handles. "The Guardia Civil said it must have been a very experienced thief, because I didn't feel a thing, and it was only my wallet that was taken."

"Only your wallet. And what did your wallet contain?"

"My traveller's cheques, and some British money, and some pesetas. And," she added, with the air of one determined to make a clean breast of it, "my return ticket."

"I see," said George.

"And the taxi-driver is waiting now, at the Cala Fuerte Hotel. For you. To pay him."

"You mean, you took a taxi from the Aeropuerto to Cala Fuerte to find me in order to pay the taxi fare. It's crazy. . . ."

"But I've explained. . . . You see, my luggage never came. . . ."

"You mean, you lost your luggage as *well!*"

"I didn't lose my luggage – *they* did. The airline."

"That's jet travel for you. Breakfast in London, lunch in Spain, luggage in Bombay."

"It got to Barcelona, but they think it must have been sent to Madrid."

"So," said George with the air of an efficient quizmaster doing a re-cap, "your luggage is in Madrid, and your wallet has been stolen and you want six hundred pesetas to pay your taxi fare."

"Yes," said Selina, delighted that he at last grasped the situation.

"And what did you say your name was?"

"Selina Bruce."

"Well, Miss Bruce, delighted though I am to have made your acquaintance, and naturally distressed to learn of your run of bad luck, I still don't see what it has to do with me."

"I think it has a lot to do with you," said Selina.

"Oh, you do?"

"Yes. You see. . . . I think I'm your daughter."

"You think . . ."

His first reaction was that she was insane. She had to be. She was one of those lunatic women who go round insisting they're the Empress Eugénie, only this one had a fixation about him.

"Yes. I think you're my father."

She wasn't insane. She was entirely innocent and she really believed what she was saying. He told himself that he must be rational. "What ever gave you that idea?"

"I have a little photograph of my father. I thought he was dead. But he has the same face as you."

"That's bad luck on him."

"Oh, no, it isn't bad at all. . . ."

"Have you got the photograph?"

"Yes, it's right here. . . ." She stooped to pick up her bag again, and he tried to reckon how old she was; he tried to remember, to decide, in a frenzied life-and-death sort of way, whether there could be the slightest chance that this dreadful accusation might be true. "It's here . . . I've always carried it around with me, ever since I found it, about five years ago. And then when I saw the photograph on the back of your book . . ." She held it out to him. He took it, not taking his eyes off her face. He said, "How old are you?"

"Twenty."

Relief made him feel quite weak. To hide the expression in his face he looked quickly down at the photograph that Selina had handed him. He did not say anything. And then, as Rodney had done when Selina first showed it to him, George Dyer carried it over to the light. After a little, he said, "What was his name?"

Selina swallowed. "Gerry Dawson. But the same initials as you."

"Could you tell me something about him?"

"Not very much. You see, I was always told that he was killed before I was born. My mother was called

441

Harriet Bruce, and she died just *after* I was born, so my grandmother brought me up and that's why I'm called Selina Bruce."

"Your grandmother. Your mother's mother."

"Yes."

"And you found this photograph . . .?"

"Five years ago. In a book of my mother's. And then I . . . was given *Fiesta at Cala Fuerte*, and I saw your photograph on the back, and it seemed to be the same. The same face, I mean. The same. The same person."

George Dyer did not reply. He came back from the open door, and gave her back the photograph. Then he lit a cigarette, and when he had shaken out the match, and placed it, dead centre, in the middle of the ash-tray, he said, "You said you were told he was killed. What do you mean by that?"

"Because I *was* told that. But I've always known that my grandmother didn't like him. She never wanted him to marry my mother. And when I saw the photograph, I thought perhaps there'd been some mistake. That he hadn't been killed at all. That he'd been wounded or something, lost his memory. That did happen, you know."

"But not to your father. Your father is dead."

"But you . . ."

He said, very gently, "I'm not your father."

"But . . ."

"You're twenty. I'm thirty-seven. I probably look a great deal more, but, in fact, I'm only thirty-seven. I wasn't even in the war – not that one, anyway."

"But the photographs . . ."

"I have an idea that Gerry Dawson was a second cousin of mine. The fact that we look alike is one of those freaks of heredity. In fact, I think we probably weren't all that alike. The photograph of your father, and the picture on the back of my book, were taken years apart. And even in my hey-day, I was never as good-looking as that."

Selina stared at him. She had never seen a man so brown, and someone needed to sew a button on his shirt because it was open right down, so that you could see the dark hair on his chest, and the sleeves of the shirt were rolled up to just below his elbows, as though he couldn't be bothered to make a proper job of them. She felt curious, as though she would have no control over anything her body might choose to do. Her legs might buckle, her eyes fill with tears, she might even start hitting him, as he stood there, telling her that he wasn't her father. That it was all true, and Gerry Dawson was dead.

He was still talking, sounding as if he was trying to be kind. ". . . sorry you've come all this way. Don't feel too badly about it . . . it's a mistake that could easily be made . . . after all . . ."

There was a lump in her throat that ached, and his face, so close to her own, began to blur and swim as though it was sinking into the bottom of a pond. She had been far too warm, but now, suddenly, she was freezing cold, her arms and her back and the very roots of her hair were crawling with goose pimples. He said, and he seemed to be speaking from a great distance, "Are you all right?" and she realised to her shame that she was not after all going to faint, nor attack him in rage, but simply dissolve, ignominiously, into tears.

6

She said, "I suppose you haven't got such a thing as a handkerchief?"

He hadn't, but he went and fetched a large box of Kleenex and thrust it into her hands. She pulled one out and blew her nose, and said, "I don't think I'm going to need them all."

"I wouldn't be too sure."

"I am sorry. I didn't mean to do that. Cry, I mean."

"I'm sure you didn't."

She took another paper tissue and blew her nose again. "I'd been waiting so long. And it was suddenly so cold."

"It is colder. The sun's gone. There's been another storm warning. Here, come and sit down."

He put a hand under her elbow and propelled her to the gargantuan couch, and because she was still shivering, pulled the red-and-white blanket down over her knees and said that he would get her some brandy. Selina said she didn't like brandy, but he went just the same, and she watched him, behind the counter of his little galley, finding a bottle and a glass and pouring her a drink.

When he brought it back, she said, "I really need something to eat."

"Drink this first, anyway."

The glass was small and thick, and the brandy neat. Selina shuddered. When it was finished, he took the empty glass, and, on his way back to the galley, kicked up the ashes in the fireplace and tossed on another piece of driftwood. The ashes rose and fell again, coating the fresh piece of wood with grey dust. Presently, as

Selina watched, there was a glow of red and a tiny flame.

She said, "You don't even need to use bellows . . . it's burning up already."

"They know how to build a fireplace here. What do you want to eat?"

"I don't mind."

"Soup. Bread and butter. Cold meat. Fruit."

"Have you got some soup?"

"A can . . ."

"Isn't that a nuisance?"

"Less of a nuisance than having you in tears."

Selina was hurt, and said, "I didn't mean to."

When the soup was heating, he came back to sit on the edge of the hearth and talk to her. "Whereabouts do you live?" he asked, reaching for a cigarette, and lighting it with a spill from the fire.

"In London."

"With your grandmother?"

"My grandmother's dead."

"You don't live alone?"

"No. There's Agnes."

"Who's Agnes?"

"My Nanny," said Selina, and immediately could have bitten out her tongue. "I mean . . . she used to be my Nanny."

"Isn't there anyone else?"

"Yes," said Selina. "There's Rodney."

"Who's Rodney?"

Selina's eyes widened. "He's my . . . lawyer."

"Does anybody know you're out here?"

"Agnes knows I was coming."

"And the lawyer . . .?"

"He was away. On business."

"Then there's nobody to worry about you? To wonder where you are."

"No."

"Well, that's something."

446

The soup in the pan began to bubble. George Dyer went back to the galley to find a bowl and a spoon, and Selina said, "I like your house."

"Do you?"

"Yes. It's got a nice feeling, as though it just happened. As though it wasn't ever planned."

She thought of the flat in London where she and Rodney were going to live when they were married. Of the time and the thought that was being put into the carpets and the curtains and the right lighting and cushions, and the wastepaper baskets, and the kitchen and the pots and the pans. She said, "I think that's the way a house should be. It should evolve. Like the people who live in it." George Dyer was pouring himself out a whisky and soda and did not reply. She went on, "You have to have some things, of course, a roof over your head, and a fire, and . . . I suppose, somewhere to sleep." He came back from the galley, carrying the bowl of soup, with a spoon sticking out of it, in one hand, and his drink in the other. Selina took the soup bowl and said, "How did you get the bed up into the gallery?"

"In pieces. We put it together up there."

"It's very large."

"In Spain it's called a *Matrimoniale*. A marriage bed."

She was slightly embarrassed. "I couldn't think how you'd got it up there. I . . . I shouldn't have looked, I'm sorry, but I wanted to see everything before you came."

He said, "What are you going to do now?"

Selina looked down at her soup, stirring it. It was vegetable soup with alphabet noodles floating around it. She said, "I suppose I'd better go home."

"With no ticket and no money?"

"If I could borrow some, I could go back to San Antonio with Toni in his taxi. And I could catch the next flight back to London."

George said, "I really was telling you the truth when I said I hadn't got that six hundred pesetas. One of the reasons I went to San Antonio yesterday was to pick up some

447

cash, but there's been some delay at the clearing bank in Barcelona, and at the moment I'm almost cleaned out."

"But what am I going to do about the taxi-driver? I have to pay him."

"Perhaps Rudolfo at the Cala Fuerte will help us."

"It seems a lot to ask."

"He's used to it."

"It isn't just the six hundred pesetas for the taxi. I'll have to buy another air ticket."

"Yes, I know."

The soup was still too hot to drink. Selina stirred it again, and said, "You must think I'm the most awful fool." He did not deny this, and she went on, "Of course I should have written or something, but I couldn't bear the thought of waiting for a reply." He still made no comment, and she felt she must try to justify herself. "You'd think that you'd get used to not having a father, particularly if you'd never known him. But I never did get used to it. I used to think about it all the time. Rodney said I had an obsession about it."

"It's not a bad thing to have an obsession about."

"I showed Agnes the photograph on the back of your book, and she was struck all of a heap, because you look so like my father. That's what really made me come, because Agnes knew him very well. And I wouldn't seem quite so stupid if I hadn't had my wallet stolen. Up to then I'd done quite well. I caught all the right connections, and it wasn't my fault my luggage got sent to Madrid."

"Did you never travel on your own before?" He sounded incredulous.

"Oh, yes, heaps of times. But only on trains going to school and things." Something in his expression compelled her to be entirely honest. "And then there was somebody to meet me. . . ." She shrugged. "You know."

"No, I don't, but I believe you."

She began to eat the soup. She said, "If my father really was your second cousin, then we must be related."

"Second cousin once removed."

"It sounds terribly remote, doesn't it? And rather royal. Did you ever know my father?"

"No, I never knew him." He frowned. "What did you say your name was?"

"Selina."

"Selina. Well, if I ever needed proof that you're not my daughter, there it is."

"How do you mean?"

"I'd never saddle any girl with a name like that."

"What would you call her?"

"A man seldom imagines daughters. He only thinks of a son. George Dyer Junior, perhaps." He raised his glass to this mythical son, finished his drink and set down the glass. "Now, come on, eat up that soup and we'll go and find the taxi-driver."

While he piled the soup bowl and the glasses into the sink and fed the hungry Pearl, Selina washed her hands and face in the sink in his bathroom and combed her hair and put on her stockings and shoes again. When she emerged, he was out on the terrace once more, his cap on the back of his head, watching the harbour through his binoculars. Selina came to stand beside him.

"Which is your boat?"

"That one."

"What's her name?"

"*Eclipse.*"

"She looks big to sail single-handed."

"She is. I usually have a crew." He added, "I get a bit edgy when this heavy weather blows up. A hell of a sea comes in round that headland, and I've known her pull anchor."

"Surely she's safe there."

"The rocks come too far out into deep water for comfort."

She glanced at the sky. It was overcast and leaden. "Is there going to be another storm?"

"Yes, the wind's changed. It was a rotten forecast." He

lowered the binoculars and looked down at her. "Did you catch the storm last night?"

"It chased us over the Pyrenees. We could scarcely land at Barcelona."

He said, "I don't mind a storm at sea, but a storm in the air scares me paralytic. Are you ready?"

"Yes."

"We'll take the car."

They went back into the house and he put down his binoculars on the desk, and Selina collected her bag and said a silent goodbye to the Casa Barco. She had thought so much about coming to it, and now, after only a few hours, she was leaving it again. For good. She picked up her coat. He said, "What the hell's that for?"

"It's my coat. It's cold in London."

"You know, I'd forgotten. Here, I'll carry it for you." He slung it over his shoulder and added, "One thing about losing all your luggage, you do at least travel light."

They went out of the house, and Selina didn't know whether his car was meant as a joke or not. It looked as if it had been decorated for a Students' Rag Week, and she longed to ask if he had painted the wheels yellow himself, but somehow hadn't the nerve. They clambered in, and George piled Selina's coat on her knee, then started the engine, jammed in the gear, and turned the car in a series of hair-raising forward and backward jerks. Disaster loomed. At one moment they seemed about to ram a solid wall. The next, their back wheels teetered at the edge of a steep alley of steps. Selina shut her eyes. When at last they shot forward and up the hill there was an overpowering smell of exhaust, and sinister clanking sounds came from somewhere beneath her feet. The seats sagged and had holes in them, and the floor, which had lost its carpeting years ago, resembled nothing so much as the bottom of a dustbin. For George's sake, Selina hoped that his yacht was more seaworthy.

But, for all that, there was something very friendly about driving through Cala Fuerte in George Dyer's car. All the children screamed with laughter and waved, and shouted joyous salutations. All the women sitting in their gardens, or gossiping at their doors, turned to smile and send a greeting after them. All the men, sitting outside the cafés, walking home from work, stopped to let them go bowling by, with shouted pleasantries in Spanish which Selina didn't understand, but which George Dyer evidently did.

"What are they saying?"

"They want to know where I found my new Señorita."

"Is that all?"

"Isn't that enough?"

They came with a flourish up to the Cala Fuerte Hotel, and stopped so suddenly that a cloud of white dust rose from their wheels and coated the tables, and the drinks of the clients who sat on Rudolfo's terrace enjoying the first aperitifs of the evening. An Englishman was heard to say, "Bloody cheek," but George Dyer ignored him, climbed out of the car without bothering to open the door, and went up the steps of the terrace and through the chain curtain with Selina behind him.

"Rudolfo!"

Rudolfo was behind the bar. He said, in Spanish, "There is no need to shout."

"Rudolfo, where is the taxi-driver?"

Rudolfo was not smiling. He poured a tray of drinks and said, "The taxi-driver has gone."

"Gone? Didn't he want his money?"

"Yes, he wanted his money. Six hundred pesetas."

"Who paid him?"

"I did," said Rudolfo. "And I want to talk to you. Wait till I serve my customers."

He came out from behind the bar, walked past them without a word, and disappeared through the chain curtain and on to the terrace. Selina stared at George. "Is he angry?"

"At a guess I'd say he was annoyed about something."

"Where is Toni?"

"He's gone. Rudolfo paid him off."

451

It took a second or so for the enormity of this to sink in. "But if he's gone . . . how am I going to get back to San Antonio?"

"God knows."

"You'll have to take me."

"I am not driving back to San Antonio this evening, and even if I did, we still can't buy you a plane ticket."

Selina bit her lip. She said, "Rudolfo seemed so nice before."

"Like all of us he has two sides to his character."

Rudolfo returned, the chain curtain clashed behind him, and he put down his empty tray and turned on George.

He did it in Spanish which was perhaps just as well, for the language he employed was not for the ears of a delicately-nurtured young English señorita. George, with spirit, defended himself. As their voices rose, Selina, unable to ignore the obvious fact that a good deal of the references were to herself, would say, "Oh, please tell me what it's all about," or "Couldn't you say some of this in English so that I could understand?" but neither of them took the slightest notice of her.

The argument was interrupted at last by the arrival of a fat German who wanted a glass of beer, and while Rudolfo went behind the bar to serve him, Selina took the opportunity to tug at George's sleeve and say, "What's *happened?* Tell me what's happened!"

"Rudolfo is annoyed because you said you would wait at the Casa Barco, and he thought that the taxi-driver would wait there with you. He doesn't like stray taxi-drivers sitting round his bar, getting sloshed, and he seems to have taken a particular dislike to this one."

"Oh."

"Yes, oh."

"Is that all?"

"No, of course it's not all. In the end, to get rid of the man, Rudolfo paid him. And now he says I owe him six hundred pesetas, and he's got cold feet because he doesn't think I'll be able to pay him back."

"But, I'll pay him . . . I promise, . . ."

"That isn't really the point. He wants it now."

The fat German, sensing a bad atmosphere, carried his beer outside and he was no sooner away than Rudolfo and George turned on each other once more, but Selina moved swiftly forward.

"Oh please, Mr . . . Rudolfo, I mean. It's all my fault, and I'll see you get paid back, but you see, all my money was stolen. . . ."

Rudolfo had heard this before. "You said you would wait at the Casa Barco. With the taxi-driver."

"I didn't know he would be here for so long."

"And you," Rudolfo turned to George again. "Where were you, anyway? Going off to San Antonio, and not coming back, and nobody knows where you are . . ."

"What the hell's it got to do with you? Where I go and what I do is my own bloody business."

"It has to do with me when I have to pay your bills."

"Nobody asked you to pay it. And it wasn't my bill, anyway. And you've loused everything up, because now the Señorita can't get back to San Antonio."

"Then take her yourself!"

"I'll be damned if I will!" yelled George. And with that, he stormed out of the bar, was down the terrace steps in a single stride, and into his car. Selina shot after him. "What about me?"

He turned to look at her. "Well, are you coming or are you going to stay here?"

"I don't want to stay here."

"Come on, then."

There was no alternative. Half the village, and all Rudolfo's customers, seemed to be enjoying the scene. George leaned over to open her door, and Selina got in beside him.

At this moment, as if on a signal from some celestial stage manager, the storm broke.

There was a flash of lightning that split the sky, a roll of thunder and a sudden upsurge of wind that sent the pines shaking. The tablecloths on the Cala Fuerte terrace rose and flapped like badly-set sails, and a hat blew from the rack outside Maria's shop, and went bowling, a big pink and yellow wheel, down the main street. Dust rose in spirals, and behind the wind came the rain, a sudden sheet of it, the drops so big and heavy that in seconds the gutters were flooded.

Everybody rushed indoors. Rudolfo's customers, the gossiping women, the scampering children, the two men who had been working on the road. There was a general air of impending disaster as though an air-raid siren had gone, and in no time the place was deserted. Except for Selina and George, and George's little car.

She started to get out, but he had the engine running and he yanked her back again. She said, "Can't we shelter too?"

"What for? You're not afraid of a little rain?"

"A *little* rain?" His profile was stony and he didn't deign to answer. "Doesn't the hood go up?"

He pushed the car into gear and they started with the suddenness of an exploding rocket.

"It hasn't done for ten years," he shouted over the din of the car and the rain and the wind. Already they seemed to be up to the hubcaps in water, and Selina's feet were awash. She wondered if she should start baling.

"Well, what's the good of a hood if it doesn't go up?"

"Oh, stop bellyaching."

"I am not bellyaching, but . . ."

He accelerated, and her words died in a grasp of fright. They roared down the road, cutting corners with screeching tyres and sending up waves of yellow mud. The sea was the colour of lead, and the gardens of the delectable little villas already devastated by the wind. The air seemed to be filled with flying flotsam – leaves and scraps of straw and pine-needles – and when at last they came over the hill and down the lane towards Casa Barco, the water, penned between high walls, had reached the proportions of a deep stream, and their progress in George's car was like shooting rapids.

The bulk of this water, by force of gravity, was diverted down the flight of steps which led to the harbour, but a good deal had invaded the old net-store where he kept his car, and which already appeared to be in a state of flood.

Despite this, he drove straight into it, stopping a perilous inch from the far wall. He switched off the engine and jumped out, saying, "Come on, get out, and help me to get the doors shut."

Selina was too frightened to rebel. She stepped out into four inches of cold, dirty water and went to help him drag shut the sagging doors. They got them closed at last, leaning against them until, by sheer brute force, George was able to jam the primitive bolt into position. This done, he took her by the wrist and ran her into the Casa Barco, as another flash of lightning split the black sky to be followed by a roll of thunder so close that she thought the roof was going to fall in.

Even in the house, they did not appear to be safe. He went straight out on to the terrace, and began to struggle with the shutters. The wind was so strong that he had to prise them away from the walls of the house. The pots of flowers had already gone, some over the edge of the wall, others on to the terrace, where they lay, a mêlée of broken earthenware and spilt mud. When at last he got the shutters closed, and the inner doors, the house seemed dark and unfamiliar. He tried the light switch, but the electricity had gone off. The rain, coming down the chimney, had put out the fire, and the well was gurgling as though it might at any moment overflow.

Selina said, "Are we going to be all right?"

"Why shouldn't we be all right?"

"I'm frightened of thunder."

"It can't hurt you."

"Lightning can."

"Well, then, be frightened of lightning."

"I am. I'm frightened of that, too."

She felt that he should apologise, but he merely felt in his pocket and pulled out a soggy packet of cigarettes. He chucked this into the spitting fireplace, and went prowling, searching for more, eventually running a packet to earth in the galley. He took one and lit it, and then, while he was there, poured himself a stiff whisky. He brought the glass to the well, let down the bucket and brought it up brimful, and, with a dexterity born of long practice, tipped the water from the bucket into the glass without spilling a drop.

He said, "Do you want a drink?"

"No, thank you."

He took a mouthful of whisky and stood watching her, and she couldn't guess if he was laughing or not. They were both of them as wet as if they had fallen into a bath. Selina had shucked off her ruined shoes and now stood in an ever-widening puddle of water with her dress-hem dripping and her hair plastered to her face and neck. Being wet did not appear to bother George Dyer as much as it bothered her. She said, "I suppose you're used to this sort of thing," and tried to wring out the hem of her dress. "There wasn't even any need for it. We could easily have sheltered till the storm was over. Rudolfo would have let us. . . ."

He set down the glass with a small clash, and went across the room, and, two at a time, up the ladder to the gallery.

"Here," he said, and threw down a pair of pyjamas. "And here." They were followed by a towelling robe. There was the sound of a drawer being opened and shut. "And here." A towel. He stood, his hands on the rail, looking down at her. "Use the bathroom. Take everything off and give yourself a rub and get changed."

Selina went to pick up the clothes. As she opened the bathroom door, a wet shirt came over the gallery rail to be followed by a soaking pair of denims. Swiftly she shot into the bathroom and locked the door.

When she emerged, dried and dressed in the over-large clothes, and with her hair wrapped in a turban of dry towel, she found a certain metamorphosis had taken place.

The fire was blazing brightly once more, and there were three or four lighted candles standing about in old wine bottles. The transistor radio was playing flamenco music, and George Dyer had not only changed and cleaned himself up, but shaved as well. He wore a white polo-necked sweater, and a pair of blue serge trousers, and red leather slippers. He was sitting on the hearth with his back to the fire, reading one of his English newspapers and looking as relaxed as any gentleman in his country home. He glanced up as she came in.

"Well, there you are."

"What shall I do with all my wet things?"

"Chuck them on the bathroom floor. Juanita can cope in the morning."

"Who's Juanita?"

"My maid. Maria's sister. Do you know who Maria is? She runs the grocery store in the village."

"The mother of Tomeu."

"So you have already met Tomeu."

"Tomeu brought us here today; he led the way on his bicycle."

"Tomeu brought a chicken in that big basket of groceries. It's in the oven now. Come and sit by the fire and get warm. I'll pour you a drink."

"I don't want a drink."

"Don't you ever drink?"

"My grandmother didn't really approve."

"Your grandmother, if you'll excuse the expression, sounds an old bitch."

Despite herself, Selina smiled. "She wasn't really."

He was surprised by the smile. Still watching it, he said, "What part of London do you live in?"

"Queen's Gate."

"Queen's Gate, SW7. And very nice too. And I suppose your Nanny took you for walks in Kensington Gardens?"

457

"Yes."

"Do you have brothers and sisters?"

"No."

"Uncles and aunts?"

"No. Nobody."

"No wonder you were so desperately in need of a father."

"I wasn't desperately in need. I just wanted one."

George rocked his glass, watching the tilting amber liquid. He said, "You know, it's occurred to me that people you . . . are fond of . . . they go on living until some meddlesome fool comes and tells you they're dead."

Selina said, "I was told years ago that my father was dead."

"I know, but today you've been told for the second time. And it was I who killed him."

"It wasn't your fault."

"I'm sorry, just the same." He added, more gently, "You could do with a drink. Just to warm you up."

She shook her head, and he let it go, but it made him feel uncomfortable just the same. He was so used to being with Frances, who could hold her own, drink for drink, even if she did get a little blurry by the end of the evening, and ready to fight at the drop of a hat; and the next day she was as clear-headed and bright-eyed as ever, if you could discount the slight tremor of her hand as she reached out for the tenth cigarette of the morning.

But this child. He looked at her. Her skin was like ivory, creamy, quite unflawed. As he watched, she took the towel off her head and began to rub at her hair to dry it, and her ears showed, touching, and vulnerable as the back of a baby's neck.

She said, "What are we going to do?"

"What about?"

"About the money. And paying Rudolfo, and getting me back to London."

"I don't know. I'll have to think about it."

"I could cable my bank in London, and they'd send me something."

"Yes, you could."

"Would it take long?"

"Three or four days."

"Don't you think, perhaps, I should try and get a room at the Cala Fuerte Hotel?"

"I doubt if Rudolfo would have you."

"I don't really blame him, you know. Even when he was sober, Toni was rather terrifying. Drunk, he must have been really scarey."

"I doubt if he scared Rudolfo."

"Well . . . where am I going to stay?"

"Where else but here? In the *Matrimoniale*. I'd go out to *Eclipse*, only not in this weather, and it won't be the first time I've slept on the sofa."

"If anyone's going to sleep on a sofa, then it should be me."

"Whichever you like. It's all the same to me. I'm sorry that the Casa Barco isn't more conveniently designed, but there's little I can do about it now. I never imagined I'd have a daughter come to stay."

"But I'm not your daughter."

"Then let's say you're George Dyer Junior."

7

Six years ago, when George Dyer had first come to live at Cala Fuerte, Juanita had presented herself at his door and announced, with great dignity, that she would like to work for him. She was the wife of a farmer from San Estaban, she had four children, who were at school in the village, and poverty was never far away. She needed the work, because she needed the money, but there was nothing in her erect and proud demeanour to give any hint of this. She was a small woman, with the square, toiling sturdiness of a working peasant, dark-eyed, short-legged, and with a smile of great charm only spoiled by the fact that she had never cleaned her teeth.

Each morning she was up at half past four, did the daily chores in her own house, fed her family and saw them off to work, and then walked down the hill from San Estaban to Cala Fuerte to present herself at the Casa Barco at half past seven. She cleaned and cooked for George, did the washing and the ironing, combed the cat and weeded the garden, and was not averse, if the need arose, to taking the dinghy out to *Eclipse* and scrubbing down her decks as well.

When *Fiesta at Cala Fuerte* was published, George gave her a complimentary copy, with a dedication written on the fly-leaf, "*Juanita from George Dyer, with love and respect,*" and it was perhaps her most precious possession, after the marriage bed which had been bequeathed to her by her grandmother, and the linen sheets, heavy as leather, which she had embroidered herself. She spoke no English and read in no language, but the book was already on show in her house, arranged, like an ornament, with a lace doily all to itself. She never let herself into his house. In Juanita's code, this appeared to be a breach of etiquette. Instead, she would sit outside, on the wall, with her hands in her lap and her legs crossed at the ankle, like Royalty, and wait for him to come and open the door and let her in. He would say, "*Buenos días*, Juanita," and they would exchange pleasantries about the weather, and she would ask how the Señor had slept. He had never discovered the reason for this strange shibboleth, and did not like to ask. Perhaps it had something to do with the fact that he did not have a wife.

The morning after the storm he awoke at seven. He had slept on the sofa, after all, because he hadn't the heart to take the comfortable bed for himself. It was very quiet. The wind had died, and when he got up and went to open his shutters and go out on to the terrace, the morning was fresh and quiet as a pearl, without a cloud in the sky, and the world smelt damp and sweet after the rain, although the water of the harbour was murky from the rough weather, and a certain amount of devastation would have to be cleared away. To start with, he picked up his rickety terrace furniture from where it had been ignominiously blown, and tipped a puddle of water from the top of the table, and then he went back inside, and lit a cigarette, and thought that he would make a cup of tea. There was, however, no water in the kettle and he did not like to let the bucket down the well for fear of waking Selina.

He looked for his clothes, but the sweater and trousers he had worn last night were unsuitable for the day's work, so he went to the gallery to fetch himself some others. Selina still slept like a child, engulfed by George's pyjamas and the enormous bed. Moving quietly, he took the first shirt and pair of pants that came to hand, and eased himself down the ladder again. He had a shower (the water was icy after the storm) and dressed, and then went to open the door for Juanita. She had not arrived, but if the door stood open, she would come in and start to cook his breakfast.

Then he went back out on to the terrace, down the steps to the slipway, pushed out the dinghy and rowed out to *Eclipse*.

She seemed to have weathered the storm with her usual calm. He checked her mooring ropes, then went aboard. With a certain amount of forethought he had secured the tarpaulin cover over the cockpit, and although this sagged with pools of water, the cockpit itself was relatively dry. He loosened off a couple of straining halyards, and went below to make sure that his forward hatches had not let in any of the rain. Reassured, he returned to the cockpit, and perched himself on the coaming and lit a cigarette.

It was going to be a very warm day. Already steam was rising from the wet decks, and the tarpaulin, which he had spread out to dry. The air was so clear that he could see far inland, beyond the distant cross of San Estaban; and so quiet that when a fisherman, busy on his boat, talked in undertones to a companion, George could hear every word. There was only the slightest movement of water. The dinghy's prow resisted this, with a soft lapping sound, but the yacht moved lightly, as though she were breathing.

Soothed by familiar surroundings, familiar smells and sounds, George felt himself begin to unwind. Calmly, now, he could consider the day ahead, and give a certain order to the problems which beset him.

The first was Rudolfo. He did not mind the row; it was not the first and it would not be the last, but Rudolfo was not a wealthy man, and somehow, and soon, the six hundred pesetas had to be paid back. George could not risk waiting until his own money was cleared by the bank in Barcelona. These delays had happened before, and he had once had to wait nearly a month before it came through. If, however, they sent a cable to Selina's bank there was the possibility that the money would be in San Antonio in three or four days, and Rudolfo, knowing this, would be only too pleased to put her up at his hotel, and that way conventions would be respected,

463

and no fine feelings, vulnerable in Cala Fuerte, would be offended.

On the other hand, there was Frances. Frances would lend him six hundred pesetas and Selina's return air fair, if George could bring himself to ask her. But with Frances, money talked. And if he was going to get into her debt, he would not do it for Rudolfo, nor a girl who had come looking for her father, but on his own account, because only he would be able to settle the bill.

A movement from Casa Barco caught his eye, and he looked up and saw that Juanita was on the terrace, hanging the red-and-white blanket from the sofa over the washing line in order to air it. She wore a pink dress and a brown apron, and she went back into the house, only to reappear with a broom, and began to clear up the debris of last night's broken flowerpots.

George wondered how he was going to explain the presence of Selina in his bed. He had always been very careful never to let such a situation arise, and as far as Juanita was concerned, he had no idea how she might react. He did not like the thought of deceiving her, but on the other hand he did not want to lose her – for any reason. He could tell her the truth, but it was so far-fetched that he doubted whether the simple Juanita would swallow it. Or he could say that Selina was a visiting cousin, who had had to spend the night because of the storm. After some deliberation he decided that this was the best story, and had the added advantage of being more or less true. He tossed his cigarette overboard, let himself down into the dinghy and rowed gently back to Casa Barco.

Juanita was in the galley, boiling a kettle for his coffee.

"*Buenos días*, Juanita."

She turned, beaming.

"*Buenos días*, Señor."

He decided to plunge straight in.

"Did you wake the Señorita when you drew the water from the well?"

464

"No, Señor, she still sleeps, like a baby."

George glanced at Juanita sharply. Her voice was lyrical, her eyes shining with sentiment. This was not exactly what George had expected. He had not even had time to tell his story about the visiting cousin, and here was Juanita already looking all dewy-eyed . . . about what?

"You've . . . been up to see her then . . .?"

"*Sí*, Señor, I went to see if she was awake. But, Señor," her voice dropped to a tone of mild reproach, "why did you never tell me that you had a daughter?"

George felt behind him for the arm of the sofa, and sat on it. "I never told you?" he said, stupidly.

"No, you have said no word about your daughter. And when Maria tells me, this morning, as I come through Cala Fuerte, that the Señor's daughter is staying at the Casa Barco, I would not believe it. But it is true."

George swallowed, and said, with forced calm, "Maria told you. And who told Maria?"

"Tomeu has told her."

"Tomeu?"

"*Sí*, Señor. There was a taxi-driver who brought her here. He spent many hours in the bar of Rudolfo, and he told Rosita, who works there, that he had taken the daughter of Señor Dyer to the Casa Barco. Rosita told Tomeu when she went to buy some soap powder, and Tomeu told Maria, and Maria told Juanita."

"And the rest of the village, I'll be bound," George muttered, in English, and silently cursed Selina.

"Señor?"

"It is nothing, Juanita."

"Are you not pleased to have your daughter?"

"Yes, of course."

"I did not know that the Señor had been married."

George thought for a second and then said, "Her mother is dead."

Juanita was devastated. "Señor, I did not know. And who has taken care of the Señorita?"

"Her grandmother," said George, wondering how much

465

longer he was going to get away from telling the truth. "Juanita, tell me . . . does Rudolfo know that . . . the Señorita is my daughter?"

"I have not seen Rudolfo, Señor."

The kettle boiled, and she filled the earthenware jug that George had taught her to keep for coffee. The smell was delicious, but did nothing to cheer him. Juanita put the lid on the coffee-pot and said, "Señor, she is very beautiful."

"*Beautiful?*" He sounded amazed, because he was.

"But of course she is beautiful." Juanita carried his breakfast tray past him and out on to the terrace. "The Señor does not have to pretend with me."

He ate his breakfast. An orange, a sweet *ensamada*, and as much coffee as the pot contained. Juanita moved about inside the house, soft-footed and making gentle sweeping sounds which indicated that she was cleaning. Presently she emerged with the round washing-basket, filled with clothes.

He said, "The Señorita got very wet last night, in the storm, and I told her to put her clothes on the floor of the bathroom."

"*Sí*, Señor, I have found them."

"Do them quickly as you can, Juanita. She has nothing else to wear."

"*Sí*, Señor."

She went past him and down the steps to her little cave of a wash-house, where she scrubbed sheets, socks and shirts impartially, boiling water in a great tub and using a bar of soap as large and as hard as a brick.

The first thing to do was go and see Rudolfo. As George went through the house, he glanced up at the gallery but there was no movement and not a sound. He cursed his visitor silently, but left her sleeping, and went out, and because he could not be bothered to open the garage doors and start up his car, began to walk to the village.

He was to regret this. For, before he had reached

the Cala Fuerte Hotel, no fewer than seven people had congratulated him on having his daughter come to stay with him. As each encounter took place, George walked a little faster, as though on some errand of desperate urgency, giving the impression that much as he would like to stop and discuss this new and happy state of affairs, he simply did not have the time. Consequently he arrived at Rudolfo's bar, out of breath and soaked in sweat, and feeling as if he had been caught in a trap. He stood in the curtained doorway, panting with exhaustion, and said, "Rudolfo. Am I allowed in?"

Rudolfo was behind the bar, polishing glasses. When he saw George, his hands were still. His smile began to spread. "George, my friend." He laid down the glass and came out from behind the bar as if to embrace George.

George eyed him warily. "You're not going to hit me?"

"It is you who should be hitting me. But I did not know. I was only told, this morning, by Rosita, that the Señorita is your daughter. Why did you not tell me last night? That she was your child. I did not even know that you had a child. And so beautiful . . ."

"Rudolfo, there's been a mistake. . . ."

"And it was my mistake. And what kind of a man must you think I am, to grudge a favour to an old friend and his child?"

"But . . ."

Rudolfo raised a hand. "There can be no buts. Six hundred pesetas, well," he shrugged, "it doesn't grow on trees, but it will not ruin me."

"Rudolfo . . ."

"My friend, if you say more I shall think that you have not forgiven me. Come, let us have a drink together – a cognac. . . ."

It was impossible. He refused to listen to the truth and George was not going to push it down his throat. He said weakly, "I'd rather have a coffee," and Rudolfo went to shout for it and George hitched himself on to one of

467

the bar stools and lit a cigarette. When Rudolfo returned he said, "You'll get your money back. We can cable to London . . ."

"You will have to go to San Antonio to send a cable."

"Well, fair enough. How long would you reckon it would take to come?"

Rudolfo shrugged hugely. "Two or three days. Maybe a week. It's of no importance. I can wait a week for six hundred pesetas."

"You're a good man, Rudolfo."

"But I get angry. You know I get angry."

"You're still a good man."

The coffee came, brought by Rosita, the unconscious source of the trouble. George watched her set down the minuscule cups and told himself that he was deeper in deception than ever. And he realised, with a slight sinking of his heart, that there was now no need to ask his second favour of Rudolfo. If Selina was to be George's daughter, there could be no point in her coming to live at the Cala Fuerte Hotel.

It was Pearl who woke Selina. She had been out all night, was tired from hunting and in need of a soft place to sleep. She came into the Casa Barco by way of the terrace, trod lightly up the stair to the gallery, and jumped, with scarcely a sound, on to the bed. Selina opened her eyes and looked straight into Pearl's white, whiskered face. Pearl's eyes were jade-green, the dark pupils mere slits of contentment. She trod the sheets for a little, making a nest, then fitted her boneless, furry body into the curve of Selina's own and proceeded to go to sleep.

Selina rolled over and did the same thing.

The second time she was awakened more roughly. "Come on, now, it's time to wake up. It's eleven o'clock. Come on, now." She was being shaken, and when she opened her eyes, George Dyer was sitting on the side of the bed. "It's time you woke up," he said again.

"Umm?" The cat was still there, deliciously heavy and

468

warm. George, once focused, loomed enormous. He wore a blue cotton shirt and a grim expression, and Selina's heart sank. She was never at her best first thing in the morning.

"It's time you woke up."

"What time is it?"

"I told you. Nearly eleven. I've got to talk to you."

"Oh." She pulled herself up and searched for pillows that had disappeared. George stooped to pick them up off the floor, and shoved them behind her. "Now, listen," he said. "I've been to see Rudolfo . . ."

"Is he still angry?"

"No, he's not angry. Not any more. You see, Rudolfo, and for that matter the entire village, believe that you really are my daughter. You know why they think that, don't you? Because your drunken taxi-driver, damn his eyes, told them so."

"Oh," said Selina.

"Yes. Oh. *Did* you tell the taxi-driver I was your father."

"Yes," she admitted.

"For God's sake why?"

"I had to, to make him bring me here. I said, 'My father will pay the taxi fare,' and that was the only thing that persuaded him."

"You had no right to do that. To involve an innocent party . . ."

"You?"

"Yes, me. I'm up to my neck in this now."

"I never thought he would tell all the village."

"He didn't. He told Rosita, the girl who works in Rudolfo's bar. And Rosita told Tomeu. And Tomeu told his mother. And Maria is the Official Receiving and Transmitting Station for this part of the island."

"I see," said Selina. "I am sorry. But can't we tell them the truth?"

"Not now."

"Why not now?"

"Because the people here . . ." he chose his words carefully, "have a very rigid standard of morals."

"Then why did you let me stay last night?"

He was exasperated. "Because of the storm. Because of the row with Rudolfo. Because there wasn't any alternative."

"And you've said that I am your daughter?"

"I haven't said that you're not."

"But you're much too young. We worked it out last night."

"No one else is to know that."

"But it's not true."

"It wasn't true when you told the taxi-driver."

"Yes, but I didn't *know* it wasn't true!"

"And I do. Is that it? Well, I'm sorry if your principles are offended, but these people are my friends and I don't want to disillusion them. Not that they have many illusions about me, but at least they don't think I'm a liar."

She still looked troubled, so he changed the subject. "Now, about this money. You say that we can cable to your bank . . ."

"Yes."

"But not from Cala Fuerte. We have to go into San Antonio to send a cable. We can either send a wire directly to your bank, or it occurred to me on the way home, we might get in touch with your lawyer . . ."

"Oh, no," said Selina, with such vehemence that George raised his eyebrows in surprise.

"Why not?"

"Let's just cable the bank."

"But your lawyer would be able to get the money through so much more quickly."

"I don't want to cable Rodney."

"Don't you like him?"

"It isn't that. It's just that . . . well, he thought this whole business of coming to find my father was crazy."

"As things have turned out, he wasn't far wrong."

"I don't want him to know what a fiasco it's all been. Try to understand."

"Well, sure I understand, but if it meant the money coming through more quickly . . ." Her face remained resolutely stubborn, and George, suddenly fed up with the whole business, stopped trying to persuade her. "Well, all right. It's your money and your time. And your reputation."

Selina ignored this. "Do you want to go to San Antonio today?"

"Soon as you can be up and dressed. Are you feeling hungry?"

"Not particularly."

"How about a cup of coffee?"

"If there's one going."

"I'll make you one."

He was halfway down the ladder when she called him back.

"Mr Dyer . . ."

He turned, only his top half visible.

Selina said, "I haven't got anything to put on."

"I'll speak to Juanita."

He found her on the terrace, ironing, with the flex of the iron trailing through the open window.

"Juanita."

"Señor."

"The Señorita's things? Are they ready?"

"Sí Señor." She beamed, delighted with her own efficiency, and handed him a pile of neatly-folded clothes. He thanked her, and went back into the house, to meet Selina coming down the steps from the gallery. Still in his pyjamas, she looked tousled and sleepy. He said, "Here," and handed her the pile.

"Oh, how wonderful!"

"Just one of the services in this hotel."

"She's been so quick . . . I never thought . . ." The words tailed to a stop. George frowned. From the top of the pile of clothes, Selina took her dress. Or what remained of

471

it. Juanita had treated the good British wool just as she treated the rest of her washing. With hot water, hard soap and much scrubbing. Selina held it out at arm's length. It might have fitted a very small six-year-old and the only thing that rendered it recognisable was the silk Fortnum and Mason label on the inside of the collar.

There was a long silence. Then George said, "It's a Little Brown Dress."

"She's washed it! Why did she have to wash it? It didn't need to be washed; it was only wet. . . ."

"If it's anyone's fault, it's mine. I told Juanita to wash it, and if I tell Juanita to do a thing, she certainly does it." He began to laugh.

"I don't think it's anything to laugh about. It's all very well for you to laugh, but what am I going to wear?"

"What is there to do except laugh?"

"I could cry."

"That won't do any good."

"I can't wear pyjamas all day long."

"Why not? They're very fetching."

"I can't come to San Antonio in pyjamas."

Still enormously amused, but trying to be sensible, George scratched the back of his head. "What about your coat?"

"I should die of heat in my coat. Oh, why do all these horrible, horrible things have to happen?"

He tried to soothe her. "Now look . . ."

"No I *won't* look!"

It was a typical example of the blind injustice of arguing with a woman, and George lost patience.

"All right then, don't look. Go and jump on the bed and cry for the rest of the day, but before you do, come and help me compose a cable to send to your bank. I'll take it into San Antonio myself, and you can stay here and sulk."

"That's the most horrible, unfair thing to say . . ."

"All right, Junior, so it's horrible. Maybe I say horrible things because I'm a horrible person. It's as well you

472

found out in good time. Now, come and sit down and put that pin-brain of yours into action and let's get this cable written."

"I have not got a pin-brain," Selina defended herself. "And even if I had, you haven't known me long enough to find out. All I'm saying is that I can't walk round in my underclothes all day. . . ."

"Look, this is Cala Fuerte San Antonio, not Queen's Gate, SW7. Personally, I don't care if you walk around stark naked, but I'd prefer to get hold of that money as soon as possible, and return you, unopened, as it were, to Kensington Gardens and Nanny." He was leaning over his desk, finding a clean sheet of paper and a pencil, but now he looked up, his brown eyes unreadable, and said, "If you were older and more experienced, I rather think you'd have slapped my face by now."

Selina told herself that if she cried, in rage, or for any other reason, she would never forgive herself. She said in a voice that shook only slightly, "The idea never entered my head."

"Good. Don't let it." He sat down at the desk and drew the sheet of paper towards him. "Now, the name of your bank . . ."

8

After the quiet, tree-shaded cool of Cala Fuerte, San Antonio that afternoon seemed hot and dusty and inordinately full. The streets were packed with traffic. Hooting cars and motor scooters, wooden donkey carts and bicycles. The narrow pavements were so crowded that pedestrians, careless of life, overflowed into the road, and George found that it was impossible to make any sort of progress without the heel of his hand more or less permanently on the horn.

The cable office and his own bank were both situated in the main plaza of the town, facing each other across the tree-lined walks and the fountains. George parked his car in a shady spot, lit a cigarette, and went, first, into the bank to see if by any chance his own money had come through from Barcelona. If it had, he planned to collect the lot in cash, tear up Selina's cable, and go then and there to the airport and buy her return ticket to London.

But the money had still not come. The cashier suggested kindly that if George would like to sit and wait for perhaps four or five hours, he would endeavour to get through to Barcelona and find out what had happened. George, in fascinated interest, asked why he would have to wait four or five hours, only to be told that the telephone was broken and had not yet been repaired.

After six years of living on the island, he was still torn between exasperation and amusement at the local attitude to time, but he said that it didn't matter, he would do without the money, and he went out of the bank, and across the square, and up the impressive stairway to the soaring marble halls of the cable office.

He copied the message out on to an official form, and then joined a slow-moving shuffling queue. When at last he reached the wire grille and it was his turn, his patience was running short. The man behind the grille had a polished brown head and a wart on his nose and spoke no English. It took him a long time to read the message, to count the words, and consult manuals. Eventually he stamped the form, and told George that it would cost ninety-five pesetas.

George paid him. "When will it get to London?"

The man eyed the clock. "Tonight . . . maybe."

"You'll send it off right away?"

The wart-nosed man did not deign to reply. He looked over George's shoulder. "Next, please."

There was nothing more to be done. He went back outside, lit another cigarette, and debated on his next move. In the end he decided that it would be worth going to the Yacht Club to pick up his mail, but not worth taking the car. He started to walk.

The crowds made him feel claustrophobic. He stayed in the middle of the streets, stepping aside every now and then to let the motor traffic brush by. Overhead, small balconies bulged with humanity. Enormous, black-clad grannies sat with their embroidery, enjoying the spring sunshine. Clusters of children, their eyes like grapes, peered through the wrought-iron lace of the railings, and washing, like celebration bunting, zig-zagged from one side of the street to the other, and over all was the San Antonio smell. Of drains and fish, and cedar wood and Ideales cigarettes, overlaid with unidentifiable harbour smells that blew in from the sea.

He came to a small crossroads and stopped on the edge of the pavement, waiting for the traffic to clear so that he could cross. A cripple, in a little booth, sold lottery tickets, and on the corner of the block was a shop, the window filled with embroidered blouses and cotton dresses and beach hats and shoes and bathing-suits.

George thought of Selina. He told himself that he could not wait to put her on the London plane, and to be rid of her, but she wouldn't be able to travel if she didn't have a dress to wear. Perhaps he should buy her a dress. But even as he went in through the door, he was visited by a second and far more amusing idea.

"*Buenos días*, Señor," said the red-headed woman, getting up from behind her small glass counter.

"*Buenos días*," said George, and, straight-faced, he told her what he wanted.

Five minutes later he was back in the crowded streets, carrying the little parcel wrapped so carefully in pink-and-white-striped paper. He was still grinning to himself, when the car horn blared behind him. He swore and stepped aside and the long black snout of a Citröen brushed alongside the seat of his trousers, and stopped.

"Well," said an unmistakable voice. "Look who just rode into town."

It was Frances. She sat in her open car, looking both surprised and pleased. She wore sun-glasses and a man's straw hat tipped over her nose and a faded pink shirt. She leaned across to open the door. "Hop in and I'll take you some place."

He got in beside her, and the leather upholstery was so hot that he felt as if he were being grilled, but before he had even shut the door Frances had moved forward again, slowly, nosing through the crowds.

She said, "I didn't expect to see you back so soon."

"I didn't expect to be here."

"How long have you been in?"

"Half an hour or so. I had to send a cable."

Frances did not comment on this. Another cluster of pedestrians had gathered ahead. Fat ladies in cotton dresses and white cardigans, with very new straw hats and painfully sun-burned faces. Frances's horn blared again, and they looked up, surprised, from the postcards they had been buying, and backed unresentfully up on to the already bursting pavements.

"Where the hell have they all come from?" George wanted to know.

"It's a cruise ship in. The first of the season."

"Oh, God, has it started already?"

Frances shrugged. "You have to make the best of it. At least it brings cash into the town." She glanced down at the little parcel in his lap. "What have you been buying at Teresa's shop?"

"How do you know it was Teresa's shop?"

"The pink-and-white-striped paper. I'm intrigued."

George thought for a moment. He said, "It's handkerchiefs."

"Didn't know you used them." They had come to the main street of the town, an artery of traffic controlled by a wickedly-tempered Guardia Civil. The Citröen moved down into second gear, and Frances said, "Where d'you want to go?"

"There might be some mail at the Yacht Club."

"Didn't you pick it up yesterday?"

"Yes, but there might be some more."

She glanced at him sideways. "Did you get home all right?"

"Sure."

"Boat O.K.?"

"Yes, she's all right. Did you get that second storm yesterday evening?"

"No, it missed us."

"You were lucky. It was a corker."

They waited at the traffic lights until the red changed to green, then Frances turned down a narrow street and on to the broad harbour road. This was George's favourite part of San Antonio, packed with cheerful little waterfront bars, and ships' chandlers, smelling of tar and grain and paraffin. The harbour was filled with craft. Island schooners, and yachts, and the Barcelona boat, getting steam up to sail, and the cruise ship, from Bremen, tied up at the north pier.

He saw a strange yacht, new since yesterday. He said, "She's flying a Dutch flag."

"A young person called Van Trikker, doing a circumnavigation." Frances made it her business to find these things out.

"Through the Mediterranean?"

"Well, why not? That's what the Suez Canal is for."

He grinned. Frances leaned forward and took a pack of cigarettes out of the dashboard shelf and handed it to him, and he took it and lit one for himself and one for her. When they got to the Yacht Club, he went inside for his mail, and Frances sat and waited for him, and when he returned with two letters stuffed in the back pocket of his trousers, she said, "Where now?"

"I'm going to have a drink."

"I'll come with you."

"Oughtn't you to be selling original Olaf Svensens to all those lovely tourists?"

"I have a young student working for me. She can take care of the Germans." She turned the car in a single sweep. "I'd much rather take care of you."

They went to Pedro's, a little way along the road. Pedro had pulled some tables and chairs out on to the wide pavement, and they sat in the shade of a tree, and George ordered a beer for himself and cognac for Frances.

She said, "Darling, you're very abstemious all of a sudden."

"I have a genuine thirst."

"I hope it isn't painful."

She reached around his back for the letters he had stuffed in his pocket and laid them on the table in front of him and said, "Open them."

"Why?"

"Because I'm curious. I like to know what's in letters, especially other people's. I don't like to think of them ageing gracefully, like well-bred old ladies. Here. . . ."

She picked a knife off the carelessly-laid table, and slit the flaps of the envelopes. "Now all you have to do is take them out and read them."

Humouring her, George did so. The first contained a letter from a yachting magazine to say that they would pay him eight pounds ten shillings for an article he had submitted to them.

He handed this over to Frances and she read it, and said, "There, what did I tell you? Good news."

"Better than nothing." He took out the second letter.

"What was the article about?"

"Self-steering gears."

She patted his back. "Well, aren't you a clever boy. . . . Who's that one from?"

It was from his publisher, but he was reading the letter, and did not hear the question.

> George Dyer, Esq.,
> Club Nautica,
> San Antonio,
> Baleares,
> Spain.

Dear Mr Dyer,

I have written you no fewer than five letters over the last four months in the hope that you would be able to let us have at least some sort of synopsis for a second book as a follow-up to *Fiesta at Cala Fuerte*. I have not had a reply to any of them. All these letters were addressed to the Club Nautica at San Antonio, and I am now wondering whether perhaps this is no longer your Poste Restante.

As I pointed out when we agreed to publish *Fiesta at Cala Fuerte*, a follow-up is important if we are to maintain the public's interest in you as a writer. *Cala Fuerte* has sold well and is into its third printing, and negotiations are under way for a paperback; but we must have

480

a second book from you soon, if your sales are not to deteriorate.

It is unfortunate that we were unable to meet personally and discuss this matter, but I think I made it clear when we agreed to publish *Fiesta at Cala Fuerte* that we could only do it on condition that it would be the first of a series, and I was under the impression that you understood this.

In any event, I should be grateful for a reply to this letter.

Yours sincerely,
ARTHUR RUTLAND

He read this through twice and then dropped it on the table. The waiter had brought their drinks, and the beer was so cold that it frosted the tall glass, and when he put his hand around it it was an actual pain, like touching ice.

Frances said, "Who's it from?"

"Read it."

"I don't want to read it if you'd rather I didn't."

"Oh, read the thing."

She did so, and he drank his beer.

She reached the bottom of the page, and said, "Well, I think that's the hell of a letter. Who does he think he is?"

"My publisher."

"For heaven's sake, you're under no contract!"

"Publishers don't like one-book men, Frances. They want either nothing at all, or a good steady stream."

"He's written to you before?"

"Yes, of course he has. He's been on at me for the last four or five months. That's why I've given up opening my letters."

"Have you *tried* to write a second book?"

"Tried? I've ruptured myself trying. What the hell am I to write it about? I only wrote the first one because I thought I was running out of money, and it was a long, chilly winter. I never thought I'd get it published."

481

"But you've been around, George . . . you've done so many things. That cruise in the Aegean . . ."

"Do you think I didn't try to write about that? I spent three weeks bashing words on to my typewriter, and it was as dull to read as it had been to write. Anyway it's been done before. Everything's been done before."

Frances took a final drag of her cigarette, and then stubbed it out, carefully, in the ash-tray. Her brown hands were as big as a man's, the nails very large and painted bright red. She wore a heavy gold bracelet and as she moved her arm, it clashed on the wood of the table. She said, carefully, "Is it really that much of a disaster? After all, you've had one successful book, and if you can't write a second, then you just can't."

A boat was moving out of the yacht club basin. Across the water came the rattle of shackles, and the sail slid up the mast. It hung slack for a moment, and then the boy at the tiller moved the boat around and the sail shivered slightly and shook out its folds and swelled into a smooth, strong curve, and the boat heeled over and ran forward, and was pulled closer to the wind and heeled some more.

He said, "I don't like to break a promise."

"Oh, darling, you talk as if it were a personal thing."

"Isn't it?"

"No, it's business."

"Would you break a business promise just like that?"

"Of course not. But writing isn't like selling stocks or doing accounts. It's creative and it doesn't work with the same set of rules. If you have a writer's block then there's nothing you can do."

"Writer's block," said George bitterly, "Is that what it's called?"

She laid her hand on his arm, heavy with the weight of the bracelet. "Why don't you forget about it? Write to Mr . . ." she glanced at the signature on the letter, "Rutland, and say, Well, O.K. if that's how you feel, to hell with any more books."

"You really think I could do that, don't you. And what then?"

She shrugged. "Well . . ." Her voice began to drawl. "There are other diversions."

"Such as."

"In two weeks it'll be Easter." She picked up the knife she had used to slit his envelopes, and began tracing the grain of the table with its tip. "I've been asked to Malaga for the Easter Sunday *corrida*. I have friends there, Americans. They are great *aficionados*. At Malaga you get the best bulls and the best *toreros* in Spain. And there are parties all day long and all night long."

"It sounds like a travel agent's dream."

"Darling, don't get sour with me. I didn't write that letter, I just read it."

"I know, I'm sorry."

"Will you come with me? To Malaga."

The waiter was hovering. George called him over and paid for the drinks and the boy took away the glasses and George gave him a tip, and when the boy had gone, he gathered up his cap and the pink-and-white-striped parcel and his two letters.

Frances said, "You haven't answered my question."

He stood up, holding the back of his chair.

"I think you've forgotten that I was never an *aficionado*. The sight of blood makes me faint."

She said, like a child, "I want you to be there . . ."

"I'd spoil it all."

She looked away, trying not to show her disappointment. She said, "Where are you going now?"

"Back to Cala Fuerte."

"Can't you stay here?"

"No, I must get back."

"Don't tell me you have to feed that cat again."

"I have more things to feed than the cat." He touched her shoulder in farewell. "Thanks for the ride."

Darkness fell as George drove back to Cala Fuerte. Once

483

the sun had slipped out of the sky, the air became chill, and at dusk he stopped by a lonely farmhouse and reached for the spare sweater he had brought with him. As his head emerged from the neck of the sweater, he saw the farmer's wife come out of her house to draw water from the well. The open door glowed with yellow light and she was silhouetted against it, and he called "*Buenas tardes*" to her and she came over to chat for a little, resting her water-jug against her hip and asking him where he had been and where he was going.

He was thirsty, so he took a drink of water from her, and then went on his way, his headlights probing the sapphire evening. The first stars began to prick the sky and San Estaban was a saucer of lights in the shadow of the mountain, and as he came down the last stretch of the road towards Cala Fuerte, the wind blew off the sea and brought with it the fresh resinous smell of the pines.

Unaccountably, but inevitably, this feeling of coming home always cheered him up. Now, his spirits lifted, and he realised how depressed and tired he had been feeling all day. Nothing, much, had gone right. The letter from Mr Rutland was an added weight to his conscience, and he was still saddled with Miss Queen's Gate. He wondered how she had spent her day, and told himself that he did not particularly care, but he could not help hoping, as he bowled down the last slope of the road towards the Casa Barco, that she would not still be in a sulk.

He put the car in the garage, turned off the engine, glanced at his watch. It was past eight o'clock. He got out of the car and crossed the lane and opened the door of the Casa Barco, and went in. There did not seem to be anybody about, although the house bore witness to a certain amount of unaccustomed care and attention. The fire was blazing, the lamps lighted, and the low coffee table by the hearth laid with a blue-and-white cloth, which George had not known he possessed, and knives and forks and glasses. There was also a bowl of wild flowers and the air was filled with the delicious smell of cooking. He laid down his cap and went out on to the terrace, soft-footed in his rope-soled shoes, but the terrace was dark and there was no sign of his guest. He went to lean over the wall, but the slipways were empty, the only sound was the whisper of water and the creak as his dinghy tugged at her mooring. Then, from one of the harbour cafés came the warm chords of a guitar, and a woman started to sing, the strange two-tone warbling that was one of the Moorish legacies of the island.

He frowned, puzzled, and went back into the house. The gallery was in darkness, but the light was on in the kitchen, and when he went to lean over the counter, he was surprised to find Selina squatting in front of the open oven, basting a casserole with enormous concentration.

He said, to the top of her head, "Good evening."

Selina looked up. He had not startled her, and he realised that she had known all along that he was there, and he found this disconcerting. It seemed to give her some sort of advantage.

She said, "Hello!"

"What are you doing?"

"Cooking dinner."

"Smells good."

"I hope it is. I'm not much good at cooking, I'm afraid."

"What is it?"

"Steak and onions and peppers and things."

"I didn't think we had any food in the house."

"We didn't. I went up to Maria's and bought it."

"You did?" He was impressed. "But Maria doesn't talk any English."

"No, I know. But I found a dictionary in the drawer in your desk."

"What did you use for money?"

"I'm afraid I put it down on your account. I bought myself a pair of espadrilles, too. They were eight pesetas. I hope you don't mind."

"Not at all."

She eyed the casserole critically. "Do you think it looks all right?"

"It looks splendid."

"I did think I'd roast the meat, but I couldn't find any fat except olive oil, and somehow I didn't think that would work."

She picked up a towel, put the lid back on the casserole, and returned the whole fragrant dish back into the oven. She closed the door and stood up. They faced each other over the counter and she said, "Did you have a good day?"

In the light of all this domesticity, George had forgotten about his day. "What . . . oh, yes. Yes, all right."

"Did you get the cable off?"

"Yes. Yes, I sent the cable." She had some freckles on her nose, and under the light her smooth hair shone with unexpected streaks of fairness.

"How long did they say it would take?"

"Just what we thought. Three or four days." He leaned on his crossed forearms, and said, "And how did you fill in the day?"

"Oh . . ." She seemed nervous, and for something to do with her hands, wiped at the top of the counter with the cloth she was still holding, like a diligent barmaid. "Well, I made friends with Juanita, and I washed my hair and I sat on the terrace in the sun . . ."

"You have freckles."

"Yes, I know. Isn't it awful. And then I went up to the village to do the shopping and that took me ages, because everybody wanted to talk to me and of course I couldn't understand a word they said. And then I came back and peeled some vegetables . . ."

"And lit the fire . . ." George interrupted. "And did some flowers . . ."

"You noticed! They'll be dead tomorrow, they're just wild; I picked them on the way back from the village." He did not comment on this, and she went on, quickly, as though nervous of any lull in the conversation, "Have you had anything to eat today?"

"No, I skipped lunch. I had a glass of beer at four."

"Are you hungry?"

"Ravenous."

"I just have to make a salad. It'll be ready in about ten minutes."

"Are you hinting that I should go and put on a dinner jacket and my bow tie?"

"No, I'm not doing anything of the sort."

He grinned at her, straightened up and stretched. "I'll make a bargain with you," he said. "I'll go and wash the dust out of my ears and you can pour me a drink."

She looked doubtfully. "What sort of a drink?"

"A Scotch and soda. With ice."

"I wouldn't know how much whisky to put in."

"Two fingers." He showed her how to measure. "Well, maybe three of your fingers. Got the idea?"

"I can always try."

"Good girl. You do that."

He collected a clean shirt and took a swift and icy shower and had dressed again and was combing his hair when his reflection told him that he needed a shave.

George squared up to his reflection and told it, without mincing words, that he needed that drink far more.

The reflection acquired a sanctimonious inner voice. *If she can lay a table and be bothered to pick a bunch of flowers you can surely shave.*

I never asked her to pick the bloody flowers.

You never asked her to cook the dinner either, but you're going to eat it.

Oh, shut up! said George, and reached for his razor.

He did it in style, finishing off with the remains of some aftershave which had been so little used that it had started to congeal in the bottom of the bottle.

Oh, very nice, his reflection said now, standing back to admire him.

Satisfied? George asked, and his reflection gave him a sardonic grin.

The whisky was waiting for him, on the table by the fire, but Selina had gone back to the kitchen, and was tossing a salad in his big wooden bowl. He picked up his transistor and went to sit with his back to the fire, and tried to find some music they could listen to, and Selina said, "They're having some sort of a party down on the harbour. You can hear the singing."

"I know; it's riveting, isn't it?"

"It doesn't sound like a proper tune."

"It wouldn't. It's Moorish."

The transistor, from squeaks and warblings, moved into warm guitar music. George laid it down, and picked up his glass, and Selina said, "I hope your drink's all right."

He tried it. It was too strong. He said, "Perfect."

"I only hope the dinner's perfect, too. I should have bought some fresh bread at Maria's as well, but there seemed to be masses of bread, so I didn't."

"Juanita is a secret bread addict. She has it for elevenses every day with goat's cheese and a tumbler of *vino tinto*. How she keeps awake, I don't know."

Selina picked up the salad bowl and came out from behind the counter to put it in the middle of the laid table. She was wearing a blue-and-green-striped shirt which George had never liked till now, and a pair of navy-blue trousers, very neat and trim, and belted around her waist with a narrow strip of leather. He had genuinely forgotten what their row this morning had been about; the whole ridiculous business had gone clean out of his mind, but now his subconscious did a swift double-take, and he recognised the belt as one of his own, and as she moved away from him, back towards the galley, he reached out and took hold of it.

He said, "Where did you get those trousers?"

Selina, held like a puppy by its tail, said, "They're yours."

Her casual tone was not convincing. "They're *mine?*"

They were, too. They were his best navy-blue serge trousers. He set down his glass and turned her to face him. "But they fit you." She met his eyes, but only just. "What have you done to my best trousers?"

"Well . . ." Her eyes widened. "You know, when you'd gone this morning, well, I didn't have anything much to do so I was tidying around and I noticed, well, that these trousers you had on last night were rather dirty. I mean, there were marks down the side of the leg, like gravy or something. So I took them down and showed them to Juanita, and Juanita washed them for you. And they shrank."

After this outrageous fabrication, she had the grace to look a little embarrassed. George said, "That is a flaming lie, and you know it. Those trousers had just come back from the cleaners, and ever since *I* got back from San Antonio, you've been looking like a cat with two tails. And I, poor mistaken fool, imagined it was because you'd been clever and cooked poor old George a good dinner. But it wasn't, was it?"

Selina said, plaintively, "But I didn't have *anything* to wear."

"So you took your revenge on my best trousers."

"It wasn't revenge."

"Just because you can't take a joke against yourself."

"Well, you don't seem to be taking this one very well."

"This is different."

"How different?"

He glared at her, but already he realised that his initial rage was wearing thin, and the humour of the situation was getting the better of him. Also, there was a gleam in Selina's eye which suggested an entirely unsuspected side to her character. He said, "I never thought you'd have the guts to stand up for yourself."

"Is that why you're angry . . .?"

"No, of course it isn't. I'm glad you've got guts. And anyway," he added, remembering delightedly that he could cap the dirty trick she had played on him. "I have something to give you."

"You do?"

"Yes." He had thrown the parcel down with his cap and now went to retrieve it. "I bought you a present in San Antonio. I hope you like it."

She looked at the tiny package doubtfully. "It couldn't be anything to wear . . ."

"Open it and see," said George, picking up his drink again.

She did, meticulously untying the knots in the string. The paper fell away, and she held up the two halves of the minute pink gingham bikini he had bought her.

He said, very seriously, "You seemed so upset this morning, about having nothing to wear. I do hope the colour will suit you."

Selina could think of nothing to say. The bikini seemed to her to be both suggestive and shocking. That she had been given it by George Dyer made the situation too embarrassing for words. He surely wouldn't imagine that she could ever put it on?

Blushing, not looking at him, she managed to say, "Thank you."

He began to laugh. She glanced up, frowning, and he said, quite gently, "Did nobody ever tease you before?"

Selina felt a fool. She shook her head.

"Not even Nanny?" He put on a ridiculous voice, and at once it was not embarrassing any longer, but funny.

"Oh, be quiet about Nanny," said Selina, but his amusement was as catching as the measles, and he said, "Don't try to stop smiling. You should smile all the time. You're really very pretty when you smile."

9

At half past seven the next morning, George Dyer opened his door to Juanita, and found her, as usual, sitting on the wall with her hands in her lap and a basket at her feet. The basket was covered with a clean white cloth, and Juanita beamed self-consciously as she picked it up and came into the house.

George said, "Now what have you got in there, Juanita?"

"It is a present for the Señorita. Some oranges from the tree of Pepe, Maria's husband."

"Did Maria send them?"

"*Sí*, Señor."

"That was kind."

"The Señorita is still asleep?"

"I think so. I haven't been to look."

While Juanita was drawing water to make his coffee, he opened the shutters and let the morning into the house. He went out on to the terrace and the stone floor was cool beneath his feet. *Eclipse* lay quietly, her crosstrees white against the pines of the far shore. He decided that perhaps, today, he would take out the new propeller. Otherwise there was nothing that he had to do. The day stretched ahead of him, blissfully empty, to use as he chose. He looked up, and thought that the sky looked good. There was a certain amount of cloud inland, beyond San Estaban, but rain always gathered around the high peaks of the mountains, and out to sea it was clear and cloudless.

The clangour of the bucket as it went down the well had wakened Selina, and presently she joined George, wearing the shirt she had borrowed last night, and apparently not much else. Her long, slender legs were not pale any more, but tanned lightly to the colour of a fresh egg, and she had bundled up her hair into an ingenuous knot from which trailed one or two long strands. She came to lean over the terrace wall beside him, and he saw the thin gold chain which she wore around her neck and which doubtless supported a childhood locket, or a gold Confirmation cross. He had always disliked the word innocence, associating it as he did, with fat, pink babies and shiny postcards of winsome kittens; but now, unbidden, it sprang to his mind, as clear and unmistakable as the chime of a bell.

She was watching Pearl, who performed her morning ablutions in a small patch of sun on the slipway below them. Every now and then a fish would dart in the shallows, and Pearl would stop washing herself and freeze to stillness, back leg erect as a lamp-post, only to return to the business in hand.

Selina said, "The day Tomeu brought us to the Casa Barco, there were two fishermen down there, cleaning fish, and Tomeu talked to them."

"That was Rafael, Tomeu's cousin. He keeps his boat in the pen next to mine."

"Are all the village related to each other?"

"More or less. Juanita has brought you a present."

She turned to look at him, her escaping strands of hair hanging down like tassels. "She has? What is it?"

"Go and see."

"I already said good morning to her, but she didn't say anything about a present."

"That's because she doesn't speak English. Go on in, she's longing to give it to you."

Selina disappeared into the house. A strange exchange of conversation could be overheard, and presently she reappeared, carrying the basket with the cloth off the top.

"Oranges."

"*Las naranjas*," said George.

"Is that what they're called? I think she said they were from Maria."

"Maria's husband grew them himself."

"Wasn't that kind?"

"You'll have to go up and thank her."

"I can't do anything unless I learn to speak Spanish. How long did you take to learn?"

He shrugged. "Four months. Living here. I didn't speak a word before that."

"But French."

"Oh, yes, French. And a little Italian. Italian is a great help."

"I must try to learn just a few words."

"I have a grammar I'll lend you, and then you can mug up some verbs as well."

"I know *Buenos días* is good morning . . ."

"And *Buenas tardes* is good afternoon, and *Buenas noches* is good night."

"And *Sí*. I know that. *Sí* is yes."

"And *No* is no, which is a much more important word for a young girl to learn."

"Even I, with my pin-brain, can remember that one."

"Oh, I wouldn't be too sure."

Juanita came out with the breakfast tray and began to lay the cups and plates and the coffee things out on the table. George spoke to her, telling her that the Señorita had been made very happy by Maria's gift, she would doubtless be going up to the village later on in the day, in order to thank Maria personally. Juanita beamed more widely than ever, and tossed her head, and carried the tray back to the kitchen. Selina picked up an *ensamada* and said, "What are these?"

He told her. "They are made each morning by the baker in San Estaban, and Juanita buys them for me and brings them, fresh, for my breakfast."

"*Ensamadas*." She took a mouthful off the end of one, and soft, flaky bread and sugar encrusted her mouth. "Does Juanita work for anybody else, or just for you?"

"She works for her husband and her children. In the fields and in the house. She has never done anything but

493

work, all her life. Work and get married and go to church and have babies."

"She seems so content, doesn't she? Always smiling."

"She has the shortest legs in the world. Have you noticed?"

"But having short legs has nothing to do with being content."

"No, but it makes her one of the few women in the world who can scrub a floor without kneeling down."

When breakfast was over and before it got too warm, they walked up to the village to do the marketing. Selina wore George's shrunken navy-blue trousers and the espadrilles she had bought in Maria's the day before, and George carried the baskets, and as they walked he taught her to say *"Muchas gracias para las naranjas."*

They went into Maria's shop, through the front section, where the straw hats were piled, and the sun oil and the camera films and the bathing-towels, and into the high, dark room at the back. Here, in the cool, were barrels of wine and bins of sweet-smelling fruit and vegetables, and loaves of bread as long as your arm. Maria, and her husband Pepe, and Tomeu, were all busy serving, and there was a small gathering of waiting customers; but when George and Selina came in, they all stopped talking and looked around, and George gave Selina a prompting dig, and she said, "Maria, *muchas gracias para las naranjas*," and there was much gap-toothed laughter, and back-slapping as though she had done something enormously clever.

Their baskets were filled with groceries and wine-bottles and bread and fruit, and left for Tomeu to deliver at the Casa Barco on his bicycle. George accepted the glass of brandy offered him by Pepe, and then he and Selina walked over to the Cala Fuerte Hotel to see Rudolfo. They sat at the bar and Rudolfo gave them coffee, and was told that a cable had been sent to England for the money and that very soon, in days, they would be able to repay him, but Rudolfo only laughed and said he did not care how long he had to wait, and George had another brandy and then they said goodbye and walked home again.

Back at the Casa Barco, George dug out the Spanish grammar which had eased him through the intricacies of learning a new language, and gave it to Selina.

She said, "I'm going to start right away."

"Well, before you do, I'm going out to *Eclipse*. Do you want to come too?"

"Are you going to take her for a sail?"

"Take her for a sail? This isn't Frinton, you know." He put on a comic Cockney voice. "Once round the island, arf a crown."

"I just thought you might be going out in her," said Selina, mildly.

"Well, I'm not." He relented. "But I have to take that new propeller out some time, and it might as well be today. You could swim if you wanted, but I warn you the water'll be frigid."

"Can I bring the grammar book with me?"

"Bring anything you like. We could take a picnic."

"A picnic!"

"Juanita'll put some food in a basket, I'm sure. It wouldn't exactly be a Fortnum and Mason hamper . . ."

"Oh, do ask her. Then we wouldn't have to come back for lunch."

Half an hour later they piled into the dinghy. Selina sat in the stern, with the box containing the propeller between her knees. She had the grammar book, and a dictionary, and a towel in case she wanted to bathe. The picnic basket lay in the bottom of the boat at George's feet, and George rowed. As they moved away from the slipway, Juanita hung over the terrace and waved a duster, as though she were saying goodbye for ever, and Pearl walked backwards and forwards along the edge of the water mewing plaintively because she had wanted to come too.

"Why can't we take her?" Selina wanted to know.

"She'd hate it once she got there. Too much water gives her traumas."

495

Selina trailed her hand and gazed down at the depths of waving green weed. "It's like grass, isn't it? Or a forest in the wind." The water was very cold. She withdrew her hand, and turned back to look at the Casa Barco, fascinated by this novel view of it. "It's quite a different shape from all the other houses."

"It was a boat-house. *Barco* is boat."

"Was it a boat-house when you came to live here?"

George rested on his oars. "For the Organising Secretary of the George Dyer Fan Club, you seem to have read my book with remarkably little attention. Or did you read it at all?"

"Yes, I did read it, but I was only looking for things about *you*, because I thought you might be my father. And, of course, there was really nothing about you. It was all about the village and the harbour and *Eclipse* and everything."

George began to row again. "The first time I ever saw Cala Fuerte was from the sea. I'd come from Marseilles, single-handed, because I couldn't pick up a crew, and I had the devil's own job finding the place. I brought *Eclipse* in under power, and I anchored, not a few feet from where she's lying now."

"Did you think then that you'd stay here, and live here, and make it your home?"

"I don't know what I thought. I was too tired to think. But I remember how good the pines smelt in the early morning."

They moved in under *Eclipse*'s hull, and George stood up and took hold of the guard-rail and, holding the painter, climbed up on to the stern deck and made the dinghy fast, and then returned to help Selina unload. She handed up her towel and her book and the picnic basket and then scrambled up herself while George returned to the dinghy to deal with the heavy box containing the propeller.

The tarpaulin cockpit cover was still draped over the coach roof as George had left it, and bone-dry again after its soaking. Selina stepped down into the cockpit and put

496

the picnic basket down on to one of the seats, and looked about her with the confused admiration of one who has never been in a small boat in her life.

She said, "She seems terribly small."

"What did you expect? The *Queen Mary*?" George dumped the propeller on to the floor of the cockpit, and squatted to shove it, out of harm's way, under one of the slatted seats.

"No, of course not."

He stood up. "Come along; I'll show you around."

The steps of the main hatch led down into the galley, a portion of which had been fitted out as a navigation table, with drawers beneath wide enough for charts. Beyond this was the cabin, with two berths on either side of a folding table. Selina asked if this was where George slept, and when George said it was, she pointed out that while he was a good six feet, the bunks could only be four and a half feet long. George, with the air of a conjurer, showed her how the ends of the bunks extended beneath the sideboards.

"Oh, I see. So you sleep with your feet in a hole."

"That's the idea. And very cosy it is, too."

There were a great many books, held in position on their shelves by retainer bars, and the cushions on the berths were blue and red, and a paraffin lamp swung on gimbals. There were some photographs of *Eclipse* under sail, complete with the ballooning stripes of a massive spinnaker, and a locker door, left open, bulged with yellow oilskins. George went forward, easing his way around the white painted column of the mast, and Selina followed him and in the tiny triangular forepeak there was a lavatory, and the chain and sail lockers.

She said again, "It seems so small. I can't imagine living in such close quarters."

"You get used to it. And when you're single-handed, you live in the cockpit. That's why the galley's so handy, so that you can reach in and grab sustenance when you're under way. Come on, let's go back."

Selina went ahead, and behind her ne paused to unscrew

497

the portholes and push them open. In the galley, she reached through the hatch for the picnic basket and brought it in, out of the sun. There was a slim-necked bottle of wine which felt sadly warm, but when she told George about this, he produced a length of twine and tied it around the neck of the bottle and hung it overboard. Then he went below again and returned, carrying one of the foam-rubber mattresses from the cabin berth.

"What's that for?"

"I thought you'd like to sunbathe." He heaved it up on to the coach roof.

"What are you going to do? Are you going to fit the propeller?"

"No, I'll wait till the sea warms up a bit, or get someone else to do it for me." He disappeared below again, and Selina took the Spanish grammar and climbed up on to the coach roof and draped herself over the mattress. She opened the grammar and read, "Nouns are either masculine or feminine. They should always be learned with the definite article."

It was very warm. She dropped her head on the open book and closed her eyes. There was the lap of water and the smell of pines and comforting heat of the sun. She spread her arms to its warmth, and her hands and her fingers, and the rest of the world slid away, so that reality was here and now, a white yacht anchored in a blue inlet, with George Dyer moving about below, in the cabin, opening and shutting lockers and occasionally swearing when he dropped something.

Later, she opened her eyes, and said, "George."

"Umm . . .?" He was sitting in the cockpit naked to the waist, smoking a cigarette, and winding a rope into an immaculate coil.

"I know about masculine and feminine now."

"Well, that's a good start."

"I thought I might swim."

"Well, swim then."

She sat up, pushing her hair back from her face.

"Will it be terribly cold?"

"After Frinton, nothing could be cold."

"How did you know I used to go to Frinton?"

"It's a primeval instinct I have about you. I see you spending your summers there with Nanny. Blue with cold, and shivering."

"You're right, of course. And there are pebbles on the beach, and I always had an enormous sweater over my bathing-suit. Agnes used to hate it, too. Goodness knows why we got sent there."

She stood up and began to unbutton her shirt.

George said, "It's very deep. You can swim?"

"Of course I can swim."

"I'll keep the harpoon handy in case of man-eating sharks."

"Oh, funny!" She pulled off the shirt, and she was wearing the bikini he had given her. He said, "Good God!" because it had been meant as a joke, and he had never imagined that she would have the nerve to put it on, but now he felt as if the joke had back-fired and he was left standing with egg all over his face.

Again the word innocence stood up and hit him, and he thought, unfairly, of Frances, with her weather-beaten, black-tanned body and the raffish bikinis which on her could never be anything but vulgar.

He was never sure whether Selina heard his astounded exclamation, for at that moment she dived, and he watched her swimming, neatly and without a splash, and with her long hair fanning out in the water behind her like a new and beautiful species of seaweed.

When at last she came in, shuddering with cold, he shoved a towel at her, and went down to the galley to find something for her to eat; a round of bread with some of Juanita's goat's milk cheese. When he returned, she was back on the coach roof, in the sun, rubbing her hair with the towel. She reminded him of Pearl. He gave her the bread and she said, "At Frinton it was always a ginger snap. Agnes used to call them shivery bites."

"She would."

"You mustn't say things like that. You've never even met her."

"I'm sorry."

"You'd probably like her. You'd probably find a lot in common. Agnes always looks desperately cross, but it doesn't mean a thing. Her bark is much worse than her bite."

"Thank you very much."

"It's meant as a compliment. I'm very fond of Agnes."

"Perhaps if I learn to knit you'll grow fond of me too."

"Is there any more bread? I'm still hungry."

He went below again, and when he returned she was lying on her stomach once more, with the grammar book open. She said, "*Yo* – I. *Tú* – you, (familiar), *Usted* – you (polite)."

"Not *Usted*. *Usteth* . . ." He gave it the subtle Spanish lisp.

"*Usteth* . . ." She took the bread and began to eat it, absently. "You know, it's funny, but although you know quite a lot about me . . . I've had to tell you, of course, because of thinking you were my father . . . I don't really know anything at all about you."

He did not reply, and she turned to look at him. He was standing in the cockpit, his head on a level with hers and not two feet away, but his face was turned from her; he was watching one of the fishing-boats move out of the harbour across the pellucid, blue-green water, and all she could see was the brown line of forehead and cheek and jaw. He did not even turn when she spoke, but after a little, he said, "No, I don't suppose you do."

"And I was right, wasn't I? *Fiesta at Cala Fuerte* wasn't about you. You hardly came into the book."

The fishing-boat edged between the bearings of the deep-water channel, and George said, "What are you so anxious to know?"

"Nothing." She was wishing already that she had not

500

broached the subject. "Nothing in particular." She turned down the corner of the page of his grammar, and then smoothed it out again quickly because she had been taught that this was a bad habit. "I suppose I'm just being inquisitive. Rodney, my lawyer – you know, I told you – it was he who gave me your book. And when I told him that I thought you were my father and that I wanted to come and find you, he said that I should let the sleeping tiger lie."

"That sounds a very imaginative thing for Rodney to have said." The fishing-boat passed them, moved into deep water, quickened her engines and headed for the open sea. George turned to face her. "Was I the tiger?"

"Not really. He just didn't want me to stir up a lot of complications."

"You didn't take his advice."

"No, I know."

"What are you trying to say?"

"Just that I'm naturally nosy, I suppose. I'm sorry."

"I haven't anything to hide."

"I like to know about people. Their family and their parents."

"My father was killed in nineteen forty."

"*Your* father was killed, too?"

"His destroyer was torpedoed by a U-boat in the Atlantic."

"Was he in the navy?" George nodded. "How old were you?"

"Twelve."

"Did you have brothers and sisters?"

"No."

"What happened to you then?"

"Well, let's see . . . I stayed at school, and then I did my National Service, and then I decided to stay on in the army and take a commission, which I did."

"Didn't you want to be in the navy like your father?"

"No. I thought the army might be more fun."

"And was it?"

"Some of it. Not all of it. And then my Uncle George suggested that as he had no sons of his own, it might be a good idea if I went into the family business."

"What was that?"

"Woollen mills in the West Riding of Yorkshire."

"And you went?"

"Yes. It rather seemed to be my duty."

"But you didn't want to."

"No, I didn't want to."

"What happened then?"

He looked vague. "Well, nothing. I stayed in Bradderford for five years, which I'd agreed to do, and then I sold up my share of the business and got out."

"Didn't your Uncle George mind?"

"He wasn't awfully pleased."

"And what did you do then?"

"I bought *Eclipse* on the proceeds and after a few years of wandering I fetched up here and lived happily ever after."

"And then you wrote your book."

"Yes, of course, I wrote my book."

"And that's the most important thing of all."

"Why so important?"

"Because it's creative. It comes from inside you. To be able to write is a gift. I can't do a single thing."

"I can't do a single thing either," said George, "which is why Mr Rutland sent me that cryptic message through the medium of you."

"Aren't you going to write another book?"

"Believe me, I would if I could. I did start off, but the thing was such a grinding failure I tore it up into little pieces and had a sort of ritual bonfire. It was discouraging, to say the least of it. And I promised the old boy I'd produce a second effort, even if it was only an idea, within a year, but of course I haven't. I've been told I'm suffering from a writer's block, which, if you're interested, is like the worst sort of mental constipation."

"What did you try to write the second book about?"

"A voyage I did to the Aegean, before I came to live here."

"What went wrong?"

"It was tedious. It was a super trip, but the way I wrote about it, it sounded about as exciting as a bus ride through Leeds on a wet Sunday in November. Anyway, it's all been done before."

"But that isn't the point. Surely you have to find an original angle, or a new approach. Isn't that how it works?"

"Well, of course." He smiled at her. "You're not as green as you're cabbage-looking."

"You say nice things in a horrible way."

"I know. I'm twisted and warped. Now, how about those personal pronouns?"

Selina looked back at the book. "*Usted*. You. *El*. He. *Ella* . . ."

"You pronounce a double 'l' as though it had a 'y' behind it. *Elya*."

"*Elya*," said Selina, and looked up at him again. "Were you never married?"

He did not reply at once, but his face tensed up as though she had switched on a light and held it to his eyes. Then he said, calmly enough, "I never married. But I was once engaged." Selina waited, and, perhaps encouraged by her silence, he went on. "It was while I was in Bradderford. Her parents were Bradderford people, very rich, very kind, self-made. The salt of the earth, really. The father drove a Bentley and the mother drove a Jaguar, and Jenny had a hunter about ten feet high, and a patent automatic horse-box, and they used to go to San Moritz to ski, and to Formentor for their summer holidays, and to the Leeds Music Festival, because they thought it was expected of them."

"I don't know whether you're being kind or cruel."

"I don't know either."

"But why did she break it off?"

"She didn't. I did. Two weeks before the biggest

wedding Bradderford had ever known. For months I couldn't get near Jenny for bridesmaids and trousseaux and caterers and photographers and wedding presents. Oh, God, those wedding presents! And it began to be like a high wall between us, so that I couldn't get near her. And when I realised that she didn't mind about the wall, she didn't even know it was there . . . well, I've never had an awful lot of self-respect, but what I did have I wanted to keep."

"Did you tell her you weren't going to marry her?"

"Yes. I went to her house. I told Jenny and then I told her parents. And it all took place in a room filled with crates and boxes and tissue paper and silver candlesticks and salad bowls and tea-sets and hundreds of toast racks. It was gruesome. Ghastly." He shuddered slightly at the memory. "I felt like a murderer."

Selina thought of the new flat, of the carpets and the chintzes, the ritual of the white dress and the church wedding and having Mr Arthurstone to give her away. The panic that suddenly visited her was the panic of a bad dream. Of being lost, and knowing that you were lost. Knowing that somewhere you had taken the wrong turning and ahead there could be nothing but disaster, precipitous cliffs and every sort of nameless fear. She wanted to leap to her feet, to escape and run away from everything she had ever committed herself to doing.

"Was . . . was that when you left Bradderford?"

"Don't look so horrified. No, it wasn't; I had another two years to run. I spent them being *persona non grata* with all the debs' mums and being cut by all sorts of unexpected people. It was rather interesting in a way, finding out who my real friends were . . ." He moved forward to rest his elbows on the edge of the coach roof. "But all this is doing nothing to improve your faultless Castilian Spanish. See if you can say the present tense of *Hablar*."

Selina started. "*Hablo*. I speak. *Usted habla*, you speak. Were you in love with her?"

George glanced up swiftly, but there was no anger in his

504

dark eyes, only pain. Then he put his brown hand flat over the open page of the Spanish grammar and said gently, "Without looking. You mustn't cheat."

The Citröen nosed into Cala Fuerte at the very hottest time of the day. The sun shimmered in a sky of cloudless blue, shadows were black, and dust and houses very white. There was no living soul about; shutters were closed, and as Frances drew up in front of the Cala Fuerte Hotel, and turned off the engine of the powerful car, there was a great silence, broken only by the rustle of the pines which moved in some mysterious, unfelt breeze.

She got out of the car, and slammed the door shut, and went up the steps of the hotel and in through the chain curtain to Rudolfo's bar. After the sunshine it took a moment for her eyes to become accustomed to the darkness, but Rudolfo was there, stealing a siesta in one of the long cane chairs, and he woke as she came in, and stood up, sleepy and surprised.

She said, "Well, hello, *amigo*."

He rubbed his eyes. "Francesca! What are you doing here?"

"Just drove over from San Antonio. Could you give me a drink?"

He moved behind his bar. "What do you want?"

"Any cold beer?" She pulled herself up on to a stool, and took out a cigarette, and lit it from the box of matches that Rudolfo pushed across to her. He opened the beer and poured it, carefully, without a head. He said, "It's not a good time of the day to be driving an open car."

"Doesn't bother me."

"It is very hot for so early in the year."

"This is the hottest day we've had yet. San Antonio is like a tin of sardines; it's a relief to get out into the country."

"Is that why you're here?"

"Not entirely. I came to see George."

Rudolfo replied to this in a characteristic way which was

505

to shrug and turn down the corners of his mouth. It seemed to suggest some innuendo, and Frances frowned. "Isn't he here?"

"But of course he is here." A gleam of malice showed in Rudolfo's eyes. "Did you know that he had a visitor staying at the Casa Barco?"

"A visitor?"

"His daughter."

"*Daughter!*" After a second's astounded silence Frances laughed. "Are you crazy?"

"I am not crazy. His daughter is here."

"But . . . but George has never been married."

"I don't know about that," said Rudolfo.

"How old is she, for heaven's sake?"·

He shrugged again. "Seventeen?"

"But it's impossible . . ."

Rudolfo began to be annoyed. "Francesca, I tell you she is there."

"I saw George in San Antonio yesterday. Why didn't he say anything?"

"Did he give you no idea?"

"No. No, he didn't."

But this was not strictly true, because all his actions yesterday had been unusual and therefore, in Frances's eyes, faintly suspect. The sudden urge to send a cable when he had been in the town only the previous day, the purchase made in Teresa's, that most feminine of shops, and his final remarks about having more to feed than the cat when he returned to Cala Fuerte. All evening and most of the night, she had been chewing over these three clues, convinced that they all added up to something about which she ought to know, and this morning, unable to remain in ignorance any longer, she had decided to come to Cala Fuerte and find out what was going on. Even if there was nothing to discover, she would see George. And it was true that the congested streets and pavements of San Antonio had begun to get on her nerves, and the thought of the empty blue inlets and the fresh piny smell of Cala Fuerte was very inviting.

And now this. It was his daughter. George had a daughter. She stubbed out her cigarette, and saw that her hand was shaking. She said, as calmly and as casually as she could, "What is she called?"

"The señorita? Selina."

"Selina." She said the name as though it left a bad taste in her mouth.

"She is very charming."

Frances finished her beer. She set down the empty glass, and said, "I think I'd better go and find out for myself."

"You should do that."

She slid off the high stool and picked up her bag and made for the door. But at the chain curtain, she stopped and turned, and Rudolfo was watching her with a gleam of amusement in his frog-eyes.

"Rudolfo, if I wanted to stay for the night . . . would you have a room for me?"

"Of course, Francesca. I will have one made ready."

She drove, in a cloud of dust, to the Casa Barco, left the Citröen in the only patch of shade she could find, and crossed the lane to the house. She opened the green shutter door, and called, "Anyone around?" but there was no reply, so she went in.

The place was empty. It smelt sweetly, of wood ash and fruit, and was cool with the air that moved in from the sea through the open windows. She dropped her bag on a handy chair, and wandered round, searching for signs of feminine occupation, but there appeared to be none. From the gallery there was a small sound, but when she looked up, a little startled, it was only George's ridiculous white cat jumping off the bed, and coming down the steps to welcome the visitor. Frances did not like cats, especially this one, and gave Pearl a push with her foot, but Pearl's dignity was not impaired. Her back view speaking volumes, she left Frances and walked, tail erect, out on to the terrace. After a moment Frances followed her, lifting George's binoculars off his table as she went by. *Eclipse* lay quietly at anchor. Frances raised the binoculars and focused them and the yacht and her occupants sprang towards her. George was in the cockpit, at full length on one of the seats, his old cap tipped over his eyes, and a book on his chest. The girl was draped over the coach roof, an arrangement of boneless-looking limbs and a quantity of pale fawn hair. She wore a shirt which looked as though it might belong to George, and Frances could not see her face. The little scene was one of content and companionship, and Frances was frowning when she lowered the binoculars. She returned them to the table, and then went to draw herself a glass of George's sweet, cool well water. She brought the glass back on to the terrace, pulled the least lethal of his terrace chairs back into the shade of the split-cane awning, stretched herself gingerly out, and settled down to wait.

George said, "Are you awake?"

"Yes."

"I think we should get straightened up and go back. You've been out in the sun for long enough."

Selina sat up and stretched. "I went to sleep."

"I know."

"It was all that gorgeous wine."

"Yes, I expect it was."

They rowed back to the Casa Barco, the dinghy suspended like a cloud over the peacock-coloured water, her shadow drifting through the weeds below them. The world was still and hot and quiet, and seemed to contain only the two of them. Selina's skin prickled and felt tight, as though, like an over-ripe fruit, she might burst out of it, but this sensation was not unpleasant – merely a part of the splendid day. She pulled the empty basket between her knees and said, "That was a good picnic. The best I ever had," and waited for George to come back with some crack about Frinton, but to her surprised

508

delight he said nothing, only smiled at her as though he had enjoyed it too.

He brought the dinghy up to the jetty and stepped ashore and made her fast with two loops of the painter. Selina handed out all their gear, and then stepped after him, the jetty burning hot on the soles of her bare feet, and they crossed the slipways, and started up the steps to the terrace, George going ahead, so that Selina, behind him, heard Frances Dongen's voice before she ever saw her.

"Well, now. Look who's here!"

For a split second George appeared to be petrified into stillness. And then, as though nothing had ever been said, he went on, up to the terrace.

"Hello, Frances," he said.

Selina, more slowly, followed him. Frances lay in the old cane chair, with her feet up on the table. She wore a blue-and-white-checked shirt, knotted to expose her dark-tanned midriff, and white duck pants, skimpy and tight. She had kicked off her shoes, and her feet, crossed on the edge of the table, were dark and dusty, the toe-nails lacquered bright red. She made no effort to sit up or get up, but merely lay there, supine, her hands resting on the floor, and surveyed George from under her thatch of short blonde hair.

"Isn't this a nice surprise?" She looked over his shoulder and saw Selina. "Hi, there!"

Selina smiled weakly. "Hello."

George put down the basket. "What are you doing here?"

"Well, San Antonio's pretty hot and full and noisy, and I thought I might give myself a couple of days off."

"Are you staying here?"

"Rudolfo said he'd give me a room."

"You've seen Rudolfo?"

"Yeah, I had a drink with him on my way here." She eyed him, her eyes malicious, teasing him because he didn't know how much Rudolfo had told her.

George sat on the edge of the table. "Did Rudolfo tell you I had Selina staying with me?"

"Oh, sure, he told me." She smiled at Selina. "You know, you're the biggest surprise that ever happened to me. George, you haven't introduced us yet."

"Sorry. Selina, this is Mrs Dongen . . ."

"Frances," said Frances quickly.

"And this is Selina Bruce."

Selina moved forward with her hand outstretched to say "How do you do," but Frances ignored the tentative gesture.

"Are you here on a visit?"

"Yes, I am. . . ."

"George, you never told me you had a daughter."

George said, "She isn't my daughter."

Frances, blank-faced, seemed to accept this. Then she lifted her foot from the table's edge and pulled herself into a sitting position. "Are you trying to tell me . . ."

"Hang on a moment. Selina . . ."

She turned to look at him, and he saw that she was confused and embarrassed, and even, possibly, a little hurt. He said, "Would you mind if I spoke to Frances alone, just for a moment?"

"No. No, of course not." She tried to smile, to show how little she minded, and swiftly laid down the things she had been carrying, the towel and the Spanish grammar, as though to lighten herself before making a swift escape.

"Just for five minutes . . ."

"I'll go back down to the dinghy. It's cool there."

"Yes, do that."

She went, swiftly, away and out of sight down the steps. In a moment Pearl, who had been sitting on the terrace wall, stood up and stretched, leapt lightly down, and went off after her. George turned back to Frances. He said again, "She isn't my daughter."

"Well, who the hell is she?"

"She arrived here from London, out of the blue, looking for me, because she thought I was her father."

510

"What made her think that?"

"The photograph on the back of my book."

"Do you *look* like her father?"

"Yes, I do. In fact, he was a distant cousin of mine, but that's beside the point. He's dead. He's been dead for years. He was killed in the war."

"She surely didn't imagine he'd come alive again?"

"I suppose if you want something badly enough you can believe in any miracle."

"Rudolfo told me that she *was* your daughter."

"Yes, I know. The buzz got round the village, and for her sake it seemed kinder not to deny it. She'd already been here for two days."

"Living here – with you? You must be out of your mind."

"She had to stay. The airline had lost her luggage, and her return ticket was stolen at the airport."

"Why didn't you tell me about her yesterday?"

"Because it didn't seem to be any of your business." This sounded ruder than he had intended. "Oh, God, I'm sorry, but it's just the way things are."

"What are your friends in Cala Fuerte going to say when they know she isn't your daughter? When they know you've been lying to them. . . ."

"I'll explain when she's gone."

"And when might that be?"

"When we get some cash from London. We already owe Rudolfo six hundred pesetas, and we have to buy another air ticket, and my own money's been held up in Barcelona . . ."

"You mean it's only money!" George stared at her. "That's the only thing that's kept her here? That's the only reason you didn't send her straight back home?"

"It's as good a reason as any."

"But, for Pete's sake, why didn't you come to me?"

George opened his mouth to tell her why and then shut it again. Frances was incredulous. "Does she want to stay here? Do you *want* her here?"

"No, of course not. She can't wait to get back, and I can't wait to be rid of her. But meantime, the situation's quite harmless."

"Harmless? That's the most naive thing I've ever heard you say. Why, this situation is about as harmless as a barrel of dynamite."

He did not reply, but sat, shoulders hunched, his hands closed so tightly over the edge of the table that the knuckles shone white. Frances, with a show of gentle understanding, laid her hand over his, and he did not try to move away. She said, "You've confided in me now, so let me help. There's a seven o'clock plane this evening from San Antonio to Barcelona. There's a connection to London, and she should be back by midnight. I'll give her enough for the journey, and to get her back to where she lives." He still said nothing, and she went on, gently, "Darling, this isn't any time to dither. I'm right, and you know it. She can't stay here any longer."

Selina was sitting on the end of the jetty, with her back to the house, trailing her feet in the water. He came down the steps from the terrace and across the slipways and down the sagging planking, his footsteps echoing, but she did not turn around. He said her name, but she would not answer. He squatted to her height.

"Listen. I want to talk to you."

She leaned away from him, out over the water, and her hair parted on the nape of her neck and fell down on either side of her face.

"Selina, try to understand."

"You haven't said anything yet."

"You can go back to London, tonight. There's a plane at seven; you should be home by midnight, or one in the morning at the latest. Frances says she'll pay for your ticket . . ."

"Do you want me to go?"

"It's not a case of what I want, or what you want. We have to do what is right and what is going to be best for you.

512

I suppose I should never have let you stay here in the first place, but circumstances did rather run away with us. Let's face it; Cala Fuerte isn't exactly the place for someone like you, and poor Agnes is bound to be anxious about what's happening. I really think that you should go."

Selina took her long legs out of the water, and pulled her knees up to her chin, hugging them as though she were trying to hold herself together, to stop herself from falling apart.

He said, "I'm not sending you away . . . it has to be your own decision. . . ."

"It's very kind of your friend."

"She wants to help."

"If I'm going to go back to London tonight," said Selina, "I haven't very much time."

"I'll drive you to San Antonio."

"No!" She startled him with her vehemence, turning to look at him for the first time. "No, I don't want you to come. Surely someone else can take me! Rudolfo, or a taxi or something. There must be someone."

He tried not to show his hurt. "Well, of course, but . . ."

"I don't want you to take me."

"All right. It doesn't matter."

"And in London I'll call Agnes from the airport. She'll be home; I can get a taxi, and she'll be waiting for me."

It was as though she had already gone, and they were both alone. She was alone in the plane, alone in London, cold, because after San Antonio it would be very cold; trying to ring Agnes from a call box. And it would be past midnight and Agnes would be asleep and would wake slowly. The telephone would ring in the empty flat, and Agnes would get up and pull on her dressing-gown and go, switching on lights as she went, to answer the call. And after that to fill a hot water bottle, to turn down a bed, put milk on to heat.

But beyond, he could not see.

He said, "What will you do? When you get back

513

to London? I mean, when all this is over and forgotten?"

"I don't know."

"Hadn't you any plans?"

After a little, she shook her head.

"Make some," he said, gently. "Good ones."

10

It was decided that Pepe, the husband of Maria, should be approached and asked if he would take Selina to the airport. Pepe did not run an official taxi service, but on occasion he would clean his aged car of the old straw and hen manure and such agricultural flotsam as it was normally encrusted with, and convey stray travellers to wherever they wanted to go. George, driving Frances's car, went to seek Pepe out, and ask if he would do this thing, and Selina, left alone with Frances and Pearl at the Casa Barco, prepared for her departure.

It did not take very long. She took a shower and dressed, in George's trousers that Juanita had so lovingly shrunk, and the striped shirt, and the espadrilles that she had bought in Maria's shop. Her good jersey dress had already been bequeathed to Juanita as a duster, and her bikini was so small that it fitted without fuss into the bottom of her handbag. That was all. She combed her hair and put her coat over a handy chair, and reluctantly, because she did not want to talk, went out on to the terrace, where Frances had collapsed once more into the long chair. Her eyes were closed, but when she heard Selina approach, she opened them and turned her head to watch Selina as she came to sit on the terrace wall, facing her.

"All packed?" she asked.

"Yes."

"That didn't take long."

"I didn't have any clothes. I lost my case. It got sent to Madrid by mistake."

"Those sort of mistakes are always happening." She sat up and reached for her packet of cigarettes. "Smoke?"

"No, thank you."

Frances lit one for herself. "I hope you don't think I'm interfering, chasing you out of the place like this."

"No. I had to get back anyway. The sooner I get home the better."

"Do you live in London?"

"Yes." She made herself say it. "Queen's Gate."

"How nice. Have you enjoyed your visit to San Antonio?"

Selina said, "It's been very interesting."

"You thought George was your father."

"I thought he might have been. But I was wrong."

"Did you read his book?"

"I haven't read it properly yet. But I will when I get home. I'll have time then." She added, "It's been a great success."

"Oh, sure," said Frances, dismissing the book.

"Didn't you think it was good?"

"Yes, it was good. It was fresh and original." She took a long pull on her cigarette, dropped the ash on to the floor of the terrace. "But he won't write another."

Selina frowned. "What makes you say that?"

"Because I don't think he has the self-discipline to get down to a second book."

"He's been told he's suffering from writer's block."

Frances laughed. "Look, darling, it was I who told him that."

"If you don't think he is capable of writing a second book, why did you say he was suffering from writer's block?"

"Oh, because he was depressed, and I was trying to cheer him up. George doesn't need to write. He has money of his own, and the sheer hard labour of writing simply isn't worth the candle."

"But he *must* write another book."

"Why?"

"Because he agreed to. Because the publisher is waiting for it. For his own sake."

"That's just a lot of hooey."

"Don't you *want* him to go on writing?"

"What I want or what I don't want is immaterial. I am merely stating an opinion. Look, honey, I run an art gallery. I deal all the time with these temperaments, these artists, these moods. I just don't think George is a creative artist."

"But if he doesn't write, what will he do?"

"What he did before he wrote *Fiesta at Cala Fuerte*. Nothing. It's easy to do nothing in San Antonio, to say '*Mañana*,' to everything." She smiled. "Don't look so shocked. George and I are twice your age, and at forty some of your illusions and your bright dreams get a bit bumped at the corners. Life doesn't have to be so real and so earnest as it does at eighteen . . . or whatever you are. . . ."

"I'm twenty," said Selina. Her voice was suddenly cold and Frances was pleased, because she thought she had annoyed her. She lay, watching Selina, and she was not afraid any more, as she had been when she first saw her, because Selina was going; in half an hour she would be on her way. To the airport, to London, back to a life in Queen's Gate about which Frances was content to remain in total ignorance.

The sound of the returning Citröen disturbed their uneasy silence, followed by the less sophisticated grinding of Pepe's ancient car. Selina stood up. "There's the taxi, now."

"Oh, fine!" Frances stubbed her cigarette out on to the floor. "Here, I'll give you the money."

She could scarcely bear to take it, but it was being counted into her palm when George came through the house to join them. He looked as uncomfortable as Selina about the whole business, but only pointed out that Selina would need sterling in London, whereupon Frances signed one of her American Express cheques and handed that over too.

"You can get it cashed at the airport."

"It's very kind of you."

"Oh, it's a pleasure," said Frances. "Think nothing of it."

"I . . . I'll make certain you're paid back . . ."

"Yes, of course you will."

George said, "Where's your bag?"

"Inside."

He went to get it, and it was he who took the money from Selina and stowed it away in a secure and well-hidden inner pocket. "Don't lose it again," he said; "I couldn't stand the strain." It had been meant as a feeble joke, but was instantly regretted because it sounded as though he couldn't bear the thought of once more being landed with her. He said, quickly, to cover up, "You've got your passport?" She nodded. "You're sure?"

"Yes, of course."

"I think perhaps you should make a start. There's not all that much time to spare. . . ."

She was being eased, gently, but firmly, away. She would never come back. Slowly, she followed George back into the house. He picked up her porridge-coloured coat, and moved aside, as though to let her go ahead of him. Behind her, Frances Dongen stood in the open terrace doorway.

He said quite gently, "Pepe's waiting . . ."

Selina swallowed. She said, "I'm suddenly very thirsty. Have I got time to have a drink . . .?"

"But of course." He moved towards the well, but Selina said, "No. I'd rather have soda water, it's more refreshing and so cold. Don't bother. I'll get it. There's some in the fridge. I won't be a moment."

They waited while she went for the drink, slipping behind the counter of the galley, and stooping to open the refrigerator and take out a frosty bottle. For a moment she was invisible, and then she stood up, holding the bottle, and opened it, and poured it into a tumbler, and drank it so quickly that George said that she would surely explode.

"I won't explode." She put down the empty glass and

518

suddenly smiled. It was as though the glass of soda water had solved all her problems. "It was delicious."

They went out into the sunshine, and Pepe waited for them. Pepe took Selina's coat and laid it with care over the hastily-cleaned back seat, and Selina said goodbye to Frances, and thanked her for all her help, and then she turned to George. She did not hold out her hand and he could not kiss her. They said goodbye without touching, but he felt as though he were being torn apart.

She got into the old car, erect and touching and hideously vulnerable, and Pepe got in beside her, and George gave him half a dozen last-minute instructions, and threatened death if anything should go wrong, and Pepe understood, and nodded, and even laughed toothlessly as he put the old car into gear.

It ground away up the hill and away from them, and George went on watching, long after it was out of sight, because he could still hear the sound of the engine.

There was a great party that night in the Cala Fuerte Hotel. It was not planned, but it evolved, in the way that the best parties do, growing and expanding to include a dozen different nationalities and a terrifying amount of drink. Everybody got very gay. A fat girl decided that she would dance on the table, but fell off into the arms of her boyfriend and remained there, asleep, for the rest of the evening. One of the boatmen from the harbour produced his guitar and a Frenchwoman did a mock flamenco which seemed to George the funniest thing he had ever seen in his life. At about one in the morning, however, he suddenly announced that he was going home, back to the Casa Barco. There was a great howl of protestation, taunts of being a kill-joy, claims that it was his turn to stand the drinks, but he remained adamant, because he knew that he must get out before he stopped laughing and started to cry. There was nothing worse than a maudlin drunk.

He stood up, pushing back his chair from the table with a head-splitting sound. Frances said, "I'll come too."

"You're staying here, remember."

"I'll drive you home. What's the good of walking when there's a perfectly good car at the door?"

He gave in, because it was simpler and less effort than having a scene. Outside, the warm southern night was bright with starlight. The Citröen was parked in the middle of the square, and as they walked towards her, Frances slid the car keys into George's hand and said, "You drive."

She was perfectly capable of driving herself, but every now and then liked to pretend that she was helpless and feminine, so George took the keys and got in behind the wheel.

It occurred to him that while his own ridiculous little yellow-wheeled car was merely a method of getting about the island, Frances's Citröen, fast and powerful, was somehow a sexy extension of her own personality. She sat beside him now with her face tipped up to the stars, her brown neck plunged into the deep V of her low-buttoned shirt. He knew that she was waiting to be kissed, but he lit a cigarette, before he started the engine, and she said, "Why don't you kiss me?"

George said, "I mustn't kiss you; I don't know where you've been."

"Why do you have to turn everything into a joke?"

"It's my British defence mechanism."

She glanced at her watch, clear in the starlight. "It's one o'clock. Do you think she'll be back in London?"

"She should be."

"Queen's Gate. Not really our line of country, darling."

He began to whistle, beneath his breath, a tune that had been plaguing him, at the back of his brain, all evening.

"You aren't worrying about her, are you?" she asked.

"No, I'm not worrying. I should have taken her to the airport though, not let her go with Pepe in that sewing-machine on wheels he calls a car."

"She didn't want you to take her. She would have howled all over you, and you would both have been embarrassed." He made no answer to this, and she laughed. "You're like a stubborn bear that won't bait."

"I'm too drunk to bait."

"Let's go home."

He drove back, still whistling that damned tune. When they got to the Casa Barco and George killed the engine and got out of the car, Frances got out too. As though it had been planned, she came in with him, and the house was cool and dark, but he turned on the lights and went, automatically, to pour himself a drink, because without a drink he would die, or go to sleep and burst into tears, and he was damned if he would do any of these things with Frances watching him.

She flopped, entirely at home, on to his sofa, her feet on one arm, and her curly head propped up by a sky-blue cushion. He fumbled his way through pouring a couple of drinks, dropped the opener and spilt the ice, and Frances said, "That's the hell of a tune you're whistling. Don't you know any other?"

"I don't even know what it is."

"Well, stop anyway."

His head was thumping, there seemed to be pools of water and melting ice everywhere and he couldn't find anything with which to wipe it all up. He picked up the drinks, and took them over to where Frances lay, and she took hers, but all the time her eyes were on his face, and he sat on the hearth with his back to the empty fireplace, and his own drink cradled between his hands.

She said, untroubled, "You know, darling, you're mad at me."

"I am?"

"Sure you are."

"Why?"

"Because I got rid of your little girl-friend. And because you know in your heart of hearts, you should have done that for yourself. And right away."

"I couldn't buy an air ticket without any money."

"That, if you don't mind my saying so, is the feeblest excuse any man gave to himself."

He looked down at his drink. "Yes," he said at last. "Maybe it is."

The tune went on and on in the back of his mind. After a little, Frances said, "When you went off to find Pepe and that child was getting ready to go, I had a little mosey round your desk. You don't seem to be exactly productive."

"I'm not. I haven't written a word."

"Have you replied to dear Mr Rutland?"

"No. I haven't done that either. But," he added with a touch of malice, "I've consulted a specialist and been told I'm suffering from writer's block."

"Well," said Frances, with some satisfaction, "at least that's a flash of your ornery self. And if you take your kid gloves off, then I can too. You see, darling, I don't think you're ever going to write that second book."

"What makes you so sure?"

"Just you. The way you are. Writing's hard labour, and you're one of those classic, no-good, expatriate Englishmen who do nothing more gracefully than any race alive." He acknowledged this with a spontaneous gleam of amusement, and Frances sat up, encouraged, because she had not lost her gift for making him laugh. "George, if you don't want to go to Malaga, if you don't enjoy the bull-fighting, then I don't want to go either. But why don't we get away together? We could take *Eclipse* to Sardinia, or go overland to Australia, or . . . ride a camel through the Gobi desert . . ."

"Bags on the front hump."

"You're turning everything into a joke again. I'm serious. We're free and we have all the time in the world. Why flog yourself to bits over a typewriter? Is there anything left, in the world, that you can write about really well?"

"Frances, I don't know."

She fell back on to the cushion. She had finished

522

her drink, and dropped the empty glass down on the floor beside her. She was sprawled, seductive, raffish, frighteningly familiar. She said, "I love you. You must know that."

There seemed no reason not to make love to her. He set down his glass, and went to sit beside her, to pull her into his arms, and kiss her as though he wanted to drown himself. She made small, pleasurable noises, and writhed her hands in his hair, and he took his mouth from hers and rubbed his cheek down the sharp angle of her jaw, and could feel the roughness of his beard scraping her skin, and she buried her face in his shoulder and her strong arms were like a vice about his neck.

She said, "Do you love me?" but he could not answer, so she said instead, "Do you like me? Do you want me?"

He took her arms from his neck, and pulled himself free, and was left sitting, holding her forearms as though they had been fighting.

She began to laugh. Her resilience and her good-humour were two of the good things that he had always liked about her. She said, "Why, I believe you're punch drunk."

He got up and went to find some cigarettes, and behind him Frances pulled herself off the sofa, and ran her fingers through her hair. She said, "I must patch myself up before I go back to Rudolfo. He's old-fashioned, you know, about so many things. Mind if I used your bedroom?"

"Go ahead," said George, and switched on the upstairs light for her.

She ran up the steps, the heels of her sandals slapping on the wooden treads. She was singing the song that had been tormenting him all evening, and still it did not have any words, and then, as though someone had switched off a radio, the teasing tune was stopped, and Frances was silent. The silence caught at George, as surely as though she had suddenly screamed. He stopped prowling, and pricked up his ears like a suspicious dog.

Presently, Frances came down the steps again, with an

expression on her face that he could not begin to decipher. He said stupidly, "What's up? No comb?"

"I don't know," said Frances. "I didn't look. I didn't look farther than the bed . . ."

"The bed?" He was completely mystified.

"It couldn't be a joke? Not another example of that peerless British sense of humour?"

He realised then, to his horror, that she was really angry. Beneath the careful control of her voice was the tremor of an incipient explosion.

"Frances, I don't know what you're talking about."

"The girl. Your daughter. Selina. Whatever you like to call her. You know where she is? Not in London. Not even at the airport at San Antonio. She's up there . . ." She pointed a shaking finger and her control, like an over-stretched rubber band, suddenly cracked. "*In your bed!*"

"I don't believe it."

"Well, go and take a look. *Go on up and take a look.*" He did not move. "I don't know what's going on here, George, but I didn't hand over a considerable amount of pesetas just to find that little tramp back in your bed again . . ."

"She isn't a tramp."

". . . and if you're going to try and give me some sort of an explanation, it had better be good, because I'm not going to swallow a second load of hog wash about losing luggage and thinking you were her long-lost daddy. . . ."

"It was true."

"True? Look, you bastard, who do you think you're kidding?" She was shouting at him now, and it was the one thing that made him mad.

"I didn't know she'd come back . . ."

"Well, kick her out now . . ."

"I'll do no such thing . . ."

"Right." Frances swooped to gather up her handbag. "If you feel inclined to set up house with that mealy-mouthed little tramp, that's O.K. by me . . ."

"Shut up!"

524

"   but don't involve me in a complicated scheme to protect both your reputations, because as far as I'm concerned, they're simply not worth protecting." She made for the door and flung it wide, turning back to deliver a final broadside, as she did so, but the effect was slightly spoiled by the entrance of Pearl, erect and dignified. She had been outside the door waiting for someone to let her in, and when Frances did just this thing, entered with a faint mew of appreciation and thanks.

"You'd better go," George said, as calmly as he could, and Frances said, "Don't bother; I've gone!" and pausing only to give Pearl a vicious kick in passing, she was out of the door, and slamming it so hard behind her that the whole house shook.

In a moment the quiet night was torn asunder by the sound of the Citröen being brutally started and driven up the hill in bottom gear at a speed that set George's teeth on edge.

He stooped to pick up Pearl. Her feelings were hurt, but there was no further damage, and he sat her gently on her favourite cushion on the sofa. A slight movement above him made him look up. Selina was standing, her hands on the rail of the gallery, watching him. She was wearing a white nightgown with blue ribbons framing the neck, and she said, anxiously, "Is Pearl all right?"

"Yes, she's all right. What are you doing here?"

"I was in bed. Asleep."

"You're not asleep now. Get something on and come on down."

A moment later she descended from the gallery, barefoot, but tying the ribbons of a ridiculous white silk negligee that matched the nightgown.

He frowned and said, "Where did you get those?"

Selina came across the floor towards him. "My suitcase had come. From Madrid." She smiled, as though he should be pleased, and he was forced to resort to sarcasm.

"So you did get as far as the airport?"

"Oh, yes."

"And what happened this time? The flight was cancelled? There wasn't any room on the plane? Pepe had a puncture?"

"No, none of those things." Her eyes were so wide that the blues were entirely ringed with white. "I lost my passport."

"You *what*?" To his annoyance it came out as an incredulous yelp.

"Yes, it was most extraordinary. You know you asked me, before I left, if I had my passport. Well, it was in my bag then, and I don't remember opening it again, but when I got to the airport and I was buying my ticket and everything, I opened my bag. And it had gone."

She looked at him to gauge his reaction to this piece of information. George's reaction was to lean against the back of his sofa and maintain a monumental calm.

"I see. So what did you do then?"

"Well, I told the Guardia Civil, of course."

"And what did the Guardia Civil have to say?"

"Oh, he was most kind and understanding. And after a little, I thought I'd better just come back here and wait until they found it."

"Who's they?"

"The Guardia Civil."

There was a small silence, while they watched each other. Then George said, "Selina."

"Yes?"

"Do you know what the Guardia Civil do to people who lose their passports? They throw them into jail. They intern them as political prisoners. They let them rot in dungeons until the passports get found again."

"Well, they didn't do that to me."

"You're lying, aren't you? Where did you put that passport of yours?"

"I don't know. I lost it."

"Did you leave it in Pepe's car?"

"I tell you, it's lost."

526

"Look, Junior, in Spain passports aren't things you play games with."

"I'm not playing games."

"Did you tell Pepe about the passport?"

"I can't speak Spanish, how could I tell him?"

"You just got him to bring you back?"

She looked disconcerted, but only said, bravely, "Yes."

"When did you get here?"

"About eleven."

"Did we wake you up when we got in?" She nodded. "Then you heard most of our conversation?"

"Well, I did try to put my head under the blankets, but Mrs Dongen has a very carrying voice. I'm sorry she doesn't like me." There was no comment to be made on this, and she went on, in social tones that would have done credit to her grandmother, "Are you going to marry her?"

"Do you know something? You make me ill."

"Is she married?"

"Not any more."

"What happened to her husband?"

"I don't know . . . how should I know? Maybe he's dead."

"Did she kill him?"

His hands seemed, suddenly, to have taken on an independent personality of their own. They itched with the desire to take Selina and shake her till her teeth rattled, to box her ears, and slap that smug expression off her face. George slid his hands into his pockets, and balled his fists against these purely primitive instincts, but Selina seemed innocent of the turmoil that was going on within him.

"I suppose it was rather annoying for her, finding me here, but she wouldn't stay and listen to any explanations. She just kicked poor Pearl. . . . It would have been much more fair if she'd kicked me." She looked George straight in the eye and he was shattered by her nerve. "She must know you very well. To talk to you like that, I mean.

527

Like the way she is tonight. She wanted you to make love to her."

"You're asking for trouble, Selina."

"And she seems to think that you'll never write another book."

"She may not be wrong at that."

"Aren't you even going to try?"

George said, slowly, "You mind your own bloody business," but even this did not deter her.

"It seems to me that you're afraid of failing before you've even made a start. Mrs Dongen was right; you've been cast in a classic mould, one of those no-good expatriate Englishmen" (here Selina gave a startling imitation of Frances's drawl) "who do nothing so gracefully. I suppose it would be a pity to spoil the image. And after all, what does it matter? You don't need to write. It isn't your living. And as for Mr Rutland, what is a broken promise? It doesn't count for anything. You can break your word to him just as easily as you broke it to the girl you were going to marry."

Before he could think, or control himself, George's right hand had escaped from the prison of his pocket and he had slapped her face. The sound of the blow was as loud a crack as the explosion of a bursting paper bag. The ensuing silence was painful to a degree. Selina stared, incredulous but curiously unresentful while George rubbed his stinging palm against his side. He remembered that he had never got those cigarettes. He went to find them now, to take one out and light it, and he was horrified to see how his hands were shaking. When at last he turned around, he realised, to his horror, that she was trying not to cry. The thought of tears, and the subsequent recriminations and apologies, was almost more than he could bear. Besides, it was too late to start apologising. He said, impatiently, but not unkindly, "Oh, go on, buzz off!" and when she turned and fled, in a flurry of long bare legs and white silk, back up to his bed he called after her, "And don't slam the door," but the joke was a sour one, and fell as flat as it deserved.

11

It was late when he woke. He knew by the angle of the
sunshine, by the reflected water-shadows on the ceiling, by
the gentle sounds of sweeping which indicated that Juanita
was cleaning the terrace. Instinctively tensed against the
hangover which he knew was going to hit him, George
reached for his watch, and saw that it was half past ten.
He had not slept so late for years.

He moved his head carefully from side to side, waiting
for the first stab of his well-deserved agony. Nothing
happened. Pushing his luck, he tried rolling his eyes and
the sensation was in no way painful. He turned aside the
red-and-white blanket, and cautiously sat up. It was a
miracle. He felt quite normal; better than normal, bright
and alert and full of energy.

Gathering up his clothes, he went to shower and shave.
As he scraped away at his face, the tune of last night came
back to him, but this time it had words, and he realised,
too late by now, why Frances had been so annoyed with
him for whistling it.

> *I've grown accustomed to her face.*
> *She almost makes the day begin.*

Well, he asked his sheepish reflection, *and how corny can
you get?* But when he had dressed, he went and dug out
his old record-player, and rubbed the dust from the Frank
Sinatra disc, and put it on.

Juanita had finished scrubbing the terrace, and now,
hearing the music, she laid down her brushes and came
in, her wet brown feet leaving marks on the tiled floor.

"Señor," she said.

"Juanita! *Buenos días*."

"The Señor has slept well?"

"Too well, perhaps."

I've grown accustomed to the tune
She whistles night and noon.

"Where is the Señorita?"

"She has gone out to the Señor's boat, to swim."

"How did she get there?"

"She has taken the little boat."

He raised his brows in mild surprise. "Well, good for her. Juanita, is there any coffee?"

"I will make some."

She went to draw a bucket of water, and George realised that he felt well enough to want a cigarette. He found one, and lit it, and then said, cautiously, "Juanita?"

"*Sí*, señor."

"An Americana stayed at the Cala Fuerte Hotel last night . . ."

"No, señor."

He frowned. "What do you mean?"

Juanita was in the kitchen, putting on a kettle. "She did not stay, Señor. She drove back to San Antonio last night. She did not use the room at the hotel. Rosita told Tomeu and Tomeu told Maria, and . . ."

"I know; Maria told you." But Juanita's news filled him with a shameful sort of relief, although the thought of Frances hurtling back to San Antonio through the night in that lethal bomb of a car, gave him the shivers. He prayed that nothing had happened, that she had not had an accident, was not, even now, trapped in some distant ditch with the car on top of her.

With the air of a man cornered on all sides by trouble, he scratched the back of his neck, then went out on to the terrace to search for his other headache. He took his binoculars and focused them on *Eclipse*, but although the

530

dinghy bobbed peacefully at her stern, there was no sign of Selina.

It was, however, a beautiful day. Just as bright as yesterday, but cooler, with a good sea running in from the harbour mouth. The pines tossed their spicy heads in the breeze, and small waves slapped cheerfully on the slipways below him. He was filled with pleasure by every prospect. Blue sky, blue sea, *Eclipse* dipping serenely at her moorings, white terrace, red geraniums, all dearly familiar, and yet, this morning, magically fresh. Pearl was sitting on the end of the jetty, consuming a delicious morsel of fish-offal she had found; Frances was back in San Antonio, and Juanita was making him a pot of coffee. He could not remember when he had felt so well, so hopeful or so optimistic. It was as though he had been living for months in the murky gloom of a potential storm, and now the storm was over and the pressure had lifted and he could breathe freely again.

He told himself that he was a heel, that he should be grovelling in a pit of self-hate and remorse, but his sense of physical well-being was too much for his conscience. All this time he had been leaning, with his hands flat, on the wall of the terrace, and now, when he straightened and stood up, he saw that his palms were chalked with whitewash. His automatic reaction was to wipe them clean on his jeans, but all at once his attention was drawn to the convolutions of his own fingerprints, outlined in the whitewash and as delicately drawn as a microscopic chart. A chart of himself, unique to George Dyer, just as the life he had led, and the things he was doing now, were unique.

He was not especially proud of himself. He had, over the years, hurt and offended too many people, and last night, the climax of it all, did not even bear thinking about. But none of this could take away from his present elating sense of identity.

I've grown accustomed to her face.

531

The record ended and he went inside to turn it off. As he shut the lid of the player he said, "Juanita."

She was spooning coffee into his jug.

"Señor?"

"Juanita, did you know that Pepe, the husband of Maria, had taken the Señorita to the airport yesterday afternoon?"

"*Sí*, Señor," said Juanita, but she was not looking at him.

"Did he tell you that he brought the Señorita back again?"

"*Sí*, Señor. All the village knows."

It was inevitable, and George sighed, but persevered in his interrogation.

"And did Pepe say that the Señorita had lost her passport?"

"He did not know that it was lost. Just that she did not have it."

"But she told the Guardia Civil at the airport?"

"I do not know, Señor." She poured boiling water into the coffee jug.

"Juanita . . ." When she did not turn, he laid his hand on her bare forearm, and her head swung round, and to his amazement he saw that she was laughing at him, her dark eyes bright with amusement. "Juanita . . . the Señorita is not my daughter."

"No, Señor," said Juanita, demurely.

"Don't tell me you already knew."

"Señor," she shrugged, "Pepe did not think that she was behaving like your daughter."

"How was she behaving?"

"She was very unhappy, Señor."

"Juanita, she is not my daughter, but my little cousin."

"*Sí*, Señor."

"Will you tell Maria? And tell Maria to tell Tomeu, and maybe Tomeu will tell Rosita and Rosita will tell Rudolfo . . ." They were both laughing. "I did not tell a lie, Juanita. But I did not tell the truth either."

532

"The Señor does not need to worry. If she is a daughter or a cousin . . ." Juanita shrugged enormously as though the question were too trivial for consideration. "But to Cala Fuerte, the Señor is a friend. Nothing else matters."

Such eloquence was foreign to Juanita, and George was so touched he could have kissed her, but he knew that this would have embarrassed them both enormously, so instead he said that he was hungry, and, feeling companionable, he joined her in the kitchen to look in the bread jar and find something that he could smother in butter and apricot jam.

As usual the bread jar was full and had been replenished on top of the old bread. He said, reproachfully, "Juanita, this is very dirty. The bread at the bottom has got a blue beard." And to prove his point, he turned the crock upside down and emptied all the bread out on to the floor. The last mouldy crust fell out, and then the sheet of white paper with which Juanita had lined the bottom of the jar, and finally a slim, dark-blue folder.

It lay on the floor between them, and they stared at each other in question, each imagining that the other must be responsible.

"What is that thing?"

George picked it up, and turned it over in his hands. "It's a passport. A British passport."

"But who does it belong to?"

"I think, the Señorita."

The idea was to start, not at the beginning of the voyage, but in the middle – the week that *Eclipse* had slid into the harbour at Delos. And then he would go back to the beginning to show, in a series of back-flashes, how the voyage had taken shape, how it had all been planned in the first place. His typing-paper felt thick and smooth and his typewriter was running as sweetly as a well-tuned engine. Selina was still swimming, and Juanita was in her wash-house, beating hell out of George's sheets with her bar of soap, and warbling away at some local love-song, so that when the knock came at the door, he did not hear it.

It was a very discreet knock and scarcely audible above the pounding of his typewriter, and after a little the door was pushed open, and this movement caught George's eye and he looked up, his hands suspended over the typewriter keys.

The man who stood there was young, tall, and very good-looking. He wore a suit, a regular business suit, and a stiff white collar and a tie, and yet he managed to look maddeningly fresh and cool, and he said, "I am sorry to disturb you, but I got no reply to my knocking. Is this the Casa Barco?"

"Yes, it is."

"Then you must be George Dyer."

"Yes, I am. . . ." He stood up.

"My name is Rodney Ackland." He obviously felt that the conversation should not go further without some sort of ritual recognition. He came across the room to shake George's hand. "How do you do?" George thought *Firm grip. Keen, straight eye, thoroughly reliable.* And then, as an unworthy afterthought, *Dead bore.*

"I believe Selina Bruce is staying here?"

"Yes, she is." Rodney looked around in mild question. "She's swimming just now."

"I see. Well, in that case, perhaps I'd better give you some sort of an explanation. I'm Selina's lawyer." George did not comment on this. "And I'm afraid that, indirectly, it was my fault that she made this trip to San Antonio in the first place. It was I who gave her your book, and she saw your photograph and became convinced that you were her father. She spoke to me about it; she told me that she wanted to come and find you, and suggested that I should accompany her, but unfortunately I was forced to make a business trip to Bournemouth to see a very important client, and when I returned to London, Selina had gone. By then she'd been away three or four days. So, of course,

534

I caught the first available plane to San Antonio, and . . . well, I think I should take her back." They eyed each other. Rodney said, "Of course, you aren't her father."

"No, I'm not. Her father's dead."

"There is, however, a singular resemblance. Even I can see that."

"Gerry Dawson was a distant cousin of mine."

"What an extraordinary coincidence!"

"Yes," said George. "Extraordinary."

For the first time, Rodney looked a little discomfited. "Mr Dyer, I have no idea of the circumstances of this . . . rather unconventional visit of Selina's, or even how much she's told you about herself. But she's always had a great desire . . . an obsession, really, about her father. She was brought up by her grandmother, and her childhood was different, to put it mildly . . ."

"Yes, she told me."

"In that case, as you know the facts, I'm sure we're batting on the same side."

"Yes, I expect we are." He grinned and added, "Purely out of interest, however, what would your reactions have been had I really turned out to be Selina's father?"

"Well . . ." Caught for the moment without words, Rodney floundered. "Well, I . . . er . . ." And then he decided to turn it into a joke, and laughed gamely. "I suppose I should have caught you over the port and nuts, and asked your permission."

"My *permission*?"

"Yes. A bit late, of course, because we're already engaged. We're getting married next month."

George said, "I beg your pardon," and the words themselves were an indication of his state of mind. He had not used the outmoded formality for years, since the Bradderford days of polite parties and Hunt Balls, and had imagined that it was consigned to oblivion. But here it came, back again, jolted out of his subconscious by sheer shock.

"We're already engaged. You surely knew that?"

"No, I didn't know."

"You mean Selina didn't tell you? She is an extraordinary girl."

"Why the hell should she tell me? It's nothing to do with me if she's engaged or not."

"No, but you'd think it would be important. The first thing she'd talk about." George thought, *You conceited clothes-horse*. "But that's beside the point. Now that you're in the picture, I'm sure you'll realise that I should take her back to London, and as quickly as possible."

"Yes, of course."

Rodney eased past him and went out on to the terrace. "What a splendid view! Did you say Selina was swimming? I can't see her."

George joined him. "No, she's, uh, out beyond the yacht. I'll fetch her for you. . . ." And then he remembered that he couldn't, because she had taken the dinghy. And then he remembered that he could, because he would borrow the boat of Rafael, Tomeu's cousin. "Look . . . can you wait here? Take a seat. Make yourself at home. I won't be long."

"You wouldn't like me to come with you?" Rodney sounded unenthusiastic, and George said, "No, it's all right. The boat's full of fish-scales, and you'd ruin your suit."

"Well, if you're sure . . ." and before George's eyes, Rodney pulled a cane chair forward into the sun, and subsided gracefully into it, the picture of the well-bred Englishman abroad.

George dragged the boat of Tomeu's cousin Rafael down the slipway and into the water, swearing with every breath. It was long and heavy and awkward to handle, and there was only one oar so he had to scull, which he did inexpertly, and this in itself was infuriating, because Rodney Ackland, with his smooth bland face and his smooth bland voice and his uncreased charcoal-grey suit was watching him from the terrace of the Casa Barco. He made his way, rocking and sweating and swearing, across the water to where *Eclipse* lay, but when he called Selina's name there was no reply.

With some difficulty he manoeuvred his unwieldy craft around *Eclipse*'s stern mooring-rope, and immediately spied Selina, perched like a mermaid on one of the rocks on the far shore. She had climbed up the bathing steps of one of the little wedding-cake villas that nestled in the pine trees and she sat with her arms wrapped around her knees and her hair lay close and wet to her neck like the fur of a seal. Rafael's boat slid beneath *Eclipse*'s port beam. George shipped the heavy oar, and stood, cupping his hands to call her again.

"*Selina!*" It came out as an infuriated yell, and she looked up at once. "Come on in, I want to talk to you."

After only a second's hesitation, she stood up and came down the white steps, and let herself into the water and swam back towards him. When she reached the boat, the gunwales were too high for her to climb over, so he had to put his hands under her shoulders and lift her in, wet and dripping as a freshly caught fish. They sat on the two thwarts, facing each other, and she said, "I am sorry. Did you want the dinghy?"

It occurred to him that any other woman would have demanded, before another word was spoken, an apology for his behaviour of the night before. But Selina was not any other woman.

"I hope you didn't mind my taking it . . ."

"No of course not."

"You were asleep when I came down. I had to let Juanita in." He watched her speak, not hearing what she said, trying to reconcile himself to the shattering knowledge that she was going to marry Rodney Ackland, had been engaged all the time, had never told George.

". . . and is your friend all right? She wasn't too angry, I hope."

"My friend? Oh, Frances. I don't know if she's angry or not. She drove back to San Antonio last night. Anyway, it wasn't your fault. She'll simmer down and it'll be all forgotten."

"I shouldn't have come back to the Casa Barco, I do see that now, but . . ."

He could bear it no longer. "Selina."

She frowned. "Is something wrong?"

"Listen. There's someone waiting for you at the Casa Barco. He's come to take you back to London. Rodney Ackland."

She seemed to freeze to stillness. Her lips said "Rodney" but no sound came out.

"He flew from London last night. He got back from Bournemouth and realised that you'd come to San Antonio on your own, so he caught the first available flight. I told him that I wasn't your father, and I must say, he didn't seem particularly surprised. But he does want to talk to you."

The breeze blew coolly and Selina shivered. He saw the thin gold chain, disappearing into the top of the little bikini he had bought her, but now he knew that it was not a Confirmation cross that hung there. He reached out and took hold of the chain and lifted it free, and the sapphire and diamonds of Rodney Ackland's engagement ring swung and spun before his eyes, sharp arrows of sunlight darting from every facet.

"Selina. Why did you never tell me?"

Her eyes at that moment seemed almost as blue as the sapphire that he dangled beneath her chin. "I don't know."

"You are engaged to Rodney?" She nodded. "You're going to marry him next month." She nodded again. "But why does it all have to be so secret?"

"It isn't secret. I told Rodney about you. I told him I thought George Dyer was my father. And I wanted him to come with me and find you. But he couldn't. He had business to see to in Bournemouth, and he never thought I'd come alone. He said that if you were my father, then you'd be embarrassed by my sudden appearance. And if you weren't my father, then it was a wild goose chase

538

anyway. He didn't seem to understand how important it was; to have roots and a family, and really belong to somebody."

"Have you known him a long time?"

"Since I was a little girl. His firm has always looked after my grandmother's affairs. She liked him very much, and I know she hoped I would marry him."

"And now you're going to."

"Yes. I usually ended up by doing what she wanted." George's dark eyes were suddenly compassionate and Selina could not bear him to be sorry for her. "We're moving out of Queen's Gate. We've found a lovely flat in a new block. I wish you could see it. It's full of sunshine and it's got a wonderful view. Agnes is going to come and live with us. I've even bought my wedding dress. It's white, and very long. With a train."

"But you wear your engagement ring hidden away, not even on a finger."

"I thought you were my father. I wanted to meet you, for the first time, just as myself. Not belonging to any other person, or any other way of life."

"Are you in love with him?"

"I asked *you* that question yesterday, and you wouldn't reply."

"That was different. We were talking about my past and this is your future."

"Yes, I know. That's what makes it so important."

He did not reply to this. Now Selina put up her hands to the back of her neck and unfastened the gold chain. The ring slipped free and she caught it and put it back on her finger and then re-fastened the chain once more about her neck. All these actions were deliberate and entirely composed. She said, "I shouldn't keep Rodney waiting."

"No, of course not. Take the dinghy back, and I'll follow on in this great crate of Rafael's. But don't sneak off without saying goodbye."

"I'd never do that. You know I'd never do that."

After a little, Rodney had found it too hot to wait on the terrace. He could have taken off his jacket, but he was wearing braces, and there seemed something almost indecent in sitting about in braces, so he got out of the cane chair and went into the cool of the house. He was prowling to and fro, trying to make head or tail of its unconventional design, when Selina, unnoticed and unheard, came up the steps of the terrace, and said his name.

Stopped short in his prowlings, Rodney swung round. She stood in the open doorway and he stared in disbelief. He could not believe that in such a short time one person could have altered so much. He had always thought of her as a monotone person, fawn skin and fawn hair, only relieved by the bright blue, Siamese-cat eyes. But now she was very brown and her hair, still wet from swimming, was bleached in streaks by the sunshine. She wore a bikini which to Rodney's eyes seemed one step short of sheer bad taste, and as she stood there, regarding him, the large white cat which had been sunning itself on the terrace came to wrap itself affectionately around her bare ankles.

The moment was fraught with a strange embarrassment. Then Selina said, "Hello, Rodney. This is a surprise." She tried to put a lift in her voice but it fell sadly flat on the last syllable.

"Yes," said Rodney, "I thought it would be." It was not easy to believe that he had just made the journey from London, had sat up all night in his clothes, had walked from the village down the stony, dusty road to the Casa Barco. Admittedly, his shoes were lightly veiled in white, but otherwise he looked as immaculate as he did at home. He came to give her a kiss, his hands on her shoulders, and he held her off to raise mildly disapproving eyebrows at her bikini. "What's this you're wearing?"

She shrugged, "It's all I have to swim in." There was an old towel coat of George's draped over the washing-line, and she went to collect it, and put it on. The towel was hard and dry with salt and sun and smelt of George. She wrapped it tightly about her, and in

540

some inexplicable way it comforted her, and bolstered her courage.

He said, "You were naughty to come out without letting me know. I might have been out of my mind with worry."

"I knew you were in Bournemouth."

"I called the flat as soon as I got back to London and Agnes told me where you were." He added, "I came straight out, of course, on the first available flight."

"That was very kind of you, Rodney."

"How do you feel about coming home?"

"I would have been back before, only I had all my money stolen at the airport, and I couldn't buy a return ticket."

"You surely could have let me know; I'd have cabled you some by return."

"I . . . I didn't want to bother you. And," she added on a burst of honesty, "I thought you'd just say 'I told you so.' Because you were right and I was wrong, and George Dyer wasn't my father . . . isn't my father . . ."

"No, I rather gathered that."

"But you do see that I had to find out?" It was a plea for sympathy, but Rodney misunderstood her.

"I'm afraid I still feel it would have been better had you let me do the finding out for you."

"But I asked you to come with me. I wanted you to come, but you wouldn't."

"Not wouldn't. Couldn't. You know that."

"You could have put off Mrs What's-her-name."

"Selina!" He was deeply shocked, and realised then, perhaps for the first time, that the changes in her were not merely physical, but deeper and far more subtle.

She took a deep breath.

"Anyway," she said, "I don't regret any of it. I'm glad I came, even if George isn't my father. And if I were asked, I'd do it all over again."

It was an invitation to a stand-up battle, but before Rodney could think up any reply, they were joined by

George Dyer himself, who came up the terrace steps, gathered Pearl into his arms, and chipped cheerfully into the conversation.

"Well, now, isn't this nice? You've found each other again. How about a drink to cool us all down?"

"I won't have a drink, thank you," said Rodney stiffly.

"Cigarette, then?"

"No, not just now." He cleared his throat. "I've been telling Selina that I think it would be a good idea if we were to return to London as soon as possible. My taxi's waiting now at the Cala Fuerte Hotel; we can go straight back to the airport."

"Good organisation," said George.

Rodney glanced at him swiftly to see if George was laughing at him, but the dark eyes were very solemn. Not entirely reassured he turned back to Selina. "Perhaps you should pack. Where have you been staying?"

There was a long silence. Rodney looked at Selina. Selina looked at George and then back to Rodney. George, with great nonchalance, stroked Pearl.

Selina said, "Here."

Rodney seemed to blanch visibly. "*Here?*"

"Yes. Here. At the Casa Barco."

"*Sleeping* here?"

"There wasn't anywhere else to go. . . ."

She shivered slightly and George knew that she was nervous. Rodney, however, did not seem aware of this, for when he spoke it was in tones of ice.

"Wasn't that just the *slightest* bit unconventional?"

Abruptly, George tipped Pearl into a handy chair and joined in the discussion. "I don't think so. After all, let's not forget, Selina is a cousin of mine."

"And let's not forget how distant. Besides, that is scarcely the point."

"Then what is the point?"

"Well, Selina turned up here, uninvited, unannounced, a complete stranger to you, and you let her *stay*; living in this house – practically, as far as I can see, sleeping in the

542

same room. I quite appreciate that you don't necessarily have to consider your own reputation, but for Selina's sake you could surely have made some other arrangement."

"Perhaps we didn't want to," said George. Rodney lost his temper. "I'm sorry, Mr Dyer, but we obviously don't speak the same language. I find your attitude insufferable."

"I am sorry."

"Do you always have such scant regard for the normal, decent rules of behaviour?"

"Yes, always. And they aren't my rules."

For a moment Rodney toyed with the thought of knocking him down, but then decided that George was beyond contempt and only fit to be ignored. He turned to Selina.

"Selina . . ." She seemed to start visibly. "I'm sorry about this, but I give you the benefit of believing that it was none of it your fault. I'm quite prepared to forget about it all, but we must make sure that no whisper of what has happened ever reaches London.":

Selina regarded him gravely. His face was smooth and well-shaved. He didn't seem to have any lines on it at all, and it was impossible to imagine him growing old, experienced and pleasantly worn-looking. He would be like this when he was eighty, as impersonal and unruffled as a newly-laundered shirt.

She said, "Why, Rodney?"

"I . . . I wouldn't like Mr Arthurstone to hear of it."

It was such a ridiculous reply that she wanted to laugh. Mr Arthurstone, with his arthritic knees, who was going to give her away . . . what on earth had it got to do with Mr Arthurstone? "And now" – Rodney glanced at his watch – "there's no more time to waste. Get on some clothes and we'll get going."

George was lighting himself a cigarette as Rodney said this. Now he shook out the match, took the cigarette out of his mouth and said, "She can't come to London with you. She's lost her passport."

"She's . . . *what*?"

"Lost her passport. It happened yesterday. Most extra ordinary."

"Is this true, Selina?"

"Oh. I . . . well, yes . . ."

George bulldozed her into silence. "Of course it's true. My dear Mr Ackland, you can have no idea what it's like out here. They'd steal the gold out of your teeth if they could lay their hands on it."

"But your *passport*. Selina, do you realise how serious this is?"

"Well . . . I . . ." Selina floundered.

"Have you informed the British Consul?"

"No," said George, taking charge once more, "but she told the Guardia Civil at the airport, and very understanding and helpful they were, too."

"It amazes me that they didn't throw her straight into jail."

"I was pretty amazed too but of course it's wonderful what a pretty smile can do, even in Spain."

"But what steps are we going to take?"

"Well, now you ask me, I would suggest that you go and get into that taxi and go back to London, and leave Selina here with me . . . No," he halted Rodney's infuriated protests, "I really think this is the best plan. You can possibly pull some strings at your end and between us we ought to be able to keep her out of prison. And don't worry too much about the conventions, old boy. After all, I'm probably Selina's nearest relative, and I'm perfectly prepared to take responsibility for her. . . ."

"Responsibility? You?" He made a final appeal to Selina. "Surely you don't *want* to stay here?" Rodney nearly exploded at the thought.

"Well . . ." Her very hesitation was enough to convince him.

"You amaze me! Your selfishness amazes me! You don't seem to realise that it isn't just your good name. I have a certain reputation to keep up as well, and I find your attitude incredible! What Mr Arthurstone will have to say, I dread to think."

"But you'll be able to explain to Mr Arthurstone, Rodney. I'm sure you'll be able to explain. And I think . . . while you're explaining, you'd better tell him that he won't have to give me away after all. I really am awfully sorry, but I'm sure, in a way, it's a relief to you. After all, you wouldn't want to be saddled with me, not after what's happened. And . . . here's your ring. . . ."

She held it out in her palm, the winking diamonds and the deep blue sapphire that he had imagined would bind her to him for ever. He longed to be able to make the grand gesture to take the ring, and fling it out over the terrace wall and into the sea beyond, but it had cost him a great deal of money, so he swallowed his pride and took it back.

"I am sorry, Rodney."

It seemed most dignified to maintain a manly silence. Rodney turned on his heel and made for the door, but George was there first, holding it open for him. "A shame you've had such an unproductive visit. You should come to Cala Fuerte later on in the year when there's more going on. I'm sure you'd enjoy the waterskiing and the aqua-lunging and the spear-fishing. It was good of you to come."

"Please don't imagine, Mr Dyer, that I or my partners will let you get away with this."

"I don't imagine so for a moment. I'm sure Mr Arthurstone will have some bright ideas up his sleeve, and in due course I shall be on the receiving end of a stiff letter. Sure I can't run you to the village?"

"Thank you, I prefer to walk."

"Oh well, *chacun à son goût*. It's been splendid meeting you. Goodbye."

But Rodney did not reply, merely marched in silent fury from the house. George saw him safely on his way up the hill, and then closed the door behind him.

He turned. Selina stood, still in the middle of the room

where Rodney had left her. She looked as if she were expecting another violent scene, but he only said, in his most reasonable of tones, "You ought to get your head examined, thinking you'd ever marry a man like that. You'd spend half your time changing for dinner, and the other half looking up all those long words in the dictionary. And who's Mr Arthurstone, anyway?"

"He's the senior partner of the firm Rodney works for. He's very old and he's got arthritis in his knees."

"And he was going to give you away?"

"There wasn't anyone else."

It was a forlorn admission. George said, "Are you talking about Mr Arthurstone, or are you talking about Rodney?"

"Both, I suppose."

"Perhaps," said George gently, "perhaps you were suffering from a bad attack of father-fixation."

"Yes. Perhaps I was."

"And now?"

"Not any more."

She shivered again, and he smiled. "You know, Selina, I would never have believed it possible how much you can learn about another person in such a ridiculously short time. For instance, I know that when you lie, which is sadly frequent, your eyes get so wide and so big that the blue bits are almost entirely surrounded by white. Like islands. And when you're trying not to laugh at some outrageous thing I've said, you turn down the corners of your mouth and somehow conjure up a very unexpected dimple. And when you're nervous you shiver. You're nervous now."

"I'm not nervous. I'm cold from swimming."

"Then go and put some clothes on."

"But I must tell you something first. . . ."

"It can keep. Run along and get dressed."

He went out on to the terrace to wait for her. He lit a cigarette and the sun was hot on his shoulders, burning through the thin cotton of his shirt. Rodney Ackland had

546

gone, away from the Casa Barco, out of Selina's life. Just as Jenny had gone, her ghost laid for ever, the unhappy affair exorcised for ever by the simple act of telling Selina about her. Jenny and Rodney were both in the past, and the present felt gay and good, and the future as hopeful and as filled with pleasant surprises as a Christmas package.

Below him, in the garden, Juanita was pegging out sheets, still singing happily to herself and apparently unaware of the drama that had taken place while she tackled the morning laundry. He was filled with a sudden surge of affection for her. No one knew better than himself that George's own personal road to hell had always been paved with good intentions, but now he promised himself that when the new book was published he would give her, not merely a presentation copy to sit on a lace doily, but something more. Something that she wanted badly, that she would never be able to buy for herself. A silk dress, or a jewel, or a fine new gas stove.

Selina's footstep behind him made him turn. She wore a sleeveless linen dress the colour of apricots, and sandals with little heels that made her almost as tall as he, and it astounded him that it had taken so long to realise that she was beautiful. He said, "This is the first time I've seen you properly dressed. I'm glad you got your luggage back."

Selina took a deep breath. She said, "George, I have to talk to you."

"What about?"

"My passport."

"What about your passport?"

"Well. You see. It isn't lost at all."

He started, and frowned in enormous surprise. "It *isn't*?"

"No. You see . . . well, yesterday afternoon, before I went off with Pepe . . . I hid it."

"Selina." He sounded deeply shocked. "Why did you do a dreadful thing like that?"

"I know it was dreadful, but I didn't want to go. I didn't want to leave you with Mrs Dongen. I knew she didn't want

547

you to write that second book. She wanted you to go off to Australia or the Gobi desert or somewhere. With her. So when I went to the kitchen to get the soda water out of the refrigerator, I . . ." she swallowed. "I hid my passport in the bread jar."

"What an extraordinary thing to do!"

"Yes, I know. But I was only thinking of you, and what I'm trying to say is that there's no reason now why I shouldn't go back to London with Rodney. I mean, I shan't get married to him, of course. I see how stupid I was even to imagine that I could. But I can't stay here indefinitely." Her voice began to tail away. George was being absolutely no help at all. "You do see that, don't you?"

"Well, of course I do." He assumed the expression of a man who would go to any lengths to see fair play. "And we must do the right thing."

"Yes . . . yes; that's what I thought."

"Well," he went on bracingly, glancing at his watch, "if you're going with Rodney, you'd better get your skates on, otherwise he'll be in his taxi and away before you've even reached the Cala Fuerte Hotel. . . ."

And before her incredulous eyes, he stood up, dusted the whitewash from the seat of his jeans, and the next moment was back at his typewriter, working away as though his life depended upon it.

It was not exactly the reaction Selina had hoped for. She waited for some sort of reprieve, but none came, and so, trying to swallow the lump in her throat and blink away a ridiculous burning suspicion of tears, she went to the kitchen, and took out the bread jar and emptied it, loaf by loaf on to the counter, eventually removing the sheet of paper under which she had slipped her passport.

It was not there. Tears, disappointment, everything was drowned in a wave of sheer panic. Her passport was really lost.

"George!" He was typing so hard that he did not hear her. "George, I've . . . *I've lost my passport*."

He stopped typing and raised polite eyebrows. "Again?"

"It's not here! I put it at the very bottom, and it's not here! I've lost it!"

"Good Lord!" said George.

"What could have happened?" Her voice rose to a wail. "Could Juanita have found it? Or perhaps she cleaned out the jar and she's burned it. Or thrown it away! Perhaps it's been stolen. Oh, what will happen to me?"

"I don't like to imagine. . . ."

"I wish I'd never put it there in the first place!"

"You've been hoist with your own petard," said George in sanctimonious tones, and returned to his typing.

Suspicion nudged at Selina at last, and she frowned. Surely he was behaving in an unnaturally calm fashion? And there had been a gleam in his dark eyes that she had learned not to trust. Had he found the passport? Had he found it, and hidden it, and never told her? Leaving the empty bread jar, she moved around the room, casually searching for clues, lifting the corner of the magazine, peering behind a cushion, as though she were playing a game of Hunt the Thimble.

She finished up behind him. He wore his worn, salt-stained jeans, and the back pocket on the right hip looked curiously square and stiff, as though it contained a small book, or a large card. . . . He was still typing full blast, but, when Selina reached out her hand to investigate the pocket, his own hand came round and slapped it away.

The panic was over. She laughed, in relief; in happiness; in love. She put her arms around his neck and nearly strangled him in her embrace and she said, "You've got it! You found it! You had it all the time, you brute!"

"Do you want it back?"

"Not unless you want me to go to London with Rodney."

"I don't," said George.

She kissed him, rubbing her own soft cheek against his rough, bristly one, and it was not smooth and scented with aftershave, but creased and sun-browned and netted with lines, as worn and familiar as one of his own rough-dried

549

cotton work shirts. She said, "I don't want to go either."
He had written a full page of typescript. Selina rested
her chin on the top of his head and said, "What are
you writing?"

"A synopsis."

"For the new book? What's it about?"

"The cruise to the Aegean."

"What's it going to be called?"

"I haven't the faintest idea, but I'll dedicate it to you."

"Is it going to be good?"

"I hope so. But in fact, I've already got an idea for a
third book. Fiction this time. . . ." He took her hand, and
pulled her around so that she was sitting on the edge of his
desk, facing him. "I thought it could be about this chap,
living in some quiet little spot, not doing a living soul a
mite of harm, minding his own business. And then, along
comes this tramp of a girl. She has an obsession about him.
Won't leave him alone. Alienates all his friends, spends all
his money, drives him to drink. He becomes a derelict, a
social outcast."

"What happens in the end?"

"He marries her, of course. She tricks him into it.
There's no escape. It's tragic."

"It doesn't sound tragic to me."

"Well, it ought to."

"George, are you, by any chance, asking me to marry
you?"

"I suppose, in my warped, twisted way, I am; I'm sorry
about last night. And I do love you."

"I know you do." She leaned forward to kiss his mouth.
"I'm glad you do." She kissed him again, and he pushed
his typewriter out of the way, and stood up to gather her
into his arms. Later, Selina said, "We'll have to let Agnes
know."

"She won't come out here and try to throw a spanner
in the works?"

"Of course not. She'll love you."

"We'll have to send her a cable. From San Antonio.

This afternoon, if it's to get to her before Rodney Ackland does. And while we're in town, we'll go and pay our respects to the English padre and find out what the delay is. And we'll ask Rudolfo to be my best man . . ."

"I wish I could have Juanita as a bridesmaid."

Juanita. They had forgotten Juanita. Now, still laughing, hand in hand, they went out to find her, to lean over the wall of the terrace and call her name. But Juanita was not as simple as she sometimes appeared. Her peasant instincts seldom let her down, and already she was on her way up from the garden, erect as ever and beaming with pleasure, and with her arms outstretched as though to embrace them both.

ROSAMUNDE PILCHER

THE SHELL SEEKERS

Artist's daughter Penelope Keeling can look back on a full and varied life: a Bohemian childhood in London and Cornwall, an unhappy wartime marriage, and the one man she truly loved. She has brought up three children – and learned to accept each of them as they are.

Yet she is far too energetic and independent to settle sweetly into pensioned-off old-age. And when she discovers that her most treasured possession, her father's painting, *The Shell Seekers*, is now worth a small fortune, it is Penelope who must make the decisions that will determine whether her family can continue to survive as a family, or be split apart.

'A deeply satisfying story written with love and confidence'
  Maeve Binchy, in the New York Times Book Review

'A beautiful, haunting story . . . that will tug at your heart strings'

Prima